10/2

$2.00

<u>The Anumal Empire Series</u>

Lazarball

Alpha

Reaper

ANUMAL EMPIRE

Book Two

ALPHA

By
David Ayres
&
Darren Jacobs

CHAPTER ONE

A TIME FOR PLAY.

Nightmare turned, wiping the sweat from his face. A trail of blood smeared across his cheekbone, halting just shy of his ever-present shades. Inhaling a lungful of air, he caught the scent of his pursuer.

The ground trembled.

"You're a persistent one, I'll give you that," he growled, and set off, darting along the potholed path between the abandoned buildings.

Cradling a large pincer with one hand, he plunged the other inside the bloody shell and yanked out its innards. With deft flicks, streams of scavenger blood and flesh flew from his ebony fingers, splattering brick, boulder, and stone, as he passed. His long, leather coat whipped along in his wake, ethereal-like in the graceful pursuit of its leader.

A giant bellow trumpeted through the cherry-plum sky.

"Someone really isn't a happy boy…"

The panther pounced atop a fallen stone statue and dove through the opening of an abandoned house. Tumbling forwards, he sprang to his feet, vaulted a collapsed wall, and continued to run.

"One…two…three…four…five…six…sev—"

The building behind him exploded.

Stones slammed into his back, and a hail of shingle pattered his skull, losing its battle against gravity with unforgiving fury.

"That's it. Keep coming."

Adrenaline fuelled his muscles. He pushed his legs harder, gaining speed and kicking up a trail of grit along the road. Numerous clan statues lay crumbled across his path. The shattered wings of a flyer, erected in honor of the Imperial Ivory Stratos clan, laid half hidden in the long grass. Next to that, the toppled torso of a bull, wielding a double-handed battle hammer, sat overwhelmed with moss and fungi. Further down the road were more remnants honoring the feline Air Spikes clan, and even the Crimson Watchers. But the presence of these stone testaments came as no surprise to him...considering he was charging through the abandoned player's village in the foothills below Samanoski stadium.

The panther plunged his hand into the pincer and ripped out what was left. Casting the shell aside, he swung his fist in an arc above his head, coating as many of the statues with the gore as possible. The last piece of scavenger meat slipped through his fingers and he sped off again, dropping to all fours in order to gain speed. Before him, the village boundary approached; the grassland dipped away before climbing again into a small hill, supporting a huge boulder. Within moments, Nightmare vaulted the rock and planted his back against its far side. He turned towards the finely tailored tiger hunched next to him.

"Sorry to keep you waiting," he panted.

The tiger shook his head and clutched his left shoulder. Blood seeped through his orange-furred fingers, darkening his slashed robe. "You think you are so damned clever."

Nightmare sniffed the cut. "How bad is it?"

"It is nothing."

"Why Dallas, I only have your best interests at—"

"I can take care of myself, Wade, Nightmare...or whatever you choose to call yourself."

The panther smirked and picked up a rock the size of a small karla fruit. The ground rumbled as another angry screech sliced through the air.

"Well?" asked Dallas, fidgeting. "What now? Are we to hide here until the light fades?"

"Hide?" Nightmare tossed the rock back and forth in his hands, rubbing more of the blood onto it. "Well, you could keep running I suppose, and gain a head start for yourself, but then again, our pursuer won't quit. Rest assured, though, it will track you down, and by the time your wound saps your energy, and your muscles fail, it will tear you to pieces. "

Dallas snarled.

Nightmare chuckled. "However, don't fret. I'm here to keep you safe."

2

"I do not need protecting."

The panther slipped into a crouch and patted the tiger's shoulder. "Just stay here, Shadow Soul. Wouldn't want you getting any more scratches, now would we?"

Before Dallas could reply Nightmare sprung on top of the boulder and left him behind.

The village spread out before the panther in all its newly created devastation. He knelt as still as stone, feeling the wind blow against his face, ruffling his fur. A tremor vibrated through the boulder, growing in intensity, until…

Plumes of dust burst upwards like geysers as a fully-grown kraggon ploughed through its final obstruction. The building crumbled, bouncing off the burgundy spikes lining the creature's spine. With a triumphant scream, it snapped its huge pincers together and scuttled forward, five powerful legs propelling it at great speed. Where its sixth leg should have been hung a grisly stump. The scavenger's spiky tail curled high over its exoskeleton, weaving back and forth in angry spasms.

Nightmare smiled and swelled out his chest with anticipation. For too long had he drifted across Nomica as a powerless wretch, sporting gray fur and withered muscles. Yet the power that buzzed inside him now had channeled his ascension from the cripple he had once been, to the predator he had now become.

"So nice of you to join us," he whispered, barely containing his fervor.

He dropped from the boulder to land in a crouch. Letting out a defiant roar, he protracted his claws before sprinting towards his foe. He whipped out his knife from his leather jacket, gripping the finely crafted handle. "*Roh-khen!*" he yelled, and the dagger's blade glowed a deep crimson as it grew in length. Within a few heartbeats, the blade had transformed into a long katana.

The distance between the two foes receded.

Darting forwards, the kraggon stabbed a pincer at the panther's head. Nightmare flipped through the air, easily avoiding the strike, and with a flick of his wrist, sliced through the monster's exoskeleton and muscle, ridding it of another leg. The kraggon screamed a trumpeting wail before lashing out with its needle-like tail. The deadly barb whooshed towards Nightmare's face, but he dove to his side and into the grass.

"Come on now. You aren't even trying," he grinned, spinning to the left just as the kraggon's teeth snapped where his head had been. "You can do better than that."

Nightmare rolled under the monster and jabbed his glowing sword upwards, stabbing it into the creature's black shell. The kraggon's stomach armor split open and the blade sliced into the buttery flesh beneath. Yanking it free, Nightmare lifted the blood-covered rock close to his mouth.

"*Ni kanx thum xoolaray,*" he whispered, letting his breath engulf the stone.

The rock suddenly felt heavier as power coalesced within his hand. Thrusting upwards, he rammed the glowing rock through the crack in the exoskeleton and deep into the kraggon's stomach. The scavenger shrieked. It reared back into the air, shaking its head from side to side.

"W-Wade?" he heard Dallas call from atop the boulder. "What are you doing?"

Nightmare whipped his hand up for silence, but the kraggon's head slowly swiveled in the tiger's direction, catching the scent of Dallas's blood.

"Fool!" hissed Nightmare.

The kraggon's body turned and it charged Dallas.

Nightmare sighed and activated his incantation.

A low rumble rippled across the landscape.

On the grass in front of the panther, a blood-soaked rock slowly swayed back and forth in the undergrowth. Clan statues trembled, inching across the ground in his direction. Nightmare's forehead creased. He lifted his sword and pointed it at the attacking scavenger. Like an explosion, clouds of dust burst skywards from the village behind him as huge slabs of bloody stone blasted towards his foe.

The wounded kraggon bore down on the tiger with terrible energy. It skidded to a stop before him and reared onto its back legs, whipping its tail from left to right. The kraggon screeched, widening its maw to engulf Dallas in one bite.

A slab of stone sped past Nightmare and hurtled into the kraggon's stomach, exactly where Nightmare had shoved the glowing rock. With bone shattering force, it smashed into its thorax, knocking the monster sideways and onto its back. The monster's feet waggled in the air like an overturned nutcrab.

Dallas dove away to safety.

A pained cry filled the air. The kraggon struggled to regain its feet while another blood-smeared statue slammed into it, followed by another, and then another.

Every rock Nightmare had coated in kraggon blood smashed against the scavenger. Clan statues trailed across the grass before they pummeled into it too. The kraggon's legs kicked wildly, knocking away any rocks it could, but there were just too many. Rocks struck more rocks, shattering anything in their path, and a cloud of dust twirled amongst the bedlam. Pained screams echoed in the air, gradually fading into a fluid-filled gurgle.

Within moments, a mountain like cairn of stone had completely covered the giant; a last thumb-sized pebble fell from the pile and settled by Nightmare's feet. As the dust dispersed, a single leg poked out from beneath the rubble, twitching one last time before thudding against the ground with finality.

The panther lowered his sword and turned back to the destroyed village. Broken walls were mingled with splintered wood and twisted girders.

Dallas glanced out from behind his boulder.

"Is…it dead?"

"Yes, but with no help from you," replied Nightmare.

"Well, I have never seen anything like that before."

"*Noh-khune!*" whispered the panther, and the long, glowing katana shrunk back to the size of a dagger. He bent down and wiped the wet blade against the grass. "And your loud mouth nearly kept you from seeing anything like it again."

"Oh, do not start lecturing—"

Nightmare's hand whipped up, stopping his complaints. "You

almost died!" he hissed. "I *told* you to wait, but surprise, surprise, you had to have your own way."

"I drew him away from you!" yelled the tiger, gripping his bloody shoulder.

Nightmare sighed. "Let me inspect that."

The tiger pulled away.

"Fine. Have it your way."

Nightmare set off for the destroyed village, before muffled footsteps eventually fell in behind him.

"So...will there be more?" asked Dallas, finally reaching his side.

"Possibly."

"Well, I hope not...for their sake, that is. I mean it was stupid to just attack us."

"It wasn't attacking. It was defending...because it was petrified."

"A kraggon? Petrified? Why?"

"A kraggon it may have been, but a small male at that." Nightmare shrugged. "Easy prey."

"Look, it caught me by surprise okay."

"So you keep saying."

The panther continued to walk.

Dallas continued to follow.

Neither spoke.

* * *

To the right of the destroyed village loomed a sheer cliff with Samanoski stadium roosting at its pinnacle. Stone stairs zigzagged up the mountainside, chiseled deep into the rock, until they gradually vanished, eaten away by the elements. Hand and footholds replaced the stairs, leading up onto the mountain's heights.

Fear lingered in the air.

"Blood. A couple of days old," said Dallas, finally breaking the silence and coming to a stop by Nightmare's side. "But some of it is fresh too."

Nightmare nodded in agreement. "Follow me."

Picking up his pace, he rounded the jutting rocks before halting again.

The ground sloped down into a bowl-shaped blemish where numerous shredded kraggon carcasses littered the land. Limbs had been torn free, exoskeletons cracked open, and internal organs yanked out to slowly bake under the setting sun. Blood splatters decorated the rock face like ghastly murals, and thousands of buzzing sectoids hummed everywhere. Scuttlers, such as rat-sized meyarks, hissed noisily, defending their spoils. The air felt damp. A sour odor tickled the back of Nightmare's throat.

Dallas covered his nose. "What in Skorr?"

"Seems like we missed the party."

A gigantic kraggon carcass was in the center of all the carnage. Unlike the others, though, this one had been smashed to pieces, not so much shredded, but splattered, as if it had fallen from a great height. The cliff face also had streaks of blood smeared down its side.

"Come on," hissed Nightmare, wading into the heart of the carnage.

"What? Go in there? No."

But the tiger followed, nonetheless.

Bones cracked and rotten flesh squelched under their feet, emitting clouds of sectoids.

"So...what happened?" asked Dallas.

Nightmare pointed to the largest kraggon. "The others are smaller, but this one was—"

"The pack leader."

"No." Nightmare shook his head. "A female."

He pointed to a crystal-like substance that had spilled from her stomach and created slanting cascades of hard, frosted glass. "The web sacks in her stomach exploded and dried. Looks like she was pregnant."

"Pregnant? Well, what about the pups then?"

"Highly sought after by the herd fathers. Only the strongest could have claimed them…" He motioned to the surrounding chaos. "As you can see."

Nightmare's brow creased. He knew carnage, yet here, the pureness of death felt tainted with the presence of something else: something ancient.

A small click rang in his ears.

From out of the female kraggon's carcass scuttled a single black sectoid. Nightmare plucked it up between his finger and thumb and sniffed it. The same ancient aura clung to the tiny creature: a lingering sense of earth and nature, combined with deep magic.

"*He* was here," said Dallas, slowly approaching Nightmare. "The lion, I mean."

"You can tell?"

"I can sense it."

Nightmare felt the sectoid wriggle. He squashed it without thought. "He wasn't alone."

The panther set off towards the cliff side.

"What do you mean?" shouted Dallas.

Nightmare sniffed deeply and smelled the same earthy scent as before. He followed the aroma around the base of the cliff before halting at a point where the land spread out before him. The Ridgeback Mountains continued off into the distance.

Resting on the horizon, the sky coated the land with a claret glow. Patches of trees blotted the landscape, before creeping up the mountain range like a green, breaking wave.

Dallas finally caught up with him.

"For Skorr's sake, will you stop running off and tell me what is going on?"

"Events have moved faster than planned. I believe the time for play is over."

"Play? You call what happened today *play*?"

The panther protracted his claws. "Compared to what you will face ahead. Yes."

"What are you doing, Wade? What's going on?"

"Watch and learn."

He slashed his sharp claws against a nearby boulder, creating shallow gouges in its surface. Turning to face his companion, he drew his blade and pressed his thumb against the edge. Blood dribbled from the wound, but he ignored it and wiped the gash across the boulder, creating a swirling symbol with what looked like an eye in the center.

Nightmare reached out and grabbed the tiger's hand. "Hold out your thumb."

"What—"

Before Dallas could protest, Nightmare sliced into the tiger's thumb. A moment later, blood dripped onto the grass by his feet.

Dallas snarled and clutched his hand close to his chest. "What are you doing?"

The panther simply wiped the blade against his own thumb, and then stabbed the weapon into the grass, between them both. Touching the silver handle, he hissed, *"Ghyll-bor!"*

Dallas suddenly dropped to one knee. "What the… What's happening?"

"Weaver Magic." Nightmare stepped away. "Your weakness will pass. Yet at the cost of a drop of life energy, I have made it so that no scavengers will come near the blade…or us."

Dallas stared down at the protruding hilt. The grass around the blade was beginning to brown and wither. "My life energy?" He scowled. "Is it dangerous?"

Nightmare chuckled. "This is blood magic. What do you think?"

Saying no more, Nightmare turned to the symbol on the boulder and slammed his open paw against it. He felt a surge of lectric spike through his muscles. A familiar feeling stirred within him; a powerful presence buried in his very being flooded his consciousness, obscuring his senses and ability to move. The familiar sound of wailing hissed in his ears. Countless brittle-toned voices cried in unison before two blazing-red eyes flamed into existence behind his closed eyelids, regarding him from within.

Nightmare, rasped the Shadow Seeress, coldly, in his mind. That single word ricocheted through his every fiber, sending shivers through his body.

Sorry to summon you in such a manner, Marama, Shadow Seeeress, but I have urgent news.

The flaming eyes narrowed.

Speak.

We have reached the Idlefields, Mistress. It seems the Crystal Soul has passed this way a few days ago...but he was not alone.

The Guardian? she hissed. *Are you certain?*

Without a doubt. Traces of Sensor magic linger. I believe they headed north.

Through the Ridgeback? So their journey begins...

Yes, towards their sacred grounds, Mistress. Perhaps they never truly abandoned the older camps?

His words were met with Marama's rasping breath.

I am gathering our forces to the east, but they are not at strength yet. The Crystal Soul will indeed be protected. Her eyes changed to a deep burgundy color. *Already barriers are being erected to hinder our objectives.*

Then what do you suggest?

What we set out to do...

A buzzing sound tickled Nightmare's ears and pressed against his temple, growing more intense with every passing moment. He resisted the temptation to cover his ears.

The Shadow Seeress's eyes suddenly widened. Her voice found an edge of steel.

Where calm now reigns, we must usher in chaos. Divide...fracture...alienate. Only when we threaten to take away their possessions and status will we see them take action. And when their backs are turned, struggling blindly to preserve what is already lost, will we slice through them unnoticed...to claim our spoils.

Nightmare smiled through the insistent buzzing. He lurched forward as his mouth grew dry; his stomach twisted like a knife had been plunged into it.

Mistress? He gritted his teeth, forcing down the bile. *What is happening?*

An oily obstruction began to rise from his belly and into his chest. Acid licked his throat. He gasped through his nose, yet nothing would fill his lungs. Beads of sweat trickled down his fur as panic washed over him.

What…is happening, Mistress?

Within you resides the path forward.

Claw Point flashed to his mind: the old farmhouse, the ghastlings, Marama's lair…and the pain he felt as she lanced him with power, reviving his husk of a body.

He suddenly realized.

Leaders. Marama laughed. *And these Generals within you shall become the artists of destruction.*

Nightmare felt his throat bulge. He stumbled to his knees, hand still glued to the blood sigil. With one final lance of pain, he slammed his head back, opened his mouth, and retched out an oily plume of shadows that shot up into the air in a smoky vortex. The black cloud whirled, and then exploded outwards, dispersing in different directions. Five fragile-looking shadows sped away, streaking towards the horizon.

With one last gasp of air, Nightmare's head drooped and he toppled onto his back. He opened his eyes to see Dallas looming over him.

"So how do you explain that?" asked the tiger.

Nightmare's lips curled upwards, trickling into a smile. "I believe I just called the old race to arms again." He forced himself into a sitting position, staring after the departing shadows. "A new era is being ushered in, Dallas. The ascension…has begun."

CHAPTER TWO

OLD VOICES AND NEW PLANS.

"Y'see, if it were up to me, I'd've sent hunters out long ago." The raccoon took a swig of his foamy grain water, ignoring the drips spilling onto the tavern floor. "Drag all the primates back in chains is what I say. So what if they complain!"

"Exactly!" grunted the grimy bear seated next to him. He snatched his glass of fire liquor in his meaty hand and knocked it back in one gulp. "Save us decent anumals a whole lotta work, I'll tell you that much."

Above them, cart wheels dangled from the roof's beams, candles burning at the end of every spoke. Yellowed grack and leece skulls decorated the walls.

From his usual spot at the end of the bar, Vincent huffed. "What hunters? We haven't got any left. What was left of Galront's crew split weeks ago after that business with the sandstorm."

The raccoon cackled and turned to face him. "And what'd you know, Vince? It's all right for you. Too old to work, and killin' your days sat here drinkin' in this hole. It must be so hard on you."

"Oi! You watch your mouth. Don't be disrespecting my establishment like that," snapped Jasper, packing his pipe with burlico. The old canine grabbed Vincent's half-filled glass and topped it up. "Here you go, pal, on the house."

Vincent took a gulp, wiping his mouth with the back of his hand.

"Look, Jasper," said the raccoon, "all I'm saying is the village is dying. And rebuilding the stadium? Pah! That's nothin' but monkey work."

The bear shrugged. "It's been so long since I've seen a primate I've almost forgotten what they look like."

"Oh, they're so high, stink of piss, and look like *humans*," laughed the raccoon.

At the mention of mankind, every anumal in Jasper's tavern hissed or spat on the floor.

The raccoon took another swig of his grain water. "I'm just waiting for the whole thing to come collapsin' round the mayor's ears. He can't keep treatin' us honest citizens like slaves."

"Honest?" chuckled Jasper. "You?"

"Ahh, bog off!"

As Jasper and the raccoon bickered back and forth, Vincent sighed. He adjusted his large backside on his stool and leaned against the bar top again, feeling his rolls of stomach fat squash together.

"...If Dallas was here," the raccoon shouted. "He wouldn't have us workin' mornin' an' night-"

Jasper slammed down his pipe. "Well, Dallas ain't here! And I doubt things'd be better even if he was."

The tavern door burst open.

A gust of wind swept through the room, causing the candles to flicker as two shadows lingered in the doorway.

"WHAT DO YOU THINK YOU'RE PLAYIN' AT?" Jasper shouted, jumping to protect the bottles wobbling on the shelves behind him.

Vincent quietly slipped from his stool and stepped into the shadows. Anumals shuffled backwards, dropping their drinks and trying to hide their faces.

Jasper bared his teeth and leaned over the bar. "What do you want? I don't want no trouble in—"

"Shut it, dog!" boomed one of the figures, walking under the chandelier's glow to reveal a huge coyote sporting a scar across his nose. A dented helmet covered the majority of his face, molded to fit his head, and a battered breastplate and gauntlets over a bottle-green tunic protected his chest and hands. He gripped a spiked hammer, while a towering black bear lumbered in next to him, wearing similar armor.

"Well, this looks *verrrry*...cozy," snorted the bear, flicking out his wrist to crack a huge whip against the floor. "Anyone care to explain what's goin' on?"

The raccoon gulped. "P-Please. We were...It's just...It's our break—"

"SHUT IT!" The bear stamped his foot, causing bottles and glasses to topple from the tables. "Y'think we were bred by monkeys, huh? Y'think we're stoopid? Time's runnin' short, raccoon. The new season's comin', an' that stadium's not gonna build itself."

"We…We'll go back straight away, I promi—"

The coyote grabbed the raccoon by the chin and lifted him up like a rag doll. "So…it looks like this place 'as become quite an 'aven for skivers." He glanced across the tavern. "All o' ya! Scroungers! You know the mayor's law: anyone caught offsite, shirkin' their duties, is to be dealt with…appropriately."

He tossed the raccoon aside, watching him slam into a table. Glass flew everywhere.

"Watch what you're doing!" yelped Jasper. "There's no need to smash the place up."

"What you say? No need, huh?" grumbled the black bear. He swept his arm across the nearest tabletop. "We all 'ave our parts to play, Jasper. An' it seems to me like yours is to 'elp these lazy scruds get outta their work."

"They deserve a break."

"Not on the mayor's time they don't. Simple enough to remedy, though. After all, where are you gonna 'ide out when there's nowhere to 'ide out…in?" The bear peered around the tavern before a smile crept across his face. He turned to the coyote. "Get a torch."

The coyote chuckled and headed for the door. "My pleasure."

"N-now, there's no need for this," Jasper stammered. "Call him back. What the…"

The raccoon dragged himself to his feet. "H-he's right. Things were never like this when Dallas was here."

"WELL, THINGS'VE CHANGED!" The bear slammed his fist against another table. "So deal with it."

The coyote burst through the door clutching a burning torch. He passed it to the bear. "Here you go."

"These scumbags 'ave been moaning about Dallas."

The coyote's nostrils flared. "Have they now?"

"Yes!" shouted the raccoon. "And when he retur—"

"He ain't returning. Dallas deserted us!" The black bear swung the torch in a slow circle, addressing the entire tavern. "And the Sabers 'ave been silenced. So now when the mayor gives the orders, *we're* the one who make sure it happens."

"An' the orders are for you to work," said the coyote. "So you'll work day an' night until the stadium is rebuilt. An' the sooner you realize that the better."

"Are you bloody blind?" yelled Jasper. "Ferris can't keep driving them to exhaustion like this; they need rest."

"Rest doesn't get stadiums built, or streets cleaned, or food caught." The black bear held the torch up and stared into the flames. "But you lot don't seem to understand that. Well, let's see if you understand it a bit better when I burn this place to the ground."

"No!" shouted Jasper. He vaulted over the bar and jumped for the torch, but the bear batted him away.

"If you value your lives," yelled the bear, "I'd shift your backsides outta 'ere pretty quick."

Every patron around Vincent stared nervously at one another, unsure what to do; yet no one moved. Vincent felt the urge to act: to break free from the shadows and tear into their flesh, but he too remained rooted to the spot.

The black bear snorted. "Don't believe me, huh?" He glanced at his comrade before touching the torch against an overhead beam. The fire licked hungrily against it.

Jasper scrabbled to his feet. "STOP!"

"Frag off," said the bear, swatting him away again.

The ceiling began to smoke.

Jasper crawled forwards, trying to snatch at the torch. "Please...Someone..."

"And who's gonna help you, huh, dog?" laughed the bear. "No one's got the guts."

"I have."

Every pair of eyes swung toward Vincent.

"Have you now?" The bear slowly lowered the torch to look

closer at his victim.

Vincent carefully waddled out from the comfort of the darkness, and with thick, stubby fingers, yanked his heavy cloak aside. His belly stuck out, too big to be covered by the grack-skin material.

"Yes," he replied, his jowls wobbling with every word.

The bear let out a gigantic belly laugh. "You hear that?" He tapped the coyote on the side of his helmet before turning back to Vincent and pointing the torch at him. "The old cat's grown a backbone. Seen it all now, I have. Come on then. How are you gonna stop us?"

The puma smirked. "I have ways."

"*Ways*, huh?" chortled the coyote.

The bear nodded. "Maybe 'e'll squash us flat."

Vincent gritted his teeth, but kept his anger in check. "Well, to be honest, I think it would take a gorespine to flatten the likes of you two."

A fist lashed out and struck the puma's jaw, sending him spinning to the floor. The coyote loomed over him.

"Shut your mouth and know your place. Felines are nothing these days, you hear me? Nothing."

"You can't do that to Vince!" Jasper shouted.

A dull ache burned Vincent's cheek. He crawled to his knees, trying to clear his ringing head. "I-it's alright, Jasper. They're only...doing their job."

The coyote raised his fist. "You bein' funny, glux?"

"No...no, please. I-I'm sorry." He raised his hands in surrender.

The bear snorted before cracking his whip. "Enough! Everyone outta this tavern now or else burn with it."

"Gentlemen, please!" said Vincent, struggling to his feet. "I know you've got orders, but give these anumals a chance. At least let them finish their drinks. Then, I assure you, everyone will return to the stadium and work even harder. And when Ferris sees that...just think how happy he'll be." Vincent smiled and reached under his cloak for a small pouch. "And after, well, I'm sure you'll be able to have a few well deserved drinks yourselves, huh?"

The coyote eyed the pouch greedily before snatching it from his outstretched hand. He untied the drawstring and his eyes widened at the sight of the nugs and bitz inside. Snapping his hand closed, he stuffed the pouch under his armor. "I think that should do."

"So we're going to check out the rest of the street. But if you scruds are here when we get back…" The bear raised the torch up to the blackened beam again.

"Sure!" Jasper nodded. "They understand."

The bear snorted as they stormed out of the tavern, slamming the door behind them. The flickering candles finally settled back to steady flames.

Vincent rubbed his sore face and wobbled over to his seat. He sat down and took a long draft of his grain water, draining it empty. As he put the glass on the bar, he saw Jasper staring at him, shaking his head.

"What?" he asked, repositioning his bottom on the stool.

"Are you…are you okay, pal?"

Vincent held up his empty glass. "Will be when I get another one of these."

A tankard of grain water almost immediately appeared in front of him. He took a deep gulp, and wiping his jowls, turned to face the stares still squarely pinned on him.

"I'd finish up if I were you lot," he muttered. A perfectly timed drop of blood trickled from the corner of his mouth. "I don't have enough credits to stop them next time."

He snatched up Jasper's cleaning rag and wiped away the blood, leaving behind only a slight smear…and a silent grudge to settle.

* * *

Old, fat puma, thought Vincent, making his way through Wooburn's twilit streets. The moon had risen, framed by a luxurious cobalt blue sky. The sound of clinking metal and the rhythmic sawing of wood could be heard coming from the distant half built stadium. A warm breeze tickled his fur, promising yet another hot day for those forced to work in the morning. The coppery smell of blood pricked his nose as he sidled by a boarded up butcher's shop. Passing through the closed market square, he headed towards an alley adjacent to Wooburn's justice house. He looked up and scoffed. The sight of the lone candle, flickering in the mayor's office window, always made him sneer.

It had been burning there since Dallas disappeared a week ago.

Within days of the tiger's disappearance, gossip had buzzed through the village like a swarm of sectoids: Dallas had discovered the identity of his birth parents: Dallas had been savaged: Dallas was in hiding, ready to plot the mayor's downfall: Dallas was suffering from a fatal case of skin lice. The spin mayor Ferris and his officials had finally put on the situation, however, was that Dallas had embarked on a mission to find the mayor's son, Harris, who had departed Wooburn only a few days after the fire.

He shook his head at the thought of the mayor.

"Moronic scrud."

The puma's eyes wandered towards the large glass window with the odd symbols on it, and he shuddered before quickly entering the alley.

A shadow flickered ahead of him.

Vincent stopped dead in his tracks, claws slowly poking from the tips of his fingers. His lip curled back to reveal vicious looking fangs.

"Who's there?" he hissed, hunkering down, ready for an attack.

Nothing moved.

The puma waited, before slowly exhaling and moving forward again.

"Get a grip, Vince," he muttered, shaking his head. "Getting all jumpy."

A garbage can toppled behind him, spilling its contents. Vincent spun on his heels as a shadow slipped past his shoulder.

"Who...who's there?" The puma's heart pounded, fueled by trepidation. His voice echoed along the alley with no response.

Nothing moved. "What do you want?"

Complete silence.

The guards from Jasper's tavern sprang to mind.

"If you've come for more credits, then you're out of luck. I haven't got anything else. You took—"

His world spun.

The puma fell to the ground as a jolt of pain lanced through him. He rolled onto his back and a high-pitched ringing buzzed in his ears. Stars spiraled through his blurred vision, leaving wavy tails in their wake.

A black shadow loomed over him.

Vincent pressed his hands over his ears, trying to block the noise. "Y-you don't know who I am," he gasped, kicking his boots into the grit.

The shadow leaned over and stroked the side of his face. Its touch felt like death.

"Get away!" yelled Vincent.

The shadow slowly smiled, and its mouth opened wide to reveal long, needle-like teeth.

Fear snaked through Vincent as its stick-like fingers twined around his face.

"No...Please."

The shadow moved closer.

"No! No...NO!"

The shadow grabbed Vincent's mouth and yanked it open, shoving its fingers into the gap between the puma's teeth. It forced itself down his throat, distorting its shadowy head and shoulders in order to slither into the puma's belly. Vincent's eyes bulged as tears leaked down his cheeks. The shrieks in his head intensified. The ground spun beneath him, gaining momentum, while an alien feeling gripped his insides. His vision clouded. His stomach distended. Coldness gripped his soul. His heart felt like it was about explode, when...

Everything stopped.

He sat upright, grit trickling from his robes.

A searing pain crawled up his right forearm. He clutched it to his chest and heaved himself to his feet.

"Wh..." He rubbed his throat, looking around the empty alley. "What the—"

Go to the felines.

Vincent staggered and fell against the wall, his body trembling with fear.

"Who—"

The time isss now, hissed a voice inside his head.

Vincent paused. Deep inside a dormant flicker of hope ignited. "The felines? You mean the Sabers?"

Yessss.

A slow smile replaced his fear.

Staggering back down the alley, Vincent passed through the market square again, retracing his steps by the empty butcher's, and heading in the direction of the stadium. Veering away from the main street, he navigated the twisted warren of Wooburn's back alleys, before finally reaching a flight of stairs that descended into a tunnel. Filthy water sweated from the walls, creating rancid puddles for him to wade through. Reaching the tunnel's end, he came face to face with a large, iron door.

The time isss now, whispered the voice.

He pounded on the door four times and lowered his hand. "The time...is now..." he repeated.

"Speak!" snapped a voice through a small hole.

Vincent took a deep breath, feeling power building inside him, and said, "Preserving our rights. Protecting our race. Dominating the weak through speed, strength, and grace."

He rubbed his aching arm as numerous bolts and chains were unlocked behind the door. It swung open with a creak. Heat enveloped him, and he stepped inside.

"Sir, what an unexpected surprise," said the feline guard. He bowed quickly and shuffled out of the way.

Vincent nodded. Before him hung a pleated velvet curtain, muffling the raised voices hidden beyond.

"Well, what else are we supposed to do?" someone yelled. "We need to take back control."

"How?" replied a croaky voice. "The guards are no pushover, and we lack focus—"

"They've already targeted our younger members," interrupted a female. "They threatened 'em with the junk mines if they so much as put a whisker outta line."

"Scrudding Ferris and his scare tactics."

"Oh, this ain't no scare tactic; he'll do it. Look at what he did to Narfell."

"Enough!" shouted another aged voice. "We need change. Maybe we should alter our mindset and look more towards acceptance and equality between us felines and the others?"

The younger Sabers hissed and booed.

"Acceptance?" shouted one. "Be quiet, old fool! The Fangs have heard about this kind of stupid talk and they'll surely manipulate the situation. And then what are we gonna do? Our clans'll sway in their direction when they see their strength, and then we'll be disbanded."

"We need to weapon up and hit Ferris now."

Vincent whipped back the velvet curtain. "And hit him we shall. With all our might."

The cavernous hall fell silent. Everyone ground to a halt. Smoke swirled teasingly around the still inhabitants, its exotic scent fused with the richness of nagey spices from beyond the continent. Lined with plush fabrics and hanging clan flags, ornate thrones ran in parallel lines facing Vincent, stretching far off into the darkness of the room. Felines lounged in every one of them.

Vincent faltered for a moment under their unified gaze.

"S-Sir," said a Saber, dropping to one knee, followed quickly by the room. "We weren't expecting you."

Vincent smiled. He turned to his left to study the most elaborate throne of all. Positioned on a raised platform, the wooden masterpiece towered above the others. Carvings adorned the seat, depicting anumals bent in supplication to the intricate feline skull set at the throne's pinnacle. Vincent unclasped his cloak, letting it fall to his feet. He raised his arm for the room to view it. The twisted tribal markings that had been seared into his flesh countless years ago now glowed a bright bismuth-yellow. He smiled; the ocelot brand had never appeared so beautiful. A gasp swept through the room, followed by excited murmuring.

"Brothers and sisters," he said, casually approaching the throne. Placing his hands on the canine skull armrests, he lowered his bulk into the chair. "Be seated."

As one, every feline sat. Vincent poured his gaze over his audience, inspecting the junior ranked Sabers such as Gizi, Jakz, and Kayn, occupying the furthest thrones from him. Those of higher rank sat closer, with the most senior members positioned on the front row. The front, central throne – set directly before Vincent – remained unoccupied.

Dallas…thought the puma, scratching his chin.

Yes, the key to dominance has not disappeared, whispered the voice in his head. *He will help us rise.*

Vincent chuckled, feeling everything suddenly fall into place.

"Fellow Sabers, it has been far too long since I've met with you…and, as I entered today, I heard your concerns."

"Sir!" said an older feline, his gray fur dulling. He climbed to his feet on the front row. "We were merely discussing our future. This lair has become more a sanctuary of late. Many dare not leave its walls."

"An' that makes us about as useful as primate dung! We're caged in like bloody *animals*," shouted a young feline from the rear. "We need to strike."

A female stood up straight. "The Air Spikes have already started to show public animosity to our beliefs. If this carries on, and the other feline clans follow suit, then the Sabers will be no more."

"Ferris and his guards should be reminded of their position, which will also restore lost faith from the clans," snarled Gizi, pounding his fist against his palm. "*We* are the ruling order."

"Jus' say the word and I'm with you, bro, but we should hear what the Ocelot Master has to say first," said Kayn, loud enough for Vincent to hear.

"Yeah," mumbled Jakz, chomping into a half eaten leece leg.

"Enough words!" yelled a voice. "We want action!"

"Silence!" snapped an elder. "If we instigate battle, the guards will pound us all to a pulp. They have more weapons and greater power—"

"No one possesses greater power than us felines. No one is above us, nor shall they ever be," cut in Vincent, calmly silencing the debate. "And as I promised, all those years ago, our time has finally come."

"W-with all due respect, sir," stammered the older feline. "Your decision to remain camouflaged within the village has distanced you from us Sabers. Many feel you are no longer fully in…touch with our struggles."

"I am more in touch than you realize, Basrah, and I am far more aware than most of you would like. I hear every rumor, betrayal, and loyal act each Saber commits, so have more faith in my words." Vincent raised his glowing brand high into the air again. "As was written in the Ocelot scriptures; 'A sign shall light our bodies, defining our moment of glory.'"

His smile widened.

Mutters surged through the crowd, voicing both approval and uncertainty.

"They think we are silenced; they think we are beaten. Yet how little they know." He leaned forward, dropping his voice to an urgent whisper. "Our missing brother is the key. He is the one who shall lead us to victory."

"Dallas deserted us!" snapped a withered old female near the front. "He is nothing to this order—"

"He *is* the order!" retaliated Vincent, slamming his fist against his armrest. "For he is the only one who can help us obtain what we deserve."

Younger Sabers jumped to their feet, howling their agreement.

"We must find him," urged Vincent. "Immediately!"

Bottles and jars flew against the walls, sending glass raining down on the older members. Some hissed with annoyance, while others rose to their feet and headed for the exit, leaving the youngsters, and the Sabers, behind.

"This is not the path of the wise!" shouted an elder as he left the hall.

"Good riddance!" yipped a youngster.

Younger minds are better to mold, whispered the voice in Vincent's mind. *Only the strong shall survive...*

The head of the Sabers, Vincent, the Ocelot Master, sat back in his throne, and smiled.

CHAPTER THREE

BURNICK BLIND.

"Stay there!" Clinton's mother shouted, charging down the hallway. Crunching over smashed glass, she headed for the back door. "Don't move!"

Clinton ignored her orders and scrabbled after Loretta. Snarling cries met him as he raced along the hallway. Gusts shook the house, rattling ornaments from the walls and shelves. The breath snagged at the back of his throat.

Loretta entered the kitchen.

Moonlight flooded through the window, bouncing off Clinton's new armor as he ran to her side. Shadows flickered. The noise intensified. Loretta rammed her foot against the door. It crashed open and a blast of wind engulfed her. Without pause, she ran outside. The door slammed behind her.

Feed! Gather and feed...

Raion scampered into the room.

"What's happening?" he cried.

Clinton shoved his brother behind him and rushed for the door. "Stay there, Rai. I need to help."

"But—"

"I SAID STAY!"

Raion flinched and wiped his eyes.

Gather. Feed. Move. I must...

Clinton grasped the handle and shoved his shoulder against the door. The howling wind blasted him, making him squint.

His world ground to a halt.

This isn't real. These things aren't real. None of this is real...

"Loretta!" yelled his father, fighting the skeletal dragon. Deep gashes lined the lion's back and arms, and the moonlight in his eyes glinted a luminous green. "Get them back inside!"

Them?

Clinton turned to see Raion shivering next to him, his eyes wide like saucers.

Loretta swung around, her face a mask of terror. "Get inside now!" she yelled.

Falling to all fours, she positioned herself between the flying nightmare and her children. "Clinton, Raion, get inside! Run!"

The hive is leaving. I must rejoin...

But Clinton's feet were rooted to the spot.

The dragon lunged at Grayorr, talons the size of gateposts slashing through the air.

Ducking low, his father slipped away from the strike. Loretta dove ahead and wrapped herself around the monster's legs, tearing away one of its giant bones. The dragon shrieked. It flicked its foot, flinging the lioness high into the air. Grayorr roared louder than Clinton had ever heard, his father's defiant tones merging in a cry of anger and fear.

Loretta landed in the dirt.

"GET INSIDE!" she screamed.

The dragon forced its giant bone-wings earthwards and arched its body back. It shot up, hovering in midair for a moment, before hurtling at them again...

I must rejoin...I must leave now!

Something pricked the end of Clinton's finger.

"Ow!" he yelped, snapping his eyes open.

The lion's vision swam as he lurched back to reality to inspect the small sectoid perched on the end of his index finger. The creature spread its wings and flew back to its companions on the ground, busy transporting tiny pieces of food in a long line through the forest.

"It stung me!" complained Clinton, inspecting the jewel of blood welling on his fingertip.

Hagen looked up from his map. "What did?"

"The sectoid. It stung me." Clinton sucked on the cut and resisted the urge to stamp on the tiny procession. Instead, he jumped to his feet and kicked a dry branch deep into the undergrowth. "That's the last time I practice on one of those scruds."

"Your mind wandered."

"No it didn't."

26

"I was stating a fact, Clinton, not asking a question."

Clinton glared at the komodo sitting cross-legged, next to the map. Stones had been placed on each corner to hold the parchment in position, and smoothly polished pebbles lay dotted across it, charting the path they had taken. Herbs smoked in a clay bowl beside the lizard, filling the air with a musky scent. A large pot hung over the fire with two clawed feet poking out of it.

Hagen's gaze remained fixed on Clinton. "Did you open your mind far enough?"

"Yes." Clinton sat down beside him and shrugged. "I concentrated and blocked everything out around me. I tried to find that small speck of light, that…spark inside the sectoid. And I scrudding had it too! I could feel it, seeing what it was seeing, thinking its thoughts…and yet…"

"Well Wood?"

The komodo reached over and pulled some of the smoking herbs from the bowl. He wafted them under his nose, before ripping off the charred ends and sprinkling them into the stew.

"Yes. Well Wood. Again." Clinton picked up a twig and tossed it into the fire.

Hagen stirred the stew. "You need to focus more."

"I can't help it if my mind wanders onto the past. I'm not a machine, y'know."

"Will the past help your future?"

"I don't know. Maybe? Remembering the past is probably as useful as meditating in the middle of a forest, trying to talk to sectoids all day long." Clinton turned away, trying to ignore Hagen's gaze. After a few seconds, he looked back at the lizard and smiled. "There was no lightning this time though. At least *that* seems to have stopped."

"Clinton, you know what you are practicing and why you are doing it. Raw power can manifest in many ways until it can be controlled. And until that point, it is dangerous. Now that you are aware of the power you possess, and what you must do, you will soon realize it is not a simple a case of manipulating sectoids." Hagen scooped up a spoonful of stew and offered it to Clinton.

"Here, taste this."

The lion supped up the watery stock and felt it warm his throat.

"Listen, Clinton," said the komodo, sprinkling some salt into the stew. "I remember the fight to take my first breath after breaking out of my birthing shell, and I also remember beating every last one of my kin to assert my dominance."

"What? On the day you were born?"

"No," hissed the lizard, laughing. "That is my point. A new, raw power cannot spring to life fully formed. It must be nurtured and molded *over time*."

"Much like your cooking." Clinton passed the spoon back to Hagen. "Needs more herbs."

Hagen chuckled and his yellow, forked tongue snaked out of his mouth. He snapped off more of the smoking herbs and sprinkled them into the mix.

Clinton yawned and leaned against a tree.

Night was drawing in, and the forest's branches swayed gently, masking the darkening sky. The cool breeze would soon drop to present them with another freezing evening.

Since leaving Samanoski, Clinton and Hagen had trekked for many days up into the Ridgeback Mountains. At first the dense forest appeared magical to the lion, having never seen so many trees in his life. Yet, as their seemingly endless trek continued, he yearned to see an open patch of land once more.

He leaned over to get a better look at the map.

"So are we getting closer?"

Hagen adjusted one of the stones marking their path. "I assume so. The ground at this height is undisturbed and off the beaten track. This morning we passed some kamrik roots that had been fouled on, so trackers may have led a party though here recently. When we reach higher ground we will have a broader perspective of the landscape."

"Great. Higher and colder. Who could ask for more?" Clinton pulled his cloak tight, and rolled his eyes. "Why do your tribesmen have to make things so difficult?"

Hagen grinned and pulled two wooden bowls out of his bag.

"The term 'hidden camp' would be redundant if it did not live up to its description. Give it time, Clinton; we will find it."

The lion stared back at the fire. "Time is all we seem to have at the moment—"

"Correction," interrupted Hagen. "Time…and wefring stew."

He held the steaming bowl under Clinton's nose. With a chuckle, the lion grudgingly took it from him and began to eat.

That night Clinton drifted off into a fractured sleep where rest seemed to elude him. Since his first experience with the sectoid at Samanoski stadium, Hagen had instructed him to practice with more and more of the tiny creatures. At first he had found it difficult to lock onto them and to enter their alien minds, yet, with practice, he had managed to gain control. The process, however, often left him feeling distanced from his own being. He felt stretched and drawn out, like part of him had been stolen or damaged. Physical rest did not ease the feeling either; his exhaustion spread far beyond the body.

When morning finally arrived, sleep crusted Clinton's eyes, and a twinkle of frost layered the cloak and blanket covering him.

Hagen sat with his back to the lion while the promise of cooking eggs drifted on the breeze. "Eat quickly and gather your things," he said. "We have a long day's journey ahead of us."

Clinton let his head fall back against the ground. He looked up into the morning sky, wondering when things would return to normal…and he could return home to his brother.

When the thought hit him that normal seemed less and less likely to ever return again, he closed his eyes and sighed.

* * *

By the time the sun rose, the morning frost had melted, soaking the plants with dew. Sunlight sneaked through gaps in the forest canopy, spearing beams of light along the path they were traveling. Flocks of ayvids screeched above as they flew over the trees, wafting the earthy smell of wet foliage through the air.

As their journey wore on and the sun reached its peak in the sky, Hagen took to singing the same folk song he had been reciting since Samanoski.

"...*But Burnick sped to the bloody fight,*
Come, Burnick, friend, let us help your plight,
Your strength may win, but your sight will not,
You live in the dark, lest you have forgot,
But Burnick again, he refused their plea,
To the heart of the battle did this warrior flee,
Through the light of day and the depths of night,
Made no difference to his vanished sight,
When he dropped to the ground and his life was done,
Forever shamed of the aid he shun—"

"What's it about?" Clinton picked up his pace to walk by the lizard's side. "The song. Every time we walk, it's 'Burnick this' and 'Burnick that'."

"You have folk songs in Wooburn, do you not?"

"Do we just! You only have to mention songs to Arkie and he's off for the night...Most of his are about scantily clad anumals though."

The two chuckled, but the mention of Clinton's friend caused a wave of loneliness to surge through him.

Arkie. Wooburn. Well Wood. Raion.

Everything led back to his brother.

"It is about Burnick of the Hand," said Hagen, interrupting Clinton's thoughts. "One of the greatest warriors of my tribe."

Clinton wiped the sweat from his brow. "But?"

"But Burnick could have become one of the strongest Sensors to have ever lived...if he had been less stubborn."

"I have sneaky suspicion this Burnick was blind then?"

"How ever did you guess?" Hagen smiled. "Yes, blind from the moment he was born until the moment he died. They say he had better 'sight' than most, but, in reality, Burnick had trained himself to fully utilize his remaining senses. What magic he could not conjure, or weapon he could not wield was not worth knowing."

The two anumals stepped over a trickling stream and continued up along a track that wound away from the dense forest.

Clinton nodded. "Sounds like he was pretty formidable."

"Oh, he was. He had strength, speed, intelligence, and power...However, he had great pride too. Which was his undoing."

"Why?"

Hagen pushed a low-slung branch out of their path. "Well, Burnick survived skirmishes with the Grayscales, the Technals from the Ice Lands, the Spikes, Humaneers, Horn Heads, and even deformed Bes from the Wastelands. However, as the seasons drifted by, and Silania's law brought peace into the lands, Burnick lost his edge. When a new threat surfaced, Burnick did not study it, he approached the problem in his previous manner."

"Why would he do that?"

The komodo stopped and looked at Clinton. "Stubbornness? Pride? Overconfidence?"

"Okay, okay, I get the message." Clinton clambered over a large rock blocking their path. "You're about as subtle as a stunpike, lizard."

"I have been likened to worse things."

"So who were they then, this new threat he was facing?"

"They called themselves the Cult of Shar, or the Shar Zuul. At least those were some of their earlier names."

"Never heard of them."

"Most had not," replied Hagen. "Which was why Burnick dismissed them as a threat. His fellow Sensors offered their help, and cautioned him of underestimation, but to a seasoned warrior like Burnick, the Shar Zuul were nothing. He refused assistance even from his own *quintad*."

"What's that then?"

"A group of five Sensors that work and train together. Almost like a family."

Clinton and Hagen finally mounted the crest of the hill. Ahead, on the horizon, a mist had settled over another sprawling forest. The two anumals began their descent.

"So what happened?"

"The Shar Zuul fought like beasts; they slipped, ghostlike, over the earth, stinking of death, and hindering Burnick's senses. They tore him limb from limb."

"What? How?"

"He miscalculated. He had his tribe and his *quintad* around him, each with tremendous abilities and powers, yet he ignored them. This is where the phrase *Burnick-Blind* derives from: when pride impedes the wisdom of combining strength."

Clinton pondered his words.

"I've never heard that phrase before, but it certainly sounds true about most anumals I know. Burnick-blind Ferris Lakota. Burnick-blind Council official Farl. In fact, most of Wooburn is Burnick-blind."

As Clinton entered the forest's shade again, his thoughts slowly dispersed along with the light. He walked in silence. The only sound to be heard was the twitter of ayvids and the crunching of fallen twigs and leaves underfoot. Soon the terrain began to change. The constant maze of trees no longer blocked their path, and demolished walls and iron girders stuck out sporadically from the undergrowth. When they finally cleared the last row of trees, they found themselves at the base of a hill that led into the mountains. Abandoned buildings lined the incline and then branched out upon entering a village at the top. At the far end of the village fell a sharp cliff, overlooking a forest as far as the eye could see.

"Beautiful, is it not?" muttered Hagen, inspecting the view. "Yet tragic."

Clinton ran his hand down one of the buildings, knowing what Hagen was referring to.

Ravaged by time and nature, part of it had collapsed into rubble. The whole area seemed untouched by anumalkind, with no modified entrances for larger-sized anumals, or even smaller abodes built within the trees.

Verging off the steep path, Clinton wandered further into the village proper. Empty window frames hung flaccidly from twisted hinges. Rusted girders sprouted from the ground like defiant flowers, surrounded by patches of needle bushes and itching grass. Overhead, shrubs and weeds cascaded over the rooftops like jade waterfalls.

The crunch of footsteps on broken glass echoed behind the lion.

"Y'know, I don't think anumalkind has ever lived here," said Clinton, investigating a boarded up shop. "I reckon we could be the first anumals to have entered this place since..."

He turned to face the komodo, but his words lodged in his throat. He froze. A small anumal lingered down the street, floating like an apparition, coughing and spluttering from under its hood. Yet Clinton did not need to see its face to recognize who it was.

"Y-you!" he gasped, approaching the badger.

The creature shuffled away.

"I'm...I'm not going to hurt you. Please, I—"

"You're blind!" snapped the badger. "Blind!"

"Why?" The closer Clinton came to him, the more the light illuminated his horrid features: a thin layer of flesh clung to his sunken face. "What do you want?"

"Trust!" He pulled his hood up to shield his features from the sun. "Takes seasons to earn and moments to shatter. You give it too freely."

"Who to?"

"Someone. Everyone. Everything! They will turn..." From under his hood his eyes caught the light, and flickered green. "Trust no one!"

With that he and set off down the street, gliding through anything that blocked his path.

"Wait! You can't keep doing this. Explain!" yelled Clinton, racing after him. He chased the badger down a flight of stone steps, plowing through debris and overgrown foliage, until he emerged into the village square. Charred, derelict buildings surrounded him. He vaulted the skeletal remains of a car.

"WHERE ARE YOU?"

But his cry was left unanswered.

With a huff, he kicked a stone across the street and watched it tumble through the glass-sprinkled undergrowth. Every wall on every building had been covered with lines of small holes, as if blasted by something. The trees swayed in the breeze. Scuttling sounds sneaked out from the lonely structures.

Clinton paused.

"Fine." He took a second to survey the area. "Have it your way. But next time I'm just…"

A scent pricked his nose: acrid and festering.

Clinton sighed.

"So you've seen sense…"

He turned.

A heavy weight slammed into Clinton. He toppled backwards and his head bounced against the moss-covered bricks. An unyielding weight pressed on his chest, restricting his breathing. Without a second thought, Clinton snapped his leg up, aiming for his attacker's stomach, but his boot smashed against something hard. A mouth, full of needle-sharp teeth, snapped at him, hissing a mist of spittle over his face. Dried blood and sinew coated the scavenger's maroon exoskeleton, and long fractures ran along its carapace, evidence of a heavy blow to its head. One of the creature's pincers stabbed through Clinton's cloak, barely missing his shoulder, pinning him to the ground. A chilling panic swept over the lion.

"KRAGGON!"

One of the kraggon's pincers snapped in front of his face. Its whipping head screeched in fury, but the lion threw his hand out and grabbed its carapace, forcing it back. Clinton lifted his legs and shoved against it with all his might, but he could not slip free from the monster's grip. Spotting a brick, he grabbed the weapon and smashed it against the scavenger's injured head.

"Get…off…me!"

The lion gritted his teeth and closed his eyes.

Find its soul, he thought. *Control it.*

Yet the kraggon's being felt lost to him in a maze of anger and fear.

"Come on!" he snarled, beating the brick against its skull over and over again. More cracks appeared along the kraggon's head. Its legs buckled. Ignoring the growing pain in his hand, Clinton continued his attack.

The ground rumbled.

A blustering noise surged through the gaps in the buildings, multiplying until it reached a raucous wail. Behind the kraggon, a giant komodo reared up into the air, swathing them both in its shadow. Throwing its arms wide, the giant snapped its bulging neck forwards and hissed ferociously at the kraggon, the din causing the ground to rumble again in reply.

The kraggon scampered away from Clinton with a screech.

Feeling the pressure released from his chest, the lion lowered his bloody arm and sucked in a lungful of air. Scrabbling back, he sat upright, staring at the figure of the hissing komodo.

The kraggon shrieked defiantly at the ghostly komodo, before snapping its jaws closed and fleeing for the safety of the nearby trees.

Clinton stared at the lizard before him. It looked like a giant version of Hagen, but with a darker hide, and minus the tattoos.

"Clinton," hissed Hagen's voice.

The lion jumped and spun around to see the komodo kneeling behind him, his tattoos glowing an azure blue around the eyes. Hagen blinked slowly, causing the symbols to gradually darken. When Clinton turned back to look at the giant lizard he saw it disperse, fading away with the power of Hagen's tattoos. The village square returned to silence once more.

Clinton held his breath. A burning pain ignited his bleeding hand. Every knuckle felt raw and bloody, but beneath his confusion, anger began to simmer. He rose to his feet, gripping his hand, and staring coldly at Hagen. "I don't care what magic trick you just did, I could've killed it," he growled. "I can look after myself. I don't need you saving me every time I'm in trouble."

Hagen stood up, his tattoos now fully extinguished. "You think that was my intention?"

"How am I ever supposed to stick up for myself if everyone always gets in my way?"

Hagen stared blankly at the lion. "I was not trying to save you." The komodo turned and set off up the steps, away from the village square.

"Then what were you doing?" yelled Clinton, stomping after him.

Hagen paused and looked back over his shoulder. His eyes narrowed to slits. "I was saving the baby kraggon…from *you.*"

CHAPTER FOUR

LIONS, LIZARDS AND KRAGGONS.

"A baby?" huffed Clinton, toying with his food.

The two travelers sat by the fire in the village square, warming themselves against the night air. The komodo leaned over his map, busy charting their progress. Picking up a small amulet of green crystal set within a smooth pebble, he held it to his eye, like a looking glass, and glanced at the map again. "Not as appealing as a cubling, I concur, but an infant, nonetheless."

"Yes, well, even as a baby, that thing could have taken my head off."

"It was scarcely a few weeks old."

Clinton put his bowl down. "I know, Hagen. You don't have to remind me."

"Clinton—"

"Forget it! When I'm not totally useless, I'm busy smashing in baby's skulls. Why is everything such a mess? When will things *finally* get better for me?"

"When you finally put them into order. And to do that takes effort and patience." The komodo placed the amulet down on the map. "But you will strive onwards, because that is what you always do."

Clinton ran his hand through his hair. "I lost it, didn't I?"

"A tad, yes."

"But I tried, Hagen. I searched for its soul."

"Too hard."

"What?

"You searched too hard for its soul."

Clinton leaned back against a rock and folded his arms. "Oh, this is ridiculous! First I don't do enough, and now I'm doing too much."

"Clinton." The komodo rose to his feet. "It is not a simple cantrip or cub's trick that I am expecting of you. This is not floor magic, where you merely create potions to heal a cut. The spirits know how long a Sensor takes to master his own body before he can master his mind, and what I ask of you surpasses all expectations. I tell you to focus and not let your mind wander; yet you must first free your mind in order to achieve that goal. You must protect and take flight, but are expected to also fight. You must learn to concentrate on yourself while influencing what others around you are doing. Finally, you need to master the art of drawing a soul from a source, gather it, and then utilize its power without the threat of repercussion. Now, I am sure most anumals would have trouble even understanding what I just said, let alone executing it, however, this is what is expected of you…at its simplest."

"Yeah." Clinton grabbed his bowl and stirred the wefring stew. "Simple."

"A jumble, Clinton. That is what you must become: a paradox. The fight *and* the flight. Only then can you find an anchor strong enough to ground yourself and make your first reaction the correct one. And that is what you must do; you must learn to take control, manipulate, and harvest souls…whilst also respecting them."

Clinton's embarrassment rose. "And today?"

Hagen crouched down before the lion. "Do not worry, we all have bad days."

"Bad days, huh? I can't remember the last time I've had a good one."

After finishing his food, Clinton drew closer to the fire, but even its warmth could not thaw his mood. Surrounded by the abandoned town, he heard water running though the pipes below the circular holes in the streets and wondered where the injured kraggon pup had escaped to. The image of the badger infected his thoughts again, and the ghostly warning he had been given plagued his worries.

Trust no one.

Opening an eye, he watched Hagen plotting their path through the Ridgeback Mountains on the map. At that moment Hagen felt like the only person he had left; he had to trust him, like it or not. Pondering those thoughts, his vision slowly clouded over, before sleep enticed him into a much needed respite.

* * *

The twitter of ayvids pulled Clinton from his dream of grack steak. The sun was rising and the air felt fresh and crisp. He yawned.

"Yes, I know. I'll pack my things and get ready," he said, predicting the komodo's morning greeting. Yet, when Clinton looked up, Hagen was nowhere in sight.

The lion sat up, but a searing pain shot through his wrist. He glanced down at his hand and noticed a fresh bandage had been wrapped around it while he slept. He smiled, shook his head, and sighed.

"Hagen..."

Cracking a couple of eggs onto a heated stone, Clinton opened up the lizard's backpack and took out some salted scavenger strips. He ripped off a piece and chewed the hard meat before sitting back against a wall, waiting for his friend to return. He basked in the warmth of the morning sun for a while, enjoying the peace, when the undergrowth to his left rustled.

Turning to meet the komodo, he said, "I'm cooking us some..."

He immediately swallowed his words.

A long, spiderlike leg edged out of the dense bushes, before the kraggon pup's head slowly inched into view. Clinton remained deadly still, the dried meat clutched tight in his fist.

Okay, he thought. *Okay, it's just a baby. Keep calm. It's only a...*

The kraggon limped forwards, closer to the fire, its head roving, sniffing at the scent of eggs in the air. It hummed a low warble while chattering its jaws together. Clinton stared at its tiny, black eyes, before a sudden idea struck him.

Tearing off a chunk of meat, he tossed it at the pup. The kraggon yelped and scuttled back a few steps, hissing vehemently. When Clinton remained passive, however, it warbled again and edged closer. The scavenger snapped the meat up in a pincer and scampered away, gulping down its spoils in one ravenous bite.

Climbing to his knees, Clinton held out another strip of meat and waited.

The kraggon slowly edged closer. Its pincers clicked against the stone, while one of its back legs hung limply, scraping against the ground. Clinton winced, feeling his guilt surge. The left side of the pup's mouth and eye had caved in from the lion's attack, and was now caked in dried blood. Long cracks ran along its carapace with white slime oozing from it.

Come on, it's okay, thought Clinton. *I won't hurt you.*

The cautious pup approached, nostrils flaring, tasting the air. Almost touching his hand, a long tongue slipped out of the scavenger's mouth and clasped onto the meat, before whipping it away.

"Do you want some more?" he asked, opening Hagen's bag. The kraggon hissed and darted back a few paces, but as soon as Clinton retrieved another strip, it cautiously returned. The pup's trembling tongue extended to snatch the meat, but before it could take it, Clinton's hand slipped out and touched its injured head. The kraggon tensed, but did not retreat. It locked eyes with him, trembling under the lion's touch.

Clinton, what are you doing? he thought, but his instincts told him to continue.

He closed off everything in his mind and concentrated solely on the injured creature.

Darkness filtered his peripheral vision, and before he knew it, his breath, body, and senses, had become one with the scavenger. A hot sensation spread down his leg and the side of his face, mirroring the kraggon's injuries. Fear flooded his being. Pushing past the fright, he delved deeper, until arriving at the beast's center: the pure, glowing ball of energy that cemented its core. He reached out to touch it with his mind…

Clinton's head spun. A memory of the kraggon's life flickered in front of him, unfolding right before his eyes…

Surrounded by darkness, and encased in warmth, a tremendous crash shook the kraggon's world, sending a stabbing pain through his limbs and twisting his rear leg. He had to get out of the darkness; he had to break free before he suffocated. With his small pincers, the kraggon sliced at his leathery confines, tearing free of his mother's belly. He squeezed through the slits he made, while the sunlight bombarded his sensitive eyes. The pup squealed loudly, dazed and overwhelmed by the scent of blood in the air.

This is a memory of his birth, gasped Clinton.

As Clinton continued to view the memory, he saw the kraggon stumbling on its newborn legs, when suddenly something attacked it from the side.

As the pup adjusted to the light, another pup lashed out with its tail, fracturing its carapace like an eggshell. The baby wailed and scampered away, but the sound of tapping feet followed after, biting at him without mercy. Eventually, the pup outran his pursuer, but continued to hobble on alone.

Raion, Clinton thought, pulling away from the kraggon's memories. *Raion...Alone...In pain.*

The lion steeled his mind, forcing himself to keep his consciousness on the fringes of the alien mind, anchoring himself to the thought of Raion.

I understand, he thought, trying to communicate with the pup. *Don't be afraid.*

Energy suddenly surged through his body. A burning pain ignited his arm and spread through his chest, towards the lion's injured hand. Underneath his bandage, he could feel the kraggon's power seeping through his tendons and across his skin. His muscles hardened and his bones cracked. With a ripping sound, the bandage tore from his hand and fluttered to the ground. Fear swept through both Clinton and the kraggon, and the scavenger tried to pull free.

"No!"

Clinton held on tight, feeling the pain recede as power saturated his muscles. The kraggon, however, trembled and continued to pull away.

"Argh!"

The lion jerked his arm away. His eyes burst open. A trickle of blood dripped from his palm where the kraggon had nipped him.

Emitting a low warble, the kraggon inhaled and turned to stare at him. The cracks in its carapace, and its injured eye, now glowed a healing blue. The two held each other's stare for a moment, before the lion frowned.

"I didn't mean to...hurt your mom," said Clinton, confessing his guilt.

He reached out, but immediately stopped again. His breath snagged. The lion's sandy fur had disappeared and in its place was a hard shell. Each finger had somehow lengthened into sharp points.

"What the..."

He studied it for a second before picking up a nearby stone. He squeezed it. The rock felt like brittle charcoal that turned to powder in his grasp.

"I-I don't understand."

The kraggon nipped its jaws together, and blinking, sniffed the air before backing off into the foliage.

"What's wrong? What is it?"

Clinton spun around to see Hagen suddenly appear atop the village steps. The lion gasped and scrabbled for his cloak, pulling it over his disfigured hand, hiding it from view.

"Clinton. Good news. I..." Hagen's eyes locked onto the lion's arm. "What happened?"

"Oh...nothing," he replied, peering into the bushes.

"Are you injured?"

"I just...singed my arm on the hot stone."

"Badly?" asked Hagen, descending the steps.

"Nah!" A smoky smell wafted past Clinton's nose, and he rolled his eyes, smiling. "You know me when it comes to cooking. I'd burn water."

Hagen nodded, clutching the map and the gem amulet in his hands. "Allow me to look at—"

"It's okay. I'm fine," Clinton snapped, hiding his hand behind his back. "Besides, why are you all excited? Got some news?"

"Actually, yes. Follow me."

Heading out of the village, the two anumals jogged up the

mountain path until they reached a small ledge providing them with a clear view of the landscape. Hagen placed the map down and turned Clinton by the shoulders to face the north.

"Here." Hagen put the green gemstone amulet into his hand. "Hold this to your eye."

"Why?"

"Look north."

Clinton shrugged and placed the gem against his eye. "Errr...what am I supposed to see?"

"Just look."

Clinton continued to gaze north, yet nothing caught his attention. He sighed and was just about to give up, when he spotted a subtle change of color in the forest. He removed the amulet from his eye, and the color disappeared, but when he looked through it once more, the color reappeared again.

"What's that with the—"

"Keep looking." Hagen placed his hand on Clinton's shoulder, and slowly turned him in a northeasterly direction. "Follow the patches."

Clinton did as he was told and scanned further...only to see another patch, and another, each one more intense than before. "What the—"

"Wait for it..."

As Clinton's gaze swept north, the colored canopies flourished until they finally merged. Clinton's mouth drooped when he realized they created an intricate pattern. A giant, circular symbol spread out before him, with smaller circles shooting off and covering different sections of the forest. Miles ahead of him, far into the distance, lay the epicenter, the place where the tribal pattern seemed to radiate from. Clinton lowered the amulet and turned to Hagen, who merely nodded.

"We have found it, Clinton. We found the Sensors' camp."

"Fantastic!" said Clinton.

He smiled before looking away from the komodo. Taking a quick peek under his cloak again, his heart lurched at the sight of his disfigured hand.

CHAPTER FIVE

FANGS.

"Now *this*, Vito, is a marvel of anumalkind!" The aged hog bent down and picked up an odd-looking contraption. "Jus' look at it!"

Vito sighed and finished securing her crops onto the back of the cart. She gave the rope a good yank, and turned to inspect what he was now offering. "You never give up, do you, Marl?"

The hog smiled, revealing two tusk-like teeth. "Times is hard."

"Times are always hard where you are concerned." She eyed the mess of wires and small metal spheres that were attached to a roughly woven vest. "What is it? Something that you fix to your lazarball armor?"

"Nah, much better than that. It's a snare."

"What for?"

"Junk!" laughed the hog. "Pulls out any leftover metal from the soil, watch."

Flicking a switch, the hog held the contraption against the ground. Like a scuttler emerging from the soil, a rusty can burst from the dirt and attached itself to one of the spheres. "It's *magnomized* y'see," nodded Marl. "Attracts metal. It'll make it much easier on you to turn over those fields of yours. Heard you've been havin' a nightmare with buried scrud."

"Who told you I have been having trouble?"

"Crantie."

Vito stared at him neutrally. "Yes, well it seems that I cannot keep any information to myself these days. How much for it?"

"Twenty-five nugs."

She nodded. "That sounds—"

"And ten more for the charger."

Vito raised an eyebrow.

"C'mon, lass, think on how much it'll help you getting your farm ready for planting season."

Vito leaned against her cart. "I have no worries about that, Marl. Especially as I have already built my own planting machine."

"Bah! You? Built a machine?"

"Meaning?" she asked, in a flint-like tone that promised sparks.

"W-well, no offence, but you're a female."

"And?"

Marl grimaced. "Well…it's gotta be difficult for you. Y'know, building mech and preparing fields…"

"Why?"

"Well, you ain't a Technal…and…"

His voice trailed off when he saw her face.

Vito finally smirked.

Marl snorted. "Oh, come on! You always enjoy getting me all flustered and the like."

"What? Me?" Vito batted her eyes. "I'm just a helpless female. I would not know how."

"Oh, you'd know all right."

The lights flickered in Marl's house.

He groaned and banged a small, rusty box by his door a couple of times. "Lectric feed from Quala mus' be on the blink again."

"I suppose a female installed that as well?"

"Oh, come off it, Vito."

"Look," she said, dropping the act as she climbed aboard her cart. Taking the reins, she yanked, prompting the docile boval onwards. "I will take it for the asking price, but when Lola finally has her litter, I have a choice pick of the bunch. I get two of them. Free. That is my final deal."

"Okay," laughed Marl, smacking the lectric box a few more times before the lights finally settled. "You won't find any better whoois pups than Lola's. It's a bargain you're gettin', but consider it a deal."

"All right. I will bring the rest of the credits to you tomorrow." The fox took the odd over garment out of his hands and tucked it carefully into her backpack. Have a good evening, Marl."

"Oh, do me a favor and tell 'em the lectric juice is on the blink again when you get back to Quala?"

"Of course."

The hog stared into the sky. "Night's coming on fast. You

gonna be okay, Vito?"

She laughed, but as the wagon rolled along the dirt track back to the village, she could see that night was indeed drawing in.

"Since when has the night ever bothered me?"

A slight gust from the eastern Ridgeback Mountains ruffled her fur. She pulled her hood up and grabbed her bushy tail, wrapping it around her shoulder. Abandoned shacks lined the roadside, and a procession of vehicles from the Olde-world lay decaying nearby: a mechanical sidewalk graveyard. Useful parts had long since been stripped bare, leaving behind only metal frames.

Having found half an abandoned car close to her home, Vito had modified it, fitting two front shafts for a boval to tow it by. After repairing the rear axel, wheels, and seats, she had then made space in the back to store and transport cargo.

"You sure it'll even make it to the road?" the male villagers had laughed when she rode it through the village for the first time. "There ain't even a lectric or smoker-motor to power it."

Yet she knew better than to enter into a battle of wits against the Technals. The moment they were born, they were given wratchers and drivers to play with instead of toys.

Her regular crop and grain deliveries from beyond the village, though, had proven the vehicle's reliability time and again, eventually gaining her the Technals' respect.

The cart suddenly rocked, jostling Vito out of her reverie. The boval snorted.

"Careful there, Rosie." The fox leaned forward and stroked the boval's fur. "What has got you all in a fuss, huh, girl?"

Her nose pricked at the scent of smoke in the air. She sniffed again and peered towards the horizon to see a dull orange glow sweeping the landscape.

"Go!" She snapped the reins, her stomach lurching with panic. "Quickly, Rosie! *Yah*! *Yah*!"

* * *

Rosie skidded to a halt just outside Quala's rear perimeter. The boval's eyes rolled in panic. Flaming spires coiled and curled up beyond the metal fence, spewing smoke high into the air. Terrified cries pierced the night sky, accompanied by the crashing of toppling buildings.

Vito jumped from the cart and grabbed a wrench from the back. She tied a loose rag around her face and charged towards a small house right next to the fence. Untouched by fire, Vito kicked the door open and ran inside.

"CRANTIE? ARE YOU HERE?"

"Vito?" replied a terrified voice from the back of the room. A small prairie dog poked her head from behind a table, holding a metal poker.

Vito embraced her tightly.

"Crantie! Thank the spirits you are okay. What is going on?"

The old female coughed as smoke drifted in through the open door. The glow of the fire lit her eyes.

"The gates…The guards tried to bar them…but the attackers were too quick."

"Who? Who were they?"

"Felines. So many felines…" Crantie's voice wavered. She grasped Vito by the forearms. "They cut the power. A-and before we could run…they set the houses alight…capturing any who escaped."

"And you saw all this? You saw them attack?"

"Yes! I'd left the farmer's meet in the village hall early. B-but the felines came, rounded everyone up and herded them back inside. They blocked the doors. Please tell me they're safe."

More screams echoed from the village.

"Crantie, take my cart and go."

"But—"

"Just take it."

Vito grabbed an old sack from the floor and began to stuff it with food and supplies. "Head back to Marl's farm. Rosie knows the road, she will see you safe." She snatched up a blanket and filled a skin with water. "Tell Marl what has happened. Wait for me, but if I do not come and get you…flee from Quala as fast as you—"

"But... But what about—"

"Go!"

Vito thrust the sack into Crantie's hands and ushered her out the door. She pointed to the cart on the horizon where Rosie stood waiting loyally for her. "There! She'll be skittish, but you'll do fine. Now be off."

Crantie held her bag of supplies tightly, tears streaming down her face.

"Please," said Vito quietly, "for me."

Crantie dithered for a second before scurrying towards the cart. Her figure transformed into a silhouette, before the cart finally lumbered off into the night. Taking a deep breath, Vito turned back to the village fence and sprinted into the mayhem.

Using the support rivets to climb the fence, she reached the top and leaped into the shadows. Slipping under the smoke, she skidded under an old trailer and rolled in a patch of mud, coating her clothes and fur in the dark, wet dirt, blending into the darkness like it was an old friend. Snapping back to her feet, she whipped out two small daggers kept hidden in each boot and set off in the direction of Quala's main square.

* * *

By the time Vito reached her destination, many of the wooden buildings had collapsed. Even the newer structures had started to blacken and crumble, the intense heat twisting their supports. Quala citizens had been stripped of their armor and gadgets, and shackled together in long lines by stunpike and blade-wielding felines.

"If I see anyone move," shouted a mangy-looking lynx. "I'll zap every last one of you."

The tip of his stunpike crackled with energy.

"Orders are to keep 'em alive," shouted a young bobcat, flipping down from a nearby roof. "For the moment."

"Who the skorr do you think you are, *Saber*?" replied the lynx.

48

"Clear off. We Fangs have got work to do."

The Saber slipped a knife out of his bandolier to examine its gleaming point. "We ain't gonna have any trouble here are we, *pelt rot*?"

"What did you call me?"

"I'm callin' you a dead feline if you don't follow orders."

The Fang lifted his stunpike and boosted its charge, filling the air with a hum. "Think you're gonna hurt me with that toothpick of yours, huh?"

"*Magz!*" shouted a distant voice. "Stop fragging around and get the prisoners here now!"

The Fang lowered his stunpike and backed away. "Lucky day, Saber," he snarled, before grabbing a villager and yanking him to his feet. "Come on you lot!"

Vito watched the villagers being shoved into the main hall.

What do they want? What are they doing?

Scanning the area, she scurried towards the village temple; its cone-shaped spire was still untouched by flames.

She climbed up the temple's side with ease and flipped herself onto the roof. Finding refuge behind a statue, she surveyed the scene. The village's lectric lights had been smashed, along with the generators powering Quala's defenses. Groups of felines gathered in packs, looting properties, breaking gadgets, inventions, and religious statues. Two distinct symbols were painted on the felines' jackets and shirts: a jagged circle was one symbol, and two crossing knives was the other. Yet every feline sported a similar tribal marking branded on their forearms.

"Out my way," grumbled a voice to Vito's left.

She looked down to see a sphynx cat approaching the tavern doorway. The guards moved aside, allowing the huge, furless creature room to enter. A torrent of cheers and shouts suddenly erupted from within the tavern, and a second later, a feline crashed through the window. The figure landed unmoving in the mud.

Vito sped for the roof's edge. She dove off the side and flipped around at the last second to land in a smoldering pile of hay. Slipping across the open ground like oil, she bounded atop a stack of barrels and jumped onto the tavern's roof. Darting up the slope, she peered down through a smoke hole into the room below and watched the unfolding events.

"Any more of you scruddin' Sabers gonna get in my way?" yelled the sphynx, his eyes as wide as a full moon. He whipped a cleaver from his belt and slammed it into the tabletop. "Thought not."

The felines chuckled while gulping their grain water or puffing on burlico. Smashed glass and furniture ornamented the floor. The charred remains of a stock-carcass dangled on a spit above the dying fire.

The sphynx took out a tiny, amber pellet from his jacket pocket. He crushed it before licking the powder from his palm.

"Still on the *hive* I see, Firstang," said a voice.

Vito tried to see who had spoken, but the speaker remained out of her view.

"You might know me, Saber, but I don't know you. So tell me who you are before I rip out your tongue."

"You could try. Your demise would be of little consequence anyway."

Firstang yanked the cleaver from the tabletop.

"What did you say?"

Every Saber and Fang in the room immediately drew their weapons, while a soft laughter meandered playfully under the torrent of growls and hisses.

"Felines! I do believe we have more pressing concerns to address than petty bickering," chuckled the voice. "Firstang, I apologize. Now, please, take a seat."

Firstang snorted before nudging a chair next to a table and slumping into it. Snatching a tanker of grain water, he chugged the brew. "Why are you Sabers here anyway? Why'd you get yourselves involved? This is a Fang raid."

"There will be time for questions later," replied the voice. "Right now, we have more immediate concerns."

"Such as?"

"Such as Quala's citizens in the village hall."

"You call that a concern? Roast 'em for all I care."

The voice chuckled. "Have you ever considered the fact, Firstang, that we might need those anumals in the future? Who will we have to dominate if we only surround ourselves with equals?"

Firstang snatched up another glass. "So wadda you suggest? What can Quala possibly offer us…apart from crossbreeds and primate dung?"

The room burst into laughter and Vito's claws dug into the wooden roof.

Primates!

"Please…" continued the voice. "It is in my humble opinion that we should utilize what the village has to offer. They are Technals, after all. Their skills could prove useful. Just look at what they have constructed around you."

"It's human mech in a rebuilt shanty town. That's what this place is!" shouted Firstang.

"Yes, but think of what we could do with it; a working garrison to the lower east of the Ridgeback would be a prime position for feline territory. It would begin our domination of the southern mountains."

"The southern mountains?" Firstang snorted. "I say we head north until we reach the cities."

"And we will be decimated in the process," finished the voice. "We need numbers to fight, and even more to rule, or risk losing everything. If we don't secure our rear, we gamble fighting a war on all sides. I merely suggest inserting a few key figures in prime positions in Nomica to control the masses. Remember, our rise is in its infancy, and we need word to spread."

"I should've known!" Firstang roared. "Look at the puma, soft and fat, wanting nothing more than others to do the work for him. Is this all the Sabers have to offer? No wonder you follow us Fangs like cowards, sneaking in on raids we instigate." He rose to his feet. "We received the call, Saber, and we intend to seize the glory."

"And how did you receive the call, Firstang?"

The sphinx slowly scratched his neck. "Word was received

from the Plains."

"By who?"

Firstang paused. His jaw muscles clenched. "That...that doesn't matter. All that matters is we obeyed. We heard that the sign had been spotted in the Plains ten days ago, and our call to unite had arrived."

The puma sighed. "You have no idea..."

Firstang slammed his fist on the table. "Times are changing. Felines like you only chain us to the present, where inferiors exist above their rights. But the present is moving into the future, and your ways are dying. So I ask this." He spread his arms and glared at the unseen Saber. "Are you willing to wallow in the shame of your past? Or do we rid ourselves of the parasites sucking us dry?"

"Be mindful of your tongue, Firstang." The unseen Saber's voice dropped a pitch, causing a chill down Vito's back.

"I've had enough of this." Firstang raised his cleaver and lurched forwards.

An oversized puma suddenly sprang into view and grabbed Firstang's wrist, stopping him dead. Vito watched in horror as the puma's head trembled while opening its mouth abnormally wide, revealing countless, needle-like teeth. Firstang's eyes widened, but he could not move as the gaping maw enclosed around his face...

A deafening roar exploded through the tavern.

The roof shook, causing Vito to slip. She skidded backwards before flipping over and dropping safely to the muddy ground below. Feline howls, and pained shrieks echoed in the air, followed by the thud of bodies hitting the floor. She dashed around the side to the tavern's broken window, and chanced a peek inside.

The fat puma had released Firstang, who was holding his head, quivering on the floor. And then Vito caught sight of the figure standing in the doorway. A young tiger dressed in rich, but tattered, clothing slowly surveyed the room while entering the tavern. Felines instantly stepped back to let him through.

Dread tickled the back of Vito's skull, demanding acknowledgement. Her stomach churned, while her muscles twitched. Suddenly, every natural instinct inside her screamed that the danger in Quala had just multiplied.

The true threat had finally reveled itself.

CHAPTER SIX

BLOOD FOR BLOOD.

Vito could not take her eyes off of the newcomer.

Looking younger than the other felines, three scars ran down the tiger's left eye, accentuating his stare.

"Who the frag are you?" asked Firstang, picking up his cleaver. "Wadda you want?"

The tiger eyed the blade and then peered at him, before sidestepping.

A limp feline suddenly flew through the doorway, landing in a heap where the tiger had just been standing. Another body followed, and then another, each landing atop the other. Three felines lay in a pile by Firstang's feet, each with the Fang symbol painted on their jackets. Blood dribbled from their ears like taps, leaking thick, coppery liquid.

The sphynx bent down to examine the bodies.

"Are they dead?"

"Would you like them to be?" asked the tiger.

Firstang slowly rose to his feet, towering over the youth. He pulled another hive pellet from his pocket, crushed it, and licked it clean. "Why don't you ask your friend out there to join us?"

A promise of a smile touched the tiger's mouth, and he beckoned someone inside.

"As you wish."

Like an encroaching specter, a panther, as black as night, padded through the doorway. Felines edged away from his approach as an air of anxiety permeated the tavern, mixed with ancient wisdom, blood, and death. With Olde-world sunglasses concealing his eyes, a long, leather coat flapped behind him.

"Master?" asked the panther.

"Our friend here invited you in, probably with the intention of doing away with us both. Is that not right, mister...?"

"Firstang. Head of the Targetcha and Steppe Fangs," snarled the sphynx, tightening his grip around the cleaver. He pointed it at the heap of crumpled felines. "You did this?"

"They were silly enough to get in my way."

"And...him?" The sphinx turned towards the large puma. "Is that freak with you too?"

"He could be," nodded Dallas. "Why?"

"Listen, cub. I don't know what trick you're pulling here today, or who you are, but it's blood for blood where we Fangs are concerned, and by my reckoning, your guts belong to me."

"Is that so?"

"Quala is ours; it's Fang territory now. And you can go to skorr if you think you're taking it from us. We had the calling." Firstang's eyes narrowed. "You're Sabers, huh? So what clans do you belong to?"

The tiger smirked, but said nothing.

"This a game to you, huh?" shouted the sphynx, hunching over. "Think it's funny, tiger? Laugh at this!"

Firstang swung the cleaver at the tiger's head. It raced through the air, but a leather-clad arm shot out at the last second and blocked the attack.

The tiger yawned.

Firstang's eyes bulged. The cleaver fell from his grasp as a stream of blood dribbled from his mouth. He coughed before falling to his knees, trying desperately to draw breath while the large puma, standing behind his victim, yanked his blade from Firstang's back.

"Now, to answer your question, Firstang," yawned the tiger, "I do not have a clan, because soon I will have an *army*."

He pushed the sphynx aside, letting him crumple to the floor.

"Anyone else?" snarled the puma, cleaning his blade. The tavern remained silent, neither Fang nor Saber uttered a word. The puma slid his knife back under his grack-skin cloak. "Very well."

The tiger smiled.

Stepping over the cadaver, he embraced the puma, hugging him close. "You always pick the best moments to make your point, Vincent."

The puma shrugged and stepped back. "I did try to warn him, but he thought he knew better." He studied the tiger for a moment.

"My dear, Dallas. Wherever did you wander off to?"

"To bigger and better things, my friend," replied Dallas, patting his shoulder.

Vincent's gaze swept from the tiger and came to rest on the huge panther. "So I see..."

Dallas turned his attention to his silent companion, and in that moment, Vincent's smile disappeared. His eyes flashed yellow, and his face trembled – as if something was struggling to move beneath the skin.

The panther replied with a barely perceptible smile.

Vincent put his shaking hands on Dallas's shoulders.

"What?" asked the tiger.

"You've changed, Dallas..."

"As have we all." He shrugged off the puma and strolled closer to the fire. He slouched down into a seat and pointed at a nearby Fang. "You. Come here."

The Fang flinched before puffing out his chest and swaggering closer.

"Yeah? What do you want?"

"That jacket you are wearing...Remove it."

"What?"

Dallas's gaze bore into the feline. "Remove it."

The Fang snarled, but took off the jacket and tossed it by Dallas's feet. The tiger stared at the symbol on the back for a moment, before pointing at a young Saber. "You too, Treeg. Remove your jacket."

A puzzled expression crossed the Saber's face.

"But, sir, I—"

"Now!" ordered Dallas.

The feline slipped out of his jacket and slowly dropped it to the floor.

"Sabers and Fangs," Dallas said, picking up the clothes. "Is *this* the limit to your vision?"

He protracted his claws and swiped them through the symbols, leaving behind three long slashes. He tossed them aside. "That is what I think of your vision."

56

Hisses and snarls rumbled through the crowd while Dallas put his arms around the two young felines.

"Do you see what I just did?"

The room slipped into a resentful silence.

"Now there are no more Fangs, and there are no more Sabers. Now you are united by one symbol. Now *we* are one. Too long have we been fractured, brothers and sisters. And divided by what? Territory?" He pointed to a large feline puffing on a burlico-stick near the door. "You! Did you receive the call?"

"Heard about it five days ago."

Dallas pointed at a feline leaning against the bar. "And you?"

"I saw it with my own eyes in Wooburn, Dallas…I mean, sir. Vincent led the way."

"The message was made very clear to us, sir," finished Vincent, bowing low.

Dallas stood up and walked into the crowd. He turned a female bystander around and slashed her jacket, leaving behind three claw marks. "Alliances within feline clans like the Fang and the Saber societies are a thing of the past. And clans like the Falling Terrorz, the Silver Pelts, the Short Claws, and the Mute Stares mean nothing…without *unity*. All of you roll up your sleeves!"

Each feline slowly did as they were told, every one of them revealing an Ocelot brand.

"The mark of power has been branded onto every one of you: a pattern binding us with purpose. Not all felines have been given this honor, only those who believe in the natural order of our race. And what do we do with that honor? We squabble amongst each other." Dallas paused to stare at the dead Firstang. "We are the superiors. We were the first breed to be created. Show me, fellow felines, show me we can unite and rule!"

Turning to each other, Sabers and Fangs unleashed their claws and swept them through every clan and feline symbol in sight. Now they stood united by the brand on their arms and a symbol of three claw marks slashed into their clothing.

Vito's heart pounded. Through the buzz of activity, she studied Dallas and the tall, silent panther. She had heard tales of similar words before, words she thought long buried. Yet here was another anumal, another species, kindling the fires of war with promises of dominance. She leaned against the side of the wall, resting her head against the wood. The mud camouflaging her skin was slowly drying. Raucous cries reverberated from inside the tavern, joined by the smashing of glass and the tearing of cloth and hide. The village burned around her, but now Quala was no longer her home. The time had come for her to move on again, forced to take a step closer to a land she knew she should steer clear of.

Father...

Vito discarded the growing weed of a thought in her mind as soon as it sprouted.

A sudden cheer burst from the tavern. The fox inched her head closer to the windowsill and her vision spun with a sickly realization...

"I see that Quala has been presented with quite a quandary," said Dallas. "Do you not agree, Mayor Brarll?"

In front of the tiger now knelt a small gopher, his hands bound behind his back. Deep, bloody scores gouged his face and tail, and his broken ceremonial chain was snagged on his clothes as it dangled loosely before him.

Tears welled in Vito's eyes.

"No," she whispered.

The rodent's nose twitched, yet the mayor remained silent; his gaze held nothing but contempt. A boot suddenly shoved against the gopher's back, sending him sprawling.

"Answer him!" snarled a voice.

"Mayor," Dallas urged, as Vincent helped the rodent back to his knees, "forgive my fellow felines, they do not mean you harm."

"Really?" sneered Brarll. "So you're only here for the farmer's meet then?"

"Please, mayor, let us not turn this into something it need not be. I did not envision the destruction of your village, and, as you can see, the architect of the damage has paid the price."

Dallas motioned to Firstang's body.

"So it was this feline, acting alone, who forced the others to burn the village down, huh?"

"Oh, come now, mayor." Dallas took a seat. "If you were to instruct your Technal clansmen to sack a neighboring village, would you think ill of them for obeying orders? A soldier, regardless of rank, marches to the tune of his superiors. As did they."

Brarll's stare lingered on Dallas. "Free my villagers."

"Oh, we will," smiled the tiger. "We will...on one condition."

"There always is."

"You are of the Copper Technal clan are you not?"

"Proudly. As is most of the village, apart from a few Iron and Circuit clansmen."

"Well then, the answer is simple: command the villagers to give up their clan ties, renounce their faith in whatever spirits drive their existence, and swear fealty to the Ocelots. If the anumals recognize the three-claw mark as their master sigil, my dear Brarll, they may just survive this ordeal."

Brarll looked around the room of felines.

"It will never work."

Dallas leaned in, the scars over his eye accented by the firelight. "Why not?"

"The laws of Silania, you fool. We live in a cultured time. *Every* anumal has the right to be free."

"Oh, really?"

"Yes!" spat the gopher. "Clan dominance doesn't work. Just look at the pre-colony crusade era."

"I will make it work."

"Really? You are speaking to a Technal here, boy. My own clan tried it centuries ago. Would you like to become the emperor of the next Techang dynasty? You know what happened to their cities? Or even worse, Simanoth?"

The word Simanoth struck Vito like a spear between the ears. Primate images flickered through her thoughts.

"It never works," said the gopher. "It only creates bloodshed and death, you clueless, arrogant cub."

The atmosphere twisted into a deadly silence.

With a creak of his chair, Dallas slowly rose to his feet. "That is what you think of me…a cub?"

Mayor Brarll shuffled back slightly. "Your words scream of failure. No good will come of this."

"My words speak of things older than anumalkind itself, weakling. My words come from a place of knowledge deeper than your limited mind could ever fathom. Open your eyes, Brarll! What are you commanding here?"

"G-good anumals."

"Dirt scratchers, land foragers, and parasites. We destroyed a race of humans for using mech such as this, yet here you are, you *Technals*, lovers of the Olde-world. We felines were the first of the anumal armies, leading the way, and now is the time for us to seize control again." Dallas pointed to Vincent. "Take out your knife."

Vincent obeyed.

Dallas glared at Treeg. He beckoned him closer before saying, "I want you to kill Treeg, Vincent."

Treeg's mouth fell slack. "What? No…NO!"

Without hesitation, Vincent's arms wrapped around Treeg's head and he rammed his knee into the back of the youngster's legs. Treeg dropped like a weight. The air filled with a terrified howl as Vincent's knife touched skin.

"No!" shouted Brarll. "Wait!"

"Vincent stop!" commanded Dallas.

The puma paused.

Vito's fists clenched. Bile rose in her throat. Her anger boiled, impelling her to act, to dive through the window and save her friend, yet she remained still.

"Why does this concern you, Brarll?" asked Dallas, standing before the old rodent. "He is your enemy is he not?"

"He is also an anumal."

"And one who will live and die under my authority…is that not correct, Treeg?"

The trembling feline whimpered, but nodded.

"Clear your blinkered eyes, mayor. Do not chain your village to the past when a new dawn is rising. My power will engulf you all…Surrender your village so you may live. "

Sweat ran down the crease in Brarll's brow.

"Mayor Brarll, no more harm will come to the villagers if you meet my terms. I promise."

Brarll's head fell forward, resignation dripping from him like the sweat and blood from his skin. Vito released her breath, knowing what was surely to follow.

"Okay…" said mayor Brarll, barely above a whisper. "I surrender."

Dallas snatched a sharp breath and rose to his full height. "Very wise, mayor. I commend you." He placed a hand on Vincent's shoulder, giving the order to release Treeg. "This Technal is a brave soul and a wise mayor. Tenacious and clever… Finish him."

Vito flinched.

Brarll gasped. "But… but you said—"

"I said no harm would come to the villagers."

Dallas turned for the exit, ignoring the panther as he fell in line behind him. "I never mentioned you."

With that he left the tavern and stepped outside, into the smoky darkness.

"Felines…" said Vincent to the room of watching predators, an unnatural smile stretching across his face. "You heard our master."

The room exploded into action.

Vito caught one last glimpse of her friend before he was swept up in a sea of fur and claws. She turned away, tearing her gaze from the carnage as Brarll's screams pierced the night air. Within seconds the sound descended into gasps, before fading amid a cacophony of cheers and laughter. Tears rolled down Vito's muddy cheeks. The smell of blood tugged her senses. Sliding to the ground, the fox clutched her knees, unable to comprehend what she had witnessed.

Raised voices suddenly snatched her attention, growing louder by the second. Instinctively, the fox scurried to the wall. Using the barrel as a step, she flipped herself onto the roof just as Dallas and the panther came around the corner.

"…and a united kill will cement bonds," rumbled the panther. "A wise move, Dallas."

"It should not have been like that though. Why did it take him so long to surrender?"

The panther stood next to the barrel. "It makes no difference."

Dallas leaned against the tavern wall. "But he did not fear me."

"Yet you achieved your goal."

"If I had sent you in, you would have achieved a more efficient result. What does that say about me?"

"Give it time."

"Time? What time? We march north imminently. How am I to rule if they do not fear me, Nightmare?"

The mention of the panther's name chimed like a bell in Vito's head.

"They will." replied the panther. "Eventually."

"I want their fear *now*. I want them to know the power I wield could destroy every one of them."

"And so it shall be. The power of the Shadow Soul will build and grow…in time."

Feeling the breath stall in the back of her throat, Vito leaned forwards, soaking in their conversation.

"…As we advance northwards, our numbers will grow."

"And what of Narfell?"

"As we have always said, ultimately, he will come to you. Our rise will be too much for him, and others, to ignore."

Dallas sighed. "My fear is that the clans will not be so easy to break as these Technals."

"Often the bigger the clan, the easier to break…as long as you know where to strike. Smaller clans are bound by friendship and loyalty, but larger ones deal in power. Control their influence and what they offer and you can manipulate them."

"All good theory, but in reality…"

"In realty you find their weak spot and you exploit it, Dallas. We live in an age where vulnerability is displayed in an effort to muster power. The answer is as clear as the end of your nose."

Nightmare turned to a distant structure. Dallas followed his gaze, as did Vito, until she realized what they were looking at. The towers of the village lazarball stadium were lit up like burning beacons of destruction. As they stared, one tower toppled in on itself, crashing onto the gamefield and smashing into the bleachers.

"Come, Dallas." Nightmare stood tall, displaying his full height. "Let me show you how this game is to be played out."

* * *

Vito dropped from the roof. Gliding through the night, she sped back to Crantie's shack, her body surging with adrenalin. Untouched by the fire, the door hung limply on its hinges. The windows had been smashed, and possessions lay scattered across the floor. The fox surveilled the dark belly of her friend's home, before padding silently to its rear. She pushed an old dresser aside, and with shaking hands, yanked on the floorboards. Her ears pricked at the sound of distant destruction. Her nose twitched, yet no new scents assailed her senses. She waited a few seconds in readiness of attack, and then continued with her task.

Ripping up two wooden planks, she reached down into the opening. The smooth lid of a wooden box brushed against her fingers, and she lifted it out and placed it on her knees. Crantie had been the only one she could trust with it, fearing to keep it in her own house.

A shield emblem had been engraved on its lid, surrounded by claws and also serpent tails. The emblem's grooves had been inlaid with precious stones and a substance called coal. Her hand swept across the symbol, and she found pride swelling within her – a pride that had lain dormant for years.

"Kontipur…" she muttered.

Flicking a catch, she lifted the lid to reveal two egg-shaped stones inside. The dark green stone looked dull, like a small vegetable, while next to it glistened a polished, black stone. The fox found her hand stroking the black object, and she had a hungry urge to pick it up…

With a calming breath, she scooped up the green stone in her index finger and thumb and rotated it twice. The stone started to hum gently. She brought it close to her mouth.

"Awaken, Whim," she whispered. "Your time has come."

Nothing happened at first, and then a sheen of deep green bled along its surface. Two leathery wings, that had created the stone's exterior, unfolded to reveal a creature curled inside. Scrunched up in a fetal position, two large eyes opened, revealing onyx eyeballs. Its tiny head reared, and a high-pitched noise escaped its beak, before it rocked to its clawed feet. With a shiver, the creature ruffled its bat-like wings, shaking out the final vestiges of sleep. A gust of air blew against Vito as the creature took flight and hovered in front of her face.

"My friend," whispered Vito, holding out her hand as a perch. "It has been too long."

The creature chirped and landed.

"But the time has come. You must deliver this message to your master…"

Vito whispered everything she had learned that night, everything she had heard Dallas and Nightmare discuss. Once she had finished, she lifted her head to stare deeply into the creature's eyes.

"Be safe, and stop for no one. His council is imperative now, more than ever."

The creature squawked and took off, swooping out of the broken window. Vito rushed to the door and watched her flying friend head for the Ridgeback Mountains, fast becoming too small for her to follow.

"Take care, Whim," she muttered.

She slipped back inside and picked up the box…and again her eyes drifted to the black stone. Every ounce of pride and loyalty screamed inside her to awaken it too, but her heart told her she could not.

Vito slammed the lid shut before placing the box at the bottom of a sack. She needed to salvage a few possessions, and collect Crantie and Marl immediately. If what she had heard were to come to pass, there would soon be limited safe havens left for them to run to. She picked up the remaining scraps of food and a water skin, and wrapped a heavy cloak around herself. With one last glance at Quala, Vito set off across the field and towards the horizon.

CHAPTER SEVEN

DEATHBLOW.

Warmth surrounded Clinton. Trees in shades of vivid green and blue shimmered before him, while overhead, ayvids took to the air, leaving residual pastel-orange lines trailing behind.

"Clinton…"

From the sprigs on the forest floor, to the towering trees dwarfing him in their shade, a sense of relevance and belonging permeated through everything.

"It is time," said Hagen.

The lion felt a coldness envelop him when he began to rise from his inner self towards the surface. The closer he came to being one with his physical body again, the more he yearned to flee back to the peace of his inner being.

"Clinton, take this."

Something touched his knee. The lion jerked and opened his eyes, shielding his face from the glare of the sun. A steaming bowl of broth sat before him. He leaned forward as Hagen gradually swam into focus. Grabbing the cloak that was covering his arm, he peeked underneath, and sighed with relief.

For the last two days, he had hidden it from Hagen, fearful that the effects of his encounter with the kraggon would be irreversible. However, in that time, it had slowly returned to its normal state. Now, all that remained was a slight tingle that rippled through his fingers sporadically.

"It is still there, Clinton," said Hagen. "No one has stolen your hand away since you last checked on it."

"I…was just…making sure it wasn't infected or anything."

Hagen's eyes narrowed. "You are being very cautious to say it was merely a burn."

"Can't be too careful. I just…" He picked up his bowl of broth. "How long was I out for?"

"Morning has passed, however, I did not want to disturb you, so I allowed you more practice time."

Clinton sighed. Physically, he felt alive and refreshed, yet mentally the grogginess lingered. "This meditating certainly takes it out of you."

"It will clear faster when you become more adept." The lizard slurped his broth. "Think of it as akin to the morning after a grain water feast. While you are drinking, you feel alive, but come the morning…"

"*You've* gotten drunk on grain water?"

Hagen smiled dryly. "It is always the night prior to battle that we komodos consume the most. We drink as if it is our last day alive…and for many, that is indeed the case. On these nights of celebration we sing of better times, and dance with passion. And the females…" Hagen glanced at the ground. His smile faltered. "Nonetheless, come the morning our heads feel as if an ironback has stomped on them. However, the grogginess will pass."

The two returned to eating, sipping their broth in silence, until the lion suddenly said, "So, what was it you were saying about those females?"

"Finish your meal, Clinton." The lizard gulped down his remaining food, and shoved his bowl inside his bag. He kicked dirt on the flames and stood up. "Too much time has been wasted. We must be off."

As the day wore into the afternoon, the two companions continued their trek. Every so often Clinton would peak under his cloak, checking to see his hand was still normal, but for the remainder of the trek they mostly walked in silence.

"Hagen, are you okay?" Clinton finally asked, unable to bear the stony atmosphere any longer. "You're all…moody."

"All is well, Clinton," he replied, walking a couple of strides ahead. "All is well."

Clinton considered the lizard's words for a long time before finally braving his next question.

"So who was she then? It's obvious you're thinking about—"

"No one."

The lion's brow furrowed. He sped up his pace so that he could walk next to his friend. "So…errrrr…I can see much clearer now. When I'm meditating, I mean."

"Pardon?"

"The last time I could see the trees and sectoids and ayvids much more clearly. And their souls shimmered brighter than the rest of their bodies as they flew through the air. I recognized a few wefrings, and those big, green ayvids."

"Ponrets."

"Yeah, them."

"I believe it is growing less arduous for you because you are unafraid to glimpse their inner essence."

Clinton shrugged. "I just think of Raion. He keeps me anchored, makes me remember who I am and what I'm doing this for." He murmured the last words more to himself. "But that thicket ram last night, and even the hover grub this morning, were much easier to see. I still feel them, though, even now, when the bond is broken. It feels like a bit of them lingers inside me."

Underneath his cloak Clinton flexed his hand, feeling energy rippling through his fingers.

"Which is why meditation is vital, Clinton. You must know yourself intensely before you can possibly understand the things surrounding you. Otherwise, when you access your more potent powers—"

"I'll become lost?"

"Yes. Which is why your anchor is paramount. Raion is good. In fact, I believe he is the best anchor you could have chosen."

Clinton studied the bark of a tree. It looked so simple on the surface, but underneath, hidden from view, was concealed many complex layers. "Hagen, has there ever been anyone like me or Dallas before? Y'know, anumals who can control souls...and stuff?"

"And *stuff*?" Hagen laughed. "I have never heard anyone call it 'stuff' before."

"You know what I mean."

"Yes, there has," the komodo stopped and leaned against his thick, sturdy tail. "To varying degrees. Do not get me wrong, Clinton, what you and Dallas possess is unequalled within our time, yet there has always existed those with the ability to manipulate more than just the physical."

"You mean the Entwined?"

"The Entwined are one example, yes, but there are others. The Sensors. The Mab of Feinys-Lorr. The eastern Koldun'ai witches. The Miko. Even the deformed Bes from the Wastelands." As he mentioned the Bes, Hagen brushed his thumb over his forehead to ward away evil. "Somewhere along the evolutionary map, when humans first experimented on themselves and animals, they tinkered not only with their bodies, but with their minds and consciousness. They opened pathways to control and perform the unexplainable."

"Experiments? What kind of experiments? Do you know what they did?"

"I do not." The lizard shifted his weight. "Although I do know we all have different abilities, Clinton. Some of which can be explained, and others which cannot."

Hagen set off walking again, and Clinton followed in silence, before a question became so compelling in his mind he could not help but ask it.

"You mentioned the deformed Bes creatures—"

"The spirits save us!" Hagen interrupted. "Vile beings."

"But when you say deformed, what exactly do you mean? Are they anumals who have…changed?"

"Inbred and twisted over generations, Clinton, that is all you need to know about them."

"But their deformities? Do their…do their bodies change or something?"

Hagen stopped and looked at the lion. "Change?"

"Y'know, is their appearance altered, for example?"

"There are very few who can change their physical appearance at will, unless aided by magic, of course. Why do you ask?"

"Oh, no reason. I was just wondering. Forget it." He set off walking again, scolding himself for being so tactless. "So this female—"

"Clinton, stop!"

Hagen flung out his arm, stopping the lion in his tracks, claws digging into his chest.

"Hey, I was only joking."

"Do not move!"

The komodo's light demeanor evaporated as he took a cautious step through the undergrowth.

"Hagen, what's wrong?"

"Stay exactly where you are."

Looming trees surrounded them, while a twisted net of spiked biyemba bushes and low-lying brambles filled the gaps between the trunks. Mounds of leaves and twigs were scattered across the ground.

Hagen padded slowly towards the main thicket. "Do you not hear it?"

"Hear what? I don't hear anything."

"Exactly. No scuttlers. No ayvids. The plants seem…"

"What?"

Hagen's eyes narrowed. Tasting the air with his forked yellow tongue, he leaned forwards and inched aside the bushes.

"What is it?" gulped Clinton, the smell of decay suddenly tickling his nose.

Underneath the foliage hid a brightly colored flower. Its indigo petals reached out like tense spider legs, and hair-thin tendrils attached it to the surrounding plants. A yellow stamen protruded from the center of the flower, sporting a bulbous pumpkin-colored tip.

Hagen gently nudged more leaves aside with his foot to reveal numerous scuttler, sectoid, and ayvid carcasses in varying states of decay, orange pollen coating their beaks, mouths, or probes.

"Cover your mouth and nose," instructed Hagen, quickly untying a rag attached to his belt.

"Hagen?"

"Do it now!" He handed him the rag, and covered his own mouth with his hand while carefully backing away from the bright purple flower. "Clinton, I need you to search the area and fully see what surrounds us."

"But, you told me not to move."

70

"With your mind. Look with your mind."

"Now? On my feet?"

"I need you to see the extent of the danger we are in."

The lion closed his eyes. He slowed his breathing and tried to let his fear melt away, turning his consciousness inwards. Within a few breaths, he found himself drifting away from the physical world.

Clinton inspected the clearing.

White cobweb-like strands suddenly glistened around him, stretching over the tops of the leaves. Blotches of purple and orange highlighted numerous flowers hidden within the bushes, and on the ground, shades of brown marked the countless ayvid and scuttler carcasses masked by the foliage.

"Do you see them?" Hagen's voice swirled around him in a cloud of tones. "How many corpses are there?"

"Hundreds."

"Alright. Do not touch anything. Keep your arms by your side and keep your tail perfectly still."

"But what is this place?"

"A trap," Hagen replied. "A deathblow snare. You can see the white tendrils?"

The more the lion looked, the more he could see hair-thin tendrils wafting in the air, while the small veins also ran along the forest floor.

"Touch the strands and the plants will release their spore. The next thing they will do whilst we are immobile…is attack."

"The *flowers*?" Clinton's heart raced in his chest. "Will attack us?"

"No, not the flowers, I mean…"

An arrow suddenly slammed into the ground near the lion's feet.

A loud hissing noise rang in Clinton's ears. Jets of orange pollen pumped into the air like steam, filling the clearing with a putrid stench that stung his nose.

"Don't breathe! Go!" Hagen shouted.

Clinton turned to run, but stumbled backwards.

A blurred figure loomed before him, pressing the tip of an arrow against his forehead.

"On the ground now!"

Before Clinton could think, he roared and slammed his hand towards the bright glowing soul residing in the creature's chest.

There was a blip of silence.

Clinton made contact.

Energy blasted from the lion's hand and smashed into his attacker...

"NO!" yelled Hagen.

The creature flew backwards through the bushes, landing with a sickening crunch against a tree trunk. More pollen jettisoned into the air. Clinton shook his head, bringing himself out of his meditative state. He gasped, accidentally inhaling some of the poison. The vivid colors of the life around him sharpened into focus...as a komodo burst from the bushes.

"GET ON THE GROUND NOW!" it shouted, drawing its bowstring tight, ready to release an arrow into Clinton's head.

"Who are you..." spluttered the lion, scrabbling back. He growled and protracted his claws. "Leave us alone!"

The komodo towered over him, its skin a green and yellow color. A mask fashioned from strips of leather, twigs, and leaves, covered its mouth and nose.

"No, Clinton!" yelled Hagen, jumping between the two anumals and knocking the weapon away.

The newcomer dropped its bow and slashed its claws at Hagen's head. Hagen blocked the attack and flipped his opponent to the side, sending him smashing into the bushes and releasing more spores.

Clinton's legs suddenly buckled. His vision swirled and he rubbed his eyes, trying to stop his head from spinning. The cloth over his face fell away. Another two figures burst into the clearing and charged directly at Hagen.

"Do not hurt him!" yelled the komodo. He shoved his hand out in surrender, but his words sounded like a distant echo in Clinton's ears. "Leave him alone."

Another figure loomed over Clinton, its weapon cocked and ready to fire. Three more stalked out from the bushes, shouting and wielding spears and bows.

"What did he do to Nyugon?" asked a deep voice. "He killed Nyugon!"

"The lion is under my protection!" shouted Hagen.

"GET DOWN ON YOUR KNEES, TRAITOR!"

Clinton only just saw a komodo slam the end of his spear into Hagen's head. His friend stumbled back and dropped to one knee.

"Hagen, what's happening?" coughed Clinton, before his arms buckled and he fell onto his back.

The forest canopy swirled in blurs of green and brown above him. Blood trickled down the back of his throat, before he coughed it out the sides of his mouth.

"That is it, little feline," said a komodo, standing over him with a nocked arrow aimed directly at his face. "Do not fight it…or you will die."

CHAPTER EIGHT

RHYNIUN.

"Nyugon is not dead, but he is weak. He needs immediate help from a shaman or scent-Sensor."

"I agree," answered a deeper voice. "Make all haste with Riyam and Ha'pa and bring aid from the camp. We will convene with you three when we can."

Footsteps led off into the distance.

"You must understand," said Hagen, "the lion cannot fully control his powers yet. It was an accident."

"An accident? He almost killed one of us, and you defend him?"

"His actions were not intentional. Had you not set the trap in the first place, then this would never have occurred."

Clinton slowly opened his eyes.

Night had fallen. A small campfire swam into focus with four komodo dragons sitting around it. Wearing battle armor, fashioned from leather and bone, each appeared even larger than Hagen. The light caught the ridges in their youthful skin, highlighting white tribal markings painted on their hands and arms.

Hagen sat between two komodos, his hands bound before him. "We were searching for the camp."

"Then it was fate that our paths crossed, fugitive," replied a smaller, female komodo, sharpening a bone arrowhead on a whetstone.

"Trust me, Clinton will be truly sorry to hear that he hurt one of your tribe."

"Trust you?" snapped another komodo. "If Nyugon dies then the lion will be truly sorry."

The female shook her head, and turning away from the group, sat by the litter carrying the injured komodo. Hagen sighed and faced the tall warrior sitting by him.

"Tell me, why a deathblow snare?"

"Detaining you was paramount."

Hagen nodded. "What is your name?"

"They call me Heylo. I lead this troop."

"And I presume from your markings it was the scent master that issued the orders for our capture?"

"The orders came from every master and tribe leader collectively."

Hagen's eyes widened. "They are all here?" He paused for a second. "And the patriarch too?"

"He has been here for seven cycles of the sun."

"Really?" Hagen looked into the fire. "It is rare for him to leave the homeland…"

"Oh, come now, Hagen-Jin," scoffed a female, biting into the leg of a roasted scavenger. "Twelve years separated from the tribes would not render you completely naive. You know the reason for their convergence."

The lion remained completely still and watched her speak. His head pounded, and he had to continually swallow the mucus blocking the back of his throat.

Hagen sighed. "Well, you have certainly detained us, and I would prefer it if you would be so kind as to remove these." He held up his hands. "We are not slaves."

The group paused to watch as Heylo pulled a curved bone blade from his belt and slashed Hagen's bonds. "They are not the true restraints anyway."

"Of which I am fully aware," hissed Hagen.

Clinton coughed and spluttered, before finally sitting upright. Every komodo turned in his direction as he asked, "What's going on?"

Hagen quickly rose to his feet and approached. Within a heartbeat, the others were shadowing him, weapons in hand.

"Clinton, how are you?" asked Hagen.

"I feel like I've been flattened by a gorespine."

He tried to take a breath, but coughed, leaving a splatter of orange blood on his palm.

Hagen spun to face Heylo. "He has to be purged. We need spiced wein—"

"When we return to the main camp."

"He will not last until then. He is not of our kind; he does not have our tolerance to the poison. It needs purging now."

"Not until—"

"Hagen…" coughed Clinton, shaking violently.

Blood trickled from his mouth.

"I said now!" commanded Hagen, standing to his full height. Every tattoo on his body flashed bright blue.

The group took a wary step back, each waiting for an order from their leader.

Heylo looked at Hagen for a long moment, before saying, "Gawdi, fetch the spiced wein."

Immediately, Gawdi dropped her bow and ran to the far side of the fire, snatching a scavenger skin full of liquid.

"Move," she snapped at Hagen as she approached.

"No, give it here," he replied, taking it from her.

Panic gripped Clinton. He could not breathe. Every gasp he made clogged his throat. Wasting no time, Hagen released the stopper and yanked the lion's jaws open. He poured the liquid inside Clinton's mouth, before clamping it shut again. Giant shivers wracked the lion's body. He squirmed under the restraint, desperate to spit the vile liquid out. However, with no options left, he finally swallowed. As soon as the liquid passed his throat, it felt like a fire exploded inside his chest. He bucked madly, arching his back, arms and legs flailing in all directions.

"He needs more," barked Gawdi.

Hagen tipped the wein into his mouth again. As Clinton continued to thrash, the burning spread into his stomach. From there the fire began to rise. Releasing the lion, Hagen stood back as Clinton vomited onto the forest floor, expelling the venom from his system in a cascade of orange bile. After retching out the last of the poison, he dragged in a shallow breath. Feeling the air finally reach his lungs, he flopped onto his back.

Gawdi climbed to her feet and walked back to her fallen comrade's litter. "The lion will be fine…unlike some of our party."

The other two guards followed her, leaving behind only Heylo.

Clinton could feel himself already recovering, while Hagen

poured more liquid over the lion's face, wiping clean the residual pollen from his furred skin. 'So…is that what a night of drinking grain water feels like?" he asked the komodo, inspecting the bulging wein skin. He sniffed it once and handed it back. "If so, I'm never gonna touch it."

Hagen chuckled as he examined the lion. "Many say that, young lion, but only time will tell."

The komodo lifted the skin to his lips.

"No!" Heylo barked, trying to seize the skin from Hagen's hands. "Not until we reach the camp."

"Why?" asked Hagen, holding it just out of reach.

"Orders, Hagen-Jin. Now, hand it over…please."

The two komodos stood unmoving for long seconds, before Hagen finally tossed the skin to the guard. "This does not please me."

"Your forgiveness is all we can ask for at this time," said Heylo, bowing. "Whatever reasons you had for abandoning your people are none of my business. But…may I ask, why do you travel with the lion?"

"If you have to ask, then you are not of rank to know," Hagen replied, folding his arms.

"Your *quintad*, Hagen-Jin? Where are your four?"

Hagen scratched the top of his head and looked out into the dense forest. "My *quintad* is busy elsewhere."

"I'm confused," said Clinton, his throat still burning. "Aren't you all part of the same clan? Y'know, Sensors of the Hand?"

The guard turned to Hagen with narrowed eyes. "How much does he know of our kind?"

"Only what I have mentioned in passing." Hagen took a seat next to the lion. "He has yet to encounter our...complexities."

The guard joined his comrades by the fire.

"We are *Ora'Clou*…born in the lands of the scent tribes, and we are not Sensors." He motioned towards his painted white tattoos, as if that explained everything.

Clinton nodded and turned to stare at the group of guards. His gaze fell to the litter: a limp arm hung over its edge. "The komodo

I injured, can I see him please?"

"You have already done enough," snapped Gawdi.

Clinton remained quiet, feeling the ball of guilt tighten in his stomach.

"So you are eight young guards away from the outlying islands for the first time?" asked Hagen.

"We all have to start somewhere," Heylo replied.

"Well, kudos for catching me in your trap." He put his arm around Clinton's shoulder. "This lion, nevertheless, is under my protection."

"I hope you are not going to make things difficult, Hagen-Jin, while journeying to the camp."

"Do you not mean difficult for *you*?" Hagen bowed his head slightly. "I have no such inclination. Alive, I am quite a catch, while there is little honor in dragging my poisoned cadaver back to camp. Now, if it is not too much to ask, may I suggest we pack up and get Nyugon, and myself, the attention we sorely need."

* * *

The first thing Clinton saw of the komodo's hidden camp was the towering smoke-tendrils winding high into the air. The group had journeyed through the night, veering from the forest track almost as soon as they departed. The lion had followed the komodos deeper into the darkness, but the twisting path made it impossible for him to memorize their route, and by the time the sun's rays penetrated the forest canopy, he felt completely lost.

Two komodos carried their fallen comrade, while Heylo shadowed Hagen and Clinton. Gawdi acted as a scout, maintaining her position at the head of the stretcher.

Clinton snagged his foot on an underlying root and stumbled forward.

"Not far now," said Hagen, catching the lion. "I hope."

Clinton smiled at his friend, and noticed dark rings circling the komodo's eyes. The lizard's skin looked dull and flaky, and an orange crust had formed at the corners of his mouth. "Hagen, you need to rest."

"The sooner we arrive at the camp the better."

Clinton peered at the lead guard.

"What do you think they'll do to us?"

"I am not sure," coughed Hagen. Orangey blood splashed against his hand, but he maintained his gaze and said nothing more.

A high-pitched warble trilled to the right of the group. The two litter bearers looked up sharply in the direction of the noise, before turning to their leader, relief clearly visible on their faces.

"Go!" Heylo ordered. The litter and Gawdi, immediately veered off towards the noise, leaving only Heylo, Clinton, and Hagen, behind.

"Well, that is good," commented Hagen.

"Why? What's going on?" asked Clinton.

"They will join with a shaman to help their fallen friend. His chances of survival have just increased from unlikely to slim."

Clinton looked at his hands and frowned. "I was only trying to defend myself. I didn't mean to—"

"I understand," rasped his friend, behind a wavering smile. "Your powers are still unpredictable, only time and practice can give you control of your raw energy."

By the time the sun had fully risen, ayvids had taken up their morning song while the trio traveled in silence. As they passed a line of trees, Heylo pulled back a thick curtain of branches to reveal a clearing that rose and settled at the base of a small cliff. A thin wood and rope path zigzagged up the side of the rock face. Large wooden structures loomed over the top, constructed to look like Olde-world komodos, felines, birds, and even humans. Scavenger pelts, feathers, and shredded reptilian skins had been attached to the totems, and hollow logs swung from their limbs, clattering and chiming in the breeze.

"To honor the Olde ways," panted Hagen, as they walked up the wobbling rope bridges. "Unlike many, we continue to acknowledge our origins and seek their protection."

Clinton stared at the crude effigy of a human with equal awe and disgust. "And do they protect you?"

"Let us say that we have still to be defeated."

"No wonder," whispered Clinton, when he reached the pinnacle and the camp's perimeter fence came into view.

Constructed from sharpened logs, guard towers sporting numerous arrow slits had been built at strategic positions around the fence. Two huge doors marked the entrance, decorated with countless spikes, and held up by thick, metal hinges. A troupe of armored guards muttered words in a foreign tongue at the sight of Clinton, before parting to allow them through. He felt their eyes lingering on him.

As soon as the trio cleared the perimeter, the smell of roast meat and dung assaulted the lion's nose. Komodos of every gender, shape, and size, went about their daily tasks. Some worked in armories, carving and sharpening wood and bones into wicked looking blades and spears. Carts wheeled through the narrow lanes that ran between the rows of leather tents, transporting passengers or bundles of supplies. As Clinton and Hagen passed by, every single komodo stopped whatever they were doing, making no attempt to hide the shock evident on their faces. Dark reptilian eyes bored into the lion from every direction.

Heading towards a large tent situated at the center of the camp, they passed a wooden feasting hall where komodos chatted noisily at long tables, tearing into scented bleater and boval meat. Grain water sloshed from their tankards, and pet scavengers such as baby boerbeasts and impalers fought for scraps flung from the tables. Outside, komodos practiced combat with weapons or their bare hands. Without their armor, Clinton noticed most had painted symbols on their skin, but only a handful displayed tattoos, and even less bore ones similar to Hagen.

The ground suddenly rumbled.

Clinton stopped dead in his tracks.

"What's happening?"

Hagen smiled. "Do not worry. It is only the stumpfeet." He pointed to a clear patch of ground ahead of them. "Look."

Rocks trembled. Grass and trees quivered before a small

sinkhole appeared and quickly grew in size.

Clinton's jaw sagged.

"What is it?" he gasped, walking closer, when a huge, shelled reptile – as tall and wide as a small slum structure – began to emerge from the depths.

"Watch out!"

Hagen yanked the lion back just as another of the creatures trundled by on its four, trunk-like legs. Clinton muttered a quick 'thanks', and gazed up at the mud-coated creature supporting a giant shell on its back. A squashed up, reptilian head stuck out from its front, while below its small, pinprick eyes, the creature's mouth ground mud, trees, and stones between its boulder-sized teeth.

Hagen placed his hand over his face. "I would suggest you cover your nose, Clinton. Oh, and stand back. This one is about to settle…"

Clinton stepped to the side and the creature lifted its flat, flaccid tail. Four dung boulders crashed to the ground by his feet. He fought the urge to gag, and the smell made his eyes water. Lifting its legs, one by one, the stumpfoot pounded them into the ground, embedding itself into the mud. The creature's shell slowly descended, until it finally came to rest at ground level.

"Stumpfoot…a virtual caravan on legs," said Hagen. "We use their hollow shells as shelter. Nomica has not seen this kind of beast for many years, but I suspect their hibernation is now over."

The stumpfoot lowered its face closer to the ground and started to scoop huge mouthfuls of dirt away. After that, it placed its head in the hole before flicking mud up over itself and burying its face in the earth.

"Our arrival is anticipated, Hagen-Jin," said Heylo, jolting Clinton out of his awe. "We must move on."

"Wait!" Hagen raised his bloodstained hand so the guard could view it. "I need to be purified."

"Not until you have visited the Sensors."

"I have complied with all your requests, Heylo. Had I been inclined to, I could have made your mission considerably more difficult."

Heylo's nostrils flared. "For that I am grateful."

"Then show it. I appreciate that time is of importance, but I too need to be purged of the poison." Hagen held his arms out wide. "I am surrounded. Where could I possibly escape? Trust me, I too, want to see the Sensors; especially now I know the patriarch is here."

Heylo thought for a moment, before finally tossing Hagen the skin of spiced wein. "The tent over there should be empty. "

Hagen bowed.

"All I ask for is some privacy. After that, you may deliver us to your leaders and complete your mission."

"Do not be long," sighed Heylo. "We must not keep the masters waiting."

Hagen lifted aside the tent flaps and ushered Clinton inside. A small fire burned in the center of the room, and cleanly picked scavenger bones circled the flames. A cloying scent struck the lion's senses.

Clinton covered his mouth. "What is it with you komodos and your scents?"

Hagen took a long draft of the spiced wein, picked up a wooden bowl, and placed it next to him by the fire. "Ritual, comfort, and meditation. Herbs have many functions. It all depends on the situation." He took another long drink. "Now, if you will excuse me…"

Hagen turned his back to Clinton and vomited into the wooden bowl. He sat back up and wiped his mouth with the back of his hand.

"Much better."

Clinton stole a glance out the tent and saw Heylo watching it from some distance away.

"Hagen, what in skorr is going on?"

"It seems that I am not returning to the tribes on the best of terms."

"Meaning?"

Hagen turned away and vomited again, before saying, "I have

been avoiding my people for many years…but now we need their guidance."

Clinton's eyebrows shot up. "Don't you think you could have told me you were a fugitive back at Samanoski, *before* I decided to follow you?"

"Clinton, we are here to gain their trust and help."

"Trust? Do you think they'll trust me when I almost killed one of their guards? And just how much help have they shown us since then? I almost died at their hands."

Hagen did not reply. Instead, he reached into a pouch attached to his belt and pulled out a handful of herbs.

Clinton folded his arms. "Oh, great! Avoid the question why don't you? You know what? I'm not having any more of it. I'm getting out of here."

"Impossible."

"Oh, well that's a surprise. 'Find the hidden camp,' you said. 'They'll help us.' Well, it sure as scrud doesn't look like help to me."

"Clinton, please," hissed Hagen, looking up from the herbs. "I need to concentrate."

Clinton slumped to the ground and leaned against the tent's central support.

Bloody lizards, he thought. *Arkie's just as stubborn.*

Hagen sprinkled herbs in a wide circle around himself while muttering an incantation under his breath. The lion could not understand his words, and the alien sounds seemed to rumble ominously at the back of the komodo's throat. The fire suddenly flickered. In response, Hagen flung a handful of herbs into the flames. The tent pulsed with light, before dying down into near darkness again. Thick smoke filled the air.

"I just hope he has learned to *smoketalk*…" mumbled Hagen.

"Who? What are you doing?" The lion instinctively covered his mouth, worried the smoke might affect his aching lungs. Instead, clean vapors loosened his chest, and clarity sharpened his mind. Through the smoke, Clinton watched Hagen's tattoos glow in the darkness, their azure light penetrating the hazy barrier.

"Greetings, old friend."

The lion jumped to his feet and stood next to the komodo, but Hagen's gaze remained fixed on the fire.

"Hagen, who are you talking to?" barked Clinton. "What are you..."

Behind the fire, a shrouded figure suddenly appeared through the center of the swirling smoke. The light from Hagen's tattoos picked out the newcomer's shape, but no other details could be seen. Clinton stared closely, and two orbs of light flashed from deep within the creature's hood, briefly illuminating a reptilian face. Smaller than Hagen, with sickly yellow skin, its snout protruded more than usual, and its hide seemed rougher and more bulbous. The figure suddenly stepped out of the smoke and embraced Hagen, who leaned in so that they could touch foreheads.

"The wanderer returns," said the stranger, his voice smooth and youthful.

"Rhyniun-Bo, my dear friend. The fact you are able to *smokewalk* tells me you finally found the Mab at Feinys-lorr? How did you convince them to teach you that trick?"

"My obvious abnormalities played a part in cementing the Mab's trust. I've had an eventful few years, brother-Sensor."

"As have we all." Hagen leaned back to regard the stranger with a smile. "Still living in the shadows I see."

"Much like yourself, Hagen-Jin...until of late, that is." The dark stranger turned his head towards Clinton. "And this is?"

"The one I have been guarding." Hagen looked to the lion. "Clinton Narfell, meet my *quintath* – my brother-Sensor. He is a member of my *quintad,* Rhyniun of the Mouth."

Rhyniun nodded slightly, but offered no handshake. "The Crystal Soul, in the flesh." His head snapped back to Hagen. "I trust you have questions?"

"You can say that again," grumbled Clinton.

Hagen placed a hand on the lion's shoulder. "What is happening, Rhyniun-Bo? I expected the tribes to unite, but why the ambush? Why the hostility?"

Rhyniun turned towards the wooden bowl that Hagen had just used. "Have you not heard? The great patriarch is here, and it seems they have even taken to using deathblow to catch you. Interesting."

"For seven sun-cycles the patriarch has been in the camp, I am told."

"That is not all. The heads of the Orders have gathered and await your presence. They are advising the tribe leaders under the patriarch."

Clinton noticed Hagen's posture stiffen slightly.

"But...why?"

"Word spread several moon-cycles ago, Hagen-Jin. A call to arms has swept the planet. Every komodo from Nomica to Orakomo, Ostica, Lunica and beyond knows to prepare for the inevitable. Dark powers have been seen. They know what you have done...what you may have unleashed. They *know*, Hagen. Your return is not a glorious one."

"Yet I have delivered the Crystal Soul."

"Indeed you have, friend." Rhyniun nodded. "But with complete disregard for the pact."

Hagen lowered his head.

"The pact?" blurted Clinton. "You mentioned that at Samanoski. What scrudding pact are you talking about?"

"The patriarch and the heads of each Order never stopped looking for you, Hagen," continued Rhyniun, ignoring the lion. "Twelve years you have hidden from their view, but when rumors of the dead rising and shadows blackening the skies spread through Nomica, they suspected the dark powers had been stirred from their slumber, by something...or someone."

"And they blamed me?"

"Should they have?"

"I acted because there was no other option, Rhyniun-Bo. The time had—"

"You acted in haste. And you acted with your heart."

"No!" Hagen took a deep breath and bowed his head. "No, my brother, I acted because opposing forces were making their move."

"Forces that your gaze have remained fixed on for far too long."

Clinton saw Hagen tense, but then resignation swept over him.

The sound of a rolling cart outside the tent made them pause. After a second, Rhyniun said, "My time has come. I must go before I am discovered." He offered Hagen a warrior's handshake, clasping wrists. "But I cannot tell you how pleased I am to see you, after all these years. Please tread carefully, brother-friend, be mindful of your every word, and most of all...curb your temper. Do not let them draw your anger."

Rhyniun turned towards the lion.

"And as for you, Clinton Narfell. Prepare yourself...I have a feeling you are about to be put to the test. You will need your wits, and what training you have, to keep you alive through the next few days. Fare you well."

With a swish of his cloak, Rhyniun turned and stepped back into the smoke.

CHAPTER NINE

JUH-GUHN.

"Are you ready?" asked Heylo, maintaining a discreet distance from the tent.

He was again reunited with most of his guards.

"Any news on your friend?" asked Clinton.

"The wind is with us today. Nyugon is stable. Master Jarik attended him, so Gawdi is hopeful of his recovery."

"She must hate me."

"She is Nyugon's betrothed," replied Heylo. "The couple was to take the Ceremony of Unity next moon-cycle. Yet hate is not an emotion our sister-warrior pays heed to, rather…retribution."

Hagen nudged the lion. "It was an accident, Clinton, you meant him no intentional harm."

Clinton wanted to say something more, but a noise behind the guards stopped their conversation. More komodos approached, wearing battle armor and blue markings painted on their arms.

"Master Tarat has instructed us to accompany the traitor to the *Juh-guhn*." announced the new lead guard, slamming his spear against the ground while staring at Heylo. "You may follow behind us…if you wish."

Heylo's nostrils flared. His fellow scent-guards grouped behind him. "*We* captured the fugitive and we claim the honor for Master Va'hen and the scent tribes."

"Master Tarat commands us to—"

"Master Tarat is not my concern," interrupted Heylo. "And neither are you. Now kindly step aside, unless it is your aim to keep the patriarch waiting?"

The touch-guard's eyes narrowed to deadly slits before he finally moved aside to let them pass.

"Do they always argue like this?" asked Clinton, keeping close to Hagen as they set off through the camp.

A grin crossed Hagen's face. "They are frightened and nervous…however much they try to veil it."

The group slowly made their way through the sprawling

village, towards the large tent positioned in the center of the camp. A pathway led up to the opening where many guards had gathered. Every komodo regarded the newcomers with suspicion. Clinton felt like he was about to face an execution.

The largest komodo Clinton had seen yet stepped forward from his position in front of the entrance. Dressed in the same style of armor as that of the touch-guards, a bone helmet covered his head and ran down the length of his snout. Spikes fanned down the rear, while one black eye peered at them through the eye-slits. Dark tattoos covered his body. As soon as the touch-guards saw the giant komodo, they encircled Hagen and Clinton with their weapons drawn.

"Halt!" commanded the large komodo, crossing his bulging arms. "Stand back and sheath your weapons. I instructed you to escort the scent-guards here, not dishonor them in such a fashion. Now go."

The touch-guards exited immediately.

Appearing from the tent emerged a female komodo wearing a headdress of feathers and a shawl of clinking bones. With brown and green wrinkled skin, a feral air seemed to surround her. Tiny tattoos covered her snout.

The scent-guards dropped to their knees.

Her stern eyes flickered over Clinton before locking onto Hagen. After a heartbeat's silence, she nodded.

"Hagen-Jin."

"Master Va'hen." Hagen bowed his head. "Cunning strategy with the deathblow snare. Subtle. You must be mellowing with your age. You were always the kind of warrior to use a war hammer to open a wrinkle nut."

The scent master's tongue slipped out and slowly tasted the air. "The divindi flower has many layers of petals, but its true heart is only visible when in blossom."

She disappeared inside the tent.

Clinton frowned.

"Still as wily as ever," chuckled the huge komodo, pulling off his helmet. He revealed a rugged face with scars running down the back of his head and cheek. His right eye had been gouged out and the socket sewn shut. He gave Hagen a warrior's handshake. "Hagen-Jin...Or should I call you Master Hagen?"

"I believe those days are long gone, Master Tarat."

Tarat smiled thinly. "Please, you must forgive the actions of our tribe. They were only following orders...albeit rather doggedly. They are the new batch from Orakomo."

"Eager and green?" asked Hagen, chuckling.

"Greener than a hatchling's ass," replied Tarat, loud enough to be heard by the onlookers.

Hagen peered past him, towards the tent's opening. "I trust they are waiting?"

"For over twelve years, brother." Tarat looked sternly at Clinton. "What kraggon's nest have you stirred up this time?"

If only he knew, thought the lion, shaking his head.

"One that was already stirred, Master," Hagen replied.

Tarat nodded and pulled aside the opening of the *Juh-guhn*, and ushered them inside. Clinton followed Hagen into the *heart-tent*, while Tarat followed behind, letting the tent flap fall back into place.

It took a moment for Clinton's eyes to adjust, but the heat hit him instantly. A fire blazed in the center of the room, and smoke drifted out of smoke-holes in the leather ceiling. Bone sconces decorated the perimeter, each filled with glowing embers billowing scented smoke. Furs and skins covered the walls and ground, dampening all sounds.

Three figures stood up from the five wooden thrones encircling the fire. Positioned in a semi-circle, each seat had been carved with tribal patterns running up the legs and seatbacks. Atop each throne rested a komodo skull that differed slightly from its neighbor. The eye sockets of one had complex, green patterns, while another had its nose decorated with white pebbles. The mouth of one skull had been prized open and filled with yellow herbs, and the fourth had a detailed, indigo design around its ear holes. The fifth chair had blue komodo claws spearing up from the top, resembling a form of jagged crown. A sixth throne faced them all, positioned on a slightly raised platform overlooking the others. With no decorations, carvings or skulls, Clinton could see the wood had been worn smooth with seasons of use.

"Hagen-Jin," said an old komodo, smiling sympathetically. She had a slim-looking face and wore nothing but a small, leather bikini. Black tattoos surrounded her eyes. "How the seasons have passed."

Hagen bowed. "That they have, Master Darra. Although the proof, as ever, remains elusive on your fair face."

Darra smiled warmly at the flattery, before taking a seat on the throne with the green, painted eyes.

Hagen turned towards a lean looking komodo with dark tattoos around his ear holes. He wore a long, cream tunic that split down the middle, and a belt containing countless pouches and pockets. Hagen nodded.

"Master Jarik. I trust you are well?"

"As well as can be," he answered, folding his arms and hiding his hands in the tunic's billowing sleeves.

Tarat clapped Hagen on the back and, setting aside his helmet, poured himself a tankard of grain water. He dropped down onto the throne topped with blue komodo claws. "Help yourself to refreshments, Hagen-Jin, and your friend also."

"Yes, let us all celebrate your *glorious* homecoming," interjected a voice, laced with sarcasm.

Clinton noticed that a single komodo had remained sitting on his throne with his back to them.

"Come now, Mayar-Bo," said Tarat. "Our brother-warrior has finally returned. Show some courtesy."

"Well, forgive me for failing to provide a hero's welcome. Yet, unless I am mistaken, I see no hero."

The cloying atmosphere suddenly turned sour.

Hagen stepped forward to face the hooded komodo. He bowed. "My dear, Master Mayar. It is you, friend, who I have yearned to see most."

"Is that so?" spat Mayar. "You wanted to see me in such haste that it took twelve years, and the poison of Master Va'hen's tribesmen to finally get you in front of me?"

"Clinton and I were journeying to the camp on our own accord. Forgive me for saying, but Va'hen-Gie's tribe members endangered his life—"

"Endangered his life?" Mayar sprang to his feet. "Endangered *his* life? He attacked one of our own! He endangers *us*...as always."

Mayar looked disdainfully at the lion, before pulling down his hood. Black tribal tattoos circled his mouth, but the right side of his face resembled a burnt and tenderized grack steak. Blistered, scarred skin had peeled back, revealing teeth and a charred cheekbone. Hardened flesh surrounded his right eye.

"We should have disposed of the abomination the moment it was born," sneered Mayar.

"Yet that is not our way, nor will it ever be," declared a husky voice from behind the raised throne.

Every komodo turned to regard the newcomer, who slowly approached the fire. Stooped and crooked, the komodo's wrinkled hand grasped a tall staff of smooth, gnarled wood.

"I understand tempers run high," continued the figure, his outline growing more defined the closer he came to the flames. "However, airing groundless passions will provide us with none of the answers we so desperately need."

The ancient komodo finally shuffled fully into view. At only three-quarters the size of Tarat, a white, hooded robe obscured his weathered features. He sighed and seated himself, pulling back his cowl to reveal his face and chest, covered in similar tattoos to Hagen and Tarat.

Hagen bent to one knee and held out his hand, palm upwards, in a show of fealty. "Master. My patriarch, my heart, my *Juh*. You cannot imagine the times I have envisaged our meeting again... What I would say... How sorry I—"

"And how I wish we could have reunited under less turbulent circumstances, Hagen-Jin. Yet the Great Mother has decided otherwise."

The old komodo coughed, and a flap of flaky skin quivered

below his jaw. To Clinton he looked gray and feeble, as if a stiff gust might blow him from his feet.

"It has been many seasons, yet I trust you know the reason why you were bought before the council?"

"I strayed. I distanced myself from my fellow Sensors, from my *quintad*, and from my masters. But what I did, I did for the good of all."

"You considered only yourself," hissed Mayar.

"My desires were the last thing I considered, Mayar-Bo."

Hagen turned to Clinton, and every pair of eyes came to rest on him too. "See whom I have brought."

The lion felt his cheeks reddening.

Tarat took a long gulp of grain water. "And you thought it was wise to bring him here?"

Hagen sighed. "My fellow Sensors. This is the Crystal—"

"We know who he is," said Va'hen, whipping her head in Hagen's direction, causing her feathery headdress to ruffle back and forth. "And we also know he belongs where it is safe…back in that village."

"Safe?" gasped Clinton.

From the back of the room the patriarch leaned forward and pointed a finger at him. "Step forward, lion."

Clinton slowly approached to take his place next to Hagen.

"And this is the one you believe to be the Soul of Power?"

Hagen patted the lion's shoulder. "I do not believe. I know."

The patriarch regarded Clinton with clear eyes, weighing him with a single glance. "Yet his presence brings us no comfort."

For a sickening moment Clinton found himself back in Wooburn's justice house facing mayor Ferris and the Giraffe Council again. He gritted his teeth.

"Neither does yours."

Tarat leaned forward. "Steady, boy, watch your words."

"No." The patriarch raised his hand. "Let him speak."

Tarat nodded casually and took another swig of his drink, but his gaze remained on the lion.

Clinton shrugged. "What am I supposed to say? I've only just met you and you've already told me I should have been killed at birth and that my presence here is a problem."

"Truth is a blunt weapon," replied Mayar.

"Yes, but I didn't *ask* to be here. And do you know what? I've been treated better by some of my enemies—"

"Enough!" Va'hen snapped, rising from her chair. Her necklace clinked loudly while her nose tattoos flared white.

Hagen stepped in front of the lion.

"Stop!" Jarik shouted. "This is not our way."

Clinton turned to face him. "So what is your way? Because all I've seen of you masters so far is scrud. I don't know what Hagen's supposed to have done wrong, but he's the only one who helped me when I needed him. He may not have always been there, but when I nearly died in the Plains, and at Samanoski stadium, and at Jasper's Tavern, he protected me...while you did what exactly?"

"Abided by the pact, little cub," scorned Mayar, leaning forward. "The pact that Hagen has undeniably broken on countless occasions."

Clinton's confusion churned inside. "What is this pact? How am I ever supposed to know stuff if you always keep me in the dark?"

"Patriarch, my *juh*, it is time the lion knew," said Hagen.

After a second of thought, a sad smile crossed the patriarch's face. "The soul shines brightest when fueled by passion, and you, young lion, shine bright. I trust you have seen our tribes gathering?"

"I have."

"And they gather for good reason. Several moon-cycles ago, the collective power of the Sensors – those under the command of Masters Darra, Va'hen, and Jarik, witnessed the stirrings of an ancient power in the eastern continents. It was a power we thought long dormant."

"Was it the same creatures that attacked Galront's hunters in the Plains? Those ghastling things?"

"They are but a taste of the evil out there, and their arrival is logical if we are to believe you are a Soul of Power. Do you, Clinton Narfell, believe it to be true of yourself?"

"Yes. Yes, I do."

"Yet you stand here blind to the events surrounding your existence." The patriarch breathed a weary sigh. "The search for the Souls of Power has lasted an age...

"Stories since the dawn of our time told of beings that could bring about the destruction of our race. For a time it only ever seemed a myth, or should I say, a threat, yet the Orders remained alert. To the Sensors, evolution must be protected and allowed to develop; it is not the concern of the living to exploit what is natural, rather, leave the Great Mother to maintain the balance. And while the anumal kingdom recovered from the colony crusades the Order of the Eyes diligently observed the heavens, searching for signs that the myth had become a reality...which, eventually, it did.

"As soon as we sensed the first soul arrive, the Shadow Soul, the Orders amassed and fanned out in search of it; we were aware of the power it could wield, and feared the destruction it might wreak if incorrectly nurtured. Yet others sensed its advent too."

"You know her presently as Marama, the Shadow Seeress" said Hagen. "Yet this Entwined spirit has had many aliases."

The patriarch nodded and continued. "Communities recovering after the colony crusades found their settlements attacked by Marama's decaying warriors. Under the command of the Black Death, the land was ransacked in search of the soul."

Clinton's eyebrows furrowed. "The Black Death?"

"The Harbinger," said Hagen, his gaze locking onto the Master of the Eyes.

Darra's slight frame went rigid. She lowered her tattooed gaze, and said, "The Black Death. The Harbinger. The Death Walker. These are but a few names for the leader of Marama's forces. Infused with the power of harvested souls, this monster obliterated countless villages, and was justly awarded the title of...Nightmare."

The patriarch sighed. "The Soul of Power was difficult to

locate because it changed vessels repeatedly, until it could find a fitting match. Therefore, long after its first arrival, it was finally found across the oceans on a lifeless continent called the Wastelands. And it was there eighteen years ago, on the island of Claw Point, that Marama's army fought the komodos for claim of the Shadow Soul.

"Many of our warriors were vanquished," said Darra, quietly. "Yet their sacrifice is not forgotten."

"The enemy's victory, however, was costly." The patriarch coughed, causing his rune necklaces to jingle. "Marama, also present at the battle, was overcome and fled into the depths of the earth. Foolishly, we thought her defeated, but soon discovered that Nightmare had likewise vanished...along with the newly born Shadow Soul."

Hagen folded his arms. "The Order of the Hand, though, remained actively searching throughout the bloodshed. We knew the second Soul of Power existed, and while the dark forces had their backs turned, a great warrior—"

"Hagen-Jin's mother and Darra-Sohn's sister," interrupted the patriarch, nodding towards Master Darra.

"Yes, my mother," said Hagen, proudly. "She found its location deep within the Great Plains of Nomica."

"Wooburn," muttered Clinton.

"Correct," answered the patriarch's wispy voice. "But here is where fate exceeded expectations. For reasons we could not fathom, Nightmare had likewise taken the Shadow Soul to the exact same location."

"So Dallas and I ended up in Wooburn by coincidence?"

Mayar slowly shook his head. "Not by coincidence. By powers we had yet to realize existed."

"Bereft of his mistress, we believe Nightmare was guided by another," said the patriarch. "Needless to say, ten years ago, both souls residing in one location, sparked a sequence of battles."

Tarat poured himself another drink. "Costing more lives."

"Many of which should not have been taken," added Hagen.

Tarat walked to his friend and placed his hand on Hagen's

shoulder. "And yet you claimed revenge; Nightmare was defeated. His power was expunged, reducing him to a mere husk of an anumal."

Hagen's clawed hand flexed. "He still escaped."

"We acted blindly, Hagen," murmured the patriarch, his claw trailing along his staff's wooden grain. "We believed them defeated, unsuspecting that the darkness lingered."

"Even the deadly grymrun lizard is prey for the slytherfin when it basks full-bellied under the midday sun," commented Va'hen. "No matter how wise, strong, or fierce a warrior you are, there are always others waiting to pounce."

A murmur of agreement ran though the group.

"An ancient Entwined spirit, one older than even Marama, craved your might for itself, forcing our tribes and Marama's soldiers to forge an alliance to defend you. We had no other options. A pact was forged, allowing both powers to live and grow without interference; we knew if word spread beyond the Plains of your whereabouts, then others would surface…"

"Another Entwined?" asked Clinton. "Who?"

The patriarch gripped his staff and stood. "We could not discern; the countless vessels it had previously inhabited warped its true identity. There is a handful of these creatures in hiding across the planet, Clinton, and every one of them craves a perfect vessel to inhabit…like you."

"So what were the rules of the pact then? Why did no one help me when you saw all the bad stuff happening?"

"We were helping by keeping our distance. Neither side could interfere in your life, or enter Wooburn…at risk of the pact being annulled. The united forces left, and Wooburn was neutral territory…to be monitored from afar."

All eyes slowly came to rest on Hagen.

Mayar's mouth tensed, the scarred flesh pulling tight over his teeth. "However, this was not the case, was it, traitor? And as soon as the pact was broken, the floodgates opened—"

"The Seeress had risen, Mayar-Bo. The collective powers sensed this. She was preparing to make a move."

"And why would she do such a thing?"

"Because we should never have trusted her. The souls had matured. Her strength was returning. What better time to act? It was only a matter of time before she sent her servant to re-claim the prize. The Crystal Soul needed our protection."

"Yet had you been *here*, you would have known that to be a matter for the council, as a collective, to decide."

"Please." Hagen dropped to one knee before the patriarch. "My *Juh*, I acted in haste, but I feared the pact already broken. I know I lingered in the Plains, but it was for the greater good."

"The greater good...or to quench your thirst for revenge?" asked Mayar.

Hagen slowly rose to his full height. His tattoos flashed as the two Sensors practically spat foreign words at one another.

Tarat casually placed his hand on the hilt of a curved knife at his belt. "Hagen-Jin, let us keep calm."

Clinton felt suffocated. He yearned to get away from the tent and into the fresh air, but knew only suspicion and hatred would await him outside. He resided at the heart of the controversy, and his presence in the camp only continued to spark fuses best left unlit.

With a deep breath, Hagen replied.

"I beg your forgiveness fellow Sensors. I meant no dishonor."

"Hagen-Jin, we speak thusly because we care," sighed Jarik. "Had you failed, had the Crystal Soul perished—"

"Then we would be a lot safer," snapped Mayar.

"He would not have perished," retaliated Hagen. "I am of the Hand. I may not be as powerful, but I have access to more magic than you, Mayar-Bo, and I will fulfill my destiny."

"Yet at what price, Hagen-Jin?" asked the patriarch. "We are on the brink of war, and now I am to determine whether it was caused by your disregard of the pact, or by others."

"I admit that I entered Wooburn on occasion...but I only acted because it was time to proceed."

"Were you following your destiny? Were you performing what you had been trained to do?" The patriarch's eyes narrowed. "No!

97

And your disregard makes me ponder…"

Hagen stepped forward. "I do not understand, Master."

"You are impulsive, unpredictable, and far too unreliable," answered Mayar. "Which, as we all know, is something you and your rebellious *quintad* has become egregious for."

"Leave my *quintad* out of this!" hissed Hagen.

"If the lion is indeed the Crystal Soul," commented Jarik. "Then is it wise he be left in the care of one such as Hagen? Or is it more judicious for him to be guided under our collective supervision?"

"I was raised to protect him," Hagen insisted.

"You were raised to protect your own kind, as you were raised to protect the balance and stop any manipulation of anumalkind's evolution," replied Mayar, jumping to his feet and standing eye to eye with Hagen.

"I am the Guardian."

Mayar scoffed. "No one gave you this title bar yourself. You have spent too long away from the tribes, in the presence of the selfish. And in such company, it is only natural that their traits pervaded your subconscious… Revenge… Desire."

Hagen bared his teeth. "The safety of this lion is tantamount—"

"That is where you falter, Hagen-Jin" croaked the patriarch. "I am but an outsider looking in, yet all I see is an anumal so focused on his own desires that he has forgotten the needs of his tribe."

Jarik nodded. "You removed yourself from your *quintad*, and your tribe, Hagen-Jin. The collective must be the priority, not the individual. We may indeed possess the Crystal Soul…but it will only be a matter of time before Marama's forces locate us now."

Master Va'hen suddenly began to pant and shake.

All heads snapped as one in her direction.

Va'hen's head fell back against her throne and her eyes rolled in their sockets. The tattoos around her nose glowed a soft white, and her chest trembled.

"*Marama…and others…*" she grunted, her voice deep and otherworldly. "*I see…many deaths. The lion is the catalyst for destruction. Beware the light, or it will end all.*"

"She *Speaks*" whispered Mayar, watching Darra and Jarik approach their fellow Master. "She prophesizes destruction at the hands of the lion. The Scent-Master has spoken in the *tongue*. We all witnessed. What say you to that, Hagen?"

"I…I do not know…Who is to say Master Va'hen is correct?"

"And since when have my prophecies been inaccurate?" asked Va'hen, breathing heavily as her eyelids opened to stare at him.

"We could consult the scriptures?" shrugged Tarat.

"Confusing at best," grumbled the patriarch.

"And our time is precious," added Mayar. "We must not waste time pondering; action is needed. Unity is the key here; there is no place for discord."

"You are correct," nodded the patriarch. "We have the lion in our care. As such, your task is complete, Hagen-Jin. I feel it may be time for your return to the motherland. Orakomo would be a welcome respite for you."

Clinton's stomach lurched.

"Master?" gasped Hagen.

"Your involvement with the lion is providing conflicting objectives that may threaten all. You need time to reflect."

Hagen lowered his head. "I will not abandon my charge."

"You are gripped with a vengeance that would have dispersed years ago had you stayed with your tribe. Your isolation has skewed your vision, and you lack the clarity that the temples on Orakomo will provide."

Mayar bowed. "A wise suggestion, patriarch."

"You do not understand what you are asking of me," pleaded Hagen. "I cannot leave."

"It will be for the best, Hagen-Jin," muttered the old komodo.

"No! I will not go."

Darra shook her head. Jarik stared in shock.

"Tarat-Jin," Mayar barked. "Summon your tribesmen and tell them to prepare for Hagen's departure."

Tarat slowly rose to his feet. "Patriarch?"

"Despite the Master's lack of sympathy, Mayar is correct."

"At once, *Juh, Heart Master*." Tarat bowed and exited.

Clinton turned to his friend.

"Hagen? What are they doing? Don't leave me. Please."

Hagen did not reply. His lips curled, revealing his teeth. The komodo's stance became defensive, ready to strike. Clinton stepped back as the komodo touched a tattoo on his shoulder, followed by a tattoo by his mouth. He then reached into a pouch on his belt and pulled out a handful of thorny twigs.

"*Reikken!*" he whispered.

"Hagen?" hissed Jarik. "What is the meaning of this?"

The twigs in Hagen's palms began to grow into a series of thorny spikes. With a flick of his hands, Hagen slipped his fingers through the gaps in the glowing thorns to create two lethal-looking fists.

Mayar pointed at Hagen. "Affronter!"

"If you think that I am going to abandon the Crystal Soul, then you underestimate my dedication."

Tarat rushed back into the tent. "As your master, I command you to yield!" he shouted. Behind him lingered six touch-guards wielding their weapons. "Hagen-Jin, please. Do not do this, my friend."

"My duty forbids me from abandoning him."

"A fool's duty!" cried Mayar. "And a self appointed one!"

A dark-robed female slipped into the room with glowing yellow tattoos around her mouth, followed by another male with glowing indigo tattoos around his ear holes. They took up protective stances near the tribe masters.

"Clearly your isolation has caused irrationality," snorted Mayar. He touched a tattoo around his mouth and it turned sunshine yellow as he whispered words of power at Hagen's thorned hands. The weapons began to shake and their brightness waned, fighting to maintain power.

Tarat inched closer to Hagen.

"I am warning you, Tarat-Jin," hissed Hagen. "With the greatest respect, stay back."

"Please, Hagen-Jin," begged the patriarch. "See sense."

"It is you, my *Juh*, and the masters, that need to see sense. The rising of Marama and the reappearance of Nightmare is no fault of mine. The true menace lies beyond the camp and is the one they call Dallas Sunaki. He is the Shadow Soul and will bring about our destruction...and only Clinton can be nurtured to negate that threat. No one else."

Jarik stepped closer to Hagen and pressed some markings around his ear holes. They turned indigo under his fingers.

A sudden buzzing nipped at Clinton's hearing. Nausea washed over him. He squinted towards Hagen and saw the komodo's eyes had narrowed, and his jaw clenched tight. Tears ran from the corner of his eyes.

"Hagen? What's happening?" asked Clinton.

"Halt your magic, Jarik-Ruu," replied the komodo, sweat dripping from his skin. "It will not stop me."

Jarik's gaze bore into Hagen, all his energy focused solely on him.

"What are you doing? Give up! You're hurting him," Clinton snarled.

More armed guards entered the tent and fanned out.

"I will gladly stop my magic, lion, when Hagen-Jin stops his," replied Jarik.

"NO!" shouted Hagen, his hands shaking. "I will not forsake the Crystal Soul. I am his guardian until I die."

"Then I fear I must continue."

Hagen staggered and shoved the lion behind him, barring any komodo from approaching.

Clinton gulped and stared up at the huge komodo now protecting him. His father suddenly sprang to mind. The love and security he had given him as a child was now but a memory: the time they had guarded Wooburn's graveyard: the feel of his father's heartbeat and embracing arms, keeping him safe from harm...had been stolen away. Now, though, the feeling surfaced again as he saw what Hagen would do to protect him. Never before had the komodo's commitment seemed so clear.

But he was fighting the wrong battle.

An adage that Arkie often said popped into his head: an anumal cornered is an anumal at its most dangerous.

Tarat's guards moved in.

The patriarch remained on his raised platform, his eyes glued on the drama.

"S...so be it, Jarik-Ruu," mumbled Hagen, growing with resolve. "M...may the Great Mother help you."

His breathing accelerated as he pressed his arm tattoos. The wooden spikes shone bright blue, and he set his feet wide, ready to attack.

"Hagen." Clinton placed a hand on his friend's shoulder. "Hagen, please, they're right. Stop."

The komodo remained poised, resisting the magic aimed at him...before he finally relaxed. He slowly turned to regard the lion, panting heavily as the look of anger on his face dissolved. His muscles sagged and his tattoos dimmed. The glowing wooden spikes immediately fell under Mayar's tonal magic, and dulled, before dropping to the ground.

Hagen regarded the lion with heavy-lidded eyes. "But I must protect you."

The buzzing sound disappeared. Jarik's tattoos faded.

Clinton smiled, sadly.

"But this is not the way. I'll be okay. I promise."

Hagen's emotion seemed to soften everything about him, as if buffing down his rough edges. "I will not leave you to be alone, Clinton."

"And I won't allow you to fight your tribe like this either. Not for me."

"Guards, fall back!" commanded Tarat.

As one, the touch-guards stepped aside, while various Sensors maintained a protective stance near their masters.

"Just...just go with them. I don't want to see anyone else hurt or punished because of me. It'll be for the best."

Hagen stared at Clinton for a long time before finally saying, "This is not the end." He gave the lion a warrior's handshake. "I promise that you shall see me again."

As Clinton watched, the komodo marched for the tent opening. Pulling aside the flap, he turned and bowed to the patriarch.

"My *Juh*. I hope one day you will forgive my past and today's actions. I have never forgotten who I was, or neglected my tribes, yet sometimes we must act, and not from desire, but from necessity. For to stand and idly observe with good intentions can be worse than committing the act of betrayal itself."

With that, Hagen turned and left.

For a moment the tent remained silent, soaked in a melancholic atmosphere. Clinton felt like half of him had been torn away, yet another anumal banished from his life.

Mayar finally broke the silence.

"Darra-Sohn, send me a few of your finest Sensors. I will pair them with some *Ora'klen* to question Hagen further. Between our two Orders we should find out any missing information and ascertain whether his words ring true. If indeed Marama broke the pact, then she will have had good reason…and we need to find out why."

"There is no need for such actions, Darra-Sohn," sighed the patriarch. "Today we have seen one of our own exhibit such strength and fire regarding his beliefs that he left no question as to whether we should doubt him. If all komodos acted with equal conviction, then the stronger the tribes would be."

Every komodo bowed their head at his words, before the Sensors and the guards exited the tent, leaving only the masters, the patriarch, and Clinton, behind.

"And you, young lion… The fact that Hagen believes you to be the Crystal Soul leaves little doubt in my own mind. However, many will remain skeptical. Questions will be asked. Therefore, it leaves me with no alternative but to examine the truth…"

Rhyniun's words of warning suddenly echoed in Clinton's mind. The lion's eyes narrowed. "How? What do you mean?"

"Come tomorrow, Clinton Narfell, the Sensors will see you prove whether you are truly the Crystal Soul or not."

103

CHAPTER TEN

LIKE SEAWATER AND SAP.

Hagen opened his eyes, adjusted his back into a more comfortable position against the wooden door, and peered up at the window of his makeshift cell. Moonlight slipped through the bars, striping the floor with three pearly beams. Outside, the sky had turned ultramarine, accented with pinprick stars and wispy clouds. A cold Ridgeback breeze tickled his skin. He inspected the shackles binding his wrists and feet together. A thick chain had once connected them, but as soon as he had been escorted to the cell he had yanked his hands apart, snapping the chain with little effort.

He stood up and approached the window. His cell was located inside the shell of a newly surfaced stumpfoot. The smooth walls were mottled with swirling symbols that illuminated when the moonlight bounced off them. Yet despite his strength and abilities, Hagen knew he would not be able to breach the magically fortified exterior.

Looking down into the camp, he counted the fires dotting the landscape. Scores of tents glowed with light, and in the distance, shadowy guards patrolled the perimeter fence. The whisper of music throbbed in the air, beating tribal rhythms, decorated with whistles and bells and accompanied by laughter and guttural singing. The smell of roast scavenger permeated the room, yet Hagen's thoughts were not on food. His gaze slipped over the hooded komodos lingering within shouting distance of his cell.

Still there, he thought.

Darra's Sensors had their eyes fixed on his prison, while Va'hen and Jarik's tribe sensed the air for changes in smell or sound. Tarat's guards silently patrolled the shadows, protecting them all.

Hagen nodded his head. Tarat had become a strong touch-master. He would lead the Order of the Hand well and would not be swayed by the other masters or tribe leaders. Mayar, however, was another story.

Hagen sighed, cursing himself for how his meeting with the

patriarch had turned out. He had hoped his closest friend would have come to accept the misfortunes of the past. But instead of time healing his relationship with the Master of the Mouth, it had only created a void that he knew would never be filled.

He rested his head against the bars.

Immediately around the stumpfoot, lines had been scratched in to the earth, filled with crushed herbs and sand. The *sense-snare* served to debilitate the heightened powers of a Sensor: if he succeeded in breaking through the cell's walls, his ability to fight would be childish at best when in the snare. He backed away from the window, but a fluttering movement caught his eye from the depths of the blue sky. Squinting into the darkness, the outline of wings soared up, before swooping back down and out of sight again.

At the perimeter, two komodos suddenly stared skywards. A flash of green illuminated their faces as their eye tattoos pulsed before the light slowly died again. Hagen turned from the window, only to be stopped in his tracks.

A smile spread across his face.

"Well, you certainly are a face from the past."

A small lizard-like ayvid hovered in front of Hagen, beating its leathery wings. Catching the moonlight, Hagen noticed their edges still had the red tinge of hibernation coloring them. Hagen picked up a slither of dried meat from his plate, and the creature darted forward, snatching it out of his hand, before flipping its head back and swallowing it whole. Hagen lifted his arm and the creature flapped down to perch on it.

"Whim! My faithful servant." The komodo bought the creature close to his face. "What news do you bring?"

The creature clicked a short reply, before ruffling its wings.

Hagen's eyebrows rose. "From Quala? Well, that is some distance you have flown, little one."

Whim leaped boldly from Hagen's arm. She landed on his shoulder and traversed along the komodo's shoulder, closer to his ear hole. It relayed another series of rapid clicks. As Hagen translated them, he found his heartbeat quickening. The cell walls seemed to shrink as a feeling of suffocation engulfed him.

"And this happened how many sun-cycles ago?"

Whim clicked a short reply.

Exhaling deeply, Hagen lifted Whim from his shoulder and placed her carefully on the windowsill. He dropped his voice to a whisper, cautious of Jarik's guards.

"Do you know who they were?"

Whim clicked her reply.

"And Vito set off north? That must mean…"

Hagen paused, letting the news sink in. Numerous plans of attack sprang to mind, but through them all, one remained at the forefront of his thoughts.

He scooped Whim up and held her close to his mouth. "Speed, my friend, speed is of the essence here. Fly with might." Various names flared up in Hagen's mind, before the right ones fell from his lips and into Whim's waiting ear. "Gather these anumals together. The correct ones must be selected. Our way forward is clear, for us…and for Clinton."

Whim acknowledged Hagen's instructions with a click, before Hagen lifted his hand out of the window. Whim leaped from her perch and shot skywards, vanishing into the darkness.

This was not supposed to be the way. It is too soon.

Yet the news of Quala coursed through him, turning his cold, komodo blood fiery. His forehead creased in thought for a long while. Finally, he reached into one of his belt pouches. Taking out a pinch of herbs, he sprinkled them in a circle, and then opened his mouth to sprinkle more onto his tongue. An acidic tang fizzled against it. He gagged, but chewed them into a pulp. Reaching for another pouch, he pulled out two gray shards of slate. He gritted his teeth and struck the slate together, creating small sparks with every strike. Leaning closer to the slate, he hacked up his foul-tasting spit, and with one final strike, spat the saliva at the spark. The cell flashed for the briefest second as it ignited, before darkness quashed it again.

Hagen chanced a look outside.

The guards continued their patrol, oblivious to his actions.

As green as hatchlings asses indeed, he thought, before focusing on the corner of the cell.

Smoke was slowly filling the room. Forcing his back against the window to hide the interior from anyone outside, he watched a familiar figure appear from the darkness...

Rhyniun of the Mouth gazed around the cell. His gaze lingered on the painted symbols, and he nodded in understanding before tapping some of his mouth tattoos.

Mind speak, he said, yet no words left his mouth. Instead, they rang clear in Hagen's head. *Speak this way or the guards will hear us.*

Hagen chuckled and replied in the same fashion, knowing his words would be heard.

Smoke walking, and now mind speaking. You are growing strong in your talents, Rhyniun-Bo.

As I said, it has been some years, smiled Rhyniun. *But come now, Hagen-Jin, disappearing for all this time, and now I see you twice in one day? I trust you haven't summoned me to merely discuss my progress? The masters, how did they receive you today?*

It was fragile to say the least, sighed Hagen. *It appears the tribes are not entirely stable at the moment.*

Meaning?

Hagen looked over his shoulder and out of the window. Not a single guard had noticed Rhyniun's arrival. *Much has changed during my time away from the tribes.* He shook his head. *Twelve years is but a drop in the ocean for our kind, yet during this time, the temperament and attitude of the tribes has shifted. The masters are fractured and nervous. Today they acted like cornered scavengers, protecting their territory.*

As you obviously protected yours, Rhyniun stated, rubbing his chin. *Otherwise you would not be held captive. I take it that tribe opinion differed regarding the Crystal Soul?*

Like seawater and sap. Rhyniun, the old ways are dying. Anumalkind is evolving, and so too should we, yet instead, the masters fear change. Today I not only brought change into this camp in the guise of the lion, but I threatened to kill anyone in order to protect it.

And why am I not surprised? sighed Rhyniun. *You talk of others not changing, but neither have you. You're still as stubborn as ever.*

Hagen hissed a laugh. *Yes, well, I fear this night's revelations may be the catalyst for all of us. I have received news, and I would not have risked your life coming here unless the need was dire.*

Which is why I came.

Word was sent from Quala. All is not well...An uprising has begun.

An uprising?

The felines are banding together into an army of Ocelots. They are claiming dominance. Villages are being destroyed. And guess who leads them?

Say no more, snarled Rhyniun, *Meylana predicted this may happen, but only our* quintad *had the foresight to act upon it. They said she was too young to be speaking the* Tongue. *Fools!*

And the safeguards our quintad *put in place have helped us thus far, and will continue to do so.*

True, Hagen-Jin.

The Sensor lifted his head and the soft, yellow glow of his tattoos illuminated his mouth. The only other thing to be seen under his cowl was the magic's light reflecting in his yellow eyes. Rhyniun crouched down and began to draw swirling, cloud-like shapes on the ground, scratching them onto the stumpfoot's shell. *The rest of the* quintad *have remained in position, ready for your command. I will inform them of the news.*

I know of only Quala that has been attacked so far, but that will only be the start.

It will spread, agreed Rhyniun. *Evil is a virus that multiplies.*

I received the message before I called for you, and I have sent the messenger north. Hagen crouched down in front of Rhyniun and placed his hand on top of the symbol. *From Wooburn to Middle City. They must be informed of what is happening, Rhyniun-Bo. It is time for Aegis to rise."*

Is that not what Aegis is there for?

Was *there for, and if there ever existed a time for it to rise again, then it is now.*

Rhyniun stared at Hagen from beneath his deep cowl. He remained silent for a moment, before chuckling. *And what of the Crystal Soul?*

Do not worry about him. He will remain in my care.

Rhyniun nodded and placed his hand atop Hagen's. The symbol made a hissing sound as smoke slipped through the gaps between their fingers and up their arms. The two Sensors took their hands from the symbol and stood while the smoke snaked up their thighs and torsos, completely engulfing them. Placing a hand on Hagen's shoulder, Rhyniun stood behind the tall komodo and directed him forwards, into the heart of the smoke.

Come morning they will realize you've escaped.

All I need is one night, replied Hagen. *That will be enough time to fulfill my plans. I will return then, and they will never know.*

In the meantime, let us hope they don't sense our departure. Rhyniun guided his brother-Sensor onwards, vanishing into the smoke. *Why do you always drag me into your trouble, Hagen-Jin?*

Rhyniun-Bo, when have you ever refused to be a part of it? smiled Hagen. His vision blurred as the stumpfoot shell vanished out of sight. *And when have I ever let you down?*

CHAPTER ELEVEN

THE TESTS.

Sunlight bathed Clinton in his straw bed. The lion sat up and rubbed his eyes, waiting for his vision to adjust to the brightness. Images of Hagen being banished from the patriarch's tent lingered in his mind, leaving him numb. He sighed and glanced at Tarat's ever-present guard.

"Still here?"

The guard nodded.

A tray of strange smelling bread, fruit, and some form of green paste had been placed within reach of Clinton's bed. Pushing it away, he yawned, climbed to his feet, and stared out the window. A frost had swept through the camp, causing the sunlight to shimmer off the tents and stumpfoot shells. Smoke billowed from smoke holes, forming lazy clouds that meandered in the morning air. There was a knock at the door, and the Master of the Hand entered, his physique almost filling the doorframe.

"Did you sleep well?" asked Tarat, peering down at the lion.

"What do you think?" snapped Clinton. He held his gaze for a moment and then turned back to the window.

Tarat sighed. "We have been through this."

"And that's supposed to make everything alright?"

"What happened with Hagen was unfortunate, but inevitable."

Clinton did not reply.

"Here," said the komodo, holding out a pile of clothing with a set of leather armor resting on top.

"I'd prefer my own lazarball armor, thanks. The set the scent-guards stole from me in the forest."

"Your armor is safe. In the meantime, wear this."

Clinton snatched the clothing from him and unfolded it, revealing a flexible chest plate with elbow and kneepads.

"What are you going to do to me?"

Tarat folded his thick arms. "Just do your best, Clinton Narfell, and try and eat something. It is going to be a long sun-cycle. You will need all your energy."

* * *

The deep thud of drums pounded in Clinton's ears. Flanked by guards, and lead by Tarat, the small arrowhead-procession made its way towards a distant hill. Komodos from every tribe looked on from the side of the dirt track, leading to where the patriarch and the masters were patiently waiting. Flags and banners wafted in the breeze, sporting the sigils of each Order. The crisp morning air cleared Clinton's head and energized his sleepless body. Again he felt the judgment from the crowd, watching him silently with accusing stares. His stomach twisted with uncertainty. He glanced over his shoulder at the camp, knowing Hagen was there, waiting to be escorted back to Orakomo.

If only he could be here to help me now...

Seated in his chair, the patriarch looked up from a leather scroll he was studying. Darra and Jarik stood to his left, while Va'hen and Mayar were to his right. Tarat took his place behind the five, casting a protective shadow over the ancient komodo.

"It is good to see you here, lion, considering yesterday's events," the patriarch croaked. "I must remind you that we are not forcing you to take the tests."

"Really?" Clinton scoffed, looking past the patriarch. "Sure seems like it to me."

Behind the komodos, through gaps in the crowd, Clinton snatched a glimpse of a large hole in the ground. Dirt piles lined its circumference.

The patriarch rose to his feet. "I know this may seem unnecessary, but it will help put the collective minds to rest as to whether you are truly a Soul of Power."

Clinton's face screwed up as he fought a swell of bubbling anger. "Then they should have listened to Hagen. He spoke the truth."

"Hardly a reliable source," sneered Mayar.

Clinton felt a flush of heat sweep over him. He gritted his teeth. "I'd rather trust him than a slimy, jibbar-tongued lizard like you!"

Mayar slowly pulled back his hood to peer at the lion. The morning sun highlighted every detail of his scarred face. "And this trust is based on what? The pitiful amount of time you have spent with him?" Mayar swaggered closer. "I assume your vast wisdom has ascertained everything there is to know about our wandering friend, and *that* is why you are qualified to cast such aspersions?"

"Enough, Master Mayar!" commanded the patriarch. "Allow the lion to focus."

Mayar bowed and replaced his cowl. "Of course, *Juh*."

Clinton tore his scowl away from the Master of the Mouth to stare at the hole.

"So what am I supposed to do? I take it the hole has something to do with the test?"

"What lies ahead is a simple assessment of what is assumed to be second nature to a Power."

"But as Master Mayar so conveniently pointed out: my time with Hagen was brief. My training is—"

"If I know Hagen, he will have taught you enough for you to tackle these trials," interrupted the patriarch, a warm smile crossing his face. "Clinton, whether you crawl, walk, run, or even fly, each action is a progressive extension of the previous one, all concerned with moving forwards. Simply do what comes naturally to you, and remember what you have learned. Observe your surroundings…and take nothing for granted. Judge none, and the answers will present themselves to you."

Clinton remained silent as he mulled over the advice, before finally stepping closer to the hole. The crowd moved aside at his approach, allowing him to peer over the lip. He saw a spiral path notched into the walls that disappeared into the darkness.

"Stumpfeet make them by twisting themselves into the earth," commented Tarat. He handed Clinton a burning torch, and leaned closer. "If Hagen believes in you, then so do I."

Clinton blinked and took one last look at the sea of reptilian faces around him. If he was ever going to justify Hagen's actions, or see his brother again, then he would have to follow the path set before him.

Raion, what the skorr are you getting me into this time?

He placed his foot on the top step and edged his way down into the descending gloom.

* * *

It did not take Clinton long to reach the bottom of the stumpfoot burrow. He squinted up at the opening, now only a small disc of light above, and holding the torch high, set off down the tunnel. All around, the dirt was compacted into the walls and ceiling to create an arch. Two ridges had been scored into the sides of the tunnel where the stumpfoot had dragged itself deeper into the earth. Clinton's feet sloshed through puddles, and as an acidic smell assaulted his senses, he realized what the liquid actually was.

"Are you joking?" he shouted. "Stumpfoot piss? Oh, come on!"

As he traveled deeper into the earth, the air grew humid, causing sweat to matte his skin and mane. He walked for what seemed like the whole morning, plowing through the darkness, until his torch picked out a distant wall blocking his path. He jumped over more puddles, before finally reaching the end.

"What? No, this is wrong."

He glanced back the way he had come, thinking he may have missed a turn.

I wonder if this was where it hibernated?

However, Clinton knew about scavenger nests; there were no traces of dung, or food remains anywhere. He ran his hand over the smooth wall, but it felt solid, with no breaks or cracks.

"Okay!" he shouted. "What am I supposed to do?"

No one replied.

"Is this a part of the test or what? Oh, for scrud's sake!" He kicked the tunnel wall and a clicking noise made his ears prick.

Sweeping the torch around, he saw a handful of sectoids scurrying away from the light, burrowing into the tiny holes in the mud. Clinton stared for a moment, before a sudden smile crossed his face.

"I get it." He shook his head. "Very clever. The insects can eat through the wall."

He slammed his foot against the ground, causing more sectoids to surface. As soon as they appeared, he grabbed some.

"OW!"

A burning sensation nipped at his palm, like he had shoved his hand against a needle-tree. He flicked the sectoids away and yelled, "Oh, come on!"

The tiny creatures scurried back to safety while Clinton inspected his palm. Small red spots began to blossom on his flesh.

"Little scruds," he hissed, rubbing his palms together. "Look, I'm not going to hurt you."

Yet as he watched the final sectoid burrow back into the mud, a sudden thought struck him.

"Take nothing for granted," he muttered, slowly approaching the wall again. He swept his hand over the surface. "Remember what you've learned…"

He clenched a fist.

"Do what comes naturally," he said, and with that, smacked the wall, causing more sectoids to appear.

Closing his eyes, he concentrated hard, falling through the gloom of his mind to explore deeper. Like an explosion of color, tiny specks of brown, wriggling light sprang into focus, weaving in and out of the maelstrom of movement around him. He focused on one of the lights, locking on to its existence, and assimilating its consciousness, until his physical being finally slipped away.

It felt like he was diving into water. He pushed through the heaviness, trying to sink deeper, until…

An enormous sectoid pounded towards him. Its multiple feet shook the ground when they slammed into the mud. The sectoid opened and closed its black mandibles before one of its antennas swept down the length of his body.

Move!

The impulse echoed clearly in Clinton's head, even though all he could hear was clicks. Yet he understood the message. Clinton turned to move, but found his body was not responding properly.

When he tried to step aside, his muscles not only moved two legs...but six. Two antennas flexed from the bridge of his head and translated the messages bouncing between the sectoids.

Realization struck him like a brick.

He swung his head around and caught sight of his own colossal, feline body collapsed on the ground not far from him. Meanwhile alien sensations coursed through his new, temporary body. His 'eyes' picked up multiple versions of everything, and his legs felt like roots, attaching him to the ground.

Raion!

The thought of his brother sprung to mind through the myriad of confusion. He remembered his brother's laughter; he pictured the dirt under the youngster's claws, the smell of his wet fur...memories anchoring Clinton to who he really was, preventing his identity from slipping away. Akin to a cubling's first steps, Clinton wobbled precariously on his spear-like legs, before his muscles gradually began to work in rhythm, propelling him towards the wall. A barrage of clicks echoed behind him, commanding him to rejoin the troops and protect the workers, yet he ignored his orders and continued onwards. Reaching the wall, he began to push under the mud, boring into the ground at an angle, and into the darkness. His mandibles worked at a rapid pace, stripping back layers of mud over and over again, until he finally broke through to the other side.

Firelight assaulted his senses. He wanted to retreat, but finally he scampered out to see burning torches on the other side. Thick joists propped up a false wall, obstructing his journey, while ahead the tunnel continued on with its seemingly endless descent.

Releasing his mental hold of the sectoid, Clinton felt himself sucked from the dirtmite's consciousness and dragged back through the darkness, until his feline eyes burst open. He sat upright with a gasp, and rolled his neck and shoulders, allowing time for his senses to adjust to normality again.

"A false wall, huh?" he murmured, eyeing the barrier.

He stood up, hunkered down, and charged at it with as much force as he could muster. Clinton's shoulder slammed against the wall. Crashing through to the other side, he fell face first to the ground as dried mud and wooden supports collapsed on top of him.

He smiled in triumph.

* * *

The lion continued down the tunnel, journeying along endless, snaking bends. Hope sprouted after his success at bypassing the first obstacle, but quickly waned when he realized more tests would surely be coming. The tunnel eventually came to an abrupt end, opening into an underground cavern.

As tall as Wooburn's domed temples, the ceiling arched upward, forcing him to crane his neck back to view its full height. Jagged rocks stuck up from the ground like spires, joining stalactites, and forming giant pillars of stone. Countless tunnels dotted the walls, and an acrid smell permeated the air, drifting out from the huge midden-heaps sloped against the cavern's sides.

Clinton tentatively approached the center, his mouth wide with wonder, when his gaze locked onto something very much out of place. A metal cage sat in the middle of the cavern. Inside it a scavenger grunted and snarled, pressing its nostrils against the bars.

"Mother of Treb!" huffed Clinton, remembering his childhood wound. He instinctively touched his ribs. "Why did it have to be a scrudding grack?"

The meaty scavenger bared its rotten teeth and snarled. Saliva dribbled from its lips, and a leathery paw swiped at the bars, causing the cage to shudder and creak. Clinton drew closer. "It's, okay. I'm not gonna hurt you. I'm just as confused as you are."

The grack snorted before shuffling back a few paces. It tucked its stringy tail between its legs, its ears pinned back.

"You're scared of me? Now I've seen everything."

The ground suddenly shook beneath his feet.

The grack yelped and backed into a corner. Clinton stumbled, and a low rumble groaned through the room.

"Okay, so maybe it's not me you're scared of..."

The ground trembled again.

Clinton span around to study the cavern. Wide fissures ran along the ground, creating lightning bolt patterns that split the rock and ended in holes falling away into the unknown depths. Discarded, hollow stumpfoot shells lay splintered across the ground.

"I'm guessing this is test number two, right? Well let's see what they have in store this…"

Something slapped against his ankle.

He yelped and yanked his leg away, but a mint-white tentacle coiled up his calf and tugged him to the ground.

"What the…"

Clinton protracted his claws and raked them over the white flesh, gouging four slashes in the skin. The tentacle shuddered. Releasing its hold, it whipped away through a hole in the wall.

Clinton scrabbled to his feet.

"Okay, what in Skorr was that?"

The grack barked.

The ground shuddered.

Clinton's pulse pounded.

Another tentacle whipped up through a crevice and slapped around his waist, pulling him back to the ground.

"Get off!" he snarled, as he was dragged backwards. He stabbed his claws into the white flesh again, causing blood to spray. "I said let go!"

The cavern shook. Debris trickled from the ceiling.

Releasing its hold, the tentacle unraveled and snapped back into the shadows again.

Think, Clinton. Think!

He stumbled to his feet and staggered over to the scavenger's cage. He closed his eyes, forcing his mind to switch into a more open state before surveying the area again. Swirling red lines bloomed to life, highlighting numerous tentacles weaving in and out of every opening. A swirling mass of color pulsed beneath his feet, larger than any creature he had seen before, and at its center shone a glowing, white core.

"What the…"

Clinton gulped.

Another life force came into view. A tiny glow scuttled across his arm, weaving over his furred skin, before stopping at his wrist. "I'd get away if I were you," Clinton warned the dirtmite.

The ground rumbled.

A tentacle burst through the stone, sending Clinton flying back. He clipped his head against a rock, and landed on his knees, while a long, white appendage coiled around his chest. With a bone-crunching grip, it squeezed the air from Clinton's lungs like juice from a bodando berry.

"No…" he grunted, fighting for breath. His vision blurred; bursts of color stole his sight, threatening to rob him of consciousness.

The tentacle dragged him towards a deep fissure, but the lion refused to surrender and wrapped his fingers around the bars in the grack's cage. The scavenger snarled and barked at him, shoving its mouth in his face.

Crawl, walk, run… echoed the patriarch's words.

Crawl…Walk…Run…

The tentacles tightened, tugging harder at Clinton.

Slowly the cage began to scrape across the ground, while the lion's strength slipped away quicker than a dying himperfish.

Crawl…Walk…Run…

An idea jolted through Clinton. The baby kraggon suddenly sprang to mind. It seemed impossible, yet he knew he had no other choice but to try…

Clinton reached through the bars and grabbed onto the grack's leg. He closed his eyes, anchored onto the thought of his brother, and peered at the grack again. A red glow emanated from within its chest, spreading out to the tips of its claws and the end of its stubby tail. Filtering through the scavenger's being, he focused hard, ignoring its instincts and fears, until he found what he was searching for.

Got you!

A warm sensation coated Clinton's skin. Power tingled in his fingertips to his toes, like he had lowered them into hot water. His muscles twitched. He gritted his teeth, refusing to let go of the cage, no matter how hard the tentacle yanked. A deep, feral power, like raging fire, suddenly engulfed his being and stoked his determination. He felt his shoulders bulge beneath his armor, and then great cracks ricocheted down his back, arms, and neck. Sparks of pain lanced every muscle like molten lead was oozing through his bones.

"What's...happening?"

Clinton threw his head back and yelled. His leather armor ripped. A red mist framed his vision as he watched the grack's glow fade, its heartbeat slowing with every passing moment.

"Aaaarrggghhh!"

The lion's fear and anger reached a boiling point.

Letting go of the grack's leg, he slashed his claws into the tentacle with such force it tore it to shreds. The cavern shook. The creature wailed, but Clinton held on to the damaged limb and bit into it with his powerful jaws. Gore smeared his face. He yanked his head from side to side, tearing at the tentacle until it ripped free, sending a spray of blood and green ooze in all directions. Flapping wildly, the severed stump retreated back into the darkness. Clinton dropped his prize, arched his back, and roared. His body shook. Energy, unlike anything he had ever experienced, and a taste for blood, willed him to attack and tear into something else, anything.

He growled.

Clinton's awareness slowly began to push against the grack's consciousness. He cemented himself against its power. *Raion!* he thought, anchoring his memories and quenching his bloodlust. He panted hard and stared at his hands. Hard, smooth grack skin coated them, with long, black claws extending from stump-like fingers. Underneath his torn armor he could see his fur had matted together over gray, bulging muscle.

"I don't understand," he hissed. "Is this supposed to happen?"

A tentacle whipped out at him from the side.

Clinton dove onto all fours and gnashed his teeth together,

feeling saliva splatter as he snarled. Another tentacle crashed into him from behind. He whipped around to attack, just as the cracks in the ground split open. The stone fell away, creating a gaping blemish that spread along the cavern. Huge columns fell from the ceiling, smashing all around and plummeting into the darkness. Thick tentacles suddenly whipped into the air, wrapping around rocks and slamming into crevices, before a colossal creature yanked itself up, emerging from the depths of the pit.

With a mouth wider than two standing anumals, row upon row of teeth lined the creature's lips, creating a spiky, pink maw. Two cold black eyes sat on either side of its head, nestled amongst a hide that looked like stone had been fused to its pale skin. Starting from its eyes, and working their way down the length of its neck, countless mini-tentacles wriggled and squirmed, rippling to and fro, as if blowing in a breeze. The creature reared up and let out a trumpeting blare, shaking the cavern to its foundations.

Primal fear urged Clinton to respond. He charged ahead, snarling and barking as he ran. When he reached the fissure's edge, he dove forwards, mindless of the deadly drop, and extended his claws. Crashing into the monster, he dug into its white skin and slashed at the arm-sized tentacles surrounding him. The creature roared. It flung itself from side to side but Clinton gripped on tight, scrabbling up the monster's body, towards the crown of its head. He picked up his pace, plunging his claws deeper into the creature's hide. Blood spurted from every gash he made, coating his now toughened skin.

With one last push, he struggled up onto the creature's head, and rose shakily to his feet. A field of stone and writhing tentacles spread out before him, as if growing from the creature's skull. He clawed his way onwards, until he reached one of its giant eyes…

"You think you can beat me?" he growled, flexing his claws. "Think again."

The lion slammed his hand down towards the creature's eye, but the monster bucked and suddenly shook itself. Instantly, every tentacle on its body stiffened like rods of iron, causing Clinton to miss his target and lose his footing. As Clinton fell, tentacles slammed flat against the monster's skull, creating a protective shell all over itself.

Snapping out his hand, the lion snagged his claws into the rock-like skin, managing to stop his descent. Forcing his claws into the surface, he began to drag himself back up again.

The creature started to rise, its huge tentacles pulling it towards the cavern's roof. Clinton glanced at the ceiling to see it fast approaching. Cresting the monster's head again, he dove flat, dodging another swipe from a tentacle that barely missed his face. He snapped his attention back to the tentacles protecting its skull, and spied a slight gap where one had overlapped another. Without pause, Clinton hunkered over, pulled hard at the gap, and squeezed beneath. Shoving his legs against the tentacles, he wedged himself inside the tiny space...

The monster slammed into the ceiling.

Clinton yelled as the tentacles pushed against him with bone crushing force. Almost immediately, though, the pressure released and the tentacles relaxed again.

Bright daylight burned Clinton's vision. The wind whipped over him. Clinging to the monster, the komodo's camp came into view. Beneath him, lizards scattered for safer ground as guards bellowed and hurled spears at the towering creature. Arrows clattered off its skin as the monster wailed and arched forwards, before plummeting back into the hole it had just created.

As the giant descended, speeding closer to the ground, Clinton hurled himself from the monster at the last possible moment. He slammed into the grass, knocking the wind from him, and tumbled over the bumpy soil. Rolling to a halt, he looked up just in time to see the last of the creature's tentacles slipping into the hole while it trumpeted a victorious bellow, raining mud and stones in every direction.

Panting hard, Clinton pushed the grack's energy aside, feeling it abate the more he concentrated. He stared at the hole and directed the grack's energy back to its owner, not truly knowing if it would reach its intended target or not. A thin, white mist drifted from his palm and trickled over the lip of the hole and out of sight.

Clinton's sense of self began to resurface as his body popped with unnatural cracks and judders, and his bones reset. He groaned and gritted his teeth, resisting the mind-numbing pain. He rolled back and forth as his muscles burned like fire. His armor stopped digging into his flesh, but sticky blood coated his now normal skin. As the heat of pain slowly abated, Clinton sighed, and felt the warmth of pride budding to take its place. He chanced a smile, unable to believe what he had just accomplished, and sat up.

Master Mayar's snarling face loomed over him, pushing him back into the grass.

"Bind his hands and feet! Do not let him move!"

"What…what's wrong?"

"Silence, imposter!" spat the komodo. Six spear-carrying guards rushed to flank the Taste Master's side. "Get this freak out of my sight!"

Clinton only just managed to see the small dirtmite scuttle from of his clothes, before the end of a spear slammed into his head.

CHAPTER TWELVE

GALDIIN.

"I did as you asked; I passed the test!"

"You enraged a rock louse to such extremes that it smashed through its lair and endangered the lives of the tribe," Mayar retorted. "The damage to the surrounding earth is immense, and let us not think about its appearance on the surface – alerting every scavenger and traveling anumal for miles around of our location."

The patriarch sat rigid in his chair, his unmoving gaze locked on Clinton.

Mayar slumped back and interlaced his fingers. "It is too much. Surely this proves he poses a credible danger to us all."

The tent's smoke holes had been peeled back to reveal the twinkling stars above. A fire blazed in the center of the room with the heads of the Order gathered around it on their thrones.

"*I'm* a danger?" Clinton shook his head, unable to believe what he was hearing. "I was the one forced into the pit in the first place. I did what you told me, and survived."

Mayar's malformed lip sneered. "But at what cost?"

"You live, Clinton Narfell," the patriarch finally croaked. "Yet Mayar's anger, although excessive, is valid."

"You are the ones who made me face a monster I'd never seen before…and I dealt with it. I passed your stupid trials. What more could I have done?"

"Ample," the patriarch replied, rising to his feet. "And I believe, deep down, you know your actions today were incorrect too."

The collective gaze of the komodos fell upon the lion. He looked down into the fire and sighed. A strand of his mane fell in front of his eyes, and he raised his shackled hands to nudge it away. The chains jingled in the silence.

So it has come to this again, he thought, his shoulders slumping.

"I think it unwise to be overly harsh on the boy," said Darra, breaking the tension. The bright gems fused into her skin twinkled in the firelight. "He has faced many ordeals recently. And it does not take these," she tapped her eye tattoos, "to see the truth of that."

Tarat took a sip of grain water. "I'm sure we can all appreciate that he clearly has a gift."

"But the gift of the Crystal Soul?" Va'hen asked. She wore a sleek scavenger skull on her head, the top of its jaw balancing against her brow. Its fangs jutted down like a bony sweatband. "The power he exhibited was something else. It was not normal. And my prediction still stands that he will be the catalyst of our destruction."

"Why would I ever want to destroy you? And I used the powers that Hagen taught me. I controlled those creatures, I saw their souls."

"A base talent. One that is natural to any of my Order," snorted Jarik.

"Mine also," Darra conceded. "The Order of the Eyes sees far beyond the physical, and deeper towards the soul."

"But I'm not of the Order!" Clinton gritted his teeth, feeling his arguments falling on deaf ears.

"And neither are your abnormal powers," snapped Mayar.

"There is still much we have to discover about the Crystal Soul, Mayar-Bo. However, I agree, these physical transformations were never a part of the scriptures," mumbled the patriarch. "They are something else."

"I just did what came naturally," reasoned the lion, "what felt right. Look, I don't know if these changes to my body are what you expected or not. All I know is that they just happen, okay. This is all just as confusing to me as it is to you; I only found out recently what I really was."

Clinton stepped closer to the patriarch, searching for any sign of understanding or compassion. "Please! I know what I did may seem disturbing to the tribes, but I managed to control the dirtmite, and I used the grack's powers. I did what you asked of me."

"Did you, Clinton Narfell? Did you indeed?" The patriarch narrowed his eyes and slowly stepped down from his elevated throne. He lifted one of Clinton's hands and inspected the lion's palm. "You are a survivor, there is no denying that."

"I have to be."

"Which sets you apart from most." He stared deeply into Clinton's blue eyes. "Tell me the truth. Have you or any of your family had any links to the Bes? Or studied with the Koldun'ai?"

"No. I remember Hagen mentioning them, but I've never met any."

Jarik's ear tattoos flashed. "He speaks the truth, my *Juh*. These are no Koldun'ai or Bes powers. What the lion did today is…new."

The patriarch nodded and lowered his gaze from Clinton. "Power resides in you, lion, that is a fact, but I also fear you believe…or have been led to believe, that you may be more than you actually are."

"I…I don't understand."

"Today you completed trials that many anumals would have failed from the onset…yet you are a survivor." The patriarch dropped Clinton's hand. "This instinct has been a part of you since birth, and, if I am to believe Hagen's words, has helped you safeguard your sibling after you were orphaned."

"I had no choice. I had to be strong for the both of us, just like I had to pass the test today. What I did—"

"What you did," said the old komodo, stepping back, "was savagely attack a peaceful creature."

"Peaceful?" Clinton could not believe his ears.

"Had you used the Crystal Soul's power, you would have seen what was fully around you, taken nothing for granted, and judged nothing. This is the advice I told you before you began the trials. I could not have made the answer any clearer. It was in front of you all along…and right at the very end too."

"I…I don't understand. You saw what happened to my body. I controlled the sectoid…I adopted the grack's abilities."

"And however intrigued I am of your abilities, they do not prove to us your identity as the Crystal Soul. Today, you failed the tests."

Clinton stepped back, clenching his jaw. "No. No, you're

wrong. You're all wrong. Hagen believes in me, and I know what I felt in the tunnel was real. How can I prove it to you?"

"Tell me," said the patriarch. "Do you really feel you took the best course of action?"

Mayar examined his claws and said, "He acted out of anger and desperation."

"That's not true. I did what came naturally."

"And your natural instinct was to wreak havoc," interrupted the patriarch, his wrinkled eyes looking tired. "Instincts that are not natural to the Crystal Soul."

Clinton shook his head, his rage growing.

"Clinton, the dirtmite was the answer to the trial all along. Granted, you passed the first test and proved you have a trace of ability to control a being, but by the time you reached the second test, all rational thoughts had vanished. The dirtmite was always the key."

"How?"

"The rock louse was not attacking you; it was not attacking the grack; it was attacking the dirtmite. You had two chances to discover this information, first when you controlled the dirtmite, and second when you entered the cavern."

"How?"

"By seeing what was fully around you. By judging nothing. Had the Crystal Soul truly studied these creatures, not just searched to use abilities, but filtered through their instincts, then it would have recognized this connection."

Clinton shook his head. "No...it can't be."

"The rock louse and the grack have an unusual amity. The grack keeps the lair free from sectoids, while the rock louse, in turn, protects the grack. You see, Clinton, although the dirtmite poses no threat to the grack, or to you or me, in swarms they secrete a liquid that can paralyze the louse."

"I don't—"

"The rock louse was terrified it would be affected by the poison and starve to death. It panicked. Had you looked into the rock louse's soul, you would have ascertained that it would aid you; it could have lifted you up towards the roof, for you to dig through and make a hole, as long as you agreed to take the sectoid with you. Of course, the more drastic solution might have also been to simply kill the sectoid."

"Then why was the grack caged?"

"The louse would not have let us take it away, so this was the best solution. We did not want it attacking you on sight. You are Plains born, Clinton, you know a grack's nature."

Clinton shook his head, allowing the logic to gradually fall into place.

"Not every obstruction is an enemy, Clinton Narfell, yet your natural instinct is to regard them as so. Whether small and weak, or large and powerful, with nurturing insight, you can transform your greatest adversary into an ally. You, though, did not even attempt to look." The patriarch turned and hobbled up onto the platform. He sat down. "Instead of reason, instead of calm, you attacked, inviting trouble to yourself and everyone else around you. *That* is why I believe Hagen to be incorrect, and *that*, is why you could not be the Crystal Soul."

Darra leaned closer to Va'hen and muttered something in her ear. The wilder female stared coldly at Clinton, before finally nodding, her boney headdress clinked. Tarat smiled sympathetically at the lion. Jarik lowered his head. Mayar's face held its neutral demeanor.

"I…I don't believe you," replied Clinton.

The patriarch leaned forward. "Clinton—"

"I *am* the Crystal Soul. I know I am." Tears welled in his eyes. He sniffed, attempting to keep them at bay. "I've lost too much for it to be a lie. I won't lose this. I won't let it happen."

"He clings to the hope to justify all the tragedies he has lived through." Mayar nodded. "Even if he were what he thinks he is, then there are grave flaws in his powers. Something is seriously wrong."

A tear trickled down Clinton's cheek. "Then I'll try harder. I'll train night and day. I'll do anything. Just, please…I am the Crystal Soul…I have to be."

"Why?" asked Tarat.

Jarik sighed deeply. "Because if he is not, then he will never be reunited with his brother."

A blanket of silence descended over them. Clinton felt empty, like someone had stolen every hope from him and crushed them underfoot.

Mayar finally broke the silence.

"So what now? Turn him loose? Send him away?"

Tarat rose to his feet. "He would not last a week by himself. By now many will suspect his identity. If it is not a minion of Marama, then it will be the Nightmare himself who tracks him down."

"So this fraud is to remain a problem of the tribes?" Mayar scorned. "Inviting danger to the great Wyrms?"

"Now is not the time, Mayar-Bo, for this kind of discussion. We may not be convinced of his identity as the Crystal Soul, but the boy may still be of much use to us. Until we unravel this riddle, I believe it best he stays with us."

Clinton lifted his head, gritting his teeth. "I am not a pawn in your stupid games. I am nobody's slave. If you don't believe I'm the Crystal Soul then let me go. I'll travel back to Wooburn on my own."

"And you will also die on your own, Clinton Narfell," said Darra bluntly. "Your enemies believe you to be the Crystal Soul. Given the chance, they will capture or kill you."

"Plus he has witnessed too much of the tribes," added Va'hen.

"Should the enemy capture him, he would not keep our secrets long. He is young and untrained, and poses a serious threat," Jarik warned.

"I will not have any Ora'klen put in danger because of this feline!" hissed Mayar.

"Calm down, Mayar-Bo. The tribes of the Mouth are not in imminent danger just yet. I would not allow any Ora'thon to be either. My tribes' safety comes first to me too," said Tarat.

"Then we do not have the luxury of choice." The patriarch stared deep into the fire. "Clinton Narfell shall remain as a guest with the tribes until further notice."

The masters nodded in agreement at the decision.

"You can't do this," snarled Clinton. "You can't keep me captive."

"We are not keeping you captive; we are keeping you safe," Jarik commented. He brushed a speck of dirt from the long, cream robe draped artfully over his lithe physique. "The enemy will have a hard time getting to you with so many of the Order around."

Tarat nodded his agreement as he approached Clinton. "Here." He grabbed the shackles on Clinton's wrists and opened them up. With a metallic clink, he dropped them disdainfully on the rugs. "Guards!"

The heart-tent's opening pulled back to reveal two huge guards. Both wore komodo armor, their faces masked under spiky helmets. "Take Clinton back to his tent. There are anumals in and outside the camp that are not entirely thrilled he is still alive. Let us continue to make them miserable. Keep him safe."

One of the guards nodded. "As you wish." He turned to look Clinton up and down. "Follow us."

Clinton cast a pleading glance at the patriarch. Every shred of hope vanished from him when the komodo sat unmoved, staring quietly into the flames. With slumped shoulders, Clinton stumbled from the *juh-guhn* as the masters' conversation continued on without him.

* * *

Fires dotted the landscape, but since the day's trials, calm had settled upon the camp for the night. Flanked on either side by Tarat's guards, the lion bowed his head as they made their way towards a clump of stumpfeet nestled in a pod. The taller of the two guards studied the area and then nodded to the smaller guard.

"Yaria and I expect to be joined by the next full moon. Better now than later in these uncertain times."

The smaller komodo nodded, but offered no reply.

"Are you not well, Galdiin? You are quiet tonight."

The komodo shrugged. "Just tired."

In the distance, upon the hill where Clinton had caused the rock louse to burst from its lair, countless torches burned, silhouetting figures repairing the damaged ground. Trees rustled in the wind. On the horizon, the moon highlighted the peaks of the Ridgeback Mountains.

"Word is that Tarat and Va'hen have summoned more *Ora'thon* and *Ora'clou* guards to bolster tribe numbers. I have a feeling the perimeter will have to be extended."

It took every ounce of strength for Clinton to keep his mouth shut. He desperately wanted to shout at them, to make the komodos understand his torment, but the lion stopped himself. A rebellious tear trickled down his face.

"I would hate to be a green-scale when the fighting starts. I have heard Marama's minions are a sight to behold..."

A bright light lit up the darkness.

The guards spun round as a ball of flame shot skywards, lighting the far side of the camp. The ground shook. Shocked yells called out in alarm, joined by the screams of hatchlings.

The taller guard's mouth went slack. "What is happening?"

A komodo rushed out of a nearby tent, staring towards the ruckus. A flurry of activity erupted, and more lizards appeared, running towards the explosion.

The taller guard turned to face Galdiin. "What should we do?"

"We could be under attack." The komodo's cold voice grated on Clinton's nerves. Galdiin grabbed Clinton around his bicep and yanked him closer. "Go assist the other guards. Discover what has occurred. I will take care of Narfell."

"But his safety is priority. Tarat's orders were—"

"Go back to Tarat and find out what we should do!"

"But the lion can be a handful. You saw what he did in the trials."

"Go! I will secure him until you rendezvous back with new orders."

The guard nodded before sprinting off towards the explosion. Galdiin's grip tightened on the lion's arm. He loped off, dragging

Clinton along with him.

"Ow! What are you doing? What's happening?"

"Just keep quiet!" barked Galdiin, keeping his eyes fixed in front of him.

Clinton's guts churned. "T-Tarat said I was to be protected," he stumbled. "If you're trying to hurt me as some kind of revenge for what I did to Nyugon—"

"I said quiet!" Galdiin snarled.

Their rushed walk soon turned into a jog as they ploughed against a tide of approaching komodos. Galdiin barged against anyone who hindered their journey, his grip almost crushing Clinton's arm as they were jostled from side to side.

Galdiin looked over his shoulder, back towards the explosion. "We need to hurry."

Clearing a row of weapon tents, the komodo paused to stare up at an isolated stumpfoot. A solitary hut rested on its back with bars across its windows. Clinton could see strange markings surrounding its immediate perimeter in a wide circle.

"Come on." Galdiin nodded towards the hut. "Up there. Now."

"Why? I thought I wasn't a prisoner?"

"Shut—"

"Halt!" ordered a komodo, slipping out from behind the hut, wearing hooded, cream-colored robes.

Galdiin and Clinton stopped dead in their tracks.

"What are you doing?" The lizard cautiously approached, pulling his hood down and tapping his fingers against the skin by his ear holes. Tattoos the color of the evening sky began to glow.

Clinton could feel Galdiin's hand tense.

"Who are you?" asked the Sensor.

"No concern of yours. Now either let me pass, or face Master Tarat's wrath."

The komodo's ears flashed bright indigo. "So this is the lion, the one who threatens the safety of the tribes?"

"He is nothing to do with you. Now either move aside, or I will be forced to move you myself."

The Sensor began to laugh and whipped off his long cloak. He

131

pressed more tattoos around his ear holes causing light to flare. "You may be able to trick the other guards, but there is not a lie that has yet deceived my hearing...traitor!"

Galdiin shoved Clinton aside and ripped his helmet off to reveal a battle worn and leathery skinned face. He pulled something from under his armor, and his mouth flashed blue as he said, "*Reikken!*"

A giant staff suddenly grew in the komodo's hands before he sprinted towards the newcomer. The sound-Sensor crouched and raised his hands protectively, the tattoos around his ears pulsing with every noise he heard.

Galdiin swung his staff at the sound-Sensor's head.

The Sensor gracefully twirled aside, allowing the wood to miss his face, before countering with an upward swipe of his tail. Galdiin raised his thick arm, blocking the strike, and shoved the staff forward. Again the Sensor dodged the attack, as if he could predict Galdiin's every move.

With fluid attacks, the Sensor pressed his advantage, aiming kicks at Galdiin's midsection and head, assaulting him with a flurry of precisely aimed punches. Galdiin blocked each attack with his staff, before stabbing it towards the Sensor's midsection. The komodo sunk to the ground, dodging the strike, then sprang back up, slamming his fist down into Galdiin's shoulder.

The huge komodo grunted. The staff slipped from his hand, and his arm went limp. Wasting no time, he took a step back and pressed more tattoos around his mouth. A bass-like crackle erupted from Galdiin's glowing mouth that sent goosebumps rippling across Clinton's body.

The Sensor flinched back, and his tattoos flared and then darkened while Galdiin pressed ahead with his attacks. The sound-Sensor swung out his tail, but Galdiin spun past the strike and jabbed him sharply in the kidney, before landing another two strikes against the side of his neck.

The Sensor crashed to the ground.

Galdiin closed his mouth and the bass sound stopped. His tattoos faded.

Clinton stood motionless.

"Come on!" snapped Galdiin.

Wasting no time, he grabbed Clinton's arm and dragged him towards the isolated hut. With no guards nearby, the komodo slammed his foot against the door, bursting it open with a crash. Clinton stumbled into the hut and caught sight of a motionless komodo lying on the floor. Blue painted tattoos covered his arms, yet his face was out of sight.

"What's going on?" Clinton stepped closer to the unconscious komodo. "Who is this?"

"Forget him!" Galdiin grabbed a sack stashed in the corner and pushed Clinton towards the door.

"But—"

"It does not matter—"

"No, I want—"

Galdiin slammed his hand over the lion's mouth. In the following silence, Clinton heard two figures running towards the distant ruckus. The next thing Clinton knew, Galdiin had lifted both him and the sack up under his arm, and was heading for the door. Clinton wriggled and kicked, trying to break free of the komodo's grip.

"Stop this, Clinton," snapped Galdiin.

Yet the lion wriggled even more.

Galdiin strengthened his grip.

When they finally reached the perimeter fence, Galdiin rammed his shoulder against the wood. The logs fell away before him in two precise pieces. They had been rigged to snap. Black and blue hills rolled out before them, dipping down into a forest-filled valley. Mountains fringed the horizon, highlighted by the moon and stars.

Something snorted in the darkness.

Falling from Galdiin's hold, Clinton landed on the grass and looked up to see a small cart hidden by the side of the fence with a boval tethered to the front. The stock creature snorted again, two puffs of air clouding in front of its nose. Galdiin tossed the sack onto the cart, then grabbed Clinton by the back of his cloak, hoisting him up as well. "Do not ask."

"But—"

"We are not out of danger yet. Keep quiet and we may still escape."

A strange feeling of hope washed through Clinton. The cart rocked as Galdiin jumped up onto the seat in front. He grabbed the reins and snapped them sharply. Hearing the crack, the boval set off, thundering down the grassy hill and off towards the darkness of the forest. Behind them, the cries from the village faded in the distance, yet the hue of orange and red peaked over the perimeter fence, taking much longer to disappear.

"A distraction," Galdiin said over the sound of the boval's hooves. "No one was hurt. Trust me."

The lizard reached up and scratched his forehead.

Clinton studied the komodo's wrinkled face, inspecting the dull color of his skin. Galdiin looked back, and the moonlight twinkled in his eyes, displaying a recognizable glint.

Warmth suddenly spread through Clinton. He could not stop himself from smiling.

"Mother of Treb! How did you do it? The disguise, I mean."

Galdiin's eyes narrowed. "You searched my soul?"

"Pah! A scavenger or a sectoid, yes, but another anumal…no way. I wouldn't even know where to begin. Let's just say there are some things the eyes can't hide."

A wide smile slowly grew on the komodo's face, and he ruffled Clinton's mane. "Not just a pretty face are you?" Galdiin pressed some tattoos around his eyes, and his weather beaten features disappeared, revealing the familiar face of Hagen beneath.

Clinton embraced his friend, feeling like a missing piece of himself had been returned. "By skorr, it's so good to see you. But how come the masters didn't spot your disguise when you came into the tent?"

"I did not give them time or reason to. I suspect Master Darra knew…but she would never betray me."

"And Galdiin? Was that the komodo—"

"Back in the hut. Do not worry, though, he will awaken…with

a heavy head mind you." Hagen motioned to the sack. "I brought this along for you."

Clinton leaned over and picked up the sack. He pulled the drawstring loose and peered inside. He sighed, desperate to hold back his emotions as he looked down upon his treasured lazarball armor.

"I did not want you leaving behind something as important as that."

"But the patriarch, and the masters, they said—"

"I heard what they said." Hagen snapped the reins and the boval picked up its pace. "Do not listen to their conjectures. I believe in you, Clinton Narfell, and I know others who share the same sentiment as me."

Clinton looked at his hands. "So…you know about how I change then? When I draw upon a creature's power?"

However much Hagen tried to hide it, Clinton still spotted the slightest falter in his smile.

"Who is to say that is not what is supposed to happen?" asked Hagen, staring back at Clinton. "Who cares what those dusty old scriptures state. It is all ancient dung in my opinion."

Hagen smiled before cracking the reins again. The looming forest approached as they rumbled down the hill in silence.

"So much for the komodos helping us." Clinton sighed. "So where to now?"

"I received news back in the camp. Our enemy has already taken up the fight. Now the burden has been placed solely on our shoulders, Clinton; we must prepare for our part in the war."

"And what will that be?"

"I wish I could answer that for you, but the line between friend and enemy has blurred. In a few sun-cycles though, we will reach Middle City, and then," he shook his head, "hopefully, all will be made clear to us."

CHAPTER THIRTEEN

MISS CLAWZ.

Sand swept past Hiro's feline features as she sped across the bleak terrain. She squinted through her goggles and gripped tightly to her mount's horns. Her back felt damp with sweat from the heat of the unforgiving sun. Underneath her fingerless gloves, rough calluses had formed on her hands, and her chapped thighs simmered with soreness. Five days of grime had collected in every nook and cranny of her body, from the neck of her battered leather jacket to the toes of her laceless boots. The cheetah pulled her mount's left horn, and the cruzer verged off towards the shimmering silhouette of a distant town. Glancing over her shoulder, dust clouds chased her trail, while ahead, beyond the starkness of the Upper Plains, the Hacksaw Peaks dominated her view.

"C'mon! Yup! Yup!"

She spurred her heels into the scavenger's sides, and the cruzer let out a high whine as it sped up. With two long, arching horns extending back from the top of its skull, the lizard-like creature made an easy mount for the cheetah to ride. Its meaty legs were a blur of motion, propelling them over the terrain at a breathless speed.

Hiro steeled her nerves, gripped the horns tighter, and arrowed on towards her destination. If all went well with the transaction, her run of bad luck might finally change very soon.

* * *

Hiro arrived at Havucke Town's perimeter fence without incident. Passing through its imposing gates, she came to two towers covered in corrugated iron sheets, housing guards that eyed her warily from above. Empty oil drums had been welded into panels, forming sections of the perimeter fence, while the odd, sickly-brown needle-tree clung stubbornly on to life in the parched soil.

"Pfff, what a scrag hole." Hiro patted the cruzer's head as it slowed to a plodding walk, jostling her from side to side. "Just don't you touch anything, Broxy, ya hear me? Don't want you catching anything contagious."

The cruzer warbled a reply and nudged its head back. She chuckled, hoping her frosty laughter would null the slowly baking uncertainty in her stomach. It had not been long since the incident at Biozzurd Inn had caused her to take flight. She slipped out the crumpled letter from her pocket and read it for the tenth time that day.

> *Buyer interested in bulk purchase.*
> *Havucke Town Tavern.*
> *Come alone.*

Yet the further she journeyed into Havucke, the more she found herself questioning the legitimacy of the offer.

"This place is worse than Wooburn. Who in skorr would want to meet up in a trash pile like this?"

Buildings constructed from car bonnets and lorry beds lined her path. Lights buzzed and crackled with lectric, generated by smoke-belching factories. Dominating Havucke's skyline, the famed junk towers peaked high into the air, while skeletal cranes slowly sifted through the mountains of rubbish.

Hiro scanned everyone around her. Any hint of a feline made her tense.

"Just relax," she told herself, feeling the leather bag weighing against her shoulder. "Take it nice and easy."

She crossed over an iron bridge and glanced down into the murky depths below. Discarded junk had been strewn amongst the black sludge. Coated with oil, it caught the sun's rays to create pretty rainbow patterns. The smells of sour cheese, sweat, and chemicals stung her nose. She wrapped a scarf round her face in an attempt to mask the odor.

Finally, Havucke tavern came into view.

Under the watchful gaze of some locals lazing in the shade, she disembarked from the cruzer.

"Fine scavenger there, missy," muttered a moose, nodding towards her ride. "How much distance you get out of him?"

Hiro tethered the reins to a line of rusty exhaust pipes sticking out of the ground. "About two days on a full stomach."

"That much, huh?" The moose nodded, causing the plastic hubcaps attached to his antlers to clang. Old circuit boards had been sawed and sewn together with iron wool to create a protective coat around his body, much the same as the other guards. "Well, I'd be careful if I were you, Miss Feline. Folks'll be whippin' that away from you in no time if you don't be keeping your eyes on it."

Hiro casually opened her coat to reveal a bandolier of assorted knives strapped across her chest. "Folks'll be having their guts spilled out if they so much as even look at my property. Understand?"

The moose chuckled and rocked back on his stool. "A point well made, Miss…?"

Hiro thought for a second, and then said, "Clawz."

The moose ran his tongue over his teeth and smiled. "Looks to me like you'll fit in Havucke Town just fine, Miss Clawz." He slumped back against the tavern wall. "Enjoy."

As soon as Hiro yanked open the tavern's doors, the smell of burlico and grain water bombarded her senses. A bar, constructed of worn car tires and wood, spread along the right wall. Towering shelves behind it held an assortment of dusty bottles, jars, and tin cans, while engine parts, wires, and gizmos dangled from the ceiling. A toad regarded Hiro from behind the bar; her once glossy skin was now brown and flaking.

"'Bout time you showed up," huffed the toad.

"You were expecting me?"

"Not me." She pointed a stumpy finger over to a darkened booth. "Him."

To the far left of the tavern was an occupied booth. Hiro could only just discern the outline of a figure behind one of the booth's screens. She tugged the scarf from her face, swung the leather bag off her shoulder, and turned to approach. The toad slammed her hand down on the bar top.

"It's only manners to purchase a drink when doing business in my establishment, feline."

"Okay, okay," replied Hiro. "Can I have some…water?"

"*Water*? You out-of-towners made of credits or something? That's gonna be expensive."

Hiro's jaw clenched. "Fine. Just give me something cheap."

The toad grabbed a plastic bottle that had been sliced in half, and filled it with brown liquid before sliding it in Hiro's direction.

The cheetah sniffed the contents and grimaced. "Here." She flicked a nug at the toad. "What a rip off."

"Well, you know where I am if you want any more, honey," smiled the toad.

Stomping away from the bar, Hiro checked her knives while her tail flicked back and forth.

She approached the booth.

"Stop right there!" ordered the stranger, before she could get a glimpse of him.

She tried to peer around the screen, but could only see a half-drunk glass of water on the table, with a battered briefcase placed next to it. Her eyebrows rose, and a ghost of a smile touched her lips.

The guy's got credits. Best to play it cool.

"I...I've come as requested."

"As requested?" replied the stranger, his voice youthful, but clipped.

"Yeah, as requested. I've errr...I've got the stuff..."

When only silence met her words, Hiro shrugged. "Well, aren't you gonna say something?"

"What do you want me to say? What *is* the stuff?"

"Y'know. The *stuff*..."

A small, brown-furred hand came into view and began to drum its fingers on the briefcase.

Hiro's brow creased. "Here." She tossed the leather bag on the table. "It's all in there, every last pellet."

The stranger slowly opened it up and took out a cloth bag. Tipping it slightly, a handful of clear amber-like pebbles dropped onto the tabletop.

The stranger gasped. "What the... What has this got to do with my father? Are you crazy?"

"What? I don't understand, I was told you were interested in buying—"

"Buying?" the stranger shrieked. "This crap? Do you even know what it is?"

Hiro peered warily over her shoulder, hoping the bartender was not listening. "Well it's...it's hive," she whispered. "And powerful stuff it is too."

"Get that filth away from me. Who the scrud do you think I am?"

Hiro clenched her fists and snarled. "I don't know, but you were the one who dragged me to this scrag house."

The stranger slammed his fist on top of the table. "Are you insane? You sent me a note asking *me* to come, and I do not appreciate my time being wasted by the likes of you...and this."

The stranger swept his hand across the table, scattering the pellets everywhere.

"NO!" yelled Hiro. "What've you done?"

She dropped to the floor, picking some up, before ripping open her coat and reaching for the sharpest knife in her bandolier. "You little..."

As she pounced around the corner of the booth, she saw the stranger's face. Her heart lurched.

She dropped the knife as she looked on in confusion. her features twisting into a scowl.

"Is this a joke? What the blug are *you* doing here?"

Harris Lakota rose to his feet. A look of practiced distain swept over his face. The beaver's prominent buckteeth hung unmoving, as if mimicking the tavern's decorations. "I should be asking the same of you, *Saber*," he spat. "Why am I not surprised? I should have guessed one of Wooburn's scumbags would be involved with such muck as hive, Hiro Varie."

"And I should've known Nomica's number one spoilt brat would try to stitch me up, Harris Lakota. If you even think about stealing my stash from me..."

Harris slumped down into the booth, folding his arms. "Steal? Why in skorr would I want to touch that dung? Do you have any idea what hive does to you?"

"It makes you rich!" She pulled up a chair next to him and started arranging the pellets into a pile. "And provides you with a better life."

"It rots your brains."

"So? Not my problem. Most folk nowadays don't have a brain to rot."

"I always thought you were mental."

Hiro shrugged. "Well, I don't care what you think."

The tavern door swung open.

Hiro spun around, covering the pellets from sight as she stared at the two strangers in the doorway.

"Oh, you do not care, huh? Is that why you are jumpier than a knat on hot sand?" Lakota sneered. "Look at you. You are a mess."

"Speak for yourself, vermin. At least I know how to survive by myself. If anything, you're the mess. Mommy not around to clean your suit anymore? Having to wipe your own butt now, huh?"

Harris huffed, but eyed his dusty clothes. He flicked a speck of dirt from the lapel.

"What in the name of skorr are you doing here anyway, Lakota? Shouldn't you be hiding under your daddy's coattails?"

"Oh, get with the times." He took a tentative sip of his water. "I left that scavenger pit way behind me. Said good riddance to my father and the rest of those wastrels living there too."

"But your dad—"

"Is nothing to me now. He can have his stupid little village and run it into the ground for all I care. I have moved on to bigger and better things with my life."

"What? Like peddling hive?"

Harris slammed his fist against the table. "For the love of Silania, I want nothing to do with that stuff. Although I am not at all surprised you do. You Sabers were always into that scummy kind of thing."

"*Ex*...Saber," muttered Hiro. "I don't run with them anymore. Like you, I moved on—"

"So they did throw you out. I thought so."

"No, I just—"

"Save the excuses. I know the story: something about an argument with that Narfell creature, and deserting your comrades in a fight, blah blah blah." The beaver rolled his eyes. "It is all very melodramatic."

"I just…" Hiro felt her anger bubble. She shoved the pellets back inside the cloth bag. "Look, you didn't answer my question. Why are you following me?"

"I am not following you; I was told to meet someone here: an anumal who had some…information relating to my father."

"Ahhhhh! So you're trying to bring the old beaver down are you? Trying to take his place as the mayor?"

"No!" Harris snapped. "Look…just drop it."

Hiro slipped the cloth bag back inside the leather satchel, and pulled it over her shoulder. She picked up her drink, took a sniff of it, and nudged it away. "Well, I've wasted enough time on you. And time is credits. So, good luck, Lakota, hopefully I'll never see you again."

The beaver stared coldly back at her. "I am sure you will not. Besides, it is clear that whatever trouble you have landed yourself in will more than likely see you holed up in a cool dawn cage soon enough."

"Trouble?" she laughed, swaggering backwards. "Who said anything about trouble?"

Hiro turned around to make a quick exit when something slammed against her shoulder, pushing her to the ground. The cheetah instinctively covered her face and scrabbled back. "Please don't hurt me. I've got your stuff. I'll give it back."

Harris burst out laughing. "I can see you are definitely not in any trouble."

The cheetah lowered her hand to see a giant looming above her. "What do you want? Who are you?"

The figure leaned forwards.

"Going somewhere…cheetah?"

Hiro's eyes almost popped out of her head. She backed up, forcing chairs and tables out of her way. "You! What are… What do you want? Why—"

"Hold on a moment." Harris marched around the screen to stand in front of the newcomer. The beaver's head did not even reach past the giant's waistline as he craned up to get a better view. "I know you…I have seen you before…"

The newcomer pointed a stubby finger at Hiro. "She certainly knows me. Don't you, Saber?"

"Look," she retorted. "I don't want any trouble, Ephraim. What happened in Wooburn stays in Wooburn. It's all in the past."

"For you, maybe," barked the elephant. "Although, I seem to remember you being a bit more mouthy when you had your Saber friends around."

"I don't have anything to do with the Sabers anymore," she snapped. "I left those scruds in the dirt."

Harris folded his arms. "Yeah, they threw her out."

"Don't listen to him, Ephraim. He's lying. The Lakotas are born liars."

Ephraim began to roll up the sleeves of his long, brown coat. Beads of sweat dripped down his face and arms. "I can't argue with you there, Hiro, but I swore that if I saw any of you Sabers again, I'd rip you limb from limb…just like you tried to do to me."

Hiro raised her hands in surrender. "We were young and stupid, Ephraim. Besides…" Her body tensed as anger surged through her. Her hand slipped into her jacket and unsheathed a long knife. "You started it. You ruined my life. You killed Brox."

"You were bullying innocent anumals: doing the scrudding mayor's dirty work for him."

"Hey!" barked Harris.

"Well, it's the truth," snapped the elephant.

Hiro looked from her knife, to the giant, to the beaver, and back to her knife. "Like I said, Ephraim, it's all in the past. Dead and—"

Her words were silenced as the elephant lunged forward and gripped her by the throat.

Her knife dropped to the floor.

"Still playing with weapons are we?" Ephraim snarled. His

jovial features had twisted into a mask of rage. "Nothing changes, does it?"

Hiro's mind swirled. She remembered the look on the elephant's face when they had caught him in Wooburn's backstreets, how he had squirmed under the combined weight of the Sabers, tears welling in his eyes. She had threatened to tear his ear to shreds. No matter how much he had begged, she would have done it…if she had not been stopped.

"You don't know how I've wished for this moment, Saber." His grip tightened. "Do you realize how easy it would be for me to pop your head off? It'd be just like cracking chockeral eggs."

"P-please!" she croaked. "Credits…and stuff. Check…bag. Take—"

"He does not want your dirty magic beans," hissed Harris, before peering back at Ephraim. "Do you?"

"Never!"

"Yeah!" goaded Harris. He stepped back a pace to get a better view. "You…errrr…You are not really going to rip her head off are you?"

"I don't recall her relenting when I begged for my life," he growled. "The crap she's sown is finally starting to come back to her. Isn't that right, *Miss Clawz*?"

Hiro flinched.

He knows my name. What else does he know? Is he involved with the others? Are they here too? Did they trick me into coming here?

"Hive in…bag," she spluttered. "Tell Fangs, tell them…all there. Didn't steal…"

"You think I care about that?" he snarled. "All I care about is your punishment."

"N…" squirmed Hiro, closing her eyes. The pressure increased around her neck, tilting it back. She gritted her teeth, waiting to hear the snap of bones.

"Eph!" shouted a gruff voice over by the tavern door. "That's enough!"

The pressure around Hiro's neck released.

144

Ephraim dropped her to the floor, and she stumbled against a table. Rubbing her neck, she gasped for breath.

"Had enough fun?" asked the voice, sounding deep and foreign.

Ephraim's scowl vanished and his softer features blossomed. "Yep, certainly have, Garron." He stepped aside to reveal a squat, shadowy figure. "That's all I wanted to see."

"You've had your revenge; now let's move on."

A tiny winged creature flapped up behind the stranger and landed on his shoulder.

"Errrrr…" Harris poked his head around a chair, squinting his button eyes. "And you are?"

A gnarly gator stepped out from the comfort of the shadows. Olde-world spectacles were balanced on the end of his hazel-colored snout. His olive scavenger-skin coat dragged behind him, swathing a pathway over the dusty, wooden floorboards. The coat had numerous bulging pockets sewn everywhere, giving him the appearance of a giant, Olde-world hand grenade.

"Well, I'm glad to see you've all been reacquainted." He passed by the bartender and dropped a handful of credits on the counter. "Thank you, Loola. As usual, you'll be discreet about this?"

The toad nodded sweetly. "As usual."

The tiny flying creature clicked its beak impatiently.

Hiro edged closer, rubbing her aching throat. "You work for the Fangs? If so, then this is—"

"Button it, Varie," snapped the gator. He sniffed loudly. "This ain't about the Fangs."

"B-but the letter I got? Was that —"

"We can discuss all that on the road. For now, time is short. We need to get moving."

Harris brushed the dust from his suit. "Going? I am not going anywhere."

"You got better places to be, huh, Harris Lakota?" Garron asked, revealing a long line of chipped, mustard teeth. He yanked a pocket watch from one of the coat pockets and stared intently at the glowing green numbers. "Maybe got a father to overthrow, or a village to rule, or something?"

"How did you—"

"Think again, beaver." Garron popped his watch back in its pocket. "You won't get within half a day of Wooburn before you see…things you really don't want to see. And trust me…it's gonna get worse."

Hiro huffed. "Look, I know about Wooburn—"

"Well, I don't!" gasped Harris.

"Either way." Hiro folded her arms. "Drop the act, gator, and tell me why you tricked us into coming here."

Garron leaned forward and shoved his hands into his pockets. Hiro's nose tingled with the odor of his meaty breath.

"That's a simple answer, *Miss Clawz*. I brought you both here because I need you. Y'see, you two are going to help us banish some evil folk from the land and allow goodness to reign supreme."

Hiro and Harris glanced wide-eyed at one another. Harris shrugged. Hiro raised her eyebrows. Both looked back at Garron.

"Really?" asked the cheetah.

"O' course not, you dumb scruds," snapped the gator. "But an associate of mine needs your help. So shut your traps and let's get going."

"What?" laughed Hiro. "So we're supposed to just follow you because some unknown scrud needs our help? What do we get out of it?"

"Ah ha! There's the Hiro Varie I've heard so much about," Garron chuckled. "It's always about what you can get out of something, ain't it? Well, trust me, Saber, you help me out and you'll get your just rewards."

Hiro faltered, daring to hope this could be the real deal.

Harris licked his lips. "What? You mean…anything we want?"

"Got you interested now, huh?"

"Maybe…"

"Well, you best make your mind up pronto, Lakota. Ain't nobody got time for lengthy discussions. You're either in or you're out. Just decide quick as I've got others in line for the opportunity."

Hiro and Harris shared another furtive glance, unable to resist the temptation. The cheetah shoved the beaver out of the way, before planting herself in front of Garron. "Well? Come on then, old timer, what you waiting for?"

A satisfied smirk crossed Garron's face. "I've got a feeling this is gonna be an interesting journey."

The foursome set off towards the tavern's entrance. Garron said, "Oh, and one more thing, Hiro."

"What?"

"Lose the mulch you're carrying. And if I see you handling that scrud again, I'll be biting both your hands off. Understand?"

"But—"

"He said lose it!" yelled the elephant.

Hiro flinched and took a step back.

"Oh, I'm certainly gonna be enjoying this journey," laughed Ephraim.

CHAPTER FOURTEEN

SILANIA'S CHOSEN.

Dallas's head throbbed as the whimpering cries pummeled his mind.

He crouched behind some rocks, squinting at the small group of felines far below.

Silence! he thought. *Shut up!*

Obeying his command, the cries abated, providing a blissful moment of relief for the tiger, before resuming once more. Dallas growled in frustration. Nightmare had not warned him it would be this difficult.

I said enough!

With a glance over his shoulder, he saw the three impalers sprawled out behind him, small and agile, with poisonous bites and fish-hooked claws, Dallas felt like closing his eyes and expelling their captured souls from within him, forcing them back into their bodies just so he could kill them outright. At least then the incessant din in his head would stop, and he would have some peace again.

Yet peace was not what he had been training so hard for.

Stop fighting me you idiotic beasts! Surrender your power and I will release you unharmed.

The yelps continued. Feelings of anger, confusion, and fear, bubbled to the forefront of his consciousness, like oil floating on water.

Nightmare's words rang out in his memory.

They will do your bidding. But do not ask them. Command them.

The tiger closed his eyes and dug his claws into the rock.

An alien strength coursed through his veins, and the metallic tang of blood peaked his senses. His hearing grew more acute, and he could detect subtle nuances in sounds; the breeze rattling the dry grass, sectoids burrowing into the sand, the wing beats of hungry ayvids circling above. He turned his attention to the felines in the gulley below. A red mist emanated from each of them,

148

tendrils of their inner being wafting like shifting smoke. He stroked the scars over his left eye socket and set his resolve.

You will obey me, he snarled, his anger subduing the scavengers' yelps. *You will call me master!*

Dallas sprung forwards. He leaped headfirst from his perch and flung his arms wide. Mahogany colored rocks sped past him on either side, before he flipped over and landed on all fours. Baring his fangs, he let out a defiant roar.

"There he is!" shouted one feline, pointing his blade. "Don't hold back. Nightmare ordered us to go full out."

The group of felines raised their weapons.

In a streak of orange and black, Dallas rushed into them, raking his claws through flesh before his enemy could even swing a blade.

"NO!" yelled a guard. "He killed him."

Another feline gasped. "What the…"

Dallas's prey fell to the ground.

Most of the guards stood shocked, but one of them saw the bloodlust in Dallas's eyes.

"He's gonna kill us all!"

The whistle of a machete sliced through the air, alerting the tiger to an incoming attack. Sweaty fear engulfed his nostrils. Dallas turned, dropped to a crouch, and the blade whistled harmlessly over his head, just missing his scalp.

A second guard came at him from the side.

Dallas pounced and slashed his claws through the attacker's boot, slicing the tendons on the back of his legs. A scream erupted from his attacker's mouth. Flipping to his feet, he raked his claws across the feline's shoulder, and an urge to gorge on flesh suddenly overwhelmed him. The impalers' instincts inside him piqued, demanding a taste of the crimson reward. He opened his mouth and lunged for his neck.

"NO!" screamed the Ocelot, forcing Dallas away. "Please, master…"

The air whistled with the song of an approaching blade.

Without looking, Dallas sprung sideways, just as a knife whooshed down where he had been standing. A plume of liquid erupted as the blade hacked into the feline Dallas had been attacking.

The newcomer let his blade drop, staring in horror at his mistake. "No, I didn't mean. Nightmare said…"

Dallas smiled. From where he stood, he had a perfect view of the entrance to the gorge. He could see the rocky passage open out into the desert. Clouds of dust plumed upwards in the distance, while shouts from approaching reinforcements echoed through the gully with their arrival. A dozen shimmering profiles charged to help their comrades, weapons drawn and ready. Inside Dallas, the impalers howled at the promise of even more blood.

"Take him down!" yelled a nearby attacker, bolstered by the sight of reinforcements. He swung his weapon at Dallas, but the tiger ducked and slammed his shoulder into the feline's midriff, heaving him from his feet.

Slipping his hand behind his opponent's head, Dallas yanked him close and stared into his eyes.

"You will do as I command!" he ordered, not to the feline, but to the scavengers inside his head. "You will do my bidding or you will die!"

"What…master? Please—"

Dallas forced his fingers into the feline's mouth, prizing his jaws apart. An impaler soul pulsed through the tiger's body, rising through his chest and into his throat. Dallas coughed. White mist trickled past his lips, and a scavenger's soul slipped into his captive's mouth, before the tiger slammed it shut, locking the mist inside. The feline kicked and bucked, but the tiger ignored the struggle, and concentrated.

The Ocelot jerked. His body went limp. He heaved a giant breath as his eyes glossed over with an oil-like darkness.

Dallas rolled away. "Up!" he ordered, rising to his feet.

The feline wobbled into a hunched stance, sniffing the air, ears pinned back under the gaze of his master. Dallas pointed at the final feline.

"Get him."

The tiger's slave hurtled towards his comrade. He slammed

150

into the confused feline and pinned him against the ground while Dallas slowly approached. The tiger stood over them both before leaning down and prizing the trapped feline's mouth open. The scavengers' wails escalated inside Dallas's head, until he expelled a second soul. Again the mist flowed from his mouth, into his captive, and quickly took hold.

Dallas turned to watch the newest Ocelots closing in.

"Both of you," he said, smiling at his pets. "Do as I say and you will live. Flee and you die. Do you understand me?"

The felines whimpered, but made no move as the encroaching mob spread out around the gully. Dallas closed his eyes and lifted his arms towards his slaves. Sinking into the inner calmness that Nightmare had taught him, he channeled his thoughts into action. With his mind, he transformed his feline slaves, altering their limbs and twisting their appearance. The air filled with a chorus of pained feline wails.

Dallas opened his eyes.

His slaves had become warped versions of themselves, their bodies now wiry and stretched. Their claws had elongated to become long needles, and their faces had twisted into evil masks of horror.

"Kill them all," he whispered, concentrating on keeping the *warps* under his control. "No matter your injuries, you will not stop."

The monsters sped off.

The first warp attacked a female holding a stunpike. She flinched at his nightmarish appearance as she lashed out her weapon, trying to keep him at a distance from her. His elongated claws sliced into her neck. She screamed and stabbed the stunpike straight into his chest, but the monster only shrugged off the wound and moved in for the kill, slashing and raking through anything in his path.

"Tear them to shreds," Dallas snarled, seeing blood splatter across the surrounding rocks.

The air came alive with cries of terror. Feline after feline fell while his slaves tore their way through them, oblivious to their own injuries. Sweat dripped down Dallas's back. His body shook as he maintained control.

With one final cry, the last guard turned tail and retreated, running away from the massacre.

The warps pursued.

Dallas clicked his fingers. "Here!" he shouted, sighing with exhaustion.

His slaves turned to face him, blood dripping from their jaws.

He regarded them coldly.

"You have done well, but you allowed one to escape."

The felines bowed their heads as he approached.

"Not to worry. His cowardice has been noted. He will be dealt with... As will you two..." He slipped his hands around their heads and smashed their skulls together.

The felines dropped like rocks.

Dallas knelt down and placed his fingertips on their lips. A tingling sensation tickled his palm as white mist spewed from their mouths and into the tiger's grasp. In his head he could hear the impalers' snarls joined by feline cries of terror. Terrified pleas battered him like a club, begging to be released back into their own bodies, but the impaler and feline life forces had meshed together. The tiger regarded the spirits in his hands, their pearlescent glow radiating through the cracks in his fingers. Life and death had never before seemed so tangible to him, so controllable: things he could savor or scatter on the wind at will.

Yet something made him pause.

He could sense their turmoil, their desire to return to their physical shells.

They are not where they belong.

The tiger stared at the horizon and sighed. Even when surrounded by the most powerful felines, he felt as alone and empty as the barren panorama before him. He growled and squeezed the souls, utterly destroying their essences.

A cold blade suddenly slid under the tiger's neck, and a gloved hand covered his mouth, preventing him from making a sound.

"Oops," said Nightmare. "You're dead."

Dallas snarled. Stripping off his bloody shirt, he tossed it away and yanked the tent's opening aside to look across the terrain.

"I did not delay."

As far as the eye could see, the land called the Hollow Rocks extended out in all its parched grandness. Vermillion stone had been weather-beaten and worn over time to create naturally sculpted rocks: rocks with giant holes, towering rocks reaching up into the heavens, and clusters of stunted boulders.

The panther sat motionless in his chair, shrouded by the darkness of the tent. The small, central fire reflected in his sunglasses.

"So you were allowing me to hold a knife against your neck for fun? Is that what you're saying?"

Dallas huffed. "Oh, come on, Wade. I was merely contemplating."

"And that contemplation got you killed. Besides," he shrugged. "What was there to contemplate?"

"Well, nothing. Just life, really."

"Oh...*life*...Whose life? Yours? The captive souls?"

"Does it matter?"

"It matters a great deal, especially when a simple training session turns into a farce."

Dallas turned to his mentor. "I performed as instructed. I manipulated the souls to my advantage and I came out victorious. You told me to pay no heed to caution and to give no quarter. Would you have preferred I let them go?"

Nightmare leaned forward in his chair. "The farce I was referring to, Dallas, was your inner turmoil." He laced his finger together on his lap. "Some felines died. So what? The real problem arose when you faltered over your convictions."

"I did not—"

"You did not release the souls from your entrapment. What made you ponder over them? Pity?"

"No."

"Then what? Were you planning on saving them? Putting them all back in their bodies only to die a painful death? Would you defy nature for your own machinations, only to feel sympathy and then try to correct it? Your job is not to balance, tiger, your job is to conquer. Let nature correct itself."

An urge swelled inside Dallas to pounce, claws extended, and silence the panther forever.

And then he remembered...

The tiger released the tent flap and strode over to a small container made of bone. He opened its lid. Lifting it to his lips, he took a deep breath and spewed a white mist from his mouth and into the container. As the last tendrils petered out, he closed the lid with a snap and tossed it to the panther.

"Here. A gift."

Nightmare caught the macabre token mid air. He unfastened the lid and tipped the soul into his hand, before it slowly began to dissipate. "See?" He dropped the container. "Not that hard is it?"

Dallas shrugged.

"As long as you see your victims as living beings, they will never be useful tools."

Dallas's pride screamed at him to bark back a retort, to reject his mentor's words...yet he could not.

A feline appeared at the tent's entrance.

"Master," she said, bowing. "The shamans are here."

Dallas nodded slowly. "Very well." He waved the feline away, before turning back to Nightmare. "Are you coming? I would hate to disappoint you with ruining this task as well."

"No." Nightmare smiled, baring his fangs. "I do believe this is something best handled by yourself."

* * *

"May the light of Silania shine down upon us all." The shaman lifted his gaze from the ground to stare at Dallas. Knelt down, with his wings tied behind his back, the old eagle's eyes narrowed.

"Especially on you, my misguided boy."

Nine more eagles, tied up in the same manner, knelt by his side and muttered their agreement. Wearing simple cloaks, with patterns of Olde-world animals drawn on them, the cloth tails, hoods, and arms had been cut so that when the shamans took flight, they would fan out and create floating human silhouettes in the sky. Their airborne presence served as a warning to anumalkind of their murky past: a reminder that the spirits still watched from far beyond life.

"You will address me as Dallas." The tiger peeled back the eagle's thin, cloth hood. "Tell me, shaman, where is Silania now?"

"Everywhere," he answered, motioning out towards the rocky terrain. "Within every anumal rests the darkness of our feral past: a spirit that Silania forever keeps at bay."

Dallas threw his arms heavenwards in exultation. "I feel it! I can feel my feral past taking over me even as we speak."

The surrounding Ocelots, sprawled out on the nearby rocks, chuckled loudly.

"Mock our beliefs, boy. You are not the first, and you certainly will not be the last," squawked a middle-aged eagle. "Silania saves us from skorr, and stops us from turning into what we once were."

"That she does," Dallas nodded. "Vincent, slash their bindings. Let us show them some respect. They are not our captives."

Vincent nodded to Kayn, and they both unsheathed their blades and severed the ropes binding the eagles' wings. As one, the shamans flapped them out, beating at the air with deep thuds. Tiny feathers fluttered all around.

"My apologies for the restraints. My friends were merely protecting our territory. What with times becoming increasingly dangerous, none can be too careful..."

A larger eagle clambered to his feet. His black talons scraped the sand. "This is not your territory. The Hollow Rocks belongs to no clan. Everyone knows this. These are holy lands."

"And that is the way it shall remain," agreed Dallas. "Under our guidance and protection..."

The shamans shifted uncomfortably, their uncertainty as bright as the blue sky.

"So are we free to leave?" asked the younger eagle.

"Of course," nodded Dallas, standing back. "Revered and powerful beings such as yourselves should never be held captive."

"No anumal should! And when Silania manifests, she will rid us of concepts such as slavery, and greed, and war."

"And until the time comes when she fully manifests?"

One of the shamans spread his wings to their extent. "She is always among us, giving guidance and protection."

"Really?" Dallas peered around. "Well, I cannot see her."

"Only the most devout can. Those of us with accepting hearts and simple lifestyles."

"And what wonderfully simple lives you eagles lead," he replied. "The highest of the shamans, conduits to her words of wisdom. I am sure this position brings you more than just happiness and enlightenment though? Does it not?"

One of the eagles bowed. "No. Ours is a simple way."

"Simple? As in…easy? Or simple as in surrounded by riches collected from your gullible believers?"

A few of the eagles flapped their wings in disgust.

"We distribute donations from our followers and funnel them to the needy, the weak, and the sick."

"And not a nug or bit has ever lined your own pockets? Tell me, Shaman Ortho, did Silania reside in such a plush villa as you when she was alive? Or did she have such a fine array of mistresses like you, Shaman Daw?"

The shamans gasped.

Shaman Ortho said, "Utter nonsense."

"Please do not be ashamed," smirked Dallas, ignoring the chuckling Ocelots. "Silania certainly provides, while you each hide your secrets behind your austerity."

"You speak naught but lies!" Shaman Daw snapped. "We have no secrets! We are merely beacons of Silania's will, giving guidance and hope to those in need."

"Really? Then kindly tell me your whereabouts when my

followers marched through the village of Veron, Shaman Daw? Was that village not under your guidance? Or how about Yemene, Shaman Ortho? Or the Rust Steppes, Shaman Ost? Where were all of you when my felines took them under their care? Oh, that is right, you were...here."

The disgusted looks on the eagle's faces slowly slipped into masks of terror.

"You mean—"

"That at this very moment I have Ocelots positioned outside each of your settlements, waiting to burn them to the ground." Dallas rubbed his chin. "Possibly."

"You...you tricked us," accused Daw.

"I merely extended you an invitation to discuss your future, and to plan ways in which to safeguard your assets."

"My followers are my assets," hissed a female shaman.

Dallas slowly turned to her. "*Your* followers? Surely you mean *Silania's* followers? Yet where is she now? Why does she not retaliate? Are you not her most devout clerics, hmm?"

"She will have her vengeance, boy," Ortho promised.

"Yes, well, until that time, *flyer*, I shall have mine. You see, the power I believe in is not that of some long dead martyr. It is something far more...tangible." He barged through the shamans, who ruffled their wings, and came to a standstill by the lip of the cliff. "Bring them to me."

As if something had exploded among the group, the shamans suddenly sprang up into the air, flapping their great wings, trying to make their escape. The watching felines pounced from their rocks and caught the clerics by their legs, wrenching them back down to the ground. Dallas studied the ten struggling eagles as they were dragged closer, before turning to peer out over the valley below. Where he had expected to see a few hundred felines gathered in a collection of ragged tents, now sat thousands. Loaded wagons rolled in and out of the camp. Fires burned, and whistle-like instruments could be heard, their haunting screeches ricocheting off the rocks. Smiths sharpened curved blades or rewired lectric stunpikes. Cubs ran around gathering food and water, or carrying slops and waste to the trenches on the outskirts of the camp.

Since their departure from Quala village, Wade had kept Dallas busy in his quest to master his powers. From physical combat, to soul extraction and using his *sight*, a long trail of dead had been left in his wake. He had traveled with only a core group of felines, Vincent, Kayn, Jakz, Gizi, Treeg, and those who he knew well enough to trust. Yet now he could see it had been just the tip of the iceberg. A whole world of activity had been orchestrated right beneath his nose.

The tiger's eyes turned to slits.

Nightmare.

Ignoring his annoyance, he looked back at the struggling eagles. "This is real power, dear shamans. *This* will protect me from those who would do me harm. The foundation of our society is crumbling away with every new day. Our fragile laws are being smashed aside by my expanding forces. Silania's laws have blinkered the clans into living in unrealistic harmony, to respect the weak and accept alien customs. And in doing so, we have denied our very nature. The dominant must lead. And today you bear witness to our uprising."

Daw stepped forward. "This is ludicrous. Silania's laws have provided us with peace for countless years."

"No. They have provided a select few with the means to manipulate the masses, and the weak to think they are equal to the strong. The entitled grow fatter, while the deserving watch with hungry bellies." Dallas circled the eagles, casting his shadow over them. "But all that is about to change."

Shaman Ost began to tremble. "H-how?"

"Listen to my proposition carefully, as this is a one-time offer: you can keep you secrets, you can keep your riches, and you can keep your settlements. The Ocelots shall leave your lands and your wealth alone. All I ask of you is one thing…"

The shamans looked amongst themselves before finally nodding towards Ortho.

"Go on," mumbled Ortho.

"You are familiar with…Mar Mi-Den?"

"The Fallen City? Of course."

"Well, I need you fine folk to spread word of it for me."

Daw cocked his head. "What…word?"

"War." The tiger grinned, and his fangs peeked below his lips. "Soon clans will be facing rivals, vying for power and territory, making their behavior…unstable. Your followers will require your guidance and wisdom."

"What is going to come to pass?" asked Ost.

"Spread the word when the villages begin to burn. Spread the word when the cities fall. Tell your followers and your clerics to shout it out from every Nomican temple."

"What should we tell them?" whispered Daw.

"Tell them to gather at Mar Mi-Den. Tell them that Mar Mi-Den will provide peace. Make them remember the old times. Make them remember the colony crusades…"

Ortho gulped and shook his head. "I don't understand…"

Dallas straightened his jacket. "You will, for you are Silania's chosen shamans. The ruling powers listen to you. Holy Scripture dictates that power is to be contested fairly, and at Mar Mi-Den, this can be made so."

Sudden realization swept over the eagles.

"You wish to dominate by use of the old ways," said Daw. "Yet you know you cannot do this without the agreement of the shamans. You need us to enact the colony clause and allow the crusades to begin again."

"Exactly. I do not believe I will ever truly rule unless I use a method that everyone believes in and fully accepts. And until the mightiest rulers congregate at Mar Mi-Den to discuss amity through lazarball, I shall create suffering across this land like never before. No one will go unscathed."

"That is all you ask of us, that we give our consent and spread the word? Nothing more?" Ost wrung his hands when the tiger nodded. He turned to his colleagues with a sly glint in his eyes. "Then it is a fortunate coincidence, Dallas, for Silania has recently demonstrated her displeasure over the growing clan disputes, and solicited us to help acquire a truce throughout the lands. Only her most faithful high shamans bore witness to the miracle. Is that not so?"

The shamans slowly nodded their heads in agreement.

"How fortunate. Then you are free to go where you choose," laughed Dallas. "Leave and spread Silania's glorious word."

The shamans backed away, keeping their eyes locked on the felines at all times.

"Oh, and remember," added Dallas. "Should I hear of any kind of defiance from you, dear shamans, then each of you will discover whether you are on good terms with Silania on a more…spiritual level. Do I make myself clear?"

Dallas turned back to view the blossoming camp as the beat of thrashing wings drummed behind him. A feather fluttered past his face and over the lip, towards the mass of bodies below. He followed the feather's carefree journey, and his guts churned. Above him flew ten eagles, presenting themselves as human silhouettes, blurring the sun's rays as they escaped through the sky, back to their settlements.

Dallas sighed and his mind wandered back to Wooburn…

"Master," said Vincent, dragging the tiger out of his reflections. "Nightmare has requested your presence."

"Tell Wade to wait until I am ready to go," replied Dallas, knowing his response would rile the panther.

Nightmare had called masses of felines without his knowledge, or permission, and in doing so, had gathered an army together. But to whom did this army truly belong? Dallas did not know.

CHAPTER FIFTEEN

WEFRINGS AND TWIGS.

"And you fainted?" blurted Clinton, stifling a chuckle. "You, Hagen of the Hand, *fainted*?"

The komodo moved into an attack position.

"I collapsed like a slab of stone. It took three tribesmen to hoist me to my feet again."

Clinton noticed Hagen's muscles twitch just before the komodo's fist launched at him. The lion pivoted to the left and watched the strike pass his head.

Hagen retreated. "Good, Clinton. Very good. How are your injuries healing?"

"Much better, thanks." The lion readjusted his balance, and both anumals continued to circle. "I thought you komodos were 'one with nature' and all that? Isn't childbirth about as natural as you can get?"

"Oh, childbirth is a miracle of nature, no doubt about it." Hagen hunched his shoulders, preparing for another attack. "But beautiful? Well, that depends on the perspective."

The komodo shot forwards, his elbow racing towards Clinton's head. The lion, however, sidestepped with fluidity as another fist flew in from the side. Rolling under the punch, Clinton stood up in time to see Hagen's tail whipping around to finish his combination. The lion dove over the lashing tail and grabbed a half-buried sheet of metal. Swinging around, he whipped it in front of his face to block the attack.

"Excellent, Clinton. Even better that time."

Clinton panted. The wind teased his hair. He lowered the shield to look at it. The elements had eaten it away, but he could make out some of its markings: the numbers two, eight, and five. He dropped it as Hagen relaxed his aggressive posture and stopped to get a drink.

Below where they sparred sat a small settlement, its wooden huts bleached by the elements. A water tower sprung up in the village center, with guards carefully patrolling its perimeter walls.

Scrapped cars and wagons were heaped on top of one another, creating a jigsaw barrier around the hamlet, while the caravan they had tagged along with was camped just outside the boundaries.

Hagen took another gulp, dropped the water skin, and then began to circle. Clinton wiped his brow, readying himself for another attack. Hagen leaped. He reached for the lion, but Clinton flipped backwards, kicking the komodo's hands away. Hitting the ground, Hagen rolled to his feet and snatched up a dried log. Wasting no time, he pressed his attack and swung it repeatedly at Clinton's head. The lion ignored the swings and backed away, waiting for the right moment until...

With a perfectly timed leap, Clinton dodged another strike and vaulted over the komodo. As soon as he landed, he shoved into Hagen, slamming the komodo into a tree. Hagen hit the trunk with a thud, before reeling to the ground. Clinton immediately leaped onto the reptile's chest, extending his claws.

"Ha! That'll teach you—"

Pain blossomed in the lion's stomach. He looked down to see Hagen's claws pressed against his grack-skin vest, their points almost piercing the tough material.

The lizard's lips curved into a devilish smile. "Teach me to what?" He removed his claws. "Sorry, lion, you lost. It was an excellent attempt though."

Clinton rolled onto his back to catch his breath. His adrenalin slowly subsided as the pulse in his skull beat a rhythm in time with his heart. His smile vanished. "I should have stopped when you went down shouldn't I?"

Hagen sat up, rubbing his neck. "Well, at least in hindsight you realize your mistake. Having your guts ripped out is not the most comfortable of deaths, Clinton. Although, I have to admit, allowing you to win is becoming increasingly difficult."

Clinton lifted his head to see a smirk cross his friend's face. He burst out laughing. "Oh, shut up! Letting me win. As if!" Grabbing a handful of dirt, he tossed it at the komodo.

"Still, you really are coming into your own with this style of combat."

Clinton dropped his head back onto the grass. "You think so?"

"I know so."

Since fleeing the komodo camp, Hagen had pushed Clinton even harder. The news of the patriarch's uncertainty in Clinton had seemed to ignite a fire in Hagen to prove his *juh* wrong. As their caravan had trundled through the eastern Ridgeback Mountains and onto the Lonely Road, most of Clinton's time had been spent practicing soul manipulation or combat.

"You still need to hold back though," continued the lizard, interrupting Clinton's thoughts. "Strike only when absolutely necessary, and with minimal effort. Remember, during battle—"

"My energy needs to be preserved for the manipulation of the soul, and not physical aggression. I know, I know. I just couldn't help it; I saw the opportunity and I went for it. I thought that was the right time to strike. Obviously, I was wrong."

Hagen leaned closer. "What should your course of action have been?"

Clinton sighed. "When I vaulted over you, when your back was turned, I should have fled, or at least used my other powers. I could have done the same after you hit the tree as well."

"Exactly. The passions of battle would have subsided, and both anumals would have lived to see another day. This is what the patriarch meant: stepping back, controlling the situation, and assessing all options. Not just acting on pure impulse. You have the powers at your command, Clinton…so use them."

"So you say, but you're the only one who believes it. Everyone else thinks I'm a sham."

Hagen shook his head. "And all the more foolish they will feel when you prove them wrong."

Two low horn blasts pounded through the hills.

Hagen and Clinton turned to the camp.

"They are packing up," said Hagen. "We must return."

The two grabbed their belongings and made their way down the hillside, towards the bustle of activity. Hagen threw his large cloak over his shoulders, and pulled up the hood, masking his intimidating face from sight. As they walked, Clinton remembered their earlier conversation. He chuckled.

"You never said why you fainted. Surely childbirth can't be that scary as to topple the likes of you...whatever the amount of blood involved?"

"True. Yet I found myself facedown inside the healer's tent." Hagen rolled his eyes at the memory. "It had been a long night, Clinton, and some of the warriors, Tarat and myself included, had taken it upon ourselves to drink the grain water dry in celebration of the impending skirmishes. And to a young, foolish komodo, the thought of battle filled us with exhilaration. Yet I acted in haste."

They walked in silence until they entered the camp. Around them anumals of all species hefted bags and chests onto wagons and stock. The smell of dung piqued their noses. Many vehicles had been pieced together with old tires and axels, with tin huts acting as covers. Gorespine's groaned, gulping water in readiness for the journey.

"Had I the sense," muttered Hagen, "I would have stayed by my mate, Ta'arri's side. Yet it was not expected for her to come to term so soon. The morning after our drunken night, I remember Tarat shaking me awake, yelling that Ta'arri was giving birth."

Hagen swallowed.

"My head was pounding. My stomach churned. Yet I ran to the healer's tent, pulled back the entrance...and saw my child, my beautiful baby, being born."

"So what made you faint?"

"I do not know. It was just too much for me. I am told I smashed straight through one of the healer's tables. Others joke I nearly ripped the entire tent down." Hagen chuckled. "Either way, I do know I gave the warriors much mirth with my antics."

Clinton burst out laughing again.

"When I eventually came around I saw Ta'arri holding my son in her arms."

They came to a halt at their small wagon. Clinton pulled out some dried fruit from his pocket and fed it to the boval pulling their cart. Hagen checked their belongings over and Clinton felt relief when he heard the clink of his lazarball armor, still safe and sound, strapped beneath the cart.

Clinton let the boval eat from his hand as he stared at the komodo. "So where are your family now then?"

Hagen paused. His eyes glazed over as he stared vacantly at the cart. A few seconds dragged by. "Gone," he murmured. "Ta'arri was taken in battle ten years ago now. And my son...well my son breathed for only one sun-cycle. That was all. By the time the moon had risen the following night, his spirit had departed his physical body."

Clinton looked up from feeding the boval. His throat tightened. "Hagen, I'm...so sorry."

Hagen yanked one last time on the luggage strap and shrugged. "There are many things we cannot control, yet we do have control of our memories. For that one sun-cycle I was the luckiest komodo alive; I had everything. However brief, I tasted and lived perfection, and that is something no one will ever take from me." He shrugged. "My son's time was brief, yes, but it was perfect."

Hagen looked Clinton in the eye. It felt like the lion was gazing directly into the komodo's soul.

"I spent an age in distress, Clinton, until I realized that I should be thankful for what I had, not miserable over what I had lost. I believe that is the way we all must think." He looked down at his hands, but Clinton had seen his black eyes glistening. "Trust me, some things can never be brought back."

Clinton found himself nodding. When he thought about it, he had gained so much from the time his family had been together. It had molded him into the anumal he was today. Not some hero, but someone rich in memory, generosity, and love. He could not help but smile as memories of his childhood flicked through his mind: learning to hunt with his father, laughing and getting into trouble with his brother, and the comforting embrace of his mother.

"These things shape you, Clinton." Hagen bounded on to the cart and took hold of the reins. "They are powerful thoughts, ones you should use to keep you anchored and calm."

"ONWARD!" echoed a cry through the camp.

As one, whips cracked and wagons began to roll ahead as the

caravan resumed its journey. Clinton jumped up onto the seat next to Hagen. They rode in silence for a while, before Clinton finally smiled.

"Let me win, huh? Next time I'm gonna kick your backside, lizard."

Hagen grinned before breaking out into his odd, hissing chuckle. "Just try it, junior, just you try it."

* * *

After two days of travel, the lofty mountains that had edged the road surrendered to reveal a flatter land as far as the eye could see. They spotted the odd wild boval and krig roaming the area, a sight Clinton had never seen before. Hagen and Clinton's cart bounced along the muddy track, just one more in the long line of traveling anumals. As usual, Hagen wore his large cloak to mask his appearance. Overhead, the sun had dipped low against the horizon, its orange rays dyeing the sky. A couple of eager stars had started to twinkle, rebelling against the darkness of night.

"Me and Raion should have journeyed north a long time ago," Clinton commented, studying the silhouettes of the grazing stock.

"Well, you did attempt to leave Wooburn."

"Yeah, and we all know how that turned out. That scrudding lazarball tournament messed everything up."

"Clinton, please concentrate," urged Hagen.

Clinton peered down at his hand and the stark ball of light in his palm. Its glow lit up their faces.

"So what is your next course of action?" asked Hagen, holding the reins.

"I...I don't know."

"Well, you cannot hold it in your hands forever. I think our little friend would have a problem with that."

Clinton looked down by his feet at the motionless wefring.

That morning Hagen had instructed him to find various scavengers in order to extract their souls – a skill he had practiced under Hagen's guidance on many occasions. This time, though,

Hagen had silently scrutinized his technique. Having caught the scavenger with ease, the rest of the day had been spent attempting to tap into its life force. Clinton meditated to locate its soul, yet every time he tried to seize it, his hold slipped, and distracting thoughts would pop into his mind. And his frustration only made success even more elusive.

"Confidence and reassurance is the key," Hagen had reminded him. "Exasperation will only frighten it."

By the time the sun's light had waned, Clinton had finally succeeded...yet his lessons were far from over for the night.

Hagen tied the reins to the front of the cart, trusting the boval would keep in line with the caravan, and lifted the inert wefring onto his knee. "As long as you possess the soul, then this little fellow is completely under your control." He gently folded its wings into a more comfortable position. "You have the ability to absorb its life, or release it to the winds. Conversely, if you—"

"If I house it within me, then I'll adopt its abilities and...change?" Clinton considered the glowing orb. "Just as I did with the grack?"

"Adopt its abilities? Yes. Physically change? I do not know."

The lion looked away.

"Clinton, why you took on the physical manifestation of the grack, rather than the purity of its soul, I am still trying to understand. However, I do know this: yours is a gift unparalleled by any other, even Dallas. Therefore, I propose that you embrace it."

Clinton huffed and shrugged his shoulders, before nodding towards the wefring. "Fine, okay...but what could I possibly gain from that thing? Grow a beak? I'm sure that'll help me the next time I go foraging for sectoids in the mud."

Hagen burst out laughing. "Maybe it will."

Clinton glared at the komodo, his frustration rising.

"Relax, Clinton, you must try to keep an open mind." Hagen raised the wefring up. "To most this little fellow is nothing but a nuisance, preying on carcasses and rummaging through trash. However, if you look deeper you will see he has his own special abilities. Speed, agility, ferocity…All traits you could use."

"But surely there'll be bad elements too?"

"As there is in us all. Yet the stronger you grow, and the more resilient you become, the more accomplished you will be at extracting specific abilities that can aid you, while leaving the vessel still conscious and able to move on its own."

Clinton stared uncomfortably at the wefring, taking in its deathly pallor. "Sounds a lot better than what I'm doing to it at the moment."

"Do not worry, he is completely fine."

"Well, seeing as I've got this far, I might as well find out what he can offer me…or if it'll change me."

Clinton raised the glowing orb up to his mouth.

"No, stop!" said Hagen, forcing Clinton's hand down.

"Why? I thought you told me to—"

"That is a *soul* you have there, not a toy. However small or insignificant the creature may seem to you, it is still alive. If you make a mistake the wefring will be drained for some time, and as you know, being weak in the wild is not an advantageous situation."

Clinton nodded and moved the glowing orb away. The boval pulling them groaned as the wheels hit a bump in the road. The cart rocked, causing the passengers to sway.

"Okay…so what should I do?"

The komodo reach out and swept his hand through a low-lying branch. He snapped off a thick twig. "This should work."

"For what?"

"To use as a temporary vessel."

"That?"

"Yes."

"A twig?"

Hagen smiled. "Yes, Clinton, it is as good an object as any other."

Clinton stared at it unconvinced. "But…"

"As long as the soul is bound to a physical object or vessel, it will remain there. If set free, it will vanish."

"But…a *twig*?"

"The twig was a part of a tree, and a tree is a living, feeling organism. Why would it not be a good vessel?"

Clinton's forehead furrowed. "I suppose you're right." Another thought flashed through his mind. "Will the wefring try to fight me, though, and go back to its own vessel?"

"That depends on the strength of the soul. The stronger the willpower, the harder it is to maintain control. Whereas there are some unseen energies who would like nothing better than to be summoned."

"Like what? Ghosts?"

"No, not as such. Just those who passed before their time and feel they have unfinished business. What I describe is a power of the greatest extreme, yet, for now, we must concentrate on the task at hand, or should I say…in hand."

Clinton inspected the light. "So what are we gonna do exactly?"

"Place it in a temporary vessel."

It took a moment for Hagen's words to sink in. Firstly Clinton was supposed to study the art of controlling an anumal, then learn how to take its abilities, and now he was being told he had to learn how to store its soul for future use.

He looked uncertainly at Hagen. "So what else can you store a life-force in? Just living things? Or can you put them in a jar…or something?"

"Jars, rocks, machinery, even mech. But I believe you will find it easier to work with natural materials." Hagen held the twig up before him. "Hence this."

Clinton sighed and took the twig. "Okay, now what?"

"We will start at the beginning."

"And do what?"

"Hold the wood close to the soul…and ask."

"Ask it what?"

"Permission to be placed inside a new vessel."

Clinton raised an eyebrow.

"It is a living thing you are holding, Clinton, with feelings and fears. It will understand if you ask wisely."

Clinton scrunched over, feeling stupid, and muttered, "This is ridiculous."

"Maybe so. Nevertheless, try not to force the wefring against its will," advised the lizard, his eyes glistening. "Just because you hold its soul, does not give you the right to command it, or to control it. You must always seek permission, Clinton, or else run the risk of becoming a tyrant. Now go on. Relax."

Clinton took a steadying breath and brought the twig next to the glowing orb. "Okay...Please little wefring, could you go into the twig?"

A nearby gibbet chattered.

A ponret flew overhead.

Hagen sniffed.

Clinton raised an eyebrow and glanced over his shoulder at the cart behind them. An elderly hog sat at its front with his belly spilling over his trousers, and a wide, brimmed hat pulled low over his eyes. His beast navigated the terrain as its master dozed. "I feel like an idiot."

"No one cares what you are doing," replied Hagen. "And you should speak to the wefring in your mind. Reassure it that all will be well, and the rest will come naturally."

Clinton reluctantly nodded and looked back down at the ayvid soul in his lap.

Look, he thought. *I know I took you from your body, and it caused you stress, but please, I'm only learning. And I apologize.*

He could not think of anything else to say, so he thought about when Raion was younger and being particularly stubborn. He chuckled, and a tide of love, exasperation, and pride rushed over him.

I want to make you safe, and I promise I won't hurt you, but I really need your help. Please allow me to place you somewhere else. I swear I'll take care of you until you return to your own body. I wouldn't ask if it wasn't urgent. I need to learn, and only scuttlers like you can help me do this. Please...

He allowed the love and protectiveness he felt for his brother to flow into the ayvid.

Nothing happened.

He sighed.

A low, lectric buzz filled his ears. He shuddered as raw power swept through him, and gasped as his body began to vibrate.

Hagen held him steady. "That is it, Clinton. Do not be scared. Maintain your focus. The wefring is no longer fighting you, now you must assume control."

The lion's limbs shuddered as if he was holding a live stunpike. The buzzing grew in power. Hagen's eyes went wide and he grabbed on to Clinton as the lion began to rise from the cart's seat and into the air. The komodo ignored the crackling lectric snapping all over his student, as he anchored him to his seat. The lion's eyes opened and white light beamed from them in the early evening light.

"Oh dear," muttered the komodo. He put a hand over the lion's face to block the glow, fearful of drawing attention. "Clinton, you must take control of the soul and move it into the wood immediately."

The buzzing intensified.

"Clinton," urged the komodo. "Do as I say. We are causing a scene."

More lectric buzzed over the lion's body, making his every hair stand on end. He looked like the time he had been dared by Teya Farnik and Tanner Burnjaw to touch his tongue against the end of a live stunpike when he was eight.

"Clinton, you must do as I say right now!"

There was a soft pulse. The orb in Clinton's hands began to move, inching closer to the twig.

The buzzing began to recede.

Hagen sighed as he watched the soul completely cover and soak into it. Clinton's eyes closed as he slumped forwards. His body settled into stillness. He leaned back, panting against the cart while studying the twig, knowing that it now contained the life force of another creature.

"I...I did it," he finally mumbled, looking up. "Hagen look."

Hagen smiled back at him, until Clinton noticed the other trees by the side of the path, their branches swaying in the breeze.

Realization suddenly struck him.

Any of them could have souls hidden in them, or the rocks on the road, or the plants, or…

"Yes, Clinton," confirmed the lizard, as if reading his thoughts. He lifted the twig from the lion's grasp to inspect it. "They are all around us…and have been for a long time. Be it ancient, or newborn, the soul lives on."

Something suddenly crystallized in Clinton's head.

When Hagen had recounted his story about his son, days before, it had struck a nerve inside the lion. Yet, now he realized that beneath the komodo's sorrow laid an appreciation; he had created a life, and a soul, that lived on in the world.

However, something still troubled Clinton.

"This is all just a bit…crazy for me. And how am I supposed to do this in a battle? Look how long it took me just now, and look at what it did to me. I wouldn't have time to stop and beg a soul for its help when I'm up against the likes of Dallas."

"What would happen if I was in dire need, Clinton? Would you aid me?"

"Well, of course I'd—"

"How quickly?" asked the komodo.

"Straight away."

"Why?"

Clinton narrowed his eyes. "Because I know you."

"And there is your answer. The world will have to come to know and trust you. Word of your loyalty and kindness will eventually grow, and then filter through the land."

Hagen placed the twig on top of the wefring. He took Clinton's hand and placed it atop them both.

"I am going to need your help with this," said the komodo. He touched some tattoos around his ears and on his arms, and hummed a deep, forlorn note. The hairs on Clinton's neck rose as the buzzing in his ears started up again. Clinton could feel the wefring's soul surface, before its physical body glowed and wiggled a few times.

Hagen stopped humming. "Go now," he said.

As if waking from the dead, the scavenger rolled to its feet on top of Hagen's knees. It wobbled as it gained its balance, and then chirped loudly, before flapping its wings and jumping into an unsteady flight. Clinton smiled as the wefring took to the sky. Moments later, it disappeared into the solitude of the night.

"Our little friend seems happy enough," commented Hagen. "You fulfilled your promise, and now he will live another day. And he will spread the word of your deeds…gradually, of course, yet it will happen. He will eat the foliage, the foliage will fertilize the land, the land will house the sectoids, and the sectoids will converse with the anumals, scavengers, plants and so on and so on. And as this happens, their trust in you will be passed and solidified. Stick to your word, Clinton. Stick to your promises and treat all with the respect they deserve, and soon you will find a world willing to help you in your cause…instantly."

* * *

By the following morning, Clinton had captured and extracted the souls of numerous sectoids and scavengers he had charmed through the night.

Hagen stirred from his sleep. He yawned and stretched his arms.

"Clinton? Did you not sleep?"

The lion rubbed his eyes. "Thought I'd fit in some practice while I had the space to myself."

"And?"

Clinton picked up a rock and released the soul of a small thicket louse back into its body. The rodent-like scavenger came alive before their eyes and scuttled off towards the rear of the wagon.

Hagen exhaled. "The masters were foolish indeed to infer you were not the Crystal Soul."

"It just kind of clicked last night." Clinton watched the small scuttler disappear into the bushes. "I realized that every living soul is interlinked with everything else, and that we're all dependent on the other."

Hagen gazed at Clinton with pride gleaming in his eyes. "Well, I am guessing you are hungry after all your training. We had better fix you some breakfast." He jumped from the back of the cart, but stopped again. After reaching into one of his many pouches, he tied a leather strap to something in his hand and held it out. "A present for you. Something to mark the occasion."

Hagen handed Clinton a leather necklace with a Y-shaped twig attached. The wood was now bleached white, and had an odd luminescence to it, but it was clearly the twig Clinton had first used to house the wefring soul.

Clinton picked up the object as if it was a priceless jewel. "Hagen, I…"

"What you did just now, and what you did last night, is momentous, and I believe it needs to be marked. Congratulations, Clinton, you continue to inspire hope in me."

The lion gulped, feeling the swell of pride flowing, and allowed himself to bask in all that he had achieved. He sat back and looked up into the morning sky.

"Well then," said Hagen, finally breaking the spell. "Another day's travel and I estimate we will arrive at Middle City. And what better way to start the day than chockeral eggs? Would you not agree, Clinton?"

Clinton, however, did not reply.

His eyes were slowly closing. His head drooped to the side as sleep began to take hold of him.

CHAPTER SIXTEEN

PEACE THROUGH LAZARBALL.

By sunrise the following day, the caravan of wagons finally entered the slums surrounding Middle City. Dressed in their long, hooded cloaks, Clinton and Hagen looked like shamans with their faces hidden under their hanging cowls. The cart's wheels sloshed though muddy water, causing it to splash the guards escorting the caravan into the city proper.

Wearing battered chest plates, greaves, and shoulder pads, battery packs had been strapped to their backs with wires running to the lazarball gloves on their hands. Lectric crackled around the shooters, and Clinton suspected that something much more powerful than a simple lazar would be released if they were fired.

"'Bout time us travelin' folk were protected!" hollered the large hog, sitting in the cart behind them. "Brother's family was attacked in these 'ere streets. They were travelin' into the city, y'see, when Short Claws mugged 'em. Robbed 'em blind. Even took the shirts off their backs. Filthy scruds."

Clinton smiled thinly at the hog before turning to look at the ravaged slums. A second-story window suddenly opened up and a sack of scuttler carcasses toppled into the street below.

Hagen brushed a dollop of mud from his shoulder. "They certainly have a unique way of treating new arrivals here."

"Well, it's still nicer than our komodo welcome."

Hagen smirked. "Yes. Point taken."

Stagnant water lined the gutters of the wide, mud road, leading them into the city. A corrugated jungle of shacks and multi-story huts swept away from the roadside and off as far as the eye could see. Sweeping lines of cables crossed overhead, spanning from shack to shack, bearing a fruit of tattered clothing left to dry in the polluted air. Every wall seemed adorned with an assortment of graffiti and clan symbols, and piles of garbage, bottles, and useless mech had been bundled together into manned roadblocks.

Clinton ran his hand through his hair. Grit fell onto his lap.

"Why would anyone ever choose to live here?"

Hagen snapped the reins, and the boval picked up its pace. "Why would anyone choose to live in Wooburn?"

"Oh, come on! Wooburn isn't as bad as this."

"To those who live in the purer mountain villages it is." Hagen's gaze swept towards a bear clawing at himself on the roadside, his mouth was a dirty amber color from hive abuse. "Some anumals are born into such an existence, Clinton, and are rarely given an opportunity of escape. You of all anumals should know that."

Clinton nodded gravely, before peering down one of the vein-like side streets threading from the main road.

Armed guards were perched on top of barricades, protecting their territory. Clan sigils branded the buildings, from the three-taloned foot of the Whirling Banshee clan, to the hexagonal chain of the Technals.

"It is beginning to fracture," mumbled Hagen. "I did not think it would decline so rapidly."

The komodo pointed towards a symbol of two flaming horns scrawled above a tavern door. "That Burning Horn Head symbol means they have claimed the tavern as their own. I would not want to see the result if an opposing clan member tried to enter. It seems like battle lines are being drawn."

"You think it's gonna get bad?"

"Silania dictates we live as one: no ruling clan or species elevated above the other, but..."

"It's all very nice in theory. Yet just look at Wooburn and Ferris Lakota's little pyramid of power."

"Exactly, Clinton, but at least there existed some semblance of peace in Wooburn. Now, I fear disaster is looming. If more of the powerful clans attempt to assert their dominance, then peace will not stand a chance."

"And it doesn't take a genius to guess which species would benefit most from a clan war."

Clinton gazed up at a wall of tires and barrels blocking off a large side street. A three-clawed symbol had been scored into it, while a scattering of felines lounged on top. He instinctively pulled his hood down, while Hagen did likewise. A humming filled the air, and the guards flanking the cart boosted the power to their lectric gloves. The caravan rolled deeper into the slums, and the city's inner buildings swelled, growing nearer with every second.

* * *

As the day progressed, the slums gradually dissipated, replaced by sturdy, brick structures. By the time the sun had nearly finished its descent, Clinton found himself dwarfed by towering skyscrapers, neon lights, and the clamor of the big city. Anumals bustled through the crowded streets. The smell of meat, spices, and engine oil, assaulted his senses, and vehicles cobbled together from salvaged scrap spluttered smoke. Signs advertising everything from *Fangton's Snacks* to armor repairs and Olde-world mech clung to the buildings' lower levels. Vines sprouted from empty windows and tumbled down the walls like green stubble, while rope bridges and walkways linked the upper levels together.

A chattering sound from above made Clinton glance up to see a group of primates swinging from vines and leaping from rooftop to rooftop.

"It must be the same everywhere," mused Clinton.

Hagen waved away a raccoon touting an armload of bagged spices.

"What?"

"Primates, y'know, how every time you see monkeys, someone is shouting at them or they're running away. I feel sorry for them sometimes."

"Your pity would be crushed by the prejudice and persecution they receive. Yet answer me this, Clinton: what exactly have they done wrong in your lifetime?"

Clinton followed the departing silhouettes for a moment. "Well, it's guilty by association, I guess. They're the closest anumal species there is to mankind."

"So we are allowed to blame the children for the faults of their forefathers?"

Clinton slouched back and folded his arms. "Look, I don't agree with how they're treated, but they did try to take over the planet in the past."

"And do you think the felines will be regarded as inferior to primates if their current attempt at domination fails?"

Clinton pondered his answer. "Nah. Sharp claws, speed, and vicious teeth. We come naturally equipped to dominate. And we outnumber many. So, whatever happens, felines'll never fall to the level of a primate. We're stronger."

"You sound like a certain tiger I know."

He nudged Hagen. "You know what I mean. If you were to put felines and primates in a battle, it's obvious who'd win. The primates'd be decimated."

Hagen's eyes narrowed. "Is that so?"

"Of course!"

"Why?"

"Because...we were the first species to evolve. We are natural leaders, and we're more powerful."

"Yet there once existed a species with no fur, claws, or sharp teeth, and they had minimal strength: scrawny beings by today's standards. Yet they were pitted against the most dangerous of creatures, in the harshest of conditions, and prevailed to dominate the planet."

Clinton sighed. "Yeah, mankind, I know, but—"

"The weakest race reigned before, Clinton." He switched his attention back to the road and tugged on the reins. The cart turned to follow the caravan along a narrow side street. Loud music pounded from a rickshaw that sped past them. Cries from market sellers punched through the air. "You say we hate primates because of their association to mankind...I say we are just scared that one day they will adopt mankind's power."

"WHOA! DESTINATION! MIDDLE CITY!" cried a voice from the front of the caravan. "WE ALL ARRIVE IN ONE PIECE?"

Hagen jumped from the cart and headed to its rear. Clinton climbed down and went to the front, offering the boval a final handful of dried fruit. "Spread the word to your friends that I'm a good guy, okay?" he commented, stroking her on the nose. "Remember who it was who gave you treats."

Hagen chuckled and tossed Clinton his backpack. "Come on, good guy. I sold the cart and boval to our noisy neighbor." Hagen glanced at the hog clambering from his cart. "We need to move."

The armor inside Clinton's backpack clinked when he hoisted it over his shoulder. He pulled his hood up and followed Hagen's lead into the throng of the busy street, feeling like a gillet out of water.

* * *

"Finest mech you'll ever see! We got lectric goods and engines, lazarball armor, battery packs—"

"Try it and you'll be set for the next ten days! This'll energize even a sloth. Contains real tukk-tukk blood—"

"You look lost, my friend," said a tiny lizard, slipping in front of Clinton and placing a wiry hand on his chest. "Two nugs and I'll get you where you want."

A tide of anumals sloshed around them like sludge parting around blocked trash. A cacophony of trader's voices competed for passing business.

"I know this city like my mother's face, I do." The lizard smiled, revealing hive-stained teeth. "What you looking for, huh? A bargain? Or something with a little…edge?"

Hagen plucked the lizard's hand away. "I advise you to go about your business and leave us alone."

"Whoa!" jumped the lizard, backing away as he caught a glimpse of Hagen's face under the hood. "You can't blame a shedskin for trying."

Hagen ignored him as they battled on through the crowded square. A huge bear barged into them, and a small feline ran past, causing the lion to pause mid-stride. A middle-aged horse nudged him out of her path, huffing all the while.

Hagen peered back over his shoulder. "Keep up, Clinton. It is about to become a lot busier."

"What? As if this isn't bad enough."

The komodo stepped through an archway decorated with vine-clogged statues, motioning for Clinton to follow. "You have not seen anything yet."

More anumals than Clinton had ever seen in his life spread out before him on the market road, leading to a colossal lazarball stadium. Almost as big as Samanoski, metal lighting towers punched high into the air, flooding the area with their glow. Giant images of lazarball players had been painted along the stadium walls, and a circular logo, consisting of two crossed, smoke-belching exhaust pipes, dominated the main entrance and every flag or poster within sight. A sign saying *The Middle City Marauders* hung above the street, lit by flickering light bulbs. Stalls and carts trimmed the sidewalks, enticing passersby with the lure of roast meat. Spices wafted through the air with as much presence and potency as the blaring horns and drums emanating from the stadium.

"Today is game day. Keep your belongings in check at all times. Given the opportunity, they will be pilfered and you will be walking around as naked as the day you were born," advised the komodo, pulling his hood further down. "Oh, and, Clinton...close your mouth."

Clinton nodded. He grasped his bag, shielded his face with his hood, and followed Hagen into the crowd. He had heard of the Marauders, and could recollect the one time his father had played against them in Wooburn.

The village had been ablaze with energy. Players such as Rimikin Zona and Quirl Planter had dominated nearly every minute of gameplay. To the Wooburnians it had been akin to the biggest sporting event in history, yet now Clinton could see how insignificant the match must have been to the visitors.

The flow of the crowd soon came to a standstill, and a wall of anumals blocked their path. A voice shouted above the crowd, and Clinton had to stand on his tiptoes to see where it came from.

"The games are being played, but times are set to change!"

shouted an eagle, perched atop the marble arm of a vandalized human statue. The flyer wore a long, symbol-painted cloak with a hood obscuring his face. He raised a feathered finger and pointed it into the air. "Silania has spoken!"

Mutters ran through the crowd.

"You have seen what is happening within the city and in the lands beyond. Peace is under threat. War is coming!"

"What would you have us do then?" yelled a voice. "I have cubs to protect."

"You must pray, dear child. Silania hears your words; she will protect you. She has given guidance to those who listen. The cities of old will rise from the rubble. The glorious games of the past will pave a way to a more peaceful future."

"Words!" shouted a frightened voice. "We need action, not riddles and promises! Horn Heads threaten our families. Gray Thornfingers demand payment for protection. Dust Whirls promise violence to any not of their clan."

A female voice shouted, "Ocelots ransacked my village and made us swear an oath, naming them masters."

"Crimson Watchers plague my doorstep," brayed a mule, standing near Clinton. "They stock weapons and deal in hive."

"That's a lie!" retorted a high-pitched voice. "We Watchers are decent anumals, fighting for protection. We don't associate with such things as hive."

"You'll need protection if I find you dealing on my doorstep again!" retorted the mule, pounding a hand against his chest. "If the Union Wheel will not offer protection, then I'll take matters into my own hands."

As if a bomb had detonated, arguments burst out amongst the crowd.

"Force the Crimson Watchers to halt!"

"Just you try it!"

"The Wheel doesn't give a frag anymore!"

"Stop this absurdity!"

The sound of smashing glass echoed. Fistfights erupted.

"My dear followers!" yelled the eagle, taking to the air. The crowd subsided to gawp at the hovering shaman, his robes hanging in the shape of a human, and his wings beating a steady rhythm. "This is exactly what Silania teaches against. You may be of differing clans, yet prayer will unite you. Follow her guidance. Heed her wisdom."

"Which is?" shouted a rodent.

The eagle settled onto the statue again. "Mar Mi-Den."

A cheer erupted from within the nearby stadium. Traders continued to hock their wares, yet a silence swept through the immediate throng.

"What's does he mean?" whispered Clinton. "Didn't Mar Mi-Den crumble?"

Hagen eyed the shaman. "So they say."

"The High Shamans have decreed that peace will be found through lazarball. Clans will unite. Teams will rise," continued the shaman. "If a war for dominance is to spring, if territory is to be disputed, then Silania's ways will be the path to our salvation. Contest your rights. All will have a chance at Mar Mi-Den."

"Like the colony crusades?" asked a passerby.

"Yes!" shouted another anumal. "They are the only way to stop this mess!"

"Imperial Ivory Stratos shall prevail!" hollered a flyer to Clinton's right, taking to the air on his wings.

"The Technals will rise again. You'll see," countered another voice.

A sudden chorus of shouts arose. The crowd began to jostle against Clinton and Hagen. Fighting broke out, and the anumals in front of them surged backwards, forcing Clinton to stumble.

The komodo ducked his head and wrapped his arm around Clinton. "Time to get out of here. Lower your head and follow me."

The crowd inside the stadium struck up a distant cheer.

"Gather your clans. Choose your teams. All shall be decided at Mar Mi-Den!" screeched the eagle, taking flight above his rowdy flock.

The ruckus eventually faded as Hagen and Clinton fled to Middle City's backstreets. Slipping down an alley, the komodo picked up his pace.

"Hagen!" Clinton called, trying to keep up. "What's the sudden rush?"

Hagen stared at the sky, but did not reply. Clinton followed his gaze, noticing stars appearing in the waning light. Soaring buildings, with metal staircases attached to their sides, towered over them. Water dribbled down their sides from broken pipes, leaving patches of moss. Lines of laundry zigzagged overhead, while damp hay and the odd scuttler carcass crunched underfoot.

Hagen leaned close to a wall and tasted the air.

"Nearly there."

"Where? I thought we were gonna find somewhere to lay low?"

"We were. However, plans have changed." The lizard set off down another backstreet. "Follow me."

"What's wrong? Is it that stuff the flyer said?"

"Everything is slipping into place," muttered Hagen. He tasted the air, before his gaze came to rest on an old trashcan. He yanked off the lid, treating them both to the pungent aroma of rotten garbage. "Yes, we are on the correct path."

"Path?"

Hagen set off walking.

Clinton sighed, but followed after his friend. He felt trapped inside what was fast becoming a concrete maze. Back in Wooburn he had known the streets better than most, yet his sense of direction in this giant hive had been stolen from him.

"Hagen, where are you taking us?"

One backstreet turned into another, which rapidly turned into another. Shouts echoed along the alley, followed by the clatter of a toppling trashcan.

"That's it!" The lion stopped in his tracks. "I'm not going any further unless you tell me what's going on."

Hagen stopped, but did not look back. He bent down and yanked on a metal grate in the ground. Tasting the air again, he reached into the darkness and pulled out a glass bottle, before smashing it against the wall.

A curled up piece of paper tumbled to the ground.

Hagen snatched it up, unrolled the parchment, and smiled. He handed it to Clinton. "We need not go on."

Clinton read the words written on the paper.

You're here!

Before Clinton could ask anything more, something slipped over his head, obstructing his vision. A drawstring tightened around his neck, securing the cloth in place. The lion tugged against the hood, but someone grabbed him by the wrists, bending his arms behind his back, and tying his hands together.

"Hagen!" The lion struggled, lashing out with his feet as his heart beat a drum roll. "What's happening?"

No one replied.

Powerful arms grappled him into a bear hug and lifted him off the ground.

"I'm warning you. GET OFF ME!"

Hands grabbed Clinton's ankles and bound them together, before he was hoisted into the air and shoved on top of some wooden boards. An engine spluttered and then fired to life. He could smell oil as the wooden boards shuddered with motion.

"Hagen!" he shouted. "What do they want?"

"I hear you, Clinton," replied the lizard's muffled voice. "Calm down and do not struggle. It will only complicate things."

CHAPTER SEVENTEEN

THE LAIR.

The bag covering Clinton's head muffled his senses. Sweat clogged his fur. Dragged from the back of the truck, and lifted onto someone's shoulder, he heard the clanking of chains before a metal door screeched open. Engine fumes stung his nose again.

"Hagen? Are you there?"

There was no reply.

Clinton wriggled again, trying to break free.

"W-what do you want with me?"

Another door creaked open, before he was tossed into a chair and held in place.

"You, errrr, you think it's okay to take the hood off now?" asked a deep voice. "The kid seems mighty riled."

"What do you expect?" answered a high-pitched female, behind Clinton. "I just hope he isn't going to use his mumbo jumbo on us."

"You will be fine to unhood him now," replied a voice that Clinton recognized. "I am certain he will understand the precautions."

"Hagen!" gasped the lion. "Are you hurt? I swear if they don't let me go right now, I'm gonna—"

"Clinton, relax. You must not do anything rash," urged the komodo, a stern edge creeping into his voice. "Keep your temper in check and try to remain calm."

Clinton took a ragged breath, memories of being captured by the komodos keeping him on edge. "Let me go."

"Promise me you will remain calm," begged Hagen.

The lion gritted his teeth, but forced his shoulders to relax. "Okay...I won't do anything stupid. Just get them to take this thing off my head."

After a moment's silence, the higher voice reluctantly said, "Fine, but I'm warning you, lion, try anything stupid and you'll regret it."

The hood was yanked away.

The air smelled stale. A blinding light shone directly into his eyes, making him squint. A huge figure lingered in the shadows.

"Tell us your name!" ordered the higher voice.

"My name's Clinton Narfell."

"And where are you from?"

"I'm from… Hang on. What are you asking for?"

"He's right y'know," replied the deeper voice. "Why do you want to know that?"

"Because, Hudson, we need to know if he can keep his mouth shut under pressure, which he clearly can't."

"Whoa, Pep! What did you go and tell him my name for? We still don't know whether we can trust him or not."

"Well…hang on, you just told him my name too!"

"What? Did I? Oops. Anyway, your interrogation technique is rubbish."

"Well, you're rubbish."

"Whatever!"

Clinton began to fidget. "Errrr…are we done with the questions then?"

"Yes!" mumbled the lower voice.

"No!" snapped the higher voice.

"Look, what's going on?" he asked. "Just who are you folk?"

"Who?" The lumbering figure came to a sudden stop in front of the lion. "Me?"

"Of course you," laughed the higher voice.

Clinton craned his neck around to try and see anything of the speaker, but his bindings prevented him from getting a good look. He turned back, when a face suddenly loomed before him. A gust of breath from a pink, snorting nose, with a ring hanging from it, wafted his hair. Two horns curved out the side of its head, and a thick strand of brown fur hung between two black eyes. The bison's head hung low on its wide shoulders, jaws chewing a mouthful of greens. "He looks kinda puny to me. You sure we can trust him?"

"I am vouching for him," answered Hagen.

"Well, I trust Hagen," reasoned the bison. It shoved one of its massive hands out at Clinton. "The name's Hudson in case you missed it the first time."

The lion stared at the hand in disbelief, before slowly turning to Hagen. "Could you kindly tell your friend here that I'd shake his hand if I wasn't completely tied up."

"*Her!*" snapped the bison.

Reaching around his back, the bison tore apart the bindings as if they were made of straw.

"What?" asked Clinton.

The bison snorted with annoyance and pushed the bright light to the side.

"*Her* hand. I'm not a him, I'm a her."

Stepping back, Hudson rested her hand on the large spanner hanging from her utility belt. Oil smeared her shorts and vest.

"Ohhh," chuckled the higher voice. "Now you've upset Huddy. Wouldn't want to be in your shoes, pal."

"Excuse me," interjected Hagen. "I would love to be released too."

From out of the darkness scurried a small, white mouse. Dressed in makeshift armor, with a dagger strapped to her back, she grinned and scampered up Hagen's legs. The light reflected in her bright red eyes as she stood on Hagen's lap, yanking off his blindfold.

Hagen shook his head, allowing his eyes to adjust to the light. "Now then, Pep," he said, blinking. "There is no prettier face I could have asked to see than yours."

The mouse shrugged, but her cheeks flushed crimson. "Aww, come off it, Hagen. Besides, you can stop pretending you're captured now."

A mischievous smile crept across Hagen's face. He jolted his arms and legs apart, snapping his bindings.

Clinton rose to his feet. "Is someone going to tell me what the scrud is going on?"

"Ohhhhh." Pep giggled. "Bad language."

"Just what in skorr is happening here, Hagen?"

"I know how all this must seem bizarre." The komodo rubbed

his wrists. "Yet, it was necessary."

"Standard procedure," commented Hudson. She pulled out a small mirror from a pocket and checked the long, thick curl of hair that hung between her eyes. "Gotta be careful, honey."

"Huddy's right." Pep climbed up a tall stack of crates and nestled comfortably on top of them. "I still say we can't trust him. He's got a loud mouth, and he's weird. Smells funny too."

Hagen ignored the mouse and turned to the lion. "Clinton, trust me, Garron has good reason to demand such secrecy."

"Garron? Who's that?"

"Who's G?" snorted Pep. "Have you been living under a rock or something?"

Clinton huffed.

Pep laughed and peered down at him while swinging her legs. "That's if G even allows you to meet with him, of course. Us three are okay. But you? Well, he might not like you."

"Pep, stop aggravating him," sighed Hagen. "Garron will make you very welcome here, Clinton. And, like it or not, the lair remains undiscovered because of his propensity towards secrecy."

"You mean like putting a bag over my head and abducting me? That kind of secrecy?"

"Exactly," Hagen nodded, turning back to the bison. "Hudson, is Garron getting so paranoid these days that he binds even those he knows?"

"We had to act fast. No time for a welcome party or formalities. Too many watching eyes."

"Besides, most of the tunnel entrances are in clan territories now," Pep explained. "And only a few of those are located in the safer backstreets, if you can still call them that."

"But an abduction is hardly discreet," sneered Clinton.

"In a city of violence, an ambush is pretty much the norm these days, Clint," hissed Pep, glaring at him.

"It's Clinton," he snapped, baring his fangs.

Pep blew him a sarcastic kiss. "Sure thing, *Clint*."

"Are we just going to stand here bickering, or shall we proceed?" asked Hagen, breaking the tension.

"Yeah, I'm bored." Hudson muttered, lumbering off into the darkness. "Let's go."

With one last glance, Pep turned her nose up at Clinton before springing down from the stacked crates.

"Are you coming?" asked Hagen.

Clinton's insides squirmed with frustration. He ran his hand through his hair. "Seems like I don't have a choice. Again."

The komodo shrugged while the lion followed him into the dark passage. Dim lectric bulbs suddenly flickered to life all around, their weak glow lighting up towers of crates. In the distance, Hudson was turning a drive crank, trying to fire an engine to life.

Pep bowed playfully to Hagen. "After you, good sir." She ushered the komodo towards a row of seats situated in an open-top train carriage, before pushing in front of Clinton.

With one last crank, the engine exploded to life, belching out a cloud of fumes. Blowing her curl out of the way, Hudson pulled a pair of goggles over her eyes. She plunked herself into the driver's seat, behind an array of levers and dials, and revved the engine, causing the contraption to shudder.

"Strapped in?" she yelled, over the noise.

The passengers tied ropes around their waists to hold themselves in place. A long cylindrical nose – painted with sharp teeth – had been welded to the carriage head. Panels had been attached to the sides, and huge storage hoppers and bins had been fixed to the rear for luggage.

Clinton jumped with realization. "My bag! Where's my armor?"

"In the back," answered Pep. "You need to calm yourself, Clint. Stress is a killer."

So is a bad attitude, thought the lion.

"Well, hold on tight, folks," Hudson shouted. "Here we go!"

She yanked on a lever, and the carriage reluctantly shuddered off into the darkness at the speed of a tired tortoise walking on a sprained ankle.

The flatbed carriage slowly crept along the tracks until Clinton heard Hudson yank another lever. Wheels screeched, echoing along the tunnel, as the contraption picked up its pace.

"Scrudding breeze," muttered Hudson, checking her hair. "Plays havoc with my curl."

"Just please don't veer off course this time," begged Pep. "We can't risk losing another carriage."

Hagen's face lit up sporadically as the overhead lights zoomed past. "Has Garron not uncovered the full underground network yet?"

"Most of it I think. But only last month, old big horns here managed to get us well and truly lost...again."

"It wasn't my fault. The carriage malfunctioned!" retorted Hudson. "It wouldn't slow down."

"Come off it, Huddy," laughed Pep, shooing away her excuse. "Someone, who shall remain nameless, took a wrong turn. Too busy looking in her scrudding mirror and not paying attention."

Hudson snorted.

"Took us near on a day to find the lair again," groaned Pep. "I was fine, but believe me, bison don't do too well in small, dark tunnels."

"Yeah, and I stunk of smoke for ages after," huffed Hudson. She hunkered forwards, squinting into the distance. "Hold on! We got company!"

Hudson yanked on a chain. The tunnel filled with the resounding blast of a horn, and not long after, a carriage sped past them. Three armed anumals saluted from within its cabin.

"Just a patrol. Nothing to worry about," informed Pep, folding her arms.

The flatbed continued its journey through the darkness. Occasionally, they sped by a guarded platform, or more patrols would whip past, blasting their horns and disappearing into the darkness as quickly as they came. It was not long before Hudson started pulling levers and turning dials, causing the carriage to reduce speed.

"Here we are," she shouted, over the screeching brakes and hissing steam. "Home, sweet home."

Clinton saw a speck of light appear at the front of the carriage, and within moments, the flatbed veered to the right and exited the tunnel through a hole in the wall.

It entered a cavernous room.

The lion stared in wonder. Multiple levels seemingly hung in midair, accessed only by thick, metal staircases or rope. The train track had been fixed to the marble flooring, weaving in and out of giant statues, waterfalls, and pillars, supporting the weight of the ceiling above. Reconditioned shops lined each wall, their Olde-world signs still hanging above each door. Inside, anumals were busy crafting weapons, sleeping, or unpacking crates and unloading supplies.

"A 'mall' is what they called this place," said Pep, leaning on Clinton's shoulder. "Mankind sometimes built them underground like this. Dunno why."

Heavily supported shelves containing more boxes, crates, and makeshift dens towered all around. Small huts even hung from the balconies, or had been grafted to the sides of lift shafts, creating yet more living space for the multitude of working anumals.

A carriage sped past them.

"Quite the sight, isn't it?" smirked Pep. "Just you wait till we reach the center."

Another carriage screeched to a halt on the interweaving maze of tracks. The alighting anumals eyed Clinton's flatbed warily as it passed into another corridor and entered a domed hall. More shops had been recycled around the outskirts of the room. Steam rose from their open kitchens, and stoves blazed, cooking stews, and roasting meats.

"It is a world of its own," said Hagen. "You name it and Garron has it."

"You're telling me," added Hudson, sniffing the air. "Can we—"

"No!" shouted Pep. "Get to G first, then you eat."

Hudson began to slow the carriage, looking hungrily at the stew. "Not even for a quick—"

"After we go to the nest," replied the mouse, firmly.

Hudson huffed.

The flatbed finally came to a jolting stop, nudging the buffers at the end of the track. The passengers disembarked. In front of them stood a corrugated iron wall masking long, iron legs that housed an elevated office. Ropeways led off in numerous directions like a web, connected to the other rooms and passages.

"Password?" asked a huge guard, blocking the stairs leading up to the nest.

"Hood," Pep replied.

The guard winked at her and stepped aside, allowing the group to pass. They walked slowly up the winding stairs.

A grand water fountain, which had long since dried out, stood in the center of the room, while stone human figures, missing various limbs, decorated its circumference. Up above, the domed ceiling had been painted to depict the planets, its beauty had long since faded, assaulted by cascades of clinging weeds. Small winged ayvids nestled in the lofty heights.

The group reached the top, and Hagen pushed open two metal doors to reveal a carpeted office lined floor to ceiling with books. A large, wooden table stretched out before them with rolled up maps, technical documents, and papers strewn across it. Between each bookshelf hung mounted human skulls attached to the wall. Behind a desk, an arched window dominated the room, with thick, green curtains drawn across it. The smell of burlico greeted Clinton, and in the corner, smoke wafted from burning incense. The doors swung shut, muting the bustle of outside. Next to the desk, a small, winged lizard yawned and stretched on its perch. It eyed the newcomers and made a clicking sound.

"Damn it! Bloomin' guards!" yelled a voice from a side room. "Who's gone and woken you up now, huh, Whim? Told 'em to leave us in peace until—"

"We arrived?" finished Hagen.

Whim chirped and immediately flew to Hagen's shoulder. The

komodo smiled and tickled her belly as the ayvid chattered into his ear.

There was a moment of silence, before a squat gator burst into the room. Staring down his long, ageing nose, and through Oldeworld spectacles, his wide smile revealed sharp, yellow teeth.

"As I live and breathe…" The gator spread his arms wide and waddled over to Hagen, his leather coat dragging behind him. "Hagen, my ol' matey, how you doin'?"

Hagen hugged the gator. "It has been too long, Garron. Far too long."

"Aye, it has." He patted Hagen on the back before pulling away. "Missed you, buddy. Should've visited me sooner."

Hagen smiled. "There are a multitude of things I should have done sooner, yet duty takes precedence."

"You're tellin' me, ol' pal. You. Are. Tellin'. Me."

Both anumals silently appraised the other before Garron pointed towards some cards spread out in neat rows on the table. "I still got the lazarcard game waiting for you. Haven't peeked at your deck." He looked pointedly at Pep. "I'm not the one who cheats."

The mouse rolled her eyes.

"Ten years playing one game of lazarcards," chuckled Hagen. "That must be a record."

Garron nodded. "Ten bloody years too long! It's killin' me. And get you! Ten years and you ain't aged a bit. Do you komodo's ever get old, huh? You have put a bit of weight on, mind you, but apart from that…"

The two reptiles laughed.

"Now, Garron," said Hagen, ushering the lion forwards. "May I introduce you to Clinton Narfell."

"Ahhh." Garron peered closely at him. "So he's the one causing all the trouble, huh? The infamous Narfell. I've been running the length and breadth of the Plains for you, lion."

Clinton's face screwed up. "For me? And why am I infamous?"

"Just because," answered the gator, as if that explained

everything. "Well, you're smaller than I expected, but then again, I didn't really know what to expect."

"He's mouthy though, G," cut in Pep, now seated on top of Hudson's shoulder. "Shouts and swears all the scruddin' time. Smells funny too."

"Button it, Pep," grinned the gator, shaking his head. "I trust all's clear?"

"What?" Hudson looked up from her mirror. "Sorry."

"No followers?"

"Oh, come on, Garron!" laughed Pep. "This is us you're talking to; we got the job done exactly as instructed."

"Well, that makes a change." Garron walked over to Whim's perch and whistled. She flew over to the wooden stand as Garron pulled out a piece of dried meat from one of his leather pockets. After feeding the meat to the ayvid, he peeked through the large, green curtains behind the table. "I suggest you two get back downstairs. Time's running short, and Silania knows you need the practice."

As Hudson and Pep exited, the gator pulled a chair out from under the table and motioned for Clinton to sit. "I suspect you've got a head full o' questions, huh?"

"You could say that."

"Well, we'll get to 'em in time, matey." He took out three glasses, a jug of water, and a dusty green bottle. Placing them on the table, he poured Hagen and Clinton a glass of water, and himself a generous shot of fire liquor. He knocked it back in one gulp. "You like my home, huh?"

Clinton took a sip of his water. "I don't honestly know what to say...What is this place?"

"What it isn't is probably an easier question to answer," laughed Garron, his deep eyes boring into Clinton. "We're into everything here: a bit of this, a bit of that. Call us helpers, or fixers...or even fighters, if you will."

"And what do you fix?"

"Well, we fix stuff." He smiled, before running his tongue over his teeth and staring at the floor. "Yup, we...fix...stuff. This place has been my base and home now for…hmmm…How old are you, lion?"

"I'm nineteen now."

The komodo looked at Clinton sharply. "I thought you were eighteen."

"I turned nineteen three weeks ago."

"And you didn't say?"

"What was there to celebrate?"

The gator cleared his throat. "Then, Clinton, I've been in this lair longer than you've been alive. Seen some good times. Seen some bad." He poured himself another shot and turned to Hagen. "Wouldn't you agree?"

"It certainly seems busier than usual, yet that is to be expected."

"Yup, things ain't too good out there in the big wide world at the moment. You ever seen hostility like this before, Hagen?"

The komodo shook his head. "Not since the Wastelands. And even then it seemed less…distorted. You knew who you were fighting against, and who to trust."

"Exactly! The lines weren't blurred then. Friends were friends. I've got twelve patrols hidden in the streets right now. *Twelve.* And I'll be damn lucky if they return. Every time I send folk out, their safety decreases. I get daily reports of plundered villages and irate clans."

Garron pulled a chewed up burlico-stick out of his pocket and played with it in his hands.

"Scared anumals flock to the Union Wheel every day, but there's only so many anumals the clan can oppose at once."

"Oppose?" said Clinton. "Do you mean fight? But the Wheel is non aggressive. We don't do that."

Garron stared at Clinton for a long time before saying, "You're right, kid, we don't. No violence. No dominance. Equality—"

"For all. That's our way," Clinton cut in. He looked at his empty wrist where Ferris had stripped the rope membership bangle from him. "Or was."

"And it is because of those ideals that the Union Wheel is

being torn asunder," explained Hagen, staring at his water. "It may be the largest clan, but Silania deemed it peaceful. No violence…No war."

Garron sniffed. "Well, not essentially true."

Clinton frowned. He studied Garron's office, noticing a modified Union Wheel's sigil above the door. A shield and a skull, baring its fangs, had been etched inside the rope wheel. "I…I don't understand. What's that?"

"Well, we ain't, technically speakin', Union Wheel, kiddo," Garron replied, clearing his throat. "For simplicity's sake, let's just call ourselves an offshoot."

"Offshoot?"

"Yeah. Aegis."

"Aegis? Never heard of it."

"We are Aegis; this office is Aegis; this lair is Aegis. The anumals in here, everything around you, is Aegis," answered the gator, rising to his feet. He walked to a desk, picked up a piece of paper, studied it for a second, and then replaced it again. "You really think the Wheel survived this long without backup, huh? That we thrived because of optimism and spirit alone? No way, kiddo."

Clinton shook his head. "You mean to say the Wheel aren't pacifists?

"Oh, no, no, the *Wheel* is. It has to be; it represents peace. But sometimes peace needs protecting." He returned to pour himself another shot. "A long time ago our clan leaders realized this, but instead of going against clan law, a separate movement was born into existence. A clandestine movement called Aegis."

"Hence the security precautions," Hagen said.

"The need for an equal, mixed-species clan was paramount for ensuring peace after the colony crusades. It was a safe haven, where all were accepted, headed by the great Silania herself. As part of the Wheel's mandate, they decreed violence never to be used in matters of diplomacy. Yet, face it kid, a non-violent clan is easy pickings. After all the bloodshed and wars, the clan leaders had no stomach for a repeat story, and they knew they had to prevent this. So the most powerful leaders gathered in secret and created Aegis: a movement dedicated to protecting the Union Wheel and peace. Anumals of every species from rodents—"

"To komodos," added Hagen.

"Swore an oath of secrecy when joining Aegis."

Clinton nudged his glass of water, watching the surface ripple. "Surely other clans know of you though?"

Garron chuckled. "More than likely, yes. But tell me, have you ever heard of the Deep Well Basilisk or the Android Isles?"

Clinton smirked. "Yeah, but they're just journeytales."

"Exactly!" He wagged his finger at the lion. "As are we. Oh, folk know about us, but to most clans Aegis is nothing but a yarn, and the world is full of such tales."

Clinton remembered the tale of the Plain's Nomad who tamed wild scavengers and used them to protect his territory. This legend had been ingrained into Wooburn's culture by the village Teller, who wove his nightly stories to an audience gathered by the village's main fire.

"We've existed for so long now that any talk of Aegis is cast off as crazy talk. Only the foolish try find us. And yet, here we are: existing in the shadows. We've been around since the dawn of the Union Wheel. And by skorr," the gator slammed back his fire liquor, "we'll continue to protect it until its final days."

Garron's steel gaze lingered on Hagen, before the komodo motioned for him to continue.

"What's happening above is nothing new," said the gator. He trudged over to the window and pulled apart the curtains, allowing light to filter into the room. Clinton could not see the view from where he sat. "Clans always try to overshadow their competitors. Anumals always have; it's in our nature, no matter how hard we try to suppress it. But Aegis has always been there, in one way or another, to help ease tension before it escalates. Only…"

Garron tossed his burlico-stick into an ashtray on his desk, and sighed.

"Only what?" asked Clinton.

"Only this time it is different," replied Hagen. "This is the

197

conclusion to a web of scheming that has come to fruition over many years. This time the struggle is transpiring on a multitude of levels that the tribes, the clans, and even Aegis, have yet to fathom."

Clinton scowled. "Anumalkind has survived many wars. You've fought in them, Hagen, and yet you're still here. Why is this time different?"

"Because of you," answered Garron, quietly. "You...and your adversary."

The gator pulled a tatty sheet of paper from a drawer in his desk. Strange writing had been written on it, symbols Clinton did not understand. "I received reports from Aegis spies south of the Ridgeback a few weeks ago that felines had been on the rampage. Villages were being stormed, citizens tortured until they decreed that the felines were their masters.

"We fought back, naturally, and at first we drove away that ragtag feline sect called the Fangs. But then they joined with another sect called the Sabers. And then something changed, and the unthinkable happened. The feline clans began to enlist with the sects, creating some kind of new, unified clan, bearing a single sigil."

"What sigil?" asked Clinton.

"Three claw marks," replied Garron, leaning over to stare at the lion. "They call themselves the Ocelots. And they've gotten every clan riled up. Even now Burnin' Horn Heads, Crimson Watchers, Gray Thornfingers, Technals, Gray Scales, all of 'em, are rallying around, uniting on their own. But they just can't pull it off like the Ocelots are doing. The felines've changed; they're disciplined and are fighting without takin' any quarter. And with Aegis forced to intervene on a more regular basis, it's only a matter of time before we're exposed, or worse, defeated. We need folk to help, but vettin' 'em is hard, and trustin' 'em is even harder. Yet we need more numbers."

Clinton screwed his face up. "Surely, though, some of the clans have fought the Ocelots back?"

"Oh, yes, they have...and they lost. Clinton, understand that

Aegis, and the clans, aren't fighters. We were never meant to be an army. We're made up of anumals workin' in the shadows. We are the chief of security in a remote forest village. We are the councilor or healer in the corner of a big city. We are the garbage collector and the weaver you never pay heed to. But when duty calls, Aegis members pull together. Only—"

"Only the anumals who would fight for us are dwindling," interrupted Hagen. "They are being forced to fight for their own clans, and their own kind."

Garron nodded. "That's why everyone's fleein' to the bigger settlements like Middle City: to find safety in numbers. Because if you refuse Ocelot rule in the remote areas, then you die."

"And the city is too big for a single clan to rule," realized Clinton.

"Currently, yes. But give it time, kiddo, give it time. And just imagine the power they'll wield when they do."

Clinton's head spun with the news. His claws protracted with anger. The room fell silent, before Garron finally said, "He's back and he's fuellin' the felines like nothin' before."

"Who?" asked Clinton.

"Nightmare," Hagen hissed, baring his teeth.

"I wish it weren't true, but sources say he's back. Along with the tiger called Dallas."

Clinton rose to his feet. "So they're building an army while I waste time trying to work on my most basic powers?"

The gator raised an eyebrow and looked questioningly at Hagen. "Well, this tiger, or Shadow Soul, as you call him, seems to be at the center of the mess. Their 'poster boy' if you will."

"Which brings us full circle," said Hagen.

Garron took more dried meat from his pocket and fed it to Whim. "If I've been informed correctly, Clinton, it seems you're the only one who can stop him. Others may injure him, but only you can truly kill him. And if we destroy their messiah, then their unity'll be severed, forcing the Ocelots to disperse and finally give us a fighting chance to defeat any stragglers. But the Nightmare…"

Hagen rose, his chest expanding. "Leave him to me."

"Oh, rest assured, Hagen, I'm not going anywhere near that one."

Clinton's forehead furrowed.

"So what do we do? Get an army to go after them?"

"Oh, no, kiddo." Garron beckoned his guests over to view the scene from the window. "Wanna know how we'll stop these scruds, huh? Then just take a look."

As the lion approached, a twinkle of crystal reflected through the glass and into his eyes. His brow furrowed. On the other side of the wall was a rope bridge that led down to a large, bowl-shaped lazarball gamefield, constructed at ground level.

"Beautiful," purred Garron, rubbing his hands together.

"A gamefield? I don't understand? How will this help us defeat Dallas?" Clinton shook his head, and his gaze fell upon a group of anumals gathered in the center of the gamefield. "And who are they?"

The lion's heart suddenly began to hammer. A surge of fury flared behind his eyes before a low growl rumbled in his chest.

Clinton roared.

CHAPTER EIGHTEEN

OLD FRIENDS.

"Clinton, calm yourself!"

The lion pushed Hagen's hand away. He shoved open the small door behind Garron's desk, and stormed down the rope walkway leading to the gamefield. Rage propelled his body. His focus was locked on the squat figure standing in the center of the group.

"Clinton, this will not solve anything," warned Hagen, trailing after him.

"No, but it sure as skorr'll make me happier." Clinton snatched up a helmet from a nearby stack of equipment and slid down the gamefield's sloped wall. "Hey you! SCRUD!"

He hurled the helmet with all his might.

"What the…" Harris Lakota jumped sideways as the helmet bounced past him. "Are you stupid or…"

The beaver's words lodged in his throat.

His eyes widened as he caught sight of the snarling lion racing at him. "Oh, no, no, no. Please…"

Without a second thought, Clinton smashed into the beaver, pinning him against the floor. His claws protracted, piercing Harris's brown, furred skin.

"WHAT ARE YOU DOING HERE?"

"P-please Narfell. I-I…"

Saliva flew from Clinton's mouth as he scanned the area. "Where is he?"

Harris yelped, straining to break free. "Who? Where is who?"

"YOUR FATHER! THE ONE WHO RUINED MY LIFE!"

"I…I do not know."

"Liar!" Clinton slammed Harris against the floor. "Tell me!"

"Leave him be!" ordered Hagen, yanking Clinton back. "This is not the way to deal with this."

The lion shoved against the komodo, trying to break free of his grip. "Get off me, Hagen. NOW!"

Harris scurried away, rubbing his bleeding chest. "Has he completely lost his mind? He needs locking up—"

"Why you…"

Clinton lunged for him again, but Hagen stopped him.

"Let go of me!"

"Calm yourself," hissed Hagen.

"I *am* scrudding calm. I know exactly what I'm doing."

"Please, Clinton, this is not what I have taught you."

"Stuff what you've taught me!"

Hagen gripped on to him tighter. "Stop this right now!"

Pep shook her head in disbelief. Hudson stepped in front of Harris with narrowed eyes. Panting heavily, Clinton stared at the cluster of wary faces. He took a deep breath, and lifted his hands in submission.

"Fine. Just…Just let me go. Please."

A long moment passed, but finally Hagen relaxed his hold.

Inside Clinton, the spark to gut the beaver still existed, yet he fought the urge and ran his hands through his hair. "So…your father…is he here?"

Harris shook his head as everyone turned in his direction again. "No, he is not. I assume he must be back at the village."

"So why are you here?"

Harris dabbed a spot of blood pearling on his chest. "Ask the gator. He is the one with the answers, not me."

Clinton looked up to see Garron quietly watching the spectacle from the nest's doorway. "I will," he promised, scowling. "But my brother…is he okay?"

"How should I know? I left Wooburn weeks before you did, remember?"

"Oh, yeah, 'helping missionaries in the Plains' or some dung like that."

"Is that what my father said I was doing? Well, isn't that just typical!" Harris sighed, baring his buckteeth. "I left because I was sick of all the lies and the dirty deals. And finally because of you…"

"What? Me? Why?"

"Because, Clinton, what Dallas did to you in the stadium, and after, was wrong. And I told them so."

Clinton looked the beaver up and down, and slowly shook his head. "Why should I believe a single word coming out of your mouth? You're a Lakota."

Harris held his head high. "You know nothing of me, Narfell. And to be honest, I do not really care. Your head has never been out of your own backside long enough to see that others have their own problems too." He straightened his lazarball armor and lifted his glove to realign the shooter. "Contrary to your thinking, the world does not revolve solely around you, lion."

Clinton took a controlled breath, trying to stem his budding fury. "Look, you must've been in contact with your father at some point. You must know something."

"Mother of Treb!" Harris stamped his foot. "Are you listening to me? I. Do. Not. Know. Anything. I have not spoken to my father you stupid misbreed."

"Mind your words," Hagen warned.

"You mind yours, lizard", snapped Harris, turning to face Hagen. "And who the scrud are you anyway?"

Hudson snorted and flicked her curl out of her face. "Enough. No one talks to Hagen like that."

The beaver scoffed. "And just who is going to stop me?"

"Well, if she doesn't, bucky. I will," hissed Pep.

"Oh, here we go," sighed Harris. "The loudmouth scurrier is threatening folk again. Why not just draw your knife out too? Then you will be able to prick the Horn Head's backside when she finally does us all a favor and sits on you."

Hudson's tiny eyes bulged. "Oh, you little…"

The bison made a swipe at Harris, but the beaver evaded her swing. Pep, however, shoved him back into Hudson, who quickly hoisted him into the air and snorted in his face.

"Put me down right now!"

The shouting escalated, echoing through the gamefield, and as Clinton watched, his anger dissipated into bewilderment. A whistle suddenly blasted out, stopping the ruckus dead in its tracks.

"Now what in skorr is goin' on?" yelled a voice behind Clinton. "A lady leaves to use the bathroom for one second and it's total pandemonium."

Clinton turned to see a cheetah, wearing dented lazarball armor, swaggering down onto the gamefield. The armor's exposed wires were bound with strips of grackhide, while studs and rusty patches had been grafted to it in an attempt to rectify its deficiencies and damage. A mixture of relieved anger stirred within him.

"*Hiro?*"

"S'up, Narfell? Ohhhh, you look shocked, sugar."

"Are you kidding? I thought after Wooburn, and the cells... Well, I didn't know what to think."

She shrugged and swung her helmet in her hands. "Yeah, well, all that scrud is in the past. Now there's no stoppin' me."

The lion stared long at Hiro, but she carefully evaded his gaze. He turned back to Harris. "I don't understand. What are you both doing here?"

"We came to save your sandy ass, lion, that's what we're doing here," laughed the cheetah. She strutted to a stop in front of him and stroked his cheek. "Awww, you look petrified, Clint. It's okay. I don't bite...much."

Clinton nudged her hand away. "Seriously, will someone tell me what's going on here?"

"What? No one has told you yet?" smirked Harris, dusting down his armor as the bison finally lowered him to the floor. "Poor Narfell."

"Shut your mouth, Lakota," Clinton hissed. "Remember daddy's not here to protect you anymore."

"Yeah, 'cause daddy's too busy licking Ocelot boots," laughed Hiro.

Harris folded his arms. "Say what you will, Hiro, but—"

"What do you mean licking Ocelot boots?" interrupted Clinton.

The cheetah shook her head. "Are you serious? You *are* out of it, aren't you? No anumal with a shred of sense'd go anywhere near Wooburn nowadays...not unless they've the right...attributes, of course." She extended her claws and flicked her long tail at him.

"But...if Ocelots have taken Wooburn, then..." Clinton spun to

204

face Hagen, panic gripping him. "We can't stay. They'll kill him."

"He will be fine."

"But—"

"Trust me, Clinton."

"How do you know though?"

"Because Raion will be protected."

"Listen, we're here, and he's in danger." The lion looked at Harris and Hiro, then at Hudson and Pep, now perched on the bison's shoulder. "I'm going home."

"No," Hagen grabbed his shoulder. "Please."

"You heard what she said." He shrugged off Hagen's hand. "Raion is in the middle of a scrudding war zone, and you just expect me to stay here?"

"Did you not listen to Garron? Raion is protected by Aegis. Even a town such as Wooburn is within its reach. Trust in what we tell you." Hagen placed his hand on the lion's shoulder again. "We must take down the Ocelots, Clinton, and you must defeat Dallas to allow this to happen. Otherwise the problems will only intensify...for all of us."

Clinton gritted his teeth, but his panic withered under Hagen's stare. He felt his cheeks burning.

"Okay. If you say he's protected, then...then I trust you. But if one hair on Raion's head is hurt—"

"He will be fine."

"Good. So what do we do? Obviously there's a plan or else I wouldn't be here having to stomach these two." He indicated to the cheetah and beaver. "What exactly is Garron up to? Are we supposed to beat them at lazarball or something?"

"That is exactly the plan," answered a voice from Garron's doorway.

The group turned to see a shadow lingering behind the gator.

"Who's that you're gonna surprise me with now, huh?" huffed Clinton. "Oh, let me guess. It's Krog? No, wait...Galront, isn't it, back from the dead?"

"Do you think this is funny lion, because I do not see any reason for humor?" replied the shadow. A sleek figure removed her helmet and slipped past Garron to gracefully cross the rope bridge. She slid down into the gamefield. "We are in a dire situation. Countless anumals are being killed out there, and you think it is appropriate to make jokes?"

Clinton gulped, unable to take his eyes off the newcomer. The fox's boots clicked an angry beat against the metal floor with her every step. She unclipped her shooters and tossed them aside as her fiery gaze swept across the group, finally locking on to the lion.

Clinton tried his hardest to remain neutral, yet he felt his cheeks burning. "And...you are?"

The fox said nothing.

"Clinton Narfell," said Hagen, clearing his throat. "May I introduce Vito Inarrai. Apologies Vito, he has been through a lot these past few weeks, and is anxious about his brother."

Vito's eyes twitched, yet remained unreadable. "We all have worries, Hagen. It appears, though, that some are better at dealing with their issues than others."

Clinton stepped forwards, a retort on the tip of his tongue, yet he stopped himself. "I...I only want to know what's going on. Is that too much to ask?"

"Of course not, it is perfectly understandable. What is not acceptable, however, is acts of aggression against my team. So you all have a murky past together?" Her cold stare drifted over the Wooburnians. "Deal with it."

Clinton scowled.

"Deal with it? You've no idea what these scruds put me through. And I've only just met you, Vito, or whatever your name is, so back off. Okay?"

Vito smiled. "Sure. I know, why not go for a bite to eat so you can tell me what a horrible life you must have endured? I promise not to mention how most of my friends were recently murdered. I would not want to put everyone in a bad mood for the mission."

Clinton growled, his temper flaring. "What are you talking about? What mission?"

Vito yanked off her gloves. "I have seen him, you know. Dallas."

The lion went cold as the breath stalled in his throat. "Where?"

"He was with the creature they call Nightmare. And believe me, Dallas was anything but childish the day he torched my village, slaughtered the mayor, and took most of the villagers as slaves."

Clinton sighed, lowering his head. "Okay, I get it. I'm sorry."

"Yes, well, at least some modicum of good came from those events."

"What?"

"I discovered the Ocelots' plan."

Clinton nodded. "So what do they intend to do?"

"Dallas has invoked the old laws regarding the accumulation of land and power. I trust you have witnessed the shamans busy in the streets?"

"You mean the crazy flyers hawking on about Mar Mi-Den?"

"Indeed. Somehow Dallas has the cooperation of the shamans, who are preaching that war is upon us, and after the recent feline attacks, anumals are all too eager to believe them."

Clinton huffed and shook his head. "Well, the shaman's words sounded like a load of dung to me."

The light reflected off the fox's rippling, burgundy lazarball armor, accentuating her lithe curves. A tail, like a red and white fountain, sprouted out and curled around her feet. "When your home, family, and friends are being enslaved, you tend to sway towards possibilities that generate hope. Most ruined villages, had they been given the opportunity, would have jumped at the chance to compete…anything to stop the bloodshed. Silania's ways offer them hope, however twisted her preachers have now become."

"Okay, point taken, but how does this involve us?"

Vito looked over the gathered anumals. "Unless we intend to chase our tails wasting time trying to track down Dallas, we should head to the one place we know he is guaranteed to be at."

Clinton snatched a glance at Hagen, before turning back to Vito again. "You mean he's there now?"

"No. But he will be." Her tail flicked. "The High Shamans have invoked the colony clause, allowing the games to proceed.

There is to be a month of tournaments held within the ancient city, open to any clan or team wishing to compete. The rules are simple: you beat a team, you win a portion of their land or riches. The further a team progresses, the more likely you are to face a major team. If the spirits favor you, then even the smallest village could win territories such as Middle City."

"Huh!" shuddered the cheetah. "Just imagine what that slime ball Ferris Lakota would do with a prize like that."

Vito nodded. "Even worse, imagine what this Dallas would do if he gained not just a few, but most of the major cities in Nomica."

"It doesn't bare thinking about," said Pep, still perched on Hudson's shoulder.

"The Ocelots, however, can only go so far against joint opposition. And with resistance building from the clans, it is becoming—"

"Stupid!" interrupted Clinton. "Would you seriously do it? Would you risk losing your land for the sake of—"

"Yielding your pride and honor?" Vito snapped. "You all speak of Harris's father as if he is a monster, but do you really think the other leaders are all that different? Ferris Lakota sounds like a two-nug charlatan in comparison to some of the city rulers I have met."

"Hey!" shouted Harris, puffing his chest out. "That is my father you are badmouthing."

"Yeah, but she's right, y'know," muttered Hiro.

The beaver sighed. "I suppose."

"So what happens if you don't own land?" asked Clinton. "Not everyone has a village to put on the line."

"Well, that is where credits come into it; if you do not wager land, then you must wager credits. And the fees to play are costly."

Clinton looked skeptical. "So what would your team be wagering then? And who'd be paying for it? The gator?"

Vito looked up at Garron. "That is not your concern. All you have to worry about is competing. Well, competing…and making it into the major rounds, of course. If we make it there, then we are guaranteed a shot at confronting Dallas."

"What guarantee do we have he'll be there though?"

Vito stepped closer. "I am not usually a betting anumal, Clinton Narfell, but I would wager my very life on Dallas being present at the finals. Why would he miss the grand conclusion to a tournament he instigated?"

Clinton knew skorr would freeze over before Dallas would miss a chance to publicly flaunt his power. "But what if an Ocelot team doesn't reach the finals?"

"Oh, the Ocelots will be there, in one form or another. Their plan seems too convoluted to be merely about a lazarball tournament. The final games, however, guarantee us a chance at facing off against him." She swept her gaze over the gathering. "Depending on whether we are ready for such a faceoff, of course."

"This is madness. Pure madness." Clinton's brow creased. He turned back to Hiro and Harris. "I mean, if you need a team, then couldn't you have got some better team players?"

"You're welcome, glux!" snapped Hiro.

"Ignorant swine," added Harris.

Clinton's shoulders slumped. He saw Garron leaning against the door, smirking.

"Hang on." The lion turned back to the team. "We'll need eight players to enter, and with Hagen and me included, that makes seven."

He turned back to stare at the gator.

Garron's eyes widened and he cracked out laughing. "You wish, kiddo. Not a chance."

The gator turned, walked back inside, and closed the door behind him.

"Okay then, if it's not Garron, then who is the eighth player?" asked Clinton.

Vito smiled.

CHAPTER NINETEEN

FIRST SACRIFICE.

Later that night, Clinton and the team settled down for dinner. His meal consisted of krig meat, stewed in a thick bone marrow sauce, accompanied by hard bread and butter. It was washed down with a mug of water. Seated at the perimeter of the benches, he could feel every anumal studying him. Occasionally his name could be heard amongst the din of conversation.

Hiro nudged him.

"Don't worry, sugar," she said, scraping out every last drop of stew from her bowl. "I only arrived a few days ago and they looked like that at me too. S'what you get when you look as fine as we do."

Pep tore her bread roll in half and pointed at him. "Hardly the same, though, is it? He's supposedly going to save us from destruction. While you...well, you're here doing nothing but talking loudly."

Hiro slammed her bowl down and shoved it in front of Pep. "Shut it, scuttler. Now be a good girl and fetch me some more food."

Pep's forehead creased. She calmly swept the bowl from the table, and as it clattered across the floor, anumals stopped to peer at the group. Clinton lowered his head, trying to escape their scrutiny.

I can't even eat a meal without finding trouble.

Someone touched his shoulder. He looked up to see Vito standing there.

"Come on. You must be exhausted. I will show you to your room."

* * *

As the two walked through the lair slits of light leaked from the storefronts and makeshift rooms. The noise from the food hall soon faded away, replaced by the deep rumblings of generators.

"Anumals bed down wherever they can," said Vito. She gestured up at the hanging crates, swaying slightly against the ropes tethering them into position. "And, as you can see, the more folk that join the cause, the more limited space becomes."

They circled around a parked flatbed carriage; its engine still radiated heat.

"Does everyone join Aegis like I did?"

"Oh no, you definitely took the express train," she answered, smirking, as she led the way. "Anumals outside of the organization, those who truly believe in Aegis, will not stop until they find us, be it a day, a month, or even years. If they search, then they will be detected and watched. And only when Garron and the others are completely satisfied with them, will they be given clues to our existence. Even then it can take an age to find us. That was how things used to be anyway..."

She stopped to inspect the surrounding storefronts, and then peered back at him. "Now, well, it seems the entry requirements have altered."

Clinton pondered her words.

"Have you ever known anything like this before? With the clan friction and the talk of war?"

She stared blankly at the floor for a few seconds before eventually heading off. "Come on. This way," she said.

Clinton took the hint and decided to change the subject. "So, the newcomers, how did they get into Aegis so quickly?"

"Trust, and lots of it. Anumals want to fight, so Aegis gives them the opportunity. Of course not many know the true depth of Aegis's resolution, but I suspect this mall is probably just the tip of the iceberg...as is Garron."

Clinton nodded, grasping how much anumals had been forced to adapt to the changing world. Normality seemed to have slipped so far from his reach that he barely recognized it anymore. They cleared the main plaza and walked down a sloping gangway leading to a pair of metal doors. Vito pulled them open to reveal a long corridor lit by low-buzzing bulbs. Clinton watched the light bounce across her red fur. Having changed out of her lazarball armor, she now wore pulled-down overalls with the arms tied around her waist. An oil-stained vest showed off her slender physique and elegant neck.

"S-so, Vito, how long have you been here?"

"About a week. I have visited the lair twice previously though."

"Oh, so you don't live here permanently?"

"No, I have never really had any cause to." She looked over her shoulder at him. "Until now, that is."

They continued to walk in silence for some time. The corridors seemed to merge into one another, each constructed from the same sheet metal walls and overhead steam pipes. Eventually, the two approached another set of doors.

"Ah! At last." She held the door wide for him to walk through. "It is not much, but it beats what most have to bunk in."

"You're telling me."

A wall of eight shipping containers was stacked before him, consisting of four along the bottom row, and another four resting on top. He could see beds and furniture within each one, all illuminated by candles. A large, metal table stretched out in the center of the room, with everything from empty mugs, newspapers, hand weights, and gamefield diagrams spread across it. Overhead, a twisted puzzle of piping hissed tiny jets of steam, and from the back corner of the room thudded the sound of clanging metal.

"Will they ever clean up after themselves?" muttered the fox, lifting an empty mug from the table to sniff it. She winced, before shouting, "It is me!"

"Won't be a moment!" someone replied, over the loud clanging. "Just getting…"

There was a dull thud.

"OW!"

A tool smashed to the floor before a huge figure emerged from the corner, sucking his thumb while carrying a pile of dented lazarball armor. From his cut-off trousers to his large shirt, the elephant appeared almost exactly as he had in Wooburn.

"I'm telling you, Vito, this is a bad idea. I know how much he liked…"

The elephant looked up, and his words stopped dead. Clinton began to chuckle. He ran his hands through his hair and shook his head in disbelief.

"Mother of Treb! Ephraim? Is it really you?"

"As I live and breathe." Ephraim's face melted into a smile. He let the armor drop with a clang and rushed to embrace the lion in a hug.

"I was told I'd see you tonight, Clinton, but I thought I'd have more time." He released the lion. "Wanted to put some clean clothes on and—"

"Whoa, Ephraim, it's only me."

"Yeah, I know it's crazy, but when you picture meeting someone in your head so many times, and you think about what you should say, and then I heard you were coming, which made me anxious, because I just wanted to—"

"It's fine." Clinton raised his hands. "It's all cool."

"No, Clinton, it's not. All I've wanted to do since I left Wooburn is say I'm sorry for what happened—"

"Sorry for what?"

"Y'know, that I was too much of a coward to stick up for myself. Sorry that you got dragged into my problems. That I ran away and left you in a mess—"

"Ephraim—"

"No, I should've helped you like you helped me, Clinton, but I didn't. I ran." He bowed his head. "No one had ever stood up for me before, and then you did. But you got exiled for it, and…well, it's all my—"

"It's not your fault. And I don't blame you. If I hadn't been hauled into the cool down cage for the incident with the Sabers, then I'd've just been hauled in for something else. It was inevitable. And your part in the whole, stupid affair was tiny. And unintentional." Clinton shook his head. "I was always going to be kicked out of the village one way or another, with or without your help."

Ephraim shrugged. "I…I just always imagined we'd have a

213

chat over a grain water, and I could apologize."

"Well, I don't really like grain water, it tastes like dung, so that was never gonna happen."

Vito cocked her head to the side and smirked. "Remind me to give you some lessons in tact, lion."

"What?"

"Nothing." She placed a hand on her hip. "However, thanks to you, Clinton, I now owe Hiro five nugs."

"Why?"

"I bet her that you would try to tear Eph to pieces, and it appears I was wrong." She turned to study the lion with more intent. "You certainly are an enigma."

Clinton looked from the fox to the elephant, and burst out laughing. Ephraim joined in, and even the fox smiled. "I take it Ephraim is our eighth team member then? Let me guess, our target keeper?"

"I certainly am."

Vito patted the huge elephant on his shoulder. "Best I have seen in a long time."

"Well, I'm glad to see at least one friendly face here." He looked over at the giant shipping containers. "And I take it this is where I'll be sleep—"

Before Clinton could finish his sentence, his eyes fell upon the pile of lazarball armor by Ephraim's feet. The scuffed trims now had only the barest remnants of gold on them. A metallic-blue hue still coated the finely crafted metal, but the detailing on the attachments, and its intricate wiring, rang warning bells in the lion's head. He felt sick to the stomach.

"What...the..." He took a hesitant step closer to the armor, and picked up the dulled, gray helmet. "This is... What have you done?"

"I was told to do it," gulped Ephraim. He turned to Vito while wringing his hands. "I said we shouldn't, that it was wrong, but—"

"But you decided to trash it? Have you any idea what this armor means to me?"

"I told them. I did. I said—"

Clinton slammed his helmet against the tabletop, making the elephant flinch. "It's irreplaceable! This was the only thing I had left from my mother...from my old life, and you've completely ruined it!"

Ephraim backed away. "Please, Clinton, I—"

"Stop it!" snapped Vito. "You are acting like a fool. Ephraim is not the one to blame; he was following orders. If anyone is to be held responsible for this, then it is me."

Clinton knelt down and snatched up his breastplate, now dulled to a slate color. "You had no right."

"Clinton, it had to be done. I showed Harris your armor when you first arrived and he recognized it instantly. Just think what would happen if someone from Wooburn chanced to see you? It is too conspicuous. What if Dallas—"

"You didn't even consider asking me first?"

"Would you have allowed us to do it?" When Clinton did not reply she said, "Answer me this: would you have played a game wearing any armor other than your own?"

He studied his scuffed elbow pads and remained silent.

"I thought not." She picked up his shin pads. "Believe me, recently we have all had to make sacrifices for the greater good."

Clinton snatched his pads from her and threw them at the table, sending objects flying in every direction.

"Leave me alone."

Vito turned to Ephraim, indicating he should leave. "Your container is on the top level, Clinton, the last on the right."

Clinton ignored her and quietly gathered his armor together.

In an unforgiving voice, she said, "You may have learned a lot from Hagen in your travels, but you have still much to understand. Let me offer you a piece of advice: the actions of one often affects the outcome of many. We are all going to be faced with options we do not like, lion, and sacrifices we do not want to make. And the sooner you accept this, the easier it will become. This is not just about me." She pointed after the departed Ephraim. "Or him. Or you. It is about *everyone*. Your armor is not the first sacrifice that has been made on this journey, and it certainly will not be the last, but it might just save all of our lives."

With that, the door slammed shut, leaving Clinton alone.

* * *

The container seemed suffocating. Clinton did not know how long he had sat on the floor with his back against the wall, but his candle had long since burned away into a blob of wax. A thin blade of light sliced through the crack in his door. A deep, repetitive snore rumbled from the container below. If he guessed right Ephraim would be in that container, with Hagen in the one next to his own. He sighed and shuffled into a more comfortable position. He had heard the others in the group return, heard the creak of their doors and the muffled sound of Hiro bickering with Harris and Pep. Still dressed in his travel clothes, the fresh trousers, boots, and shirt that had been left for him remained untouched on his bed. His lazarball helmet rested on his lap.

This is madness. What the scrud am I doing here?

He ran his hand over the helmet and felt the scored metal ridges under his fingertips: metal that had once been forged with the most brilliant of sheens. His mother sprang to mind. He pictured her face and remembered the last time he had seen her, and then blanched at how her pride had twisted into terror the night his family had been attacked.

He rested his forehead against the helmet and closed his eyes. His heart raced. Warm tingling sensations coursed through his hands and up his arms, towards his chest. His head felt heavy, causing his breath to stall. A past smell lingered at the forefront of his consciousness: sweat, mixed with fur and metal, and the ever-present tinge of leather and dried blood.

"Father?" he whispered, imagining warm breath on his face, and fingers ruffling his mane. "Is that you?"

He could feel a presence next to him.

Clinton's fingers dug into the metal helmet. His body filled with energy. Hope sparked in his chest: a realization of how far he had actually come when he had thought all was lost.

216

His eyes burst open.

"Father?"

Yet there was no reply.

Everything inside Clinton screamed for him to remain completely still, for him to stay in that moment of happiness, but he knew he could not. He placed the helmet on the floor and turned.

The warmth inside evaporated and a cold wind chilled his skin. The sense of familiarity disappeared, leaving him alone again, apart from one niggling thought. He looked down at his armor and suddenly realized that whatever state of disrepair it was in, and however much anyone tried to deface it, it would always hold the same meaning in his heart, no matter its appearance.

* * *

"You hungry?" asked Vito as Clinton slowly creaked open his container door. She sat slumped in a chair with her back to him and her feet atop the table.

Clinton closed the container and looked down at the fox. "Couldn't sleep."

"Join the club," she muttered, picking up a nearby pipe. She sniffed the smoke, but did not inhale the fumes.

He frowned.

"Do not worry." She put the pipe back down again. "I do not smoke. It has just been a long time since I have smelled sunleaf. Hagen is the only one who seems to ever have any in these parts. It reminds me of home."

The lion walked along the platform and down the metal stairs towards her. "And where's that then?"

"You know, Clinton, I am not quite sure anymore." She made some room for him, giving him the option to pull up a chair, before her gaze fell to the armor in his hands. "Thinking of taking off?"

"Think I'd get far?"

"You tell me." She sniffed the air, taking in the sunleaf's bitter aroma. "After all, you are the Crystal Soul. Who could possibly stop you?"

"Right," he huffed. "Who?"

He forced a smile, but knew at that moment he would have trouble fighting his way past Harris Lakota, let alone Dallas, or anyone else who chose to oppose him. He approached a set of shabby lockers. The doors had been smashed off, but they each contained a set of lazarball armor for the team members. Clinton approached the empty locker at the end and placed his armor inside. He smiled.

"Guess my mind's made up."

"Appears so." She whipped her feet away from the table and leaned closer to him. "Everything changes, Clinton. Sometimes for the better, other times for the worse, but that does not necessarily negate their meaning."

Clinton mulled over her words before saying, "I guess not."

"I know this must feel like a blur to you. One day a Wooburnian, the next hiding out in a lair under Middle City. Nonetheless, you are not alone, and you never will be...not again."

Clinton gave Vito a tentative smile, before he finally placed his helmet on top of his armor.

The fox nodded, and said, "Now are you going to try and get some sleep, or are we going to have to put up with you dozing off on the gamefield tomorrow?"

Clinton chuckled, but offered no more conversation. However much he tried to stamp out the impulse, he still yearned to talk to her, to find out more about who she really was...yet his instincts told him to leave it alone. He walked back up to his container, and was about to shut the door, when he caught one last glimpse of her below. She stood, turned, and stared fixedly in his direction. Nestled in the darkness, he knew she could not see him staring back at her.

CHAPTER TWENTY

COLD STONES OF CONCERN.

"Vito! Heads up!"

The fox turned in the direction of the call to see a lazar speeding in her direction. It slammed into her burgundy breastplate in a hail of sparks, absorbing into it and making her chest glow an apricot orange.

A wolf dove for her.

Dropping into a sideways roll, his fingertips skimmed over her shoulder as he sailed overhead. The wolf collapsed into a heap and slowly slid to a halt by the gamefield wall. She flipped to her feet and set off running. Heading down the left flank, she tapped her glove against the glowing breastplate, transferring the lazar from her chest to her glove. Her hand lit up orange, while the breastplate dimmed back to its original color.

"I'm open!" screeched Hiro from way down the gamefield.

A large elk charged at Vito with his head bowed low, two metal-plated antlers protruding from his helmet. She glanced across the gamefield, and as predicted, defenders had begun to swarm the loud-mouthed cheetah, while Harris could not shake his own opponent.

"Oh, no you don't," shouted the elk, swishing his antlers at her.

Knowing she had only moments left before the lazar automatically fired from her glove, Vito pointed it at the gamefield wall as the ball of light exploded from it. She grabbed hold of the elk's antlers, swung herself around his body, and landed just in time to catch the rebounding lazar in her hand. Pressing her finger against the palm trigger, the lazar zipped through the glove's circuitry and, with a hiss, flew from the shooter and rocketed towards Pep. The mouse leaped high to intercept, and her small glove suddenly lit up cerise red. In a flash of white armor, she rolled to the side before immediately setting off running.

"Pep, to me!" yelled Hiro. "To me!"

Vito watched as two defenders obstructed Pep's path for the target keeper. The fox huffed. She would not normally have executed such a long pass, yet she had been left with no options. The player who should have been beside her centerfield was still missing. Her jaw clenched. Behind her, Hagen and Hudson advanced, pushing their defensive line forwards, while Ephraim, armed with his huge deflection shields, stood guarding their targets at the rear.

Clinton, though, was nowhere to be seen.

"OI! What're ya doing, ya stupid rodent?" hollered Hiro. "The lazar's gonna—"

The timer expired.

The lazar shot from Pep's glove, and ricocheting against the floor, headed off towards the opposing team's target keeper.

"I'll take that," laughed Harris, appearing almost out of nowhere. Flipping into action, he caught the lazar, spun around, raised his glove and fired. It blasted from his shooting mechanism on target just as a blurry figure dove in to intercept.

Faster than any anumal Vito had ever seen, Hiro caught the lazar midair, spun, and fired again. In a hail of sparks, the lazar smashed into the moving ten-point target, and a chorus of sirens blared to life, accompanied by bright, flashing lights. The cheetah flipped and landed on all fours, skidding gracefully to a halt. She whooped loudly and picked herself up from the floor.

"Did you see that?" she yelled.

Harris tore his helmet from his head. "What the scrud are you playing at?"

"Now *that* is how you do it, rodent," laughed the cheetah, raising her hand for Harris to high five her. "Watch...and...learn."

The beaver batted her hand away. "We are supposed to be stealing points from them, not each other! You just poached my goal. That lazar was on target."

"Oh, shut up and stop trying to hog the glory," she snapped, rolling her eyes. "Your 'shot' was heading for five points, and I just got us ten."

"Yeah, well if you try pulling any of that scrud on me, Hiro, then you won't know what hit you," hissed Pep.

"What is it with this team?" Hiro snapped, scowling down at

the mouse. "Maybe we'd be scoring more points if you, Bucky, and Miss Foxy over there decided to pass the bluggin' lazar once in a while."

The opposing players began to mutter as smirks and mocking glances were fired across the gamefield at one another.

Vito pulled off her helmet, called a quick break, and made her way to the water barrel at the side of the gamefield. She grabbed a cup and dipped it in.

"Something tells me Garron's barking up the wrong tree here," muttered an opossum to the elk.

Vito backed away, sitting down on the bleachers to listen to their comments.

"You're telling me," remarked the elk. "We've been playing against these clowns for over three weeks, and half the team still bicker like meyarks while the others sit back and do nothing. And don't even get me started on…the Spirit!"

"Ohhhh, the Crystal Soul," chuckled the opossum, his words laced with sarcasm. "Is that what they're calling him now? The Spirit?"

"Yeah. Thinks he's so good that he only ever comes to practice sessions in spirit."

The opossum shook his head. "Seems to me he doesn't give a damn."

The elk slammed his cup down. "Probably because he knows when we're all living under feline rule, he'll be taken into their ranks with open arms."

Vito's grip tightened around her cup. She stood with a retort on the edge of her tongue…

"Vito! Hiro! Harris! Pep! Eph! Hudson! Hagen! Get your backsides to your quarters pronto. We've got things to discuss," shouted a voice, slicing through the gamefield and stopping all conversations dead.

Garron walked back inside the nest and slammed the door shut.

* * *

221

The gator thumped his fist against the huge table, causing mugs to judder. One toppled over and its last dregs trickled onto the tabletop. "I don't want to hear no more of it! Stick to your bleedin' positions! Right, Hagen?"

"It is imperative," nodded the komodo.

"I'm just sayin' that I'd be better used as center attack," shrugged Hiro. She slouched back in her chair. "Makes perfect sense to me; I'm the fastest player you've got."

Pep slammed her plate of food down in front of her. "Yeah, and the dumbest."

Hiro's scowl whipped in the mouse's direction. "You what?"

Hudson and Ephraim tried to hide their smirks.

Vito sighed.

"Look, Hiro," interrupted Garron, "I picked you to play left attack for a particular reason. We need you to fall in line and stay in position. When the time comes, your speed'll be imperative to us. Clinton'll need to know where to look for you and trust you'll always be there."

The cheetah's cheeks bristled and her jaw clenched repeatedly. "Why are you always singling me out? I'm not the only one on this team you know."

"I'm not singling anyone out, I'm just asking you to do your job," sighed the gator.

"Fine! But that's it, okay? I signed up for this, and I'm doing my bit, but if any of you knew what I've got at stake here—"

"We have all got things at stake," informed Vito.

"Yeah, well, Narfell should be grateful then, 'cause I'm gettin' pretty sick of having to tiptoe around—"

The huge metal door creaked open.

Hiro stopped midsentence and everyone turned to see Clinton poke his head around the corner. Vito studied the lion's face, trying to ascertain whether he had heard any of the conversation. His features remained neutral.

"Clint, matey," chirped Garron, breaking the silence. "Good o' you to join. We were just...discussin' this morning's match."

Yet another match he did not attend, Vito thought.

When Clinton had first come to the lair, he had shown up for training as promised. On occasion, he looked as if he was enjoying himself, a small smile would even crack though his usually stern expression. Yet, as the days rolled by, Vito could not recall seeing the lion ever go to bed.

Since his arrival, she had waited up each night, hoping to catch a snippet of conversation with him. She would light a few sprigs of her dwindling sunleaf, and even prepare warm dooma milk for him to drink. Yet he never showed. The lion's life seemed to flip from training with the team, training with Hagen, to training by himself, and then back again, with never any time for anything else in between.

Clinton pulled up a chair next to Hagen.

The lizard leaned in close. "How was it?"

Clinton shrugged. "The same." He yawned. Dark circles like hanging baskets showed beneath his eyes, flowering with each passing day. His fur had lost its luster. "So…did I miss anything?"

"Nah, just the usual," Pep replied. "Hiro shouting her mouth off. Harris having tantrums—"

"We're all just trying to cement ourselves as a team," cut in Garron, "by discussing our relevant positions, and how we shouldn't deviate from them. Isn't that right, Hiro?"

Hiro huffed, but offered no reply.

Garron took a gulf of water and turned to the mouse. "Quick question, Pep?"

"Sure, G."

"Great." Garron sniffed. "Are you the…ahh… team captain?"

"Errr, no, boss. Vito is."

"Well, in that case, you can shut your mouth as well. I'm tired of hearing you point out everyone else's faults. Understand?"

Pep tutted, sighed, and folded her arms.

Ephraim raised his hand. "I have a question."

"Put your hand down, Eph, you ain't at school, kiddo."

"Errrr, well, you want us to be cemented as a team, right? To be a solid unit? But we haven't even got a name yet…"

"Ahhhhh." A wide smile crept along Garron's face. "Now, I

was wondering when someone'd mention that."

Hiro jumped up in her seat. "Oh, yeah, that's something I've been thinking about too. You see, I'm sick of all those morbid, industrial team names, y'know, like the Spratown Spine Snappers, and the Marshland Mashers. I was thinking we could go with something a bit more...dynamic, something that sticks in people's minds and rolls off the tongue. Something like...The Legion of Light."

The room was plunged into silence as every pair of eyes drifted over in Hiro's direction, and then towards one another. Slowly, the cracks of smiles escaped as the team tried their hardest not to laugh.

Garron cleared his throat. "Well...that's a fine suggestion there, Hiro, and one we may well use in the future, but I'm afraid I've already registered the team under a particular name."

"Typical." She slumped back in her chair. "So what have you lumbered us all with then?"

Garron waggled his eyebrows as he walked over to the team's tactical board. He pulled off the black cloth covering it to reveal a logo depicting a lightning bolt in the shape of a clenched fist.

"Ladies and gents, I present to you the Middle City Bolt Throwers."

A smile beamed from Pep's face. Hudson nodded in approval. Hagen remained unreadable, yet Vito thought she saw the hint of a smile cross Clinton's face.

Hiro chuckled. "Well, I think it's rubbish."

"You would," snapped Pep.

"Listen, sister, if I'm puttin' my neck on the line for you lot, then I want it to be recognized as something *vaguely* cool. Not plain old boring...drumroll...the 'Bolt Throwers.' I mean, c'mon!"

"How about the Loud Mouth Morons?" asked Pep.

"How about you *shut* your mouth?"

"How about you make me?"

"Pep! Hiro!" snapped Garron. He took a firm hold of his lapels. "Both of you shut it!"

Hiro stood up and shoved her chair away, letting it tip over.

"All I'm saying is, if we're the ones prancing headfirst into a kraggon's nest, then let's at least do it with a bit of style. Scrud, we're gonna need every drop of help we can get when the time finally comes."

Stomping over to the other side of the room, she entered her container and slammed the door shut.

No one said a word.

Garron looked at his watch.

"Just over thirty minutes this time," he noted, finally breaking the silence. "Thirty-four to be exact. Anyone close?"

Hudson tossed a slip of paper onto the table. "Nope, I had forty-five minutes."

"Twenty," huffed Pep. "The one time she lasts over thirty minutes without storming off, and I have to bet under. What was I thinking?"

Hagen smiled with his lopsided grin. "Twenty-five."

"Thirty," Ephraim linked his fingers behind his head and leaned back confidently. "Three. Zero. Read it and weep, losers."

"Well, you can take your thirty and shove it, Ephraim, because I have thirty-five," squirmed Harris, gleefully waving his slip of paper. "I believe that makes me the winner. Now, if you could all be so kind as to pay up?"

With a sigh, each anumal flicked a nug in Harris's direction. He chuckled while tucking the coins into a small belt pouch. "Right then." He smiled. "If you will excuse me, I do believe I have credits to count."

The team groaned and grumbled as the beaver practically skipped away to his container.

Vito, though, said nothing.

Laughter and bets were not going to save the day, and looking at the lion sitting across from her, she doubted very much he was going to do it either.

* * *

Hiro had slammed three mugs of grain water on the tabletop at their evening meal.

"And let that be a lesson to you all," she gloated. "Don't ever try pull the wool over a Wooburnian's eyes again. Okay?"

After that, the cheetah snatched up a mug and took a large gulp of the foamy liquid, letting it spill down the side of her mouth. "Next time you bet on me, my fellow teammates, just make sure I'm not in the know, or else me and Harris'll have to fleece you out of even more of your credits. Ain't that right, eh, Bucky?"

She nudged the beaver, who had turned bright crimson. "Mother of Treb! You have the biggest mouth, Hiro."

As the arguing began, Vito had stood up from the table and slipped away to her quarters before anyone could notice her departure. Now, the candles that she had set alight a few hours ago had all but burnt out. Laying on her bed, she stared at the thin beam of light shining through the doorway. Try as she might, though, the sinking feeling in her stomach had still to dissipate. She moved onto her side and continued to watch the light, feeling her eyes growing heavy.

Vito did not know how long she slept, but by the time her eyelids fluttered open, she heard voices nudging at her awareness from the main room. Slipping quietly from her bed, she peered through the gap in her door.

Hagen and Clinton sat at the long table below with two candles providing them minimal light. A covered cage was set between them while Hagen held its top. Her keen hearing picked up the scuttle of feet in the shadows, as if something had been let loose inside the room.

"Now, Clinton, meyarks are masters at hiding. Even with your enhanced vision they can be difficult to spot when immobile."

Clinton shrugged. "Nothing a rotten leg of leece wouldn't remedy. Offer one up, and it'd break cover."

"Good point," laughed the komodo, "if you have a leece leg in your possession. However, what would you do in the wild? Carry chunks of meat on you at all times? Make yourself the quarry to even more scavengers? No. Besides, your adversary will not always be a meyark, as you well know."

Clinton studied the shadows, looking for the scuttler. "So who are today's lucky candidates then?"

Hagen lifted the cloth covering the cage to reveal two tiny creatures beneath. Vito squinted to try and make out what they were. One looked like a fat grub, roughly the length of her finger, which squirmed and wriggled on the tabletop when the light hit it. The other creature remained curled in a ball with hundreds of tiny needles covering its spine. When Hagen nudged the creature, it raised its head a fraction to reveal two eyes that glistened in the dim light. Vito immediately recognized it.

Clinton leaned forwards on his elbows to study the creatures, before his gaze finally landed on the spiky scuttler.

"Okay," he nodded. "Okay, I think I'll use the groucher."

Hagen stepped back. "What are you waiting for then?"

Clinton lifted his hand up, and held it there, wavering, before finally turning to the grub. He placed his hand on the wriggling creature and closed his eyes. Vito's breath stalled. She felt as if she was intruding on something immensely private, yet could not avert her gaze.

Hagen observed the lion like a statue. "Concentrate," he hissed.

Clinton's forehead scrunched...

...And then Vito saw it...

Like the spiraling smoke from her burlico pipe, white misty tendrils drifted up from the grub. Pulled towards Clinton's fingertips, the glowing light smothered his hand before being absorbed into it.

Vito gasped.

So that's how he does it.

Clinton started to shake. He lifted his hands in front of his face, and his shoulders heaved. Letting out a strained growl, he slowly pushed his chair back and fell to one knee, hunkering down into a hunting position. When he finally raised his head again, he sniffed the air, before his eyes swept over the sleeping containers.

Vito jumped away from the door, her heart pounding. Nonetheless, the sight of his face lingered in her mind.

"No," she gasped, trying to catch her breath. "That's

impossible."

Clinton's face had completely changed. His eyes had widened, and had flashed green as they caught the light.

Holding her breath, she moved back to the crack in the door, only to find the lion had disappeared. Footsteps suddenly clattered above: gentle padding beats that slipped across the roof and onto the next container.

"Good, Clinton." Hagen nodded. The lizard carefully nudged the small grub-like creature in front of him, and it wriggled slowly at his touch. "Very good."

The smell of rotting meat piqued Vito's attention. She lifted her hand in front of her nose, trying to block the smell, when a high-pitched squeal rang out, before dying down again.

Vito waited in silence.

Soft footsteps moved along the roof, until something dropped down into Hagen's arms. Clinton quickly followed to land beside the waiting lizard.

"There," said the lion. "As requested."

"Excellent." Hagen patted the lion's shoulder and studied the struggling meyark. "Although you have forgotten something."

"Oh, yes, of course."

Clinton picked up the grub from the table and watched it wriggle in his hands. Grunting, the lion's features cracked and popped back to normal, and his eyes resumed their original shape. The grub went rigid as the silvery mist was returned to it. Vito snatched a slow, shallow breath, careful not to make them aware they were being observed, while Hagen carefully placed the meyark back in its cage.

"Tell me. How did that feel for you, Clinton?"

The lion picked up a tankard of water and took a sip. "Easier, I think. Although, those grubs sure leave a bad taste in your mouth."

Hagen smirked. "So why did you pick the grub?"

"Come on, Hagen." He wiped his brow. "I already told you the answer."

"Then humor me."

Clinton dropped into a chair. "Meyarks can't resist rotten meat, right? So it's only commonsense to catch them that way. The groucher, well, it has night vision, yes, but it'd only let me see where it was hidden, and not help me actually catch it. Whereas the waste grub has night vision, but also secretes an odor that attracts predators to eat it. Once eaten, it lives inside its host's stomach, feeding off whatever it devours, until it's removed or dies of old age...or of hunger."

"You are not exaggerating about the odorous secretion, Clinton. My advice is to take a shower," quipped Hagen, wafting the air. He tossed him a towel. "Although, it was the perfect choice for the trial. You siphoned just the right abilities to enable a quick capture with minimal effort. Good work, and good judgment."

Clinton took another sip of his water and inspected the grub closer. "So it was fully conscious after I siphoned its juice?"

The komodo chuckled. "Yes. You siphoned only a fraction of its energy. It was weakened, but it lived. Good work all around I would say."

"I'm just glad I didn't kill another creature." Clinton swilled some more water around his mouth. "To tell the truth, it did feel a lot easier to isolate what I needed, instead of ripping out its whole soul again."

A twinge of dread swept through Vito.

Hagen patted Clinton on the back. "It is a big step that you have taken. You should feel more confidence in your abilities. I do."

The lion shrugged. His shoulders seemed to drop with the weight of an invisible burden. "I just think we've a long way to go yet, Hagen. This evening could have just been pure luck."

Vito backed away from the door and sat on the edge of her bed. Her mind was awash with activity, processing all that she had seen and heard. Exhaling, she started to tremble, but forced herself to calm down. Since the lion had joined Aegis, a sinking feeling had festered inside her; they were placing so much responsibility on an inexperienced outsider.

A stone of anxiety dropped in her stomach. She slipped to the floor and reached under her bed. Cool, polished wood brushed against her fingers as she took out the small box. She opened it up and studied the shiny, black egg lying innocently inside. It filled her with a flight of emotions from hope, to regret, to betrayal. She reached out, but stopped herself from touching it.

"No!" she hissed. "This is not the way."

Vito slammed the lid shut and pushed the box back under the bed. She clasped her hands and lay down, staring at the metal ceiling, torn with indecision. Whatever power she had seen Clinton accomplish that night was almost insignificant when compared to the trials she knew he would soon have to face. Would the lion be enough to stop the encroaching darkness?

He will not let us down.

He cannot.

* * *

The days in Garron's lair seemed to merge into a blur of training and team talks, interspersed with food and sleep.

Vito sat apart from the others at the back of the food hall. The evening had once again crept in. Over the hum of conversation, she could hear Hiro's voice peaking above the cacophony. Gritting her teeth, the fox scooped up another spoonful of stew before washing it down with some water.

"Is…is anyone sitting here?" asked a familiar voice.

Vito turned to see Clinton clutching a bowl. The bags under his eyes had matured, and she realized it had been over five weeks since Clinton had joined them at the lair.

"Oh, I errr…"

The lion began to back away. "Don't worry. If you'd prefer to sit alone then I'll—"

"No…please." She shifted her tray to allow him some space. "I was just daydreaming."

"About anything nice?"

She smiled, but refrained from giving him an answer.

The two sat in silence as Clinton moved his stew around his plate, and Vito took awkward sips of her water. Eventually Clinton let his spoon drop to the table.

"It's coming together."

"Excuse me?"

"The team," he said. "After all this time we're finally working together now."

"Yes, well, at least Hiro is now listening to us." She glanced at his tired face. "How is everything for you?"

"Oh, it's a walk in the park," he laughed, prodding a claw into his food. "That's if the park drained every shred of energy you've got each and every day."

"I must admit you do look exhausted."

"I must admit I feel it. It's like someone steals a part of me every night, only to replace it with someone I barely recognize in the morning. Still, at least everyone's stopped talking about me behind my back now."

Vito flinched and found herself unable to hold his gaze. She had thought him oblivious to the subtle insults that followed him around the lair.

Clinton picked up his bread roll, sniffed it, and tossed it to one side. "It's fine though. Nothing I haven't heard before." She cocked her head, skeptical of his bravado. He shrugged in response. "At least the team is improving. No one's beaten us in over seven days now."

"And you are becoming far more familiar with the team's strengths."

"Oh, yes. Hagen's drilled that into me all right. 'Look up front for speed and agility, and behind for strength and power.' As for you, well, you're the brains…and you're always next to me."

She nudged his spoon to pull focus from her bristling cheeks. "You should be allowed to regain your strength. They are working you too hard."

"Not hard enough if you ask Hagen."

"I will speak to him then. You cannot keep training in this fashion. Surely he understands you need rest? Otherwise more creatures could get hurt."

Clinton snapped his head around to look at her. "Creatures?

What makes you say that?"

"N-nothing. It was…" She coughed, evading his stare. "Hagen should allow you some rest."

"He does. The problem is me. I can't switch off."

"Why not?"

"I don't know. I can't focus when needed, and can't stop thinking when I'm resting."

Vito inspected the disheveled lion for a moment.

"Clinton, what is it like? The thing you do? Does it…hurt?"

"So you've seen me change."

She nodded. "Just once. "

"Well, in answer to your question then, yes, it hurts," he sighed. "But I try to hide it."

"But what does it feel like?"

"Imagine sifting through memories, secrets, and hopes until you reach the core of a very anumal's being, its pure essence. The essence isn't fixed, though, or defined, it's malleable; coated and shaped by your memories and fears, likes and dislikes. Yet, if I was to actively take them on…" He shrugged. "Well, I don't think I could handle it."

Vito tried her hardest not to fidget with unease.

The lion took a sip of water. "From there you choose to extract the full energy, or take only the bits you need. One slip, though, and—"

"The creature dies," she answered. "So…you can delve through their thoughts?"

"Yes." He sighed as his bloodshot eyes latched onto the fox. "I'm beginning to lose myself, Vito; it's too much. I'm trying so hard, I really am, but it's just… Every day I use my powers, I feel like I'm being stuffed with other creatures' energies and less of my own, like I'm being squashed so tight, bits of me are leaking out."

He stared at his trembling hands. "I think I'm going mad."

"The fact that you think so proves you to be wrong."

The lion huffed.

"So, Clinton, I assume your next task is to ignore these feelings? To learn control?"

"Yes, and I'm trying, but when you run through rain, you've gotta get wet. It's one thing to do this on scuttlers, ayvids, and sectoids, but I haven't even tried it out on an anumal yet: they're still too complex, too…corrupt. Having a sectoid's death on my hands is bad enough. I doubt I could cope if I injured an anumal."

"Bolt Throwers listen up!" blared Garron, his voice ringing through the food hall. "Back to it. We've a journey that needs preparing."

In a burst of movement, the room erupted into action.

Vito shrugged. "Well, as Garron says, I suppose."

Clinton nodded and scooped up his helmet from the floor. He looked at the fox, and said, "Thanks," before turning and heading off.

As she watched him depart, the stone of concern in her stomach hardened. She clenched and unclenched her fingers with worry. Shaking her head, she picked up her gloves, slowly following after him.

CHAPTER TWENTY-ONE

CROSSBREED.

"Reports are coming in that the northern tunnels have caved in," hollered Garron, shuffling out from the nest and heading down the stairs to the ground floor. The gator trundled over to the team, busy loading supplies onto the flatbeds. "The tracks are littered with rubble, so I've sent a party to clear 'em, and also reinforce the roof."

Hagen heaved a large crate onto his shoulder before sliding it onto the carriage. "Have you determined the cause?"

"Rock Munchers, or some similar rodent clan," replied Garron, shoving his hands inside his jacket pockets. "Heard they've been burrowin' below the streets, tryin' to claim territory between the surface and the sewers. Problem is it's making the ground unstable."

Vito picked up a crate of bottles, making the glass clink. "Anything you can do to stop them?" she asked.

"Credits, protection, or revenge are the only currencies the rodents accept nowadays." The gator sighed. "Leave it with me though. I've dealt with 'em in the past, I think I know how to handle 'em."

"Filthy rodents," Hiro sneered, lounging lazily in the driver's seat. "Worse than primates if you—"

"No one asked you!" snapped Pep, throwing her bags onto the carriage. "So shut up and help with the packing."

Clinton tossed his bag of armor next to Pep's, and helped to load more boxes.

It did not take them too long to finish, and soon they were ready to commence their journey.

After speeding through the maze of tunnels, Hudson finally brought the carriage to a reluctant stop in a derelict station. With no idea just how far they had traveled, Clinton lugged equipment up countless stairs, before stepping out into the open. The sun tickled his face for the first time in many months. He took a deep breath or air. The breeze was tainted with the odor of sewage, but it felt good to be on the surface again.

"Refreshing, isn't it, Clint?" sighed the bison, lumbering up next to him, carrying a crate on each shoulder. "Scary how you lose track of time down there."

Clinton nodded his agreement while taking in his surroundings.

A vast sprawl of abandoned buildings, toppled barricades, and overflowing drains spread before him. Countless clan symbols had been painted on crumbling walls and overhead street signs, one on top of the other, in a continual battle for dominance.. A mammoth bridge, supported by a line of tall, concrete pillars, cast a shadow over the entire street.

"You okay?" asked Hudson. "Look as lost as a gunk eel in a leece pit."

"Me? Yeah, of course. Why?"

"Just wondering." She followed the lion's gaze towards the towering bridge. "We're going into flyer territory now y'know. They build their roosts up there, away from the surface. Last anumal I know who went up there uninvited got his eyes pecked out."

"And are we? Invited, I mean."

"Let's hope so, honey, because I'm partial to keeping my sight." She winked at him before clomping off.

A pang of uncertainty struck Clinton. Garron's lair had provided him with a sanctuary, allowing the lion to hide away from the world and its newest dangers.

But now?

Picking up his backpack, he heard the familiar clink of armor. He lifted up a heavy bundle of blankets and followed his teammates up the steel staircase, towards the looming roadway above.

* * *

The full sprawl of Middle City greeted Clinton when he reached the stair's summit. Stretching out as far as he could see, plumes of smoke smeared the skyline, while disheveled buildings stabbed defiantly into the air. A chunk of concrete had crumbled away from the road not far from where he stood, and in the distance, large, wooden nest-like structures clung to the edges of the bridge like limpets, looking out over the deadly drop below.

Suddenly a titanic crashing sound juddered through the air. The team spun around in time to see a distant building collapse near Beggar's End. A plume of dust spewed up and rippled out from that area, engulfing the surrounding blocks.

Hudson lowered her crates and shook her head. "That'll be the Rock Munchers."

"Do you think the lair'll be okay after that?" asked Ephraim, standing next to her, wringing his hands.

"Yup. It'll be safe," promised Garron, resting against a crate while peering into the sky. "But unless the bloomin' circus at Mar Mi-Den works in our favor, then those streets are gonna be a battlefield in the coming months."

Clinton followed the gator's wandering gaze. "So what are we waiting for then?"

"Flyers, mate, flyers," mumbled Garron, whipping out his flask to take a sip.

"I heard what happens if you come up here without an invitation."

"Believe me, kiddo, I wouldn't have bought us anywhere near this place if we didn't have one. No one can travel through these elevated infected territories without flyers knowing about it."

"Infected territories?"

"Yeah, this place used to be primate territory." The gator blew out a giant sigh. "When a big enough group of monkeys takes up residence in a particular spot, it's classed as 'infected'."

"Disease spreaders," tutted Harris, wrapping a handkerchief around his mouth and nose.

Clinton glanced up at the buildings enveloping the road. Smashed windows acted as gateways to their gloomy innards, allowing anything desperate enough to reside inside their bellies.

"So what happened to the primates then, G?" asked Pep.

"They were moved elsewhere while the Lilac Plumes, Nimbus

Chasers, and the Whirling Banshees assumed control. Now, if anyone wants to use the elevated roads, they have to gain permission from those particular clans, pay a toll, or suffer the consequences."

"Your eyes?"

"If you're lucky, Clint. Usually it'd be your arms or legs ripped off before you're dragged into the heavens to see whether you can fly without wings."

The gator indicated the sky above them. Clinton followed the gesture and saw movement out of the corner of his eye. A bulky figure appeared in a nearby window, before another appeared a few floors above. Slowly, more and more of the figures appeared.

Garron took out a handkerchief, wiped his forehead, and said, "Right on time."

From above, a gray-winged flyer plummeted down from the heights. Clinton snatched a breath as it swooped over his head, ruffling his hair, before landing in a crouch in front of them. Wide wings brushed against the ground, before reversing and folding carefully against the newcomer's back. The stranger lifted its head slowly and looked at Garron and then Clinton. Wearing a long, red tabard with brown, leather armor covering most of her body, the tip of the flyer's beak looked sharp enough to pierce metal.

"I've heard that Blackbeard once sailed these murky shores," said the female buzzard, cocking her head to the side and speaking with a clipped voice.

"Still does." Garron's eyes narrowed to slits as he looked her up and down. "But I've seen no waves in the sea. Have you?"

"Not this day. Only a feather or two floating freely in the wind."

Garron shrugged. "Then it's plain sailing." He turned to the komodo. "Looks like we weren't followed."

"Good news all round," smiled Hagen, bowing deeply towards the young flyer. "Your assistance, as always, is invaluable."

Garron shuffled over to the tall, feathered female, his arms wide. "It's sure good to see you, Powlar."

They tenderly hugged one another, Powlar's wings wrapping

around him, completely covering the gator in her embrace, before stepping back to examine him closer. "We are always glad to help. Like a phoenix from the ashes, we Nimbus Chasers are proud to assist your ascension—"

"Enough of that!" he quipped, letting out a nervous laugh. "No one needs to hear any of that dung right now. I-I take it everything is ready?"

"The path is clear, providing—"

"Providing we don't stray, I know, honey. Some things never change."

"New Aegis may be in its infancy—"

The gator cleared his throat, and said, "Yeah, yeah, yeah. Now, down to business." He wiped the sweat from his forehead again. "So everything's been made to my design then?"

The buzzard nodded. "Built by Reffien, and to your specifications."

"Reffien? Should have known he'd stick his talons in. He's clever enough to recognize a gem when he sees one." Garron looked back towards Powlar and winked. "You don't know how good it is to see you."

"I *do* know nothing I say will stop you from pursuing this madness. Your stubbornness is as rigid as your hide—"

"Polite as always," Garron muttered.

"...so I will not attempt to convince you otherwise. However, please try to return from this madness in one piece, father."

Garron patted her arm affectionately before hugging her again.

"Father?" blurted Clinton, letting the word sink in. He turned to Hagen. "Is she joking?"

"Long story," the komodo replied. "Very long."

Garron pulled out of the hug to face the team.

"Right, you lazy scruds!" he shouted, jolting Clinton from his thoughts. "Get off your butts and get everythin' ready. Hiro! Stop lookin' so bloody gormless and get to work!"

The cheetah picked up a small bag and tossed it over her shoulder. "Okay! Okay! Keep your scruddin' hide on. But just what, oh, leathery leader, are we supposed to load our goods onto?"

"Why this, of course," smiled Powlar, before raising her head and screeching so loud it echoed off the buildings.

A vehicle, of sorts, slowly peeked into view as it reversed around the closest wooden nest. Two Olde-world buses had been fixed together, with thick metal plating attached to the sides. Metal bars lined the windows, and two slobbering gorespines groaned loudly from the front, having just been watered.

"Aww, look at the cute 'ikle' gorespines." Pep clapped her hands together and smiled at Harris. "I think I'll name the ugly one Lakota!"

The beaver scowled. "Well, I think I will call the other one 'Pep, shut your fat mouth, you big stinking glux!' How about that for a catchy name?"

"How about we call them 'Harris and Pep, keep *both* your traps shut or else I'll personally feed the two of you to the bloody things'?" snapped Garron, stopping them from bickering. "Good. Now, Powlar, did Reffien remember the sunroof? You know how much I like to doze off in the sun. Been stuck in the dark for too long, I want to enjoy as much surface light as I can."

Powlar smirked and nodded. "Yes, father, like I said, Reffien followed your instructions to the letter."

"Looks like he came though for us then. It's big and safe enough to house a whole renegade team."

Powlar moved to his side. "Needs to be. Assaults have increased throughout the territories. Only yesterday another skirmish erupted in the Plumes' sector, causing us to retaliate. We are on edge, Garron; the clans will not tolerate much more of this." The buzzard shook her head, ruffling her feathers. "It seems the unrest is slowly spreading to the skies. Our kind is being trapped and used as scouts or carriers, and we will not allow it to continue. The clans are uniting. Why would the groundlings start something so foolish against the habrok?"

"Greed? Desperation? I'd watch your back, Powlar. Rumor is that you flyers are stashing hoards of food up in your nests. Us groundlings are starting to go hungry, we've families to feed."

"As do we habrok."

"I know that, love." He gestured out over the city. "But *they* don't. Like I said, folk are desperate, and in war—"

"Anumals will do anything to survive," she mumbled, gazing over the sprawling urban landscape. "Surely you must realize that this is some form of trap you are walking into?"

"'Course we do. And Hagen, Vito, and me have discussed hundreds of theories, but we can't be sure of what they're up to. Only thing we do know is that there's more going on than what they're spouting."

"And so you ride off into the distance looking for adventure. I do not know whether you are foolish heroes or heroic fools." She turned to stare at Clinton. The lion smiled, but could not hold her gaze for long. "You really think he is going to save us? The bison and the elephant look more the hero type to me."

"I've taught you better than to judge by appearance, Powlar."

"Of course, and I apologize," chuckled the buzzard. "Rest assured you have Nimbus eyes in the sky. I secured you safe passage through the habrok territories. You should meet no resistance from us flyers. After that, however, you are on your own."

With a nod of her head she dipped down and thrust upwards, her wings spreading wide, showing her tawny plumage in a breathtaking burst of feathers. Powlar slammed her wings earthwards and forced herself into the sky, ascending towards the heavens in a burst of majestic glory.

* * *

By the time the sun was setting, Hudson had taken the vehicle's reins and fired up the rear engines to ease some of the heavy burden off the gorespines.

"C'mon now, babies, time to get moving." She cracked the whip, and the giants jostled into action, trudging forwards and pulling the bus in their stead.

Clinton stared out the rear window and watched Middle City

disappear into the past. Every now and again he would catch a glimpse of a flying figure. Whether it was Powlar scouting for them or not, the lion could not tell.

"So, what did she mean by calling Garron father?" whispered the lion, leaning in close to Hagen. "I wouldn't have pitted Garron as a crossbreeder. You know what everyone thinks about that."

Hagen chuckled. "And there is that small town, Wooburnian attitude again."

"Hey! I wasn't saying it was my opinion."

"You were merely saying it is frowned upon for differing species to bare offspring. And after all the time we have traveled, I had hoped you would have broadened your mind to such closed thoughts. If one anumal loves another, even if it is of a differing species, then who is to say it is a bad thing?"

Clinton nodded and found his gaze drifting over to Vito. "I suppose you're right. I guess Wooburn's small-mindedness does rear its ugly head in me sometimes...but a flyer and a reptile?"

"Is just as acceptable as a feline and a canine coupling. The dominant gene will merely determine the species, and only the Great Mother can decide that fate. Besides," Hagen fidgeted into his seat, trying to get comfortable, "Garron is not Powlar's biological father. As I said, it is a long story."

Clinton looked puzzled and cast a glance in Vito's direction one last time. He rested his head against the window to watch the world pass by, and soon the darkness of the open grasslands spread out before them as far as the eye could see. The team was allotted beds, adapted from the bus's seats, and everybody finally settled down for the night without further incident.

"Right!" hollered Garron, the following morning. "We'll have just one day in Mar Mi-Den before we enter the free-for-alls, so we'd best make the most of that time. Now, this is gonna be tough. Every team who's entered'll be picked to play at random. No league or clan'll be taken into allowance. Winners'll automatically go through to the advancing stages, whereas the—"

"We don't need to hear about the losers," yawned Hiro. "We clearly won't be one of them. When's breakfast?"

"When I say so. Now shut up and listen. This isn't gonna be some fancy league match or cup-tie. Clan pride is at stake. Territory's up for grabs. Trust me, folk'll be out to win any which way they can. So just stick to what we've practiced and keep alert. Most of all, watch each other's backs."

Harris pointed at Ephraim. "Pretty hard not to when that boulder is always stood in your way."

"Careful, Lakota," smirked Ephraim, "or one of these days I'll stop standing in your way and start standing on your face."

Harris snapped back at Ephraim. Ephraim retorted, and immediately a riot of arguments exploded in the front of the bus.

From the back seats, Clinton sighed. He had the urge to bury his head in his hands, until he caught sight of Vito also sitting alone, halfway between him and the others. Dressed in a leaf-green cloak, with the hood around her shoulders, the blossoming sun cast a ruby sheen across her face. Clinton stared at her, and the buzzing voices dimmed into a mere annoyance.

"She has the correct idea," commented a voice. "Staying away from all the drama."

Clinton jumped. The back window started to rise as the komodo lifted it up and climbed inside.

"How is it up there?" asked the lion, making some space for his friend to sit next to him.

"As pleasant as traveling on a bus rooftop can be. You must remember to be careful when you meditate up there, though, and not step on that silly tarpaulin sunroof. I almost fell through it this morning."

"Now that'd be a sight," laughed the lion.

"Indeed."

"Yeah, I've gotta remember to stay injury free for the games."

"That too. However, I was referring to the fact that if you fell through the hole and landed on another member of the team, then we would not hear the last of it for at least another moon-cycle or more. And I am afraid my patience would not be able to weather that kind of battle; even I have limits."

The komodo shook his head in playful defeat.

Clinton laughed. "I'm in total agreement with you there."

"No, the roof is certainly not the most suitable retreat for meditating, but you have to make the best of a situation whenever, and wherever, you can. I would recommend you do likewise." The komodo casually glanced at Vito, and let out a low, rasping laugh. "However, I see you are...busy."

"Huh? I don't know what you mean."

"Of course not." The komodo nodded to the front of the bus. "What is the argument regarding this time?"

"Oh, the usual. Garron tried to give a talk, someone insulted someone else, the other threatened to flatten them, and then all skorr broke loose."

"So you decided to keep your distance and concentrate on...other things?"

"Hagen, I wasn't... Look, I'm just sick of the bickering. Besides, Vito's the only one who isn't shouting all the time. She's got her eyes on the bigger picture, and she's the only one who's ever talked to me about my situation. She knows this isn't all just a game."

"Some anumals view the bigger picture, while others prefer to be blinkered. However, Clinton, every member of this team is fully aware of the stakes. I presume their disputes could possibly be a way for them to deal with their doubts and air their frustrations in their own way."

Clinton sat back and folded his arms. "Yes, well, it's hardly productive is it?"

The komodo's gaze lingered on Clinton for a long moment. The lion frowned.

"What? What's wrong?"

"Be careful, Clinton. That is the only advice I can give you on this matter."

"Careful about what? What 'matter'?"

"Careful about who you offer your affections to."

Clinton's mouth suddenly went dry. "What was it you were saying last night about being closed minded, eh? Besides, I don't know what you are going on about. I've hardly even spoken to her."

"Alright." The komodo raised a placating hand. "Just remember, though, that the outcome of this mission remains hidden to us all. When the time comes, you will need to act with purpose and with conviction. Personal feelings cannot obstruct—"

"They won't. All the team has to do is get me to Dallas...and then we'll see what happens from there."

Hagen squeezed the lion's shoulder and smiled. "She *is* a fine looking vulpine. I will admit—"

"Hagen."

"Just watch your step."

Clinton slouched back in his seat.

At the front of the bus the ruckus had settled and the vehicle was slowing down. It verged off the road and onto a dirt track, where it finally ground to a halt. The team alighted as one, while Vito hung back, pulled her hood up, and slipped out alone. Clinton remained in his seat, watching her depart.

He turned to Hagen.

"Do you think Dallas has any of these problems? I doubt his followers bicker the way we do."

"No, they fight using sharpened blades. You forget, Clinton, that our team is here because it wants to be. Garron helped me pick them, but they could always have said no. I would rather bear a whole moon's cycle of Harris and Hiro squabbling than spend one single moment in the company of an Ocelot."

With a nod of his head, Hagen stood up and disembarked the vehicle, while Clinton peered out the window at his teammates.

Our team is here because it wants *to be.*

Yet, deep down, Clinton would not think twice about deserting them all if it meant him getting his brother back. It seemed that Dallas had been given an option to embark on his own calling. Whereas himself? He had never been given any choice.

If the Bolt Throwers are all here by choice, he sighed, *then that makes me the odd one out yet again.*

* * *

244

Breakfast eventually consisted of fried leece steak.

No sooner had Hiro seen the stewed grain on offer for them, than she dashed off the bus in a blur of yellow and black. When Clinton watched her skulking low in the long grass, a sense of admiration sparked inside him. He knew how the confines of Garron's lair must have felt for her. Much like himself, she was Plains born, brought into the world with nothing but wide expanses surrounding her. He smiled when she skidded to a swift halt, only a short distance from a grazing herd of leece.

The memory of the time he had confronted a herd in the Plains spiked in his mind. He remembered how they had surrounded him, moving in closer and closer for the kill...until he had commanded them to stop. He had been lucky to escape alive. Back then, he had never fully understood what he had done or how, but somehow his fear had caused him to use his raw powers. He could still remember the pounding of their hearts, taste their fear, and feel their muscles primed, until he finally released them from the spell.

I touched their souls, and I didn't even know it, he mused, watching the herding scavengers, their spider-like legs stabbing into the soft earth. *It all makes sense.*

The lion frowned.

"Even seasoned trackers hunt them in pairs," he mumbled.

Yet Hiro had decided to do it alone.

She waited like a stone, knowing the leeces' legs would pick up any vibrations from her movements.

It would all just be a matter of timing.

Timing and patience...

Like a lazar from a glove, she sped through the pack, dividing it in two and separating an old leece from the group. As the herd panicked and warbled, she pounced, and within seconds, paralyzed the creature. Instead of finishing the hunt there and then, however, she continued to attack. Raking her claws down the flank of another leece, she snapped her head to the side to avoid a sharp leg stabbing at her face.

"Hiro!" Clinton shouted, sprinting to help.

She spun to the side, narrowly avoiding being bitten and, in a flurry of claws, slashed a large male's throat before dragging its convulsing body to the ground. Blood plumed. Clinton roared loudly, causing the remaining leece to flee. He reached the cheetah and dragged her to her feet.

"Are you okay?"

"Get off!" she grumbled, flexing her fingers. She pushed his hand away as leece blood dripped from her face. "What are you doing? I didn't ask for your help."

"Clearly," he snapped, surveying the carnage. "What *was* that? You already had one, why'd you go for another?"

"Because I wanted to," she said, repeatedly clenching her jaw. Her eyes were like saucers as she hoisted a carcass over her shoulder. "Oh, you'll thank me later when you've a full belly, lion. Now stop gawking and pick that up will you? We've breakfast to make."

Having taken it upon himself to skin Hiro's catch, Garron drained the numbing poison from the leece fangs for Vito and himself to use as weapons, before stripping it of flesh. Hagen selected some of the bones to grind into various poultices, and the meat was put aside and rubbed with salt. After eating, Hagen found a spare patch of ground to bury what was left of the carcass. Bowing his head, he lowered the remains into the hole, before covering it over.

"From earth to life, and back again, your sacrifice shall be rewarded," he muttered.

"You know that saying?" asked Clinton, halting the ritual.

Hagen's eyes narrowed.

"Oh, sorry, it's just my dad taught me to say that after every kill too. 'That which we take from the earth—"

"Must be thanked for its sacrifice, and given a just reward in the life beyond," finished the lizard. "He was a wise anumal, your father."

"What? So you knew him then?"

"Not in person." Hagen carefully rubbed the dirt from his hands. "Only from a distance."

"Hagen! Clint!" shouted Garron, stood by the entrance to the bus. "Get yourselves in gear! We need to be moving."

Clinton had not realized, but the rest of the team had packed up and boarded the bus, with Hiro now fast asleep, dead to the world, after her morning's hunt. As the sound of rumbling engines merged with groaning gorespines, they set off once more for Mar Mi-Den.

* * *

The next few days dragged by as the bus ambled onwards. Rain continually poured, turning the roads into mud and sludge filled tracks. The sky spread out in a vast expanse of grayness, without even a single dark cloud to break its monotony.

"How's your sunroof working out now, Garron?" laughed Ephraim.

The rest of the team chuckled along with him.

"Oh, button it," grumbled the gator.

Cross-legged on the roof, Clinton shook his head at the ruckus below, inhaled deeply through the rain, and concentrated on clearing his mind. For too long he had let souls build inside his body without untangling their mixed energies. Throughout his initial training, and the time spent at Garron's lair, he had focused on preparing his vessel as a defensive weapon, while ignoring his growing anxieties and tensions within. Now, it seemed to be filling up, encroaching on his soul, like tiny particles of sand constantly trickling into a vat of water.

"That's it, Clinton," muttered Hagen, seated opposite, his eyes closed. Between them, a bundle of herbs smoked under an overturned pan, scenting the air with a woody aroma. The rain drummed noisily against the pan top. "Feel the life around you. Breathe the air. You are caged no longer."

A few days previously, the carriage had rolled through a village decimated by clan fighting. Now, as they meditated, Clinton could not help but ponder the incident...

Charred buildings laid crumbling, smashed to pieces.

Abandoned vehicles, shattered glass, and toys were strewn in the mud. The cloying scent of flesh and burned fur refused to disperse, and when Clinton finally saw the anumal carcasses dangling from ropes beneath a bridge, his stomach churned. Scavenging ayvids had made fast work of the hanging banquets, but three slashes could still be seen clawed into each anumal's chest.

Ephraim's bottom lip trembled as he stared out the bus window. "You think we should give 'em a proper burial? Burn their bodies for the bone collector?"

Garron wiped his thumb across his brow. "'Fraid they're beyond that now, Eph. All we can hope for is Silania to embrace their souls, and if not, that they haunt those responsible for this to the end of their lives."

"If only." Harris looked away from the brutality and patted Ephraim on the shoulder. "I hope they find the peace they deserve."

Yet as Clinton's mind snapped back to the present day, he questioned Harris's words.

He had felt something lingering in that village.

His mind kept on flashing with visions of the murdered anumals. He could feel their pain and sense their presence, as if their pleas were begging him for revenge.

He looked up and stared at Hagen.

"They will pay."

"Who?" asked the komodo.

"The scum who ransacked that village; the Ocelots. I swear they'll pay."

Hagen nodded. "I know they will."

On the sixth day the rain finally abated, and changing direction, the bus turned west. Endless brown and tan mountains framed every side of their path, but by the time night threatened to encroach, the lights of a large settlement glimmered ahead.

"Gorespines need rest, an' we need supplies," yelled Garron from the driver's seat, while Hudson cut off the engines. "This here is Blackwater. So called due to the black stuff that shoots up from the ground and infects the water supply. Just don't be drinking from any stream, y'hear me?"

"What about Daisy and Violet?" asked the bison.

"Daisy and Violet," scoffed Harris. "What scruddy names for gorespines. My suggestions—"

"You have a complaint with the names I chose?" asked Vito, slowly turning in his direction.

"Errrr...no. Very nice names. I love them," muttered the beaver, melting under her stare.

Vito cracked a smile.

"You go girl!" chuckled the mouse, from the front of the bus.

"Don't you be worrying about the gorespines," laughed Garron. "Mayor Tiliija owes me. I'm sure he's a few barrels of clean water to help us on our way."

Yet Garron's warnings had not prepared Clinton for what he saw as they slipped through Blackwater's gates.

Heavy brick, slate, and metal piping comprised most of the village's structures, with every house smeared black and barely standing. Streams of thick, black ooze dribbled down the sides of the street, and not an anumal could be seen that had not been stained in it.

"Heard this stuff used to be worth quite a bit when mankind was around. Vito and me use it when creating mech," said Hudson, whipping her head back inside the bus to avoid a jet of spray from a leaky pipe. "You ever see it in Wooburn?"

Clinton shook his head. "Nope. Besides, if mankind found it valuable, then it's bound to be destructive, isn't it?"

Hudson wiped a splatter from the widow and examined it between her fingers. "Hmmm...never thought of it like that. You've a funny way of thinking, honey."

As the sun fully set, and polelights containing phosphorescent sectoids lit the streets, the carriage pulled to a stop in a market square situated next to a black lake. Climbing out of the carriage, an acrid smell hit Clinton's nose: a mixture of tangy chemicals and decay. Various carriages had been parked along the roadside, each sporting team logos and sigils across their sides. Gorespines, iron backs, and grinders filled the air with groans and flatulence as the beasts fed, yet their volume could not mask the raucous songs spurting from the intoxicated anumals nearby. Clinton fought the urge to get back on the bus and wait out their stay inside.

"Come on," urged Hagen, nudging Clinton onwards. "You are in need of some food and rest. How terrible can this place be?"

A town security guard shoved a drunken visitor to the ground. "Mother of Treb! We've told you there's to be no naked flames in the town, you glux. Do you want to blow us all up?"

"Yeah, doesn't that scrud know anything?" said a nearby weasel, sliding his own burlico-stick back inside his pocket.

A bar stool smashed through a tavern window.

Clinton stared at Hagen with a raised eyebrow. "You were saying?"

"I think it may be prudent to find another establishment less...rambunctious than this one."

"I agree," said Vito, observing the drama from within the folds of her cowl. "I will scout ahead with the others, try to find somewhere a little more...sedate."

With that she set off, while Hagen, Clinton, and Hudson remained behind. Grabbing one of the huge water containers mayor Tiliija had left for them, the lion and Hudson struggled to push it over the muddy path. Water sloshed over the lip, splashing the ground next to a group of drunken anumals.

"Whoa, watch it, fatso!" slurred a raccoon, before fully focusing on Hudson. He began to cackle. "Well, I've seen it all now. Watch yourself with that lump, lion, she'd crush you with one hand."

"Either that, or her huge...assets," added another, bursting into fits of laughter.

"Why don't you guys just frag off!" hissed Clinton, which made them cackle even more. He let go of the barrel and huffed. "Ignore them. They're idiots."

Hudson sent him a warm smile.

"Why would I ignore them, Clint? They're right. I'd crush 'em both in a breath." She flicked her curl away from her face and gave him a wink. "Honestly, it's not the first time I've heard it, and it certainly won't be the last. Besides, I'm considered quite the catch amongst my own breed, honey."

He smiled. "I'm sure you are."

"Growing up with a boy's name sure toughens you up. You find that words don't mean much, and when someone gets a little too noisy...you just fill their mouth with one of these..."

She raised her meaty fist and smiled sweetly.

Clinton cracked out laughing. "So why did you get called Hudson anyway?"

The bison rolled her eyes. "Pappy got it into his head that mammy was having a boy, and he wanted to call me Hudson. And when I popped out, well, everyone laughed at him...which made him even more pigheaded." She smiled fondly. "I loved that silly, stubborn, old bison, and he loved me all the more for me doing whatever I wanted to."

Clinton nodded as she slowly trundled off.

Once Daisy and Violet had been tended to he went for a stroll, then decided to meet with the others at the tavern. Walking through Blackwater's streets, he listened to the sounds of the village. He had long since given up trying to keep his clothes and boots clean of the black liquid, and his feet squelched loudly in the soft mud. He yawned and stretched out his arms while peering into the star-filled sky. Tomorrow the team would be on the road again, and he could not stop the dark thoughts from creeping into his mind. Every pit stop they made could potentially be their last, and soon there would be no more pit stops before he was forced to encounter Dallas.

And then that would be the end.

Whose end, though, he did not know.

A shoulder suddenly jostled into him, snapping the lion from his musings. Plunged back into the present, Clinton watched the small, hooded anumal stumble on, completely disregarding the incident. A foul stench permeated the air.

"Sorry, friend," Clinton called. "I wasn't paying—"

The anumal growled and rocked to a sudden halt before turning its head.

A nearby polelight picked out some of the anumal's features. The lion paused as he took in the sight of the badger. "*You!*"

CHAPTER TWENTY-TWO

FORSAKEN HORNS.

The badger bolted through the oil-fused puddles.

"Wait!" yelled Clinton, charging after him. "I just…"

A pile of trash was swept into his path before he rounded a corner, heading for the tavern's rear. He bounded over the obstruction, but landed deep in the mud and toppled forwards. Scrabbling upright, he slopped through the dirt and trundled into the alley…only to be greeted by an empty backstreet.

The badger had disappeared again.

"Oh, come on! Why do you keep on doing this?" Clinton kicked an oil drum over and wiped his muddy hands against the wall. "Am I in danger? Just tell me!"

He paced back and forth, staring up and down the alley. Finally admitting defeat he leaned against the side of a building. With his adrenalin subsiding, he decided to head towards the tavern again but raised voices caught his attention through a crack in the tavern window.

"…Oh, c'mon, sister. Lighten up," drawled Hiro, over the din. "Here have a sip of mine. It won't do you any harm."

Clinton edged closer and peered through the dirt-stained pane of glass.

"Are you deaf or just plain stupid?" Pep hissed. "She doesn't want any of your grain water."

"Ha!" scoffed Harris. "Hiro leave something alone? That will be the day."

The team sat before a table crammed with plates, grubby mugs, and a stripped boerbeast carcass lying in the center. Large wooden bowls of greens, vegetables, and nuts, sat in front of Ephraim and Hudson, the bison's mouth chewed continuously as she enjoyed her food.

"Just drop it, Hiro," Vito replied, her hood pulled up, keeping her face in the shadows.

Hiro leaned back and put her hands behind her head. "Well, I don't know what's wrong with you. Free food. Free drink. We should be enjoying ourselves for Silania's sake. It might be the last scruddin' chance we—"

"Hiro!" barked Ephraim. "Just shut up!"

"Whoa, back up, tusks. Who put you in charge? Think you're the big boss now that Garron's swanned off with mayor Pillager or whatever his name is?"

"No, I'm just trying to keep my head down, which is what we should all be doing," he hissed, leaning in closer. "Folk are taking notice of us."

"Well, frag 'em!" she shouted. The cheetah grabbed her grain water and downed it in one gulp, before slamming the mug on the tabletop. "Frag 'em all."

Clinton noticed the surrounding anumals muttering amongst themselves. Some snarled. Others gazed on with stone-like faces.

"Anyway," continued Hiro picking her teeth with a small, cleanly stripped bone, "It'd take a lot more than a few brainless divs from Blackwater to silence me. I've passed harder turds—"

"You really are a revolting *animal*," hissed Vito, shaking her head in disgust.

The team all turned to stare at the fox with wide eyes. Hudson stopped chewing. Ephraim winced.

A malicious smile blemished Hiro's face, and she slowly ran her tongue over her teeth. "What did you just call me? Traitor."

Vito's eyes narrowed. "Meaning?"

"Oh, you know exactly what I mean."

"No I do not. Please, enlighten me."

Pep shook her head. "What are you going on about, Hiro?"

"This fool knows nothing!" Vito snarled. "She speaks naught but trash."

"Because trash is all that ever spills out of my mouth, huh? Isn't that right, traitor?"

Vito's hand curled smoothly around the knife on her hip. "I am warning you, feline, call me that name again and it will be the last thing that ever comes out of your foul mouth."

Hudson patted Hiro's hand. "Maybe we should all just calm down a bit?"

Hiro smacked Hudson's hand away and rose to her feet. "You think I'm stupid, don't you? I've seen the looks you all give me; heard the snarky remarks. But lemme ask you this: d'you think I'm dumb enough to blunder into this little mission without doing some research after I joined, huh? Then think again." Hiro leaned over the table to stare straight into Vito's eyes. "The first thing I did was get the lowdown on all of you. And when I mean lowdown, I mean low—"

"Enough!" Vito shot to her feet, slipping her knife from its sheath with fluidity. Her chair flew backwards and clattered against the floor.

Hiro's claws burst from her fingertips. Both females glared at each other as the table was thrown into silence. A slow smile crept across Hiro's face. She began to laugh, before slumping back in her seat.

"Whoa, well, that was exciting wasn't it?" She flopped her feet onto the tabletop. "But you, my dear, need to lighten up. Scrud, I'm only playin' with you. You've been nothin' but uptight since Narfell's pretty face bolstered the ranks."

Vito's gaze continued to bore into the cheetah.

Hiro ran her tongue over her teeth again. "I mean it's hardly surprising, though, is it? Just look at him: the 'savior' of the world. the big badass. Scrag, if we didn't have such a muddy history, I might've had a shot at him myself."

"Is that what you call it? A muddy history?" Ephraim slammed his bowl of leaves onto the table. "Are you completely thick in the head, or just plain deluded? Scrud, the last time the three of us were together in Wooburn you Sabers were trying to tear him to shreds. I'd say it was a little less muddy, and whole lot more bloody."

Hiro swept her plate onto the floor. "Oops, I made a mess. What was that you were saying, Eph—"

A large hand crashed down on the table in front of her, causing mugs and glasses to topple to the floor.

"That ain't the only thin' roun' here that's gonna be a mess if'n you don't shut that big mouth of yours, feline," grunted a bison, coming into view behind her.

Hudson and Ephraim stood and quickly closed in around him.

"All an accident, brother," laughed Hudson, flicking her curl from her face. "Conversation just got a bit heated, but we're all friends here."

The huge newcomer stopped and looked her up and down. "Where'n you from, huh? You ain't locals. Why you stopp'n' in Blackwater?"

"Just...just trying to make a journey in peace, friend." Ephraim smiled. "We're heading no place special."

"I did'n' be ask'n' you, elephant." The bison's dark eyes continued to stare coldly at Hudson. "I'm talkin' wid my own kind."

Outside the window, Clinton watched the giant bison finally tear his gaze from Hudson to glare at the others around the table.

"Six out-of-towners, huh?" The stranger stroked his hairy chin. "Hav'n' a nice rest and food? Why, if I did'n' know better, I'd say we've a team here makin' its way to Mar Mi-Den, would'n' you be agreein'?"

"Maybe to watch, but not to compete, honey," Hudson replied. "Wouldn't want lazarball to be spoiling these fine looks of mine."

The male bison chuckled. "Hey, Wex! Come 'ere a mo. Bring Dakey and Tiy wid ya."

Three figures stood up from a central table in the room. A rhino with one side of his face seared red pushed over chairs as he approached. Following him lumbered a smaller ram with greasy wool. The two horns protruding from his head ended in sharp points. The third anumal, a younger-looking elk, swished his head to the side, his antlers causing the wooden chandelier to sway. A pair of broken shackles were cuffed around his wrists, clinking as he walked.

The rhino pushed in close to the bison. "Now here's a purdy lil sight; table's practically full of chumps. And from the looks of 'em, I'd be agreein' wit' you, Uwon. Yep, def'nit'ly headin' for the comps."

"N-no, we're just passing through," stuttered Ephraim.

256

"Shut your mouth an' speak when you're spoken to," snapped the rhino. "You ain't native here. Know your place, *outlier*."

Hiro hissed, rising to her feet. "That outlier will speak when he scruddin' well wants to. Alright?"

"Siddown, *pelt rot*!" barked the ram.

"Pelt rot?" Hiro chuckled, before her smile slipped into a snarl. "I'll show you pelt rot…"

Hudson swiped out one of her giant arms and slammed the cheetah back into her seat. "Your mouth ain't gonna help the situation, Hiro."

The ram stepped towards Vito, licking his lips.

"And who's do we have here then? C'mon, beauteeeful, don't want to hide that pretty lil face from good ol' Dakey here, do's ya?"

He leaned over and yanked back her hood.

Vito slowly lifted the hood back up again. "We have no problems with you, sir, and we are asking for no trouble. Please, just leave us be."

The ram moved closer, his grinning mouth almost brushing her face. "Ha! You hear'n that, guys? The mouthy canid wants no trouble."

Clinton's stomach tightened. He gritted his teeth as heat surged through his head.

"Aww…and the little canid's tellin' ya's to scram too, Dakey."

The four Horn Heads turned to each other before cracking out into guffaws that sounded like exploding thunder.

"Come now, brothers," smiled Hudson, stepping in. "There's no need for any of this, let me buy y'all a grain water—"

"So I'm all confused," interrupted Uwon, turning to her, his giant bison head like a boulder resting on his shoulders. "Why'n a beauty such as you would'n be runnin' wid the likes of these runts?"

"Friendship."

"Wid a puny bunch of turds like'n this?"

Hudson smiled. "They take all shapes and sizes, brother—"

"You keep callin' me brother, but you're'n no sister of mine.

You're—"

"*No rock, nor stone, nor metal made, will split our kin or dull our blade*," she recited.

"*'Till death, horns locked, in unity, then life beyond will set us free*," finished Uwon.

The newcomers gazed at one another, before Uwon finally shrugged. "So you're'n a Kraytian follower then? An Horn Head?"

Hudson nodded.

The elk's head inclined. "Marshland or grass born?"

"Wetlands."

"Ahh, Kraytarr's dung heap," he sniggered. "No wonder you came north."

Hudson inhaled. "I wish it was that simple."

"What? You's in trouble?" asked the ram.

"Exiled?" smirked the elk.

The word struck Clinton like a jab in the gut.

"If only," replied Hudson, evenly. "Even the good God Kraytarr himself couldn't stop me leaving after seeing what happened to my clan."

"An' what happened to 'em then? Are'n they hurt?" asked Uwon.

A small crease dented Hudson's brow. "No, honey, just changed."

"Changed...how?"

"Changed..." She toyed with her curl. "Into dumb thugs. Pretty much like you lot."

Each Horn Head tensed. They took a deep breath, only to force it out again in sharp jets. They hunkered their shoulders and lowered their heads, pointing their horns at her.

"Really? That so? You turned your'n back on your'n clan?" snorted Uwon, scraping his foot slowly along the wooden floorboards. "You know'n the rules, bison. You know'n what happens to deserters."

Hudson hunkered down in reply, mirroring their stance.

"Forsake the clan, forsake your horns," the rhino growled. "You've no right to wear 'em."

258

"Theys be a clan prize now," Dakie the ram added. "Traitor's horns'll give us good standin' in the Kraytian Temples."

"They'n belong to us now! BY RIGHT!" shouted Uwon. "We're'n gonna give you's a good beatin' now, missy."

Opening his mouth wide, the bison released a deep, guttural bray, and stamped the floor.

Outside, Clinton heard voices pass the alley's entrance. He looked up to see moving shadows. The sound of smashing glass and toppling garbage signaled trouble. He felt his energy surging.

The four Horn Heads fanned out around the team.

The tavern doors suddenly flew off their hinges and clattered into the center of the room. Every anumal inside jumped in shock and turned to see a group appear in the doorway.

"Ocelots," commanded a feline from the entrance. "It's burning time."

In a burst of rage, felines surged into the tavern, stumbling and crawling over one another to get inside. Tables toppled and glasses smashed.

"All of you on your knees!" yelled a scrawny tiger, with bloodstained fur. He jumped up onto a table, brandishing a lit torch. "Bow and surrender... Oh, scrag it! Just burn 'em all."

A jar of black stuff slammed against the wall, smashing on impact and splashing across the bar and floor.

"Leave no traitor alive!" hollered the tiger, launching his torch at the liquid mess. The flame whooshed, instantly igniting the gunk, and a thick, suffocating smoke swirled up into the air.

Clinton gasped, shock gripping him.

He slammed his fist through the windowpane.

"Hiro! Vito!" He reached out for the fox, blood dripping from his knuckles. "Over here!"

The fire quickly took hold of the tavern; raging torrents of flame sucked the oxygen from the air. Clinton coughed as more jars of black stuff landed in the middle of the room, feeding the flames.

"Hurry!" yelled Clinton, seeing shadows slipping amongst the chaos, pouncing on anything that moved.

Vito ripped off her cloak. Curling it into a ball, she smashed the remaining glass free from the pane. Springing up onto the sill, Harris dove out the gap and into the backstreet, followed a second later by Pep in a blur of white. Hiro appeared next, clambering through the hole and landing in a forward roll. She shoved Clinton out of the way as she turned back and reached inside to help Vito.

"Here, grab this!" she yelled.

The fox grabbed her hand and pounced outside in a single, fluid motion. Relief flooded Clinton as he saw the fox land unharmed by his side.

However, no one else followed.

"Where are the others?" he shouted, turning back to the window. "What the scrud are they doing?"

Terrified wails leaked out of the tavern. An orange glow began to warm the night sky. He rushed closer.

"Hudson! Ephraim! What are you waiting..."

His words ended in a horrified gasp. Hudson stood coughing next to Ephraim and the Horn Heads, all staring at the tiny window.

"It's too small," she shouted. "We've gotta find another way out."

"There is'n none," yelled Uwon, covering his mouth and stumbling away from the raging wall of flame. "We're'n trapped!"

"No! We've gotta get out, Dakey. We gotta go!" the elk shouted, before setting off at a run from the flames. The smoke instantly swallowed him up.

"You have to keep calm," bellowed Clinton, running his hand through his hair. "Flip the table and use it as a shield!"

The ram kicked the table over and forced it in front of the flames, but immediately jumped back again when his hair began to singe. Cries intensified behind the wall of smoke, and the roof groaned like an injured gorespine.

"Out of my way!" bawled Hudson, charging towards the window with her head bowed low.

The team outside scattered as she slammed into the wall. Debris rained down from above. Tiles dislodged, skittered down the roof, and plopped into the mud.

"Again!" she commanded. "All of us. NOW!"

The ground rumbled. Clinton dove for cover as the giants burst through the wall, sending wood and bricks exploding everywhere. The Horn Heads, Hudson, and Ephraim toppled into a heap. Hudson, though, scrabbled back on her hands and knees and grabbed the ram by his horns, yanking him further from the tavern.

"Out of the way, it's coming down," she yelled as a section of the roof collapsed.

Felines yelled inside the building, and flames shot skywards.

Ephraim rolled onto his side, gasping for breath. "Everyone here?"

Uwon struggled to his knees, coughing loudly. "Just worry 'bout yourself, outlier. We're'n be fine."

Clinton scanned the distant rooftops and spotted sleek figures bounding across them. "More Ocelots are coming. We're easy pickings in a group this size. We need to split up."

"I'm gonna smash 'em to pieces," promised the rhino. "No cat ever got the better of a Horn Head. They've got blood on their hands now."

"Many a dead brother in Middle City would disagree with you," replied Hudson, wiping her hands down the front of her overalls. "Face them when you stand a chance, not now."

Uwon turned to the rooftops before grimacing back at Hudson. He shook his head. "No doubt'n our paths'll cross in Mar Mi-Den, traitor."

Hudson spat in the dirt. "Let's hope they don't."

The filthy bison nodded and pounded off down the alley and into the street beyond. The ram and rhino quickly followed after him.

"Circle back to the bus!" Clinton ordered, backing away to a nearby building. "Take any route you can, but stay out of the felines' way."

Ephraim wrung his hands together. "So we're splitting up then?"

"We can't risk being captured as a team. Just stick to the

shadows and hide as best you can." An encouraging smiled flashed across Clinton's face. "You shouldn't have any problem with that, Eph. It's not like you haven't done it before."

The team nodded.

Clinton sprinted towards the opposite building, while behind him the team dispersed, disappearing silently into the smoky night.

CHAPTER TWENTY-THREE

INTO THE MIST.

Clinton rushed to the far side of the alley and jumped onto the wall. Digging his claws into the wood, he scrambled up to the roof, but a hand wrapped around his leg, stopping him from cresting the lip. Vito shimmied up by his side, forcing her fingers into the gaps with ease.

"The Crystal Soul left unguarded? Whatever would Hagen think of me?"

Clinton grinned. "I can look after myself."

"Well, let us see if you can keep up then. I am not one to wait around for stragglers."

Whipping her tail, she sped off, powering past him for the roof. Clinton made a move to follow, but bile rose to his chest and a foul sensation swept through him.

"Wait!" he called. "Something's wrong."

Retracting his claws, he dropped back down to the ground.

"What are you doing?" she hissed, still clinging to the wall. "Clinton? Are you mad? We need to go."

Yet the lion could not shake off the sensation. The emotions felt displaced, but oddly familiar.

"I...can't."

"You have to!"

His eyes swept over the rubble. The fire's heat washed over him in waves, before a ghostly pain lanced through his leg. He groaned in agony, and then saw it: a foot sticking out of the pile of debris. Shoving away bricks and wood, he revealed the Horn Head elk trapped beneath. Clinton dropped to his knees, feeling a sliver of relief, and grasped one of his hands. The elk's shackled wrists clinked.

"It's okay. We'll help you," whispered Clinton.

The elk swallowed, and his face screwed up with pain. "My...leg..."

"Don't worry." Clinton squeezed his hand. "We just need to shift the rubble and pull you free."

Clinton stared at the burning ruin around them, unable to mask his concern; a large beam had crushed the elk's leg, and was now the only thing propping up the roof.

"Breathe too heavily near that mess and it will all come crashing down," observed Vito, appearing by the lion's side. "Clinton, you are putting yourself in danger, and we do not have the time for this. There is nothing we can do for him."

"So what? Let him die?"

"Would you prefer to take his place? Use your head, lion. We need you to stay alive so that you can save *thousands* of anumals, not one thug who was stupid enough to pick a fight with strangers."

"So death is his punishment for being a bully?"

"You are taking my words—"

"You're right, Vito, we don't have time for this." The lion turned his attention back to the elk. "Just keep calm, and I'll figure something out."

"This is futile. We should leave."

The elk's panic manifested inside the lion, stealing his breath away.

"I…I will not leave him, Vito. I can feel his pain."

"This is not a part of the plan. We must—"

"We must try to help anyone we can."

Ocelot yells echoed along the backstreets. The damaged roof groaned and inched closer to collapsing.

"If the beam breaks, Clinton, we are dead. If Ocelots capture us, the mission is over. One anumal is not worth—"

"You say I'm supposed to save thousands, but how many dead will I leave behind me, Vito? Two? Ten? A hundred? There must be another way to save him."

A sleek silhouette swaggered along a passing rooftop, grabbing Clinton's attention. Vito also caught sight of the figure.

"Why are you insisting on this stupidity? The only possible way to free him is to remove the limb."

Clinton paused. He studied the trapped leg and glanced back at her. The heat was intensifying while the flames crept ever closer.

He thrust his hand out.

"Give me a knife."

"What?" screeched the elk.

"Shhhh!" snapped Vito, her lithe body going taut. "You cannot be serious! The pain will—"

"Give me a knife, Vito," repeated the lion, his heart pounding. "I can stop his pain, and then take it off."

The elk began to shake. A small section of the roof toppled, causing a spurt of flames to whoosh into the air. Vito unsheathed one of her knives and handed it to the lion as he leaned in close.

"It'll feel weird," explained Clinton, "but focus on me and you won't feel anything. I promise."

"W-what are you gonna do?" whimpered the elk.

The lion ignored him and picked up a chunk of wood. "This'll do as a means to store your soul." He pressed his other palm against the elk's chest, and closing his eyes, forced away his doubts.

You can do this, Clint. You can do this.

The heat vanished as he slipped down into the elk's consciousness .Doubt. Fear. Desperation. Hope. They all battered against Clinton like a sand storm, assaulting his emotions. A cavernous emptiness took him in its embrace; a miasma of feelings and experiences that dwarfed everything his past subjects had felt. Panic gripped him. His whole existence dissolved only to be replaced by someone else's memories…

A young elk stared up at a bedraggled goat holding a knife. Moonlight reflected in the goat's green eyes, and his breath stank of rotten food.

"That's all you have to do, boy," promised the goat. "Jus' crawl through here an' open the door. Easy."

The elk knew it was wrong. He wanted to run away, wanted to alert the sleeping anumals inside, yet his growling stomach demanded nourishment.

"It's an even split, kid. Everything we steal gets cut down the middle. Your belly'll be full…" The goat grabbed him by the arm. "Now get in there!"

The elk dropped to his knees and wriggled through the tiny basement window...

A gray mist swirled. Clinton's vision changed.

A door creaked open. A shaft of sunlight pierced the dark. Urine-soaked straw was strewn across the floor. The elk struggled to his knees, but his chains weighed him down.

"H-hello?"

Hope dared to sprout. Surely they would release him from his cage today? They would finally believe his story that he had only stolen from the house, nothing more...

A brick of hard bread skidded across the cell towards him. He had eaten the same meal for the last few weeks, or had it been years? He could not tell anymore. The elk whimpered as he took a bite.

Clinton's sight clouded.

Life sped forwards.

"I told you where he is, bro," urged a voice through the haze.

The elk felt the weight of the coiled rope in his hand. Determination and anger swelled.

"They've blamed ya for murder already, when ya's was innocent. Trust me, they ain't gonna blame ya again for it. It's all the goat's fault; he framed ya, he did. I says kill him and take his money. And just remember old Dakey here when ya's a cashin' it in."

The mist swirled.

The elk slid his dirty hands into his pockets. The sound of creaking rope filled the air with guilty accusations. The dawn light gifted him with an outline of a goat swinging from a tree branch. He looked almost peaceful hanging there by his scrawny neck. Yet the serenity was shattered by a horrified shriek behind him.

Mist clouded in once again.

Raindrops pattered against the metal restraints around his hands as the elk stood outside the justice house. The dark clouds reflected his mood, and the giraffe council's elected voice was muffled by the wind.

"As law dictates," stated the giraffe. "The taking of a life is

against village and clan law. Burning Horn Head elders have decreed that you have acted against Kraytarr's will, and that those actions must be repaid in kind. The earth remembers, elk, and laws must be obeyed. As such, I sentence you to be stripped, bound, and thrown to the elements."

Screams erupted. Blood began to spill. Ocelot cries filled the night as his village burned.

"Raion!" gasped Clinton, overwhelmed by the chaos of the elk's memories. He had to anchor himself, concentrate on himself, or else lose his identity under the onslaught of another's consciousness.

He pictured the time he and Raion were caught throwing stones at rogue chockerals...the smell of Krog's backyard. He heard Arkie's laughter...

C'mon!

Clinton gritted his teeth. He had to find the core, yet the harder he searched, the more it appeared to be intertwined with the elk's memories and feelings.

"Clinton!" echoed a distant female voice. "Clinton, you must hurry."

Life. Love. Family. Desire. Regret. They all flashed by as Clinton desperately searched.

Are you there? shouted the lion. *Can you feel me?*

Y-yes, replied the elk, his voice echoing all around.

Good, I'll guide you to a place where there'll be no pain.

However, the elk began to panic. *You're in my mind! Get out! Leave me alone!*

Fear clouded the lion, weighing him down.

"Please," echoed the female. "We must escape."

I won't leave you to die, hissed Clinton.

Get out of my head!

I'm trying to—

GET OUT!

Forcing away the black cloud of fear, Clinton connected with the elk's soul. He tugged hard, trying to force it under his control, but it clung to the elk's senses like an unripened geanu fruit gripping to a branch.

Allow me to help you! pleaded Clinton.

The more desperate he became, the more fear flooded the elk, and the tighter his soul clung to its vessel.

"Clinton, leave him!" hissed the female.

GET OUT! screamed the elk.

No! I won't let you die.

"Clinton!" whispered Vito, her tone deadly serious. "They've found us."

GET OUT OF ME!

I WON'T LET YOU DIE.

Two hands grabbed Clinton's shoulders and yanked him away from the elk. His head swam with dizziness before he felt his consciousness slowly rising towards the sound of fighting. Noises swirled all around: angry voices, grunts, and roars. Partial reality returned, until he finally surfaced from his trance-like state. Vito slapped his cheek, trying to rouse him, and snarled, before the sole of a boot swung at his face. The fox kneed the foot away and spun, backhanding the Ocelot to the ground. Two knives appeared in her hands.

"Run, Clinton!"

Clinton rolled to his side.

A snarling Ocelot appeared in front of him, while another foot connected with his stomach. He scrabbled to his feet, but a hand gripped his shoulder, claws digging through his jacket.

"Oh, no you don't," shouted the Ocelot.

Clinton stumbled, and a blur of red fur sped past him. Vito slammed into the feline, and whipping her tail around his legs, made him fall. Before the Ocelot hit the floor, she sliced her dagger and took him out of the fight, before flipping away to land in a defensive crouch between the attackers and Clinton.

The lion gulped.

"More are arriving," she hissed, lifting the right knife above her head and flipping the left into a reverse hold. She turned and yelled, "GO!"

Clinton moved. The next thing he knew, he had scaled the

opposing wall and was on top of the roof.

Vito suddenly appeared next to him, more blood covering her cloak.

"There they are! Up there!" yelled an approaching voice.

Ocelots burst through the tavern's flames and into the cramped side street. Numerous boots trampled over the motionless bodies, including the elk, yet Clinton could do nothing about it.

Vito shoved him over the rooftops and away from the danger. "I will lead them away so you can get to the bus. Do you understand?"

Her words swirled around his head. He blinked.

She slapped him across the face again.

"*Do you understand?*"

Clinton nodded. "Yes...yes."

"Good!" She dove over the gap and landed on the next rooftop. "Now do not do anything stupid like dying on me."

Clinton stumbled up the sloped roof before sliding down the other side and leaping the gap. He ran with all his strength, fleeing over the roofs and into the quieter section of the village. The last thing he heard was the tavern's roof crashing to the ground, no doubt dragging the whole building down with it.

* * *

Panic had erupted in Blackwater like an infestation of meyarks. Residents and visitors scurried for safety, carrying with them anything they could get their hands on. Fires raged, filling the air with cloying smoke. The lion wiped dirt from his eyes and moved across the rooftops. Guilt seeped the energy from his muscles, and his every step felt weighed down with regret.

Why did I lose it? Why couldn't I keep calm? But the more questions he asked, the more they became twisted and torturous. *I wasn't ready...I lost patience.* A tear slipped down his cheek. *I...killed...him.*

The rippling black lake could be seen a few streets away, moonlight and dancing fires reflected across its mirrored surface.

Engines roared and stock groaned as ladened vehicles clogged the main street, escaping for the mountain roads.

Clinton sank to his knees by the roof's edge. Despair overwhelmed him. What use was he? He could not even save *one* anumal.

Perhaps it was for the best if the team continued on without me? Maybe pushing them away would stop their deaths when I fail them the next time?

The sound of smashing glass dragged him from his self-pity. He recoiled and tiptoed across a girder spanning two buildings, before leaping onto another roof. Rounding a corrugated chimney stack, he heard voices resonating from the alley below. He ignored them at first, before a distinctive drawl made his ears prick.

"...Honest! I wasn't hiding, sugar. I was just shieldin' my face from the flames."

"Lies!" barked a deep voice. "You were sneakin' past."

There was a dull thud followed by a yelp of pain.

Clinton slipped to the edge and inched his head over the lip. Four felines had someone pinned against the wall, and each wore the Ocelot symbol branded on their jackets. One held a blade while the other two wielded stunpikes, crackling and hissing with power. The fourth feline, a white snow leopard, whose fur had been disfigured from numerous scars and burns, towered above them all.

"Come here!" He slammed his captive against the wall. "I wanna see your face up close, Hiro Varie."

Clinton groaned.

"Well, you wouldn't be the first," she laughed, spitting blood.

"Shut it," ordered the snow leopard.

"C'mon, Zylver," she sighed. "I've been trying to find you for ages, but every time I'd turn up, you'd've moved on. I really missed you guys."

The leopard's grip tightened around her throat, causing her to gasp. "An' you know what I miss?" He snarled and snapped his teeth in her face. "The sound of breaking bones – traitorous, thieving bones – on cowards who flee their debts. You ever heard that sound, Hiro?"

"Well, I can't say I have, Zyl."

A swift backhand scuffed the cheetah's face. Zylver pulled her in close. "I'd be quiet if I were you." The Ocelots readied their stunpikes and pointed them at her chest. "I know you've been avoiding us, Hiro. What with the scrag you pulled in Biozzurd."

"I waited for you. I did. But I ran out of credits."

"And hive I imagine."

Clinton flinched. He had heard of hive back in Wooburn. He had never seen the drug, but knew of those who took it, and of those who dealt it. 'Vile vein-wrecking dirt,' he remembered Arkie telling him, before warning Clinton he would stitch the lion's mouth up if he ever so much as touched a pellet. However, everyone knew hive passed through the hands of anumals such as Galront as frequently as the food supplies did. Clinton could still picture the weasel's bulging eyes, abnormal strength, and volatility as a result of licking the amber substance.

The lion shook his head. *Mother of Treb, Hiro, what've you got yourself into?*

"We tracked you to Havucke," Zylver continued. "Caught word there that you met up with a bunch of scruds."

"I...I had no choice." She forced a smile across her swelling face. "They made me leave with 'em."

"Made you leave before, or after, you tipped our merchandise into the stream?"

"Oh, skorr. No, you've got it all wrong, Zyl—"

"No, Hiro, *you've* got it all wrong. See, you were spotted."

"But I tricked 'em. Made 'em think I'd dumped it...but I didn't. I swear."

The snow leopard slowly held out his hand. "Give it to me then."

Hiro blinked.

"Go on, Hiro, show me I'm wrong."

"But... I don't have it on me now... That'd be—"

A fist piled into her stomach. She doubled over.

Clinton's claws gouged the roof.

"Did you use it yourself? Is that what happened?"

Hiro coughed and gasped. "I...of... course...not. I never...touch the stuff."

"Course you don't." Zylver chuckled, along with the others. "Either way, it's the end of the line. As you can see, times are changing. This ain't purely a Fang thing you're dealing with now, and the Ocelot masters aren't as forgiving as we were."

The Ocelots edged in closer. Sparks crackled from their stunpikes.

"Arrrrgh! Please! Please, I have your hive. Honest. I can...I can get it for you."

Zylver smiled, revealing brown amber-stained fangs. "I'll collect it if you tell me where it is—"

"No!" she gasped. "You can't or...the others...the others'll destroy it."

"What...others?"

Clinton held his breath.

Don't say a word, Hiro. Keep your mouth shut.

"I'm traveling with a caravan," she finally answered. "It's probably fled from the village by now, but if you let me catch 'em up, then I can get it for you."

"Oh...you think so?" laughed the snow leopard.

"Zylver, you know how fast I can run."

"That's the problem, Hiro, indeed I do."

"But—"

Zylver held up his hand for silence. He thought for a moment, before saying, "Grille, go with her. And don't let her out of your sight."

The Ocelot to Zylver's left sheathed his blade, and wiped his nose on the back of his hand. "My pleasure."

"No!" she protested. "Please. I'm faster on my own. He'll just slow me down."

Zylver studied his companions before turning back to her again. His jaw clenched. "An hour," he blurted. "I'm trusting you, Hiro. Now if you're not back in time..." The snow leopard smashed his fist into the wall next to her face. "I will shred you to pieces and send what's left to the master. Do you understand?"

She nodded.

Zylver's fist opened to reveal a crushed amber pellet inside. "Something for the journey."

Hiro looked down at the hive, before staring back at the white leopard. "I've already—"

"Take it."

"But, Zylver, I've—"

"TAKE IT!"

With a sigh, Hiro closed her eyes and slowly licked the amber powder from his palm. The Ocelots chuckled. Zylver dropped her, and she stumbled before scrabbling upright again.

"Well what are you waiting for? Time's ticking." He bared his fangs. "GO!"

Hiro sidled away, and turning, set off at a sprint.

"An hour, Hiro!" shouted Zylver, his words chasing after the cheetah.

The lion rolled away from the roof edge and jumped to his feet. He raced over the rooftops in pursuit of Hiro, bounding past chimney stacks, and flipping over broken walls. Finally, he ran along the rooftops parallel to her on the ground.

"Hiro!" he shouted.

She did not stop.

"Hiro! It's me, Clinton!"

The cheetah continued to run.

Without waiting, he sprung at a protruding flagpole and swung forwards, grabbing a length of cable spanning the buildings. Yanking hard, he snapped the cable free and swung down to the street. The lion sailed through the air and slammed into the cheetah's back, sending them both flying into the mud. Clinton groaned and rolled to his knees.

"Hiro," he said, coldly, nudging her. "Get up."

But the cheetah remained motionless.

"Frag it!"

Picking her up from the mud, he slung her over his shoulder and staggered away. Anumals barged into him as he made his way along the street. Fires burned, and a barrier of smoke obstructed his path, smearing the back of his throat.

"Hiro?" he panted, swerving around a family of canines busy dragging their possessions from their home. "Hiro! Wake up!"

Yet the cheetah did not reply.

Ducking down a side street, the lion escaped the erupting mayhem, and with every step, Hiro seemed to weigh heavier on him. With one final push, he came to a low wall at the end of an alley. Pained cries and Ocelot yells echoed along the cramped confines, growing in intensity. Hoisting Hiro over the wall, he jumped after her.

A glass bottle hit the bricks next to his head, making him jump while spraying shards in every direction.

An Ocelot stalked closer, brandishing a stun pike. "An' here's another. Whole village thinks it can escape."

A gray trunk smashed into the feline's face, sending him tumbling into a pile of garbage.

Unable to catch his breath, Clinton looked up to see Ephraim rapidly approach.

"Quick!" urged the elephant shoving out his hand for Clinton to grab. He yanked the lion to his feet. "You okay?"

"Fine," he panted. "But she needs help."

The lion pointed behind him at the crumpled cheetah. Ephraim stepped past Clinton and lifted her over his shoulder with ease.

"What happened? Is she—"

"No...although I'm close to killing her myself."

"What? Why?"

The lion sighed. "Nothing."

Ephraim nodded and charged off in the direction of the bus. Clinton followed closely behind, barging through a crowd of panicked anumals. Engines revved and exhaust smoke swamped the air. Gorespines groaned and ironbacks warbled while whips cracked, urging the spooked beasts into action.

Garron's voice peaked above the melee of noise as they rounded a corner.

"Pep, what are you waiting for? Get on board!"

"Just a little more time. They'll be here, I know..." Her words died as Clinton caught sight of her clinging to the top of a polelamp. Her face lit up when she saw the trio approach. "They're here! They made it!"

She scurried back down to street level and raced off to the bus.

Barging over the wet ground, Clinton finally made it to the team...just as a bloody Ocelot flew through the air and squelched into the mud.

"Clinton, hurry!" yelled Hagen, turning as another Ocelot jumped onto the komodo's back. Before Hagen could tear the feline from him, a small blade thudded into his attacker.

The Ocelot slid to the ground.

"Do not worry, Hagen," called Vito from the bus's roof. She whipped out another knife. "I have you covered."

Harris shoved his head out the window, holding a towel against a cut on his forehead. "Are we going to get moving, or are we just going to let the cats keep attacking?"

"Looks like we're all good to go," said Garron, ushering Clinton, Ephraim, and the unconscious Hiro onto the bus.

"What happened to her?" asked Hagen, jumping on after them. He lifted Hiro's limp head to inspect it.

"Ask Clint," shouted Ephraim, disappearing down the walkway. "He's the one who found her."

"Clint?" said Garron, hanging out of the doorway to keep an eye on the rear of the bus. "So what happened?"

The lion shook his head, unsure of what to say.

"Nothing." He peered out the window to see vehicles of all sizes clogging the streets and creating a gridlock. "Let's just get out of here. I'll explain later."

Hudson cracked her whip, causing the gorespines to judder forwards. "Well, let's move then."

"Oh, no you don't!" shouted a voice.

An Ocelot dove up onto the side of the bus, trying to prize Hudson from her seat.

"Oh, get lost!" she huffed. Plucking him by the scruff of the neck, Hudson tossed him aside like a piece of trash. "They're like bluggin' sectoids. They really are."

With one final rev of the engine, the gorespines set off into the mayhem of traffic, scraping past any vehicle that obstructed their path. As other villagers made good their escape, the coach joined them and sped off along the road leading out of Blackwater.

CHAPTER TWENTY-FOUR

ELU.

The sun had sank in the sky. Deep, orange rays beamed through the smashed, curved windows surrounding Vincent. He closed his eyes and slouched back into his creaky, leather chair. The puma's feet rested against the control panel, dotted with buttons, screens, and displays. A glass dial had cracked under the weight of his boots, and his flabby stomach was pressed against an array of levers. The puma huffed and took in the sights of the cockpit. How mankind had managed to get such a huge contraption off the ground, let alone keep it airborne, puzzled him. He did not know if he should credit them for their ingenuity, or damn them for such stupidity, yet here the planes rested as a testament to their audacity.

Habrok belong in the skies, not machines or anumals, he decided, assuring himself that his feet would forever stay planted on the ground.

"Elu Vincent…Sir."

A lynx opened the cockpit door and crept inside.

"I have news—"

Vincent raised his hand, cutting off the feline in mid sentence. He sighed and pushed himself forward. "Tell me, Ocelot, when did you join us?"

"Elu?"

The puma sighed at his new military title and touched his scarred eye. Two long scabs had formed over the wounds that he had received in honor of the Shadow Master. His fist tightened around a lever. "The Ocelots. When did you join us?"

The lynx shrugged. "On the Silday before the last full moon, sir, after you took the Crimson Watcher's settlement near the Ridgebacks."

"So you're a Mountain Claw?"

"Yes, sir…I mean, no, sir. I'm an Ocelot, through and through."

"Oh, you are, are you? Then you'll know exactly who I am then."

"E-Elu, your reputation is becoming legendary."

"Is it indeed?" The puma swung his seat around to face the lynx. "Yet you burst in here, interrupting my private time, like I'm some mere *neophyte?*"

"E-Elu I—"

"I've led us through a solid month of travel, battles, and bloodshed, yet have I asked for much in return?"

The lynx frowned.

"No. All I've asked for when we reached the Winged Graveyard, ahead of schedule may I add, was that I was afforded a moment of solitude." Vincent scowled. "And did I get it?"

The lynx's eyes wandered to the floor. "Elu I—"

"NO!" The puma slammed his fist against the control panel, smashing another screen.

"E-Elu, you ordered me yourself to inform you when the final wagon was to be loaded."

Vincent glared at the feline, suppressing the dark urges coursing through his body. He pinched the bridge of his nose and took a calming breath. "And is it?"

The lynx nodded. "Soon we will be ready to set off...as commanded."

"Has the Shadow Master been informed of this?"

The neophyte slowly shook his head. "Not as yet. We were told not to disturb him."

"Good, keep it that way." Vincent regretted his next words, but said them nonetheless. "Any issues you find are to be reported directly to me. Understand?"

"Yes, Elu, of course," whispered the Ocelot, before leaving the ruined cockpit.

With a huff, Vincent swung back around and returned his feet to their resting spot. He could hear Ocelots shouting outside, their bellows gelling with the constant cough and splutter of engines and the rumbling cries of ironbacks.

Never had this trouble in Wooburn. At least I got a decent night's sleep there.

He closed his eyes...

And there it was again.

He could not last more than a few minutes before he found the ever-present darkness tainting his thoughts. Beads of sweat pearled his forehead. His body felt battered from the endless travel, while the stinging realization of his recent actions festered on his conscience. His final night in Wooburn taunted his memory.

* * *

"You...you don't have to do this," shouted Jasper. Blood trickled down the side of the canine's face. His arm hung limply while tears glistened in his eyes. "Please, Vincent! It's me, pal. It's me, Jasper!"

The smell of burning wood and flesh clogged the puma's nose. Pained yells lapped pleasingly in his ear. Too pleasingly.

Vincent thrust his flaming torch towards Jasper's face. "Are they in there?"

The canine shuffled away from the flame. "What's got into you, Vince? This isn't you! What've you become?"

Vincent blanched, feeling Jasper's words hit the mark. *What am I doing? This is wrong...this isn't what we're about. We're Sabers, not murderers.*

A rumbling sensation in his stomach made him shudder. His Ocelot brand pulsed with a green-yellow hue, and the darkness took over him again. A menacing growl escaped his lips. "I asked you a question, Jasper."

Yet Jasper remained firm, as stubborn as ever, blocking the entrance to his tavern. Darkness framed the puma's vision; swirling blackness narrowed his sights, fixing them upon his desire for revenge.

"So be it," he croaked, and turned to face the feline mob behind him. "Burn it! Burn it all!"

Upon his command, dozens of torches arced through the air, landing on the tavern roof. Jasper wailed, but his cries could not slake the fire's hunger.

Within moments the building was ablaze.

The tavern's front door smashed open and a flurry of guards and villagers dashed past Vincent and out onto the street.

"Capture all who run," ordered the puma, stalking closer to the entrance. He shoved Jasper aside, drew his blade, and waited.

Suddenly, two burly guards stumbled out of the burning tavern. Vincent, burst into action. His hand never faltered. His attacks found their mark. His blade thrust into the coyote guard's stomach, causing the anumal to collapse. The next slash found the black bear, slicing through its skin with ease. A crimson ribbon of blood splashed the tavern's decking. Grabbing their wounds, the guards collapsed, blood seeping through the cracks in their fingers, both clinging tenaciously to life.

Vincent's face quivered. He felt *it* twist inside.

They still live, echoed the voice. *Watch them burn.*

Vincent leaned over and scooped the coyote up by the neck, the inner darkness fueling his muscles. "So, felines are nothing nowadays, huh?" He tossed the guard back into the burning tavern, before hoisting up the black bear. "Time to learn the error of your ways. Think hard on your punishment as the flames engulf you."

With one final heave, he threw him into the tavern's inferno.

The puma stepped away as the guards' pained screeches fell upon deaf ears, and turned to his Sabers.

"The villagers will surrender or die!" he shouted, sheathing his knife. A euphoric energy coursed through him, feeding his ego and enticing his desires...He yearned for more..."Wooburn is ours. Nomica...IS OURS!"

* * *

Vincent's eyes snapped open. He sat upright in the cockpit's chair. Time had barely passed, yet it felt like he had been trapped in his memories for an age. He reached up with trembling hands to touch his face; something he had found himself doing more and more frequently. With a sigh, he clambered to his feet and peered out of the cockpit windows.

A graveyard of rusty, metal planes spread out before him. Most lay toppled with their wings sticking up like bizarre overhangs. Many had been cut in half, with primate sigils scrawled along their sides. From where he stood, Vincent could see Ocelot neophytes dragging tightly sealed crates out from an underground tunnel and heaving them onto wagons.

He swallowed. More than anything, he really did crave a cool mug of grain water, he had not tasted any since commencing the campaign.

"Quala," he muttered, groaning softly.

It had happened again in Quala, only worse.

Few dared to speak of the incident, but he knew his encounter with the Fang leader had garnered him their fear. As Ocelot numbers swelled, talk had trickled through the ranks about the puma's behavior. Many had started to move aside as he walked through the camp. Others looked at their feet. However, all had grown a newfound respect for him, bowing upon his approach and calling him Elu. Through the village of Barrowmarsh, the Bone Mines, and even as far north as the Sky Camps, more and more Ocelots radiated unease whenever he approached.

And he had wanted none of it.

As the Ocelots had advanced north, his facial twitches had flared, while his actions in battle were blurred in a haze of red and black. Now, when he recounted memories, he was unsure whether they were even his.

It had been three days since the sacking of the Sky Camps, where the Imperial Ivory Stratos clan had fallen to feline rule and those refusing dominion sent fleeing for Middle City. The mountains had provided the Ocelots the hardest battle to date, yet the habrok they captured would prove pivotal as airborne lookouts in future battles. Rich in credits and supplies, the mountain camps positively thrummed with Ocelot song that night. And it was then that Vincent had stalked though the village, passing a group of neophytes around a fire, gorging on a fresh roast.

"Shut your mouth, Briez," snarled a feline.

Briez took a deep gulp from his tankard. "I'm telling you. I stood next to him. There were only five of us, but we must have faced maybe twenty or thirty of those scrudding winged Imperials, yet Vincent—"

The puma's ears pricked at his name.

"*Elu* Vincent," interrupted an Ocelot. "Use his rank, you fool."

"Yeah. Elu Vincent. Well, it didn't faze him one bit. 'What do you think is the best course of action against the flyers?' he asks, all calm like. And then he just goes crazy."

The Ocelot brushed his brow to ward away evil.

"Yeah, I heard he went feral," commented another feline, gnawing on a krig bone.

"He did more than that," blurted Briez. "The rumors...y'know, what they say about him...well, they're true. His face...changed. It did. His mouth opened wide, and his eyes glossed over like the night, only with yellow fires in their center. And his fingers, well, they went all long and stretchy, like...like pointy knives. He literally tore the flyers to shreds. Whirled through them like a maniac. I'll never forget it."

"Hah! I'll believe it when I see it," laughed one of the newer felines from the Claws. "The fat sod isn't scaring anyone. All piss and wind if you ask me. I know his type; lives off dumb scrags like you who regurgitate his 'past', making him something he isn't. Gimme one moment alone with that fat glux, an I'll show him what nightmares are really made of."

Yet he did not know your type did he, Vincent? asked the voice inside the puma's head.

Vincent snapped back to reality again, and the sight of the Ocelots working amongst the planes came into focus. The puma's hands were shaking.

Calm down.

He interlaced his fingers and pressed them against his chest. It did nothing to stop the feline's dying screams looping in his memory.

I wonder if he thought of you as merely piss and wind when you flayed his fur and strung him from the tree?

"He should have kept his mouth shut," snarled the puma. He snapped his eyes closed and fell back into the chair. "No. It's not real. No…"

I am real.

"I'm just tired. I need rest."

He is here, said the awed voice.

"No…"

He is here…

A sudden darkness flourished inside the puma.

Opening his eyes, he swiveled to see a figure standing in the doorway, settled comfortably within the shadows.

"Trouble?" asked Nightmare, his voice a low, throat-tickling rumble.

Vincent felt the sweat drip down his back. He pulled a cloth from his pocket and dabbed his brow. "It's…nothing." He stood up to bow. "F-for what do I owe the pleasure, sir?"

Nightmare raised his hand. "Oh, please, be seated. There is no need for such courtesies between friends."

Friends? The word sounded foreign coming from the panther.

Vincent sat down, and Nightmare took the seat next to him. As Vincent had done, Nightmare rested his feet on top of the control panel. The felines waited, floating uneasily upon the pregnant silence. Vincent gave Nightmare occasional glances, yet refrained from lingering on him for too long. Even though Nightmare faced the window, the puma felt like he was being studied. And inside he could feel *it* stirring again.

He is here, repeated the voice.

"Are you at ease?" Nightmare finally asked.

"I'm sorry?"

"You were talking when I entered, yet as no one else is here, I assumed you were talking to yourself." The panther turned to face him, his eyes hidden behind his sunglasses. "I take it the silence shows your ease?"

Vincent forced a smile. "Just working a few things out in my head that's all. I often talk to myself."

Nightmare's eyebrow lifted while the rest of his face remained like flint.

Vincent felt his scarred eye twitch, and instinctively turned away to touch it. "I...I've had reports that the final wagon is being loaded. We should be ready to depart by sunset."

Nightmare folded his arms.

"And in good time too. You've done well, Elu Vincent."

Vincent cringed at the honorific, but merely nodded.

"Appreciated, sir."

Nightmare took his attention from the puma and turned towards the setting sun. The shadow of a smile curled along his mouth.

He knows... said the voice.

"It is interesting, this place; wouldn't you agree, Vincent?"

"A mechanical graveyard that's been picked clean by primates during the Simian Revolts. I heard it was cursed."

"So they say. The primates, however, merely scratched the surface before getting spooked off by its secrets. And now those who pass through the territory never quite return the same."

"Well, that's *journiers* for you, suspicious of every place they go. Predicting doom whenever a leaf falls from a tree. The whole planet is cursed according to them."

Nightmare cleared his throat. "You could say that. Yet I believe that where this little corner of the world is concerned, myths are rooted in fact. You see, those who delve into the ground around here, who explore mankind's discards, end up...altered."

"Altered?"

"Back to a more...feral state."

Vincent's bottom lip twitched. He covered his mouth with his hand. "How feral?"

"Primal."

When Nightmare did not elaborate, Vincent felt the need to ask more. "They turned into scavengers?"

"If only," rumbled Nightmare.

The puma's lips trembled. His mouth felt like it was stretching sideways. He looked away, fighting to control his breathing.

He senses us, laughed the voice. *He senses us.*

Nightmare put his hands behind his head and stretched languidly. "If one cared to decipher the childish scrawls the

284

primates scratched on the surfaces hereabouts, then they'd discover dire warnings. Most advise fleeing."

"I don't really care to read monkey scriptures," muttered Vincent.

Nightmare yawned. "Each to their own. Nevertheless, within the messages appears one word that is repeated over and over again, one word that permeates every warning."

"Which is?"

"Reaper."

Vincent turned to stare at the felines dragging crates out of the tunnels. "What do you mean? I thought we were here to raid a hidden weapon stockpile?"

Nightmare indicated the Ocelots. "And we are, as far as they're concerned. But in truth it's a little more complicated. The Reaper, it seems, is the answer to all our needs."

"So what is this Reaper? Is it a weapon? A vehicle? What?"

"Oh, it's a weapon, my friend, but one which you, and most of anumalkind will have never experienced. A weapon so potent, so vile in its effects, that life and sanity are risked with every second we linger near it."

"Yet look at where we are," snapped Vincent, a quiver garnishing his voice. He motioned to the busy felines and the decaying relics. "If this Reaper is so bad, then why are we delving into things best left buried?"

"Because things best left buried usually have immeasurable qualities." Nightmare rose to his feet and clicked his knuckles. "Power few would dare use."

Vincent saw his reflection in the panther's sunglasses. He looked tired. Worn down. He wished to know more of this weapon, yet his desire to distance himself from Nightmare had become too much to ignore. "Well, whatever this Reaper may be, I'm sure it's a wise move, sir, one that will garner untold rewards for the Shadow Master."

Nightmare's smile disappeared.

Vincent did not know if he should try to rally from his obvious blunder, but feeling the annoyance radiating from his companion, rose to his feet. "Well, I'll push on. I'll order the camps to be taken down in preparation for our depar—"

"It will make sense, Vincent...the voice, that is."

Vincent whimpered, and a tremble shuddered through him. "I don't know what you mean."

"Of course not. But trust me when I say that you'll emerge unscathed. And when you do, you'll not stand alone."

Vincent felt weightless. His mind spun, unable to anchor on to anything but the panther's words.

Never alone! hissed the voice.

Vincent forced a smile and tried to sway the conversation on to anything but the voice. "And...how is the Shadow Master progressing? Talk amongst the neophytes says he's becoming quite the warrior. None dare face him now."

"The tiger knows enough," replied Nightmare, flatly. "Enough to see him survive? Who knows?"

"Surely the Crystal Soul is no match for him?"

As if the moment slowed, Nightmare carefully placed a hand on the puma's shoulder. A whirlpool swirled into motion as *it* began to move inside the puma's stomach. A chill coursed through his veins, making his limbs vibrate with wintry power. Clenching his teeth, Vincent fought to keep *it* at bay. Sweat dripped from his body. He snatched tight, shallow breaths and dabbed his forehead out of habit.

"The Crystal Soul must be the tiger's concern. That alone," said Nightmare, over the drone in Vincent's ears. "And us? We must allow him his narcissistic dreams and provide assurances of his greater purpose. He must not doubt."

He is but one piece of the greater design...

Nightmare slowly pulled Vincent closer so that their faces almost touched. "Listen from within. It speaks the truth."

The puma's whole being felt drawn to the Nightmare, the darkness yearning to be born.

Your time will come, reassured the panther, inside Vincent's head.

The puma felt breathless as *it* toyed with the urge to strip him of his senses and assume control. His legs felt rooted, while his hands tingled with potential.

"No!" he muttered, grabbing the sides of his head. "What is wrong with me?"

Nothing, responded Nightmare. *Have patience, my faithful warrior. Your time is approaching.*

Raised voices dragged Vincent away from the panther's grip and back to reality. He felt air pump into his lungs as soon as Nightmare removed his hand. Vincent staggered to the window to see what the commotion outside was.

A wooden crate had smashed.

A canister shuddered on the ground as a stream of red gas hissed from its top. Instinctively, a feline dove forwards to stop the leak, and with a twist of the nozzle, turned off the hissing canister. The surrounding Ocelots cautiously backed away, keeping him directly in their line of sight.

No one said a word.

The Ocelot shuddered like someone was shaking the life out of him. Without pause, he turned tail and charged off, until Vincent could see him no longer.

"Clear out!" shouted a feline.

"What *is* that stuff?" barked another.

Engines revved. A whip cracked. The wagon trundled quickly from the area.

Vincent cleared his throat. "I...I think it best we move."

"That might be wise."

"Shall I tell the Shadow—"

"No," interrupted Nightmare. "I'll inform him when the moment is right. The last thing we need is for the tiger to get in our way yet again."

CHAPTER TWENTY-FIVE

CONFESSION.

"Drink this," ordered Hagen, passing Hiro a wooden mug.

The cheetah snatched it from him and took a sniff.

"Smells like dung."

"No doubt it'll taste like it too," added Clinton, sitting beside her on the bus. He rubbed his aching muscles, and tried to ignore his own wounds. "However, Hiro, the drink will do you some good."

For a whole night the engines had been set to full power and the gorespines barely allowed a break while the team fled westwards from Blackwater. The road had been crammed with escaping wagons and carts. Clothing, furniture, and chests, brimming with food and supplies, had been tossed on to vehicles, and droopy-eyed youngsters roused from their sleep and forced to flee. For a while the cries of battle could still be heard drifting on the breeze behind them, but the further they fled, the clearer the road became. Soon Blackwater fell from view and moved solidly into the past…yet another casualty of Ocelot dominance.

Clinton nodded, taking in the sight of the cheetah's face. One of her eyes had swollen shut, the flesh now a livid shade of purple-blue. A bandage had been wrapped around her head with an array of herbs crammed underneath to help ease her concussion. Clinton took a calming breath, yet every time she talked, all he could think about was her involvement with the felines. Where her eyes had once been alert, and her posture confident, she now appeared like a strip of worn grack skin, her fur dirty and stained with darkness.

Hiro took a sip of the drink, and immediately spat it out again.

"For the love of skorr."

Hagen pushed the mug towards her again. "Drink it, or I shall be forced to find another orifice in which to introduce the tonic into your body."

Hiro huffed, closed her eyes, and downed it in one go.

"There." Hagen placed a bowl of smoldering herbs at the head of her makeshift bed. "Now relax and allow your body to heal."

"Look, I've been knocked out before. Stop making such a big deal of it."

"I will stop making a big deal of it when you are better. And you have absolutely no recollection of who did this to you?"

Clinton tensed.

"I've already told you I don't know. I remember fleeing, then running into a small pack of Ocelots. Obviously they got the better of me. There, I said it. Good-bye. Leave me alone."

She gave Hagen a seething look, and then turned onto her side with her back to him.

"So the assailants simply knocked you out? That is it? They did not try to capture or recruit you, Hiro?"

She glared over her shoulder. "Look, Hagen, I've said I can't remember. What's your problem?"

Hagen's head slowly tilted as he studied the cheetah; eventually he nodded and motioned for Clinton to leave with him.

"It does not make sense," muttered the departing Hagen. "Why would they act so atypically?"

The truth lingered at the edge of Clinton's tongue, but seeing how pitiful the cheetah looked, he could not bring himself to reveal her past crimes. He had tossed and turned in his sleep all night, questioning whether he should divulge what had really happened with Hiro and the Ocelots, but by the time the sun had dawned, the answer had become clear. All would be well once he finally beat Dallas…if he beat Dallas.

The elk's face flashed through Clinton's mind again, and the ever-present weed of doubt strangled his insides. *Hiro'll be fine,* he reasoned. *Besides, if I tell, I'll ruin yet another anumal's life.*

He sighed and sat down while Hagen sat next to him.

"Clinton, what is wrong?"

"Oh, nothing. Just tired. It's been an eventful few days."

"Eventful being an understatement."

"Look, Hagen, I don't know why the Ocelots acted like they did…I just found her, that's all, after Vito and I separated. After…" His words faltered. He looked awkwardly into thin air. "After my pathetic attempt to help the elk."

"How many times must I tell you? You made a judgment call, and you stuck by it. You did the best you could."

"And my best got an anumal killed."

"Did you murder him?"

"No, but—"

"Did you alert the Ocelots and make them murder him?"

"No."

"Oh, so you pulled the building down on top of him? Is that what happened?"

Clinton shook his head.

"Then why, pray tell, is the fault resting at your feet?"

The memory of trying to extract the elk's soul made Clinton squirm inside.

"I wasn't ready."

"You overestimated your abilities, Clinton, yes, but to fully extract an anumal's soul without permission will take training...or ruthless disregard. Both of which are beyond your current grasp."

Clinton studied the passing landscape. Brown and green grassland spread out as far as the eye could see. "I learned so much about him, Hagen. I lived through so many of his memories. He-he'd been in jail, y'know. In jail for—"

"I do not need to know his story, Clinton," answered the komodo, in a soft voice. "And neither do you."

"It's just that...I tried to help him, regardless of his crimes. I had to or else just leave him to die."

"Then let that be a lesson well learned. From this experience you have discovered that you do not have the authority to be judge or executioner to anyone...and you have also discerned your limitations. You tried, yet failed, to disassociate, thus allowing his memories to bleed into your own consciousness."

"But I anchored myself to Raion, and I didn't allow myself to be overwhelmed. I did everything right, yet when it came to taking his soul—"

"You could not," concluded Hagen. "Nothing is more complex than the bond between the vessel and the soul. Both are entwined, each shaping the other to create the being. It is the greatest temptation to look at another anumal's past and to discover their secrets, but by doing so, you only become embroiled in them."

"It was just too difficult. I tried too hard."

"Remember, Clinton, not everything weakens and bends when subjected to pressure."

Clinton thought over his words. "Y'know, a meyark or a wefring, or even a chockeral is easy. They panic, you calm them, you do what needs to be done, and then you're finished."

"And the same applies to anumalkind. You take that which is needed and disregard the periphery." The komodo dug into a pouch and pulled out a pinch of herbs. He rolled them together against the palm of his hand, creating a small, compact ball. "To take the whole of an anumal's soul is not beyond your scope, Clinton, yet it requires much more training. For now, take only that which will aid you, and wait for your abilities to develop."

Clinton pondered his words.

"So...I couldn't have saved the elk?"

"He was beyond the help of many," replied Hagen, examining the mulch in his hand. "Here, take this."

Clinton picked up the ball and tossed it in his mouth, trusting it would benefit him somehow.

"Now rest," Hagen ordered. "As that is precisely what your body needs. Tomorrow we will be one day closer to Mar Mi-Den, and we must, all of us, be ready for what lies ahead."

* * *

No sooner had the sun peaked above the horizon than Clinton woke feeling refreshed. He could not remember falling asleep and, for the first time, had not been plagued by bad dreams. As the team slept, Clinton dressed in his lazarball skin armor and slipped from the bus. The sun beamed behind the distant mountains, while at the side of the road rested an Olde-world, human war machine. A breeze tickled Clinton as he surveyed his surroundings, before his eyes settled on some shrubs bordering a distant forest. With a smile, he dropped to all fours and ran for the trees with all his might. Before long, the trees' shadows covered him. Slowing his pace, he rose on two legs to stroll through the undergrowth.

Not everything weakens and bends when subjected to pressure, rang Hagen's words in his head.

Clinton knew he had to change his mindset; he had to improve his control.

"I've got to make sure I get in front of that scrud," he mumbled, perching on the trunk of a toppled tree. "I have to use every power, and every advantage, to get face to face with him."

With a sigh, he relaxed his mind and looked up into the leafy canopy.

Take that which is needed and ignore the rest...

The leaves swayed in the breeze. An awareness of countless living creatures washed over him. Wefrings hissed at one another from the branches. Gibbets sped through the undergrowth. Denders curled into tight balls, while sectoids chittered, and meyarks scampered. The symphony of life filled him with energy, and closing his eyes, an explosion of color blossomed in his mind. The existence of so many souls made him tingle. He sat forward and smiled, knowing the help he needed lay all around him. Ignoring his awkwardness, he spoke out with his voice and his mind...

"I'm embarking on a momentous journey, my friends, and I am begging for your help. Who here will help me learn and grow?"

The forest paused.

"I am in need of your aid. Please come to me. Please."

Even the wind seemed to take notice of his words.

A few seconds passed, before Clinton heard the creak of branches, followed by the rustle of leaves, but nothing more. He huffed, feeling his cheeks turning red. He considered backing off, when a sudden movement caught his attention. With its leathery wings spread wide, a wefring glided towards him and landed on a shrub next to the tree trunk. A second later a rodent-faced meyark scuttled out from the undergrowth, while a hovergrub landed delicately on his shoulder. Clinton's breath caught in his throat. Unable to believe that they had answered his call, he slowly leaned over to address them.

"All I ask is that you trust me. I cannot promise you'll not be harmed, but I can promise that what I am attempting to do is for the greater good, for your greater good, and for the good of every living creature out there."

As the creatures made no move to leave, Clinton realized he had been given his answer. Carefully placing a hand on the wefring's trembling wing, he closed his eyes and fell into the creature's psyche.

A beautiful, white light blossomed from their contact.

* * *

"Feeling refreshed?" asked Hagen the moment Clinton boarded the bus. The team sat outside, preparing breakfast and loading the vehicle for another day's travel, while Hagen had stayed aboard, tending to Hiro. "You were up early."

The cheetah sighed loudly as she sat up in her bunk. Her face was still a mess, and her bruises looked angry. "Look, Hagen, never mind him. Are you ever gonna chill and let me out of this prison or what?"

"When I am fully satisfied you are well enough."

Hiro groaned and slumped back again, glaring at Clinton. "What are you looking at? And what is that bluggin' awful smell you've trailed in with you? Did you step in something?"

"Oh, this?" Clinton held up a small sack. He opened it up to reveal the bodies of a meyark, a wefring, and a hovergrub. "They're my new friends."

Hagen frowned.

The cheetah's mouth sagged. "He's bloody lost it. He's gone mad. I knew this'd happen."

Clinton shrugged. "I realized that I have to be smart; I have to think differently. So I thought I'd make some preparations. They're alive, don't worry."

A hint of pride budded through Hagen's puzzled face. "So their souls are…?"

Clinton tapped his fist against his breastplate.

The corner of Hagen's mouth turned up into a smile. "Say no more, my friend."

"About what?" Hiro scoffed. "What's he prattling on about?"

"Hiro, I do believe you may be healed enough to leave the bus after all," answered the komodo. "I think you getting a bit of fresh air might do us all some good."

With a final, dramatic sigh, the cheetah whipped off her covers and climbed tentatively to her feet. "About scruddin' time."

She barged past them without so much as a backwards glance. Clinton shook his head and began to strip off his armor.

"She looks to be on the mend."

"Unfortunately so," laughed Hagen. "Although she seems to be a lot more irritable and not quite as jovial as before. Time will see her back to her old self."

Time, or hive, thought the lion.

"Well, I will also leave you to it," said Hagen, interrupting Clinton's musings. "Though I must say you seem a lot happier since we conversed last night."

"Hmm… Sometimes you just need to get out in the open."

Hagen's head tilted to the side before he turned and trundled off along the bus's walkway.

The komodo had been right. Clinton did feel happier, and also less anxious about his abilities. He did not know if it was simply the fresh air, or the fact that his idea had worked, yet something had clicked for him. As he kicked off his boots and began to unfasten his gloves, he could sense he was not alone. He turned to see Hiro glaring at him from the far end of the bus.

"Are you okay?" he asked, yanking off a glove.

"Errr…yeah. Yeah, I'm fine. I just came for… erm…these." She picked up a pair of boning knives. "Vito caught us some breakfast. It needs skinning."

Clinton nodded, but could not help notice her focus gravitating towards his discarded equipment.

"Y'know, you looked the business in your armor back in Wooburn," she said, slowly inching away. "Your mother…well, she was pretty good at what she did."

Clinton's eyes narrowed. "She was the best."

"The best, huh?" The cheetah's eyebrows rose. "If you say so."
With nothing else to add, she turned and exited.

* * *

The sun cycled over the team another two times before the Bolt
Throwers finally arrived at Rusted Canyon. On their way they
passed through Woodshack, home to a base of Humaneers, who
had preserved the white chapels, houses, and Olde-vehicles that
mankind had left behind, restoring them back to their former glory.

"I bet they have a few human skeletons in those buildings too.
My father tolerated them back in Wooburn, but I was never
allowed to go near the few families that lived in the village,"
shuddered Harris, inspecting the structures. "Freaks."

Garron turned around from Hudson's side at the head of the
bus. "Don't mock 'em, kiddo. Gotta respect anyone with such
conviction. You've seen what they've put in place to protect those
buildings; certainly don't want the likes of us enterin'
their...museum."

Clinton looked out to see the razor wired fences lining each
property. The air practically sang with the hum of the lectric
currents. Dressed in their simple robes, and shaved from head to
toe, the bald Humaneers conveyed an image of peace on the
surface, yet the farming tools they carried had obviously been
adapted for more defensive purposes as well. Like Harris, Clinton
had also steered clear of the Humaneers in Wooburn. It had been
bad enough being associated with the Narfells, let alone a bunch of
anumals who devoted themselves to the memory of humans.

Everyone wiped their thumb over their brows when they left
the settlement behind.

After Woodshack they entered Evestone, an ancient Horn Head
garrison that had been laid to waste years ago. Barely a building
had survived the attacks when earlier Horn Heads had positioned
themselves as a blockade on the westward road to Mar Mi-Den.
The only true remnant of their era came in the shape of a bronze

bison. Riddled with graffiti, it still stood staunchly over any traveler passing by; a true testament to the Burning Horn Heads' strength. Around it was scattered countless antlers and horns, hewn off and strewn across the road. Traveling caravans had crushed many to dust over the years.

"That blugging dust is still stuck in my throat," coughed Harris the following evening. He slouched back and wiped his mouth with his hand. "What was the point of all those horns anyway?"

The team had shacked up for the night in one of Rusted Canyon's many storage containers. They sat outside around a brightly burning fire, a slowly roasting bleater at its center. Above them hung a sky teeming with stars.

Hudson looked up from chewing her mound of greens. "The horns have a dual purpose really. Let's just say the last thing you'd want to do is get on the wrong side of a Horn Head, or worse, turn your back on the clan. Otherwise, they'd have these off," she tapped her horns, "quick sharp."

"Savages," huffed Hiro, sitting apart from the group, a blanket wrapped around her, staring into the darkness of the canyon.

"Nah, it ain't all that bad," replied the bison. "Y'see, some of the horns belonged to the elderly: those whose wish it was to offer them back to our god who provided them. It's an old practice now, though. Don't think many choose to do it anymore. It's called kerafreya, when you please the God Kraytarr with your gift. You're promised a reward in the life beyond for you sacrifice. It's a brave thing to do…unlike being cleaved."

"Cleaved?" asked Clinton, looking up from his bowl. "What's that then?"

"That's when you have your horns forcibly taken from you. It's the ultimate shame. For a time it was outlawed within the clans, but now it's becoming common practice again. Now, since the fighting began, any clan deserters get the chop."

"So what about you?" asked Harris. "Do you not you worry about having your horns taken?"

Garron patted Hudson on her broad shoulder. "Trust me, matey. No one's taking hers. I've seen this lady charge through whole gangs of thugs and Horn Heads alike. As soon as you see her aiming those points at you...well, you'd better start running."

The group chuckled, while Hudson's face bristled with embarrassment. She turned to Harris. "So what about you, Lakota? What's your story?"

"Where to start?" laughed Ephraim, sarcastically. He shoved a handful of greens in his mouth.

"All right, Eph," scoffed Harris. "She was talking to me, not you."

Clinton paused from eating, intrigued as to Harris's response.

The beaver tossed a bleater bone into the fire and watched the flames engulf it. "Well, there is not much to say really. I was nothing but a scragging runt, pure and simple."

Clinton's mouth gaped.

"Yep. You could not have called me the nicest of anumals." A sardonic grunt escaped the beaver's lips. "However, as the saying goes: if you are raised by scavengers, then a scavenger you will become."

"Yeah, a rich scavenger," muttered Ephraim.

Harris did not even bother to look at the elephant. His gaze remained fixed on the flames. "Maybe so, but then again, only a narrow-minded fool would presume that wealth equates to happiness. It took a lot for me to leave Wooburn."

"I bet it did," hissed Hiro.

"And why would it not, huh? Villagers practically starved while I gorged on roast boval and chockeral meat every night." He leaned forward and yanked another rib from the carcass. "I never went without anything. My house was the only one with lectric for a long time—"

"Your house?" snapped Clinton, interrupting him. "*Your* house?"

Harris chewed slowly, baring his buckteeth. "Yes." He flicked a small lump of fat from his meat. "*My* house. I lived there too, Clinton."

"You lived on stolen property. It was my house."

"But it was not stolen by me. Look, I cannot condone my

parents' actions, and I will not be blamed for them either; I was an infant, Clinton. My childhood was shaped and forged just as much as yours in Brook Manor—"

"Well Wood."

"Call it what you will, Narfell, but it does not change its meaning, or the part it played in my life."

Clinton snarled under his breath.

Harris's eyes narrowed. "You think that your life in the slums was the worst thing anyone had to endure?"

"Well, I'm sure it was a lot worse than yours."

"Well...maybe you are right, maybe you are wrong. I do not know, because I was too busy being the village whip to see much else. I was the one they quietly hated because of my family's actions. You might not believe it, Clinton, but while you lived without credits, at least you had anumals who cared for you. Me? I had everything and no one; my family preferred a foundling tiger over their own son.

"Well Wood held nothing but happy memories for you, while I lived in a house where every last shred of attention was lavished on someone else, purely for political status. Oh, but there was always mother for me to run to, wasn't there, huh?" Harris's voice trembled. "Given the choice between losing her son and losing her prized possessions, she made it obvious what she would rather do without."

Clinton blinked, feeling his anger abate. He looked at Ephraim who had bowed his head, not touching his bowl of greens.

It was Hiro who finally broke the silence.

"Oh, poor little rich boy. I feel so sorry for you."

"I would not expect you to understand, cheetah. You were a Saber, surrounded by like-minded maniacs. But still, you weren't alone, were you? You had others—"

"You know nothing!" she snapped, going as taut as a spring.

"I know that it was the Sabers who used Ephraim's attack on them as a cover so they could punish your so called boyfriend...and then blame *him*," Harris pointed at the elephant, "for it."

298

Tear's glistened in Hiro's eyes.

Ephraim edged forwards, his forehead furrowed. "What is he talking—"

"Lies!" Hiro hurled her bowl across the ground and stood up. "Brox loved me, Lakota. It was complicated."

The cheetah's words died as she walked off towards the giant storage container. She stopped and leaned against its side.

A long moment passed before Harris finally spoke.

"When I left Wooburn, do you know how many guards were sent after me by my father? Two. And one of those gave up a day later and headed to Crankton to get drunk at the mayor's expense. However, as you say, Ephraim, I am the lucky one. I had wealth...and objects...and servants...and not one anumal who really gave a damn about me." Harris tossed his bone into the fire. The flames sizzled from the fat while he walked in the opposite direction from Hiro and sat on a rock. "Out of the two of us, Clinton, I think you were far richer than I ever was."

A melancholy silence permeated the group, broken only by Ephraim.

"And...what about you, Vito?" he asked. "Sometimes you're so quiet I forget you're here."

Vito, who had been sitting against an oil drum, looked up and pulled her hood down. "There is really not much to tell."

From where he was sitting, Clinton caught Hagen glance at Garron.

"So where are you from then?" asked the elephant.

"Quala," she immediately replied.

"Oh, so how come you're Union Wheel then? I thought Quala was full of Technals?"

"It was. Yet they were open to all anumals, all clans, and all ideas. They mocked and joked with me, but they never showed me any malice. Qualians were mostly drifters who settled there because it was a refuge for Technals and the mech minded. Like the Union Wheel, freedom of individuality was always key there."

"So tell me," said Hudson. "If these Technals could construct stuff using mankind's Olde mech and junk, then why didn't they just build weapons and barricades to stop the Ocelots attacking the village?"

"Because they trusted they did not need such things, that clan harmony still held strong, that anumal society had progressed. Do not get me wrong, there were Technals I came across who had the knowledge to construct machines that could cause much damage, but that was a dark practice, and very much outlawed. 'Second only to human' is what many said it was. How I wish Quala would have embraced that knowledge now." The fire's flames reflected in her eyes like smoldering embers waiting to ignite. "It is insane how our world has descended into this madness so quickly. Peace has flourished for so many years…only for us to end up here. I was one of the lucky few to escape. Along with two friends of mine."

"But you did escape," said Hiro, from the darkness. "How?"

"By sneaking out. I was given no other option."

Pep yawned and rested her head against Hudson's leg. "You should make the journey east, Vito. You'd be shown a lot more respect there, believe me. One of my uncles told me about the Far East before he was killed in a domination battle."

"Killed?" asked Ephraim, pausing to choose a nice handful of greens to chew on.

"Oh, yes, happens all the time. When the older females come into heat every seven years, the males tend to get aggressive. Not as aggressive as the females, though," said Pep, nonchalantly. "The bigger burrows are volatile places, I'll tell you that. Anyway…what was I saying?"

"That Vito should travel east," answered Garron.

"Ah, yes. My uncle said that in the Far East, past the Wastelands, foxes are something of a special breed. I can't remember the name of the place, but he saw temples dedicated to the fox and…I can't remember the other anumal now, but he said it was rare to see one of your breed slumming it in the east. If I were you, Vito, I'd be heading in that direction once this is all over with."

"It is something I will certainly bear in mind, Pep. Thank you," answered Vito, smiling.

Clinton, though, sensed a hesitance in her words. He knew she was merely humoring the mouse.

"Well, I think it is somewhere we should all travel to once Clinton has completed his business," agreed Hagen. "It certainly sounds a lot warmer than where we are now."

"If you want warm, you should try Wooburn on a hot day." Clinton could not help but chuckle. "It got so hot you could fry a chockeral egg on the ground."

"The smell of roast krig," Ephraim cut in. "I remember that about the hot days in Wooburn. I ain't a meat eater, but the aroma would make my mouth water when they'd light the fires."

"I couldn't afford krig," admitted Clinton.

"Could anyone?" shrugged Ephraim. "Yet journeying this far north, bovals, krigs, and bleaters are as common as sectoids. It's crazy."

Clinton nodded. "I always looked forward to the arrival of the journiers and traders. They always brought their weird stuff with them. Poisons that cured ailments, and human mech that they'd salvaged. There was once a lizard who showed me this box that spoke actual words over and over again. He said a spirit was trapped inside it…a *human* spirit."

"The little box with the numbers on it? Ha! I remember that too," barked Ephraim, jumping in his seat. "I used to imitate the voice. 'This is a distress signal from Arc West, level sixteen, section D. Subjects are in stasis…'"

" 'Lockdown is now complete,' " they both said together.

Ephraim sighed. "Wonder what happened to that box? You think anyone bought it?"

"Guess so," shrugged Clinton.

He glanced over at Harris, still slumped against the rock.

Maybe he's right?

Even though Clinton had been one of the poorest anumals in Wooburn, he had certainly received a lot more love than the beaver ever had.

Garron's voice snapped Clinton out of his reverie.

"Well, we all have reasons for bein' here, and scores to settle too."

"And to that I say bring it on!" said Hudson, standing up to reveal a barrel of grain water she had been sitting on. "I've been saving this little beauty since Middle City. Might as well enjoy it now. Here."

She tossed a wooden mug to Garron, and another to Ephraim. Vito caught hers, and smiled, but placed it on the ground. Pep chuckled, clasping hers in both hands. She approached the barrel's tap, ready to drink.

"My appreciation, young lady, but I must sadly decline," smiled Hagen, tossing his mug back to the bison.

Hudson caught it, before throwing it to Clinton. "Here you go, then."

Clinton snatched the mug out of the air with one hand. He studied Pep and Ephraim filling their mugs with the foamy liquid while a long absent laughter developed around the fire. Clinton climbed to his feet.

"Go on then. Just this once." He grinned and filled his mug to the brim. He hated the taste of grain water and had always refused it, yet now he felt he needed to live his life just that little bit more.

"To the Bolt Throwers!" cried Ephraim, and as one, Clinton, Pep, Ephraim, Garron, and Hudson, clashed their mugs together.

And why the skorr not? thought the lion. *Why not enjoy tonight? For soon we will reach Mar Mi-Den...*

And then everything will change.

- - -

END OF BOOK TWO

- - -

302

Read more in

BOOK THREE

ANUMAL EMPIRE: REAPER

David and Darren would like to say thank you to their families and to all the people who have given their support to the Anumal Empire series.

Azucena Duran, Paulo Kadow, Terri Glennan, Emma Ruthven, and Jenny Jenson for your help.

Thanks to Jony Hunter for the work on the cover artwork. (jonathanhunter.co.uk)

Ben Wilkinson for the lettering.

Dedicated to Bob (Robert Ayres), and also to all the writers that gave them both the inspiration to begin this project.

Follow us on Facebook – Anumal Empire
anumalempire.com
darrenjacobs.com

@DavidAyres01
@darrenjcbs

Made in the USA
San Bernardino, CA
05 September 2016